PRIME SUSPECT

I was writing out my check at Curly's Feed Store when Curly said, "It really is a terrible thing about that murder."

"Murder? Who said it was murder?"

"Cripes, Trade, who drowns in a stock tank?"

"That doesn't mean it was murder," I said. "Besides, who'd want to murder her?"

He grinned.

"That's not very charitable, Curly."

"Just kidding. You're right, she probably drowned."

Poor J.B. No matter what way this was sliced, he'd always be under a cloud of suspicion because he was a poor cowboy married to a filthy rich older woman.

Also by Sinclair Browning

THE LAST SONG DOGS
THE SPORTING CLUB

RODE HARD,
PUT AWAY DEAD

SINCLAIR BROWNING

BANTAM BOOKS
NEW YORK TORONTO LONDON SYDNEY AUCKLAND

RODE HARD, PUT AWAY DEAD
A Bantam Book / February 2001

ISBN 0-553-58327-1

Published simultaneously in the United States and Canada

Bantam Books are published by Bantam Books, a division of Random
House, Inc. Its trademark, consisting of the words "Bantam Books" and
the portrayal of a rooster, is Registered in U.S. Patent and Trademark Office and in other countries. Marca Registrada. Bantam Books, 1540
Broadway, New York, New York 10036.

PRINTED IN THE UNITED STATES OF AMERICA

OPM   10 9 8 7 6 5 4 3 2 1

For Lance . . . who forgave me
for the lizard sandwich;
For Rowena . . . who forgave me
for the bucking pony;
For George . . . who I forgave
for the rock to the head.
I love you guys.

ACKNOWLEDGMENTS

The author wishes to thank the following people for contributing their expertise to the writing of this book: Dave Bridgman, San Diego Police Department; Lori Davisson, retired research historian, Arizona Historical Society; Michael Downing, investigator, Pima County Medical Examiner's Office; Luci Zahray; Fran Haggerty, psychologist; Lillian Roberts, DVM; Wyman Eske; Dennis Fessenmyer, Pima County Sheriff's Department; Lisa Baget; Joyce Garcia; Rosemary Minter; Ethel Paquin; Heidi Vanderbilt; and, last but not least, Kara Cesare, for wading through once again.

RODE HARD,
PUT AWAY DEAD

1

ABIGAIL VAN THIESSEN HAD BEEN LIFTED, STITCHED, TUCKED, stretched, molded, nipped, sucked, mudded and sweated and she still didn't ride worth a damn. Not that all of that remodeling should have turned her into a cowgirl, but the thousands of dollars she'd spent on horseback riding lessons could have accounted for something.

Still, with all the Choco-Willie Candy fortune behind her, I supposed she wasn't too worried about her money being flushed down the toilet.

Martín, my ranch foreman, and I sat on our horses high on the mesa watching the circus down below. We were gathering cattle and Abby and her husband of six months, J.B. Calendar, were trying to flush a Brahma bull out of the brush. By my own count, Abby had almost fallen off her horse three times in the last five minutes. But then almost only counts in horseshoes.

"J.B.'s got his hands full," Martín offered.

I nodded. "So does she."

Less than a year earlier J.B. Calendar rode into Abigail Van Thiessen's heart on a two-thousand-pound bucking, twisting, torqueing Brahma bull and never left. The wiry Arizona bull rider had been a part of the rodeo show the Rancho Los Reales entertained their corporate guests with, and that particular night had included executives from Choco-Willie. Abigail Van Thiessen and her brother, Peter, sole owners of the candy dynasty, had been in the audience.

To keep everyone glued to the performance and in their seats—just as in the real rodeos—the Los Reales crew had saved the bull riding until last. There was always something in this man-against-beast pairing that thrilled spectators. The only difference between this sport and the Christians against the lions was that today's spectators liked to see their heroes walk away from the wreck. Usually that happened. But sometimes in bull riding the good guys didn't get up.

World champion Lane Frost was one who didn't. Although he'd been killed a few years earlier, Los Reales had a spectacular finale where J.B. Calendar would ride a bull, not for the required eight seconds, but for a full sixteen—eight for himself and eight for Lane Frost. The fact that he had never known Frost, for J.B. was a second-class bull rider at best, or that national champion Tuff Hedeman had been the first to offer this tribute, never seemed to bother the Los Reales champ.

Double Indemnity, the ancient Brahma who was the class part of the act, always made J.B. look good. The two of them had perfected Calendar's dismount to the point where he'd tumble into the dirt with Double Indemnity spinning into the dust beside him.

J.B. would lie, like a broken, busted doll, face down in the arena, listening to the crowd gasp, and then become strangely silent. In the best John Barrymore tradition, Calendar would begin to twitch, first one finger, then a hand, a shudder of a shoulder and then a leg quiver, and finally slowly rise from the earth like Lazarus from the dead.

That first encounter was one that Abigail Van Thiessen often related in the ensuing months. "Like a Remington bronze come to life," she'd said. "I'd never seen anything like it."

In the time it took Abby to push through the crowd eager to congratulate the dusty cowboy on his spectacular ride, J.B. had already figured out who she was.

The fact that the Choco-Willie mistress had thirty-two years on him didn't hobble his courtship.

And now the happy honeymoon couple was down in the canyon below me trying to coax a recalcitrant Brahma from the brush. Watching Abby bounce on the seat of her saddle, I briefly wondered if I could be sued for someone falling off her horse on my land.

J.B. was doing a valiant job trying to chouse the bull out from under a mesquite tree, but he might as well have been working alone for all the help his bride was giving him. At least he rode. Unlike ropers and bronc riders, a lot of bull riders are city boys, and not all that comfortable riding horses. At the National Finals Rodeo every year a lot of them hate the grand entry where they either ride or face a $250 fine.

"*Chiquita*, they're never gonna get Freight Train out of there," Martín offered.

I wasn't surprised that even at this distance my foreman knew the beast in the brush, for Freight Train was the largest bull on the ranch.

"Looks like work for you, Blue." At the sound of her name, the Australian cattle dog jumped up from under the mesquite tree where she'd been resting. Mrs. Fierce, my cock-a-schnauz, had been left back at the ranch headquarters. While she would have preferred to come along on the roundup, she also took her job as head of ranch security very seriously, and I had left her with that important assignment.

As I rode down the mesa, the hot June sun flooded my face in spite of my cowboy hat. Dream, my bay Arabian, had his evaporative cooler already working as his neck and shoulders gleamed with sweat. I was glad we started early. While the ice had already broken on the Santa Cruz—a local euphemism for the first day of the year that hits 100 degrees—the weatherman had sworn last night that we'd only hover in the high 90s. So far, he was right.

But that's how June in the desert around Tucson is, hot and dry. While my ranch, the Vaca Grande, is thirty miles north of town and cooler than Tucson, when you're talking those kinds of degrees, it's not much help. The desert was suffering, not only with the heat, but also with the prolonged drought we'd been having.

In spite of the temperature, I was happy to be out gathering cattle this morning. It gave me a good chance to clear the cobwebs in my head, and took me away from my other job as a private investigator. All in all, I'm one of the lucky ones, for I love the ranch life and I love my work, and in both I'm self-employed, which means I can set my own hours, wear what I please and screw off when I want to.

As Martín and I rode up, Freight Train decided to amble out from under the tree. With a stern shake of his massive head and an impressive snort, he stamped one huge cloven foot at Abby's horse and started throwing dirt over his shoulder. Blue was boldly nipping at his heels in an effort to dislodge him.

"Move!" J.B. yelled.

His timing was just off, for Abby's seasoned horse knew not to get in the way of the irritated bull and the horse spun out from underneath her, depositing her at the feet of the huge Brahma. Her cowboy hat landed a few feet away.

Freight Train looked as startled as the rest of us and, thankfully, instead of charging this godsend from heaven, he stomped on her dislocated straw hat and took off in the direction of the cows.

Abby rolled on her back and gulped air.

J.B. did a quick dismount, dropped his reins on the ground and rushed to his wife before Martín and I could even get close. Abby's horse browsed nearby.

"Oh, hon." He leaned over her, brushing her blond

hair away from her face. "Don't move, just take it easy." One of his hands was on her thigh, the other holding her hand as he watched her gasp. "Are you okay?"

His bride didn't answer. She couldn't, for all of her energy was concentrated on catching her breath. J.B. looked close to tears.

Finally, Abigail Van Thiessen said, "I'm fine, sweetie," as she sat up slowly and rubbed her hip.

I was now on the ground, kneeling in the dust, beside J.B. "Don't get up too quickly, Abby," I cautioned. "Take a few deep breaths and take inventory."

The Choco-Willie heiress gave me a blurry look. "Are you part Apache?"

"What?" I said.

"J.B. said you're part Apache, is that true?"

Calendar gave me an embarrassed look.

"My grandmother is an Apache." What in the hell did this have to do with her getting dumped? Did she have a concussion?

"Who am I?" Her husband of six months asked, obviously considering the same diagnosis.

She gave him a sly grin.

"Stud Muffin McGillicutty."

"Abby, what day is it?" I asked.

She fluffed the dirt out of her blond, once perfectly coiffed hair, and as she pushed it back from her face I could see faint surgical scars, the result, no doubt, of her many rumored plastic surgeries. Even at sixty-eight, she was a strikingly good-looking woman. Her doctors had done a good job, for she lacked much of the stretched, numb look that so many face-lifted women wear. I suspected that her lips had not escaped attention either, for they were suspiciously full. Collagen injections, no doubt. She batted her crystal blue eyes at me. "Monday. It's Monday."

She was right.

"What's your name?" J.B. asked.

"Abigail Van Thiessen," she paused. "Calendar."

Martin, convinced that we were not looking at a medevac case, rode off after Freight Train.

"I don't think we need to bother with asking who the president is," I said.

"I'm not going there." Abby grinned. Her teeth were flawless and unnaturally white.

J.B. helped her to her feet and then retrieved her wide-brimmed straw cowboy hat. She was quite a bit shorter than her groom, and rail thin. At five foot seven and 125 pounds I felt like a giant standing next to her.

"It's a little the worse for wear," J.B. said apologetically, dusting her hat off against his Wrangler's. From my vantage point I could see that it was a good one—a $100 Thievin' Vaqueros. He took the tips of his fingers and gently wiped the dust from her nose. "How's my girl?"

She patted his face. "I'm fine, sweetie. Really."

He gave her a light kiss on the lips and replaced the cowboy hat on her head. Then he retrieved her horse and held it for her as she struggled to get on.

Not for the first time, I studied the odd pair before me. Like many people, I wondered what she saw in him. Average-looking, he did have a full head of hair and a great smile, punctuated by deep dimples on both sides of his mouth, which could be seen hugging his long, black handlebar mustache. J.B.'s previous zip code had been E-I-E-I-O and he'd passed time in Elko, Santa Fe, Lubbock, Sedona, and most recently in Tombstone, where he dressed up as Bat Masterson for the tourists. As for brains, any guy who'd jump on the back of a two-thousand-pound bull and tie a rope close to its balls to make it even more pissed off, certainly wouldn't qualify for a think tank in my book.

What J.B. saw in the Choco-Willie heiress was obvious. Still, for her rumored $200 million, it seemed to me that Abby could have bought more for her dough.

"Guess I'm not doing so hot on my first roundup, huh?"

"No, no, you're doing fine," I lied. Abby and J.B. had bought the old Marvin place north of Oracle. They'd renamed it the Brave Bull and, after a whirlwind remodeling job on the old house, had been living up there for the past three months.

In marrying Abigail Van Thiessen, J.B.'s fondest dream had come true. Suddenly the itinerant bull rider found himself wearing glass slippers. Abby's wedding present to her thirty-six-year-old husband had been four magnificent bucking bulls including the elderly Double Indemnity, and J.B. now had his own bull riding school. The plan was to have one-week sessions four to five times a year, sandwiched in between the Calendars' trips to Abby's beach home in the Bahamas, her hunting lodge in Montana and her apartments in Milan and New York.

Since J.B. had no herd of cattle and Abby had been eager to learn about his life—Arizona ranching and cowboys—I had been happy to include them in our roundup.

J.B. grabbed his canteen from his saddle and offered it to Abby, who declined. As he took a long slug from it, I wondered if he'd cut his water with something stronger, for Martín and the cowboys had told me that J.B. had taken to drinking a lot lately.

"Why don't you guys head down to the holding pasture," I suggested. "I'll meet you there."

As I rode off in search of Martín and Freight Train it hit me. Could that business about my being Apache have been Abby's way of deflecting attention from herself? Since she was so much older than J.B., was she sensitive about being more frail?

All in all it seemed a pretty stupid idea, since any one of us could have fallen off our horses today.

Briefly, I wondered if Abby had died from her fall if J.B. would have been set for life or once again be out in the cold.

As it turned out, I wouldn't have to wait long for the answer to that question.

2

I WAS AT THE KITCHEN TABLE WORKING ON THE RANCH BOOKS later that afternoon when Martín knocked at the door.

"Come in," I hollered, as I recorded the last cow/calf entry in the old-fashioned ledger.

My foreman threw his hat on the counter, brim down, and pulled up a chair.

"Iced tea?" I held up my frosted glass.

He shook his head and placed a crumpled newspaper clipping in front of me. I grabbed it before the evaporative cooler blew it off the table. It was a Mexican newspaper, *El Imparcial* from Hermosillo. While my Spanish is passable—by that I mean I can usually carry on a conversation as long as it's punctuated with a lot of *cómo se dices*—how do you say?—I'm by no means a fluent reader of the language.

But the picture on the front page told volumes. Young Mexican soldiers wearing rifles across their uniformed frames were guarding a courtyard in which two dead bodies lay sprawled on the dark ground. Had blood darkened the soil? A couple of Big Wheels, the kind toddlers like to use, and a broken wooden chair littered the yard. My mouth went dry as I studied the picture.

"Does this have anything to do with Cori Elena?"

He nodded.

Martín's old girlfriend, Cori Elena Figueroa de la Fuente Orantez, had reappeared in his life over a year ago. Martín, after taking a month's vacation in Mexico, had returned with his childhood sweetheart.

A few months later all hell had broken loose when Cori Elena's great secret had been unmasked. A short time after ditching Martín years ago to marry a nightclub owner in Magdalena, Sonora, she'd given birth to a daughter. That baby girl, Quinta, was now twenty-two and Martín and his daughter had only found out about each other last November.

Since Quinta and her mother had some serious issues to deal with she was now living with her grandfather, Juan Ortiz, Martín's father, in the old adobe house on the ranch. Juan was getting old and was hard of hearing, but his granddaughter's presence rejuvenated him.

"Is this about Lázaro Orantez?" I waved the clipping at Martín. Orantez had been Cori Elena's husband. Definitely not a nice man. After finding Cori Elena in bed with one of his bartenders, he'd pushed her down a flight of stairs, breaking her leg.

Orantez had turned up with his throat slit and a short time later Cori Elena had arrived at the Vaca Grande with Martín. While both Martín and Cori Elena had sworn to me that they had nothing to do with Orantez's death, she was still wanted for questioning by the Mexican authorities.

Unfortunately they weren't the only ones looking for Martín's girlfriend. It turned out that Orantez had some unsavory business associates. Like the Mexican Mafia.

Those first few months after I found out about Orantez I spent a lot of time looking over my shoulder. I was concerned that somehow Cori Elena would be traced to the Vaca Grande and her presence would jeopardize all of us. Months had gone by and I had become fairly complacent about the whole thing. Until now, because there was a damned gruesome newspaper clipping sitting on my kitchen table.

I grabbed my reading glasses.

"Rafael Félix?" I asked, making out the name under the captioned photograph.

"Cori Elena says he was one of Lázaro's *amigos*," Martín said.

"Victim?" I asked hopefully.

Martín shook his head. "No, *chiquita*."

"Shit." I knew that if Rafael Félix was not one of the featured players in the photograph, then he had to be the one responsible for their appearance in the newspaper.

"Fermín Talavera was muscling in on the action in Ciudad Juárez."

"And he's one of these guys?" I asked, pointing to one of the dead bodies.

"I don't know. It says he was one of the fifteen killed."

I whistled. "Fifteen."

"They usually only execute one or two people, not entire families." Martín waited a minute to let me assimilate this information. "Lázaro Orantez is mentioned in the story. They say rumors are that he died owing Félix a lot of money."

"Cori Elena took it," I said dully.

"She says no."

I bit my tongue. There was nothing I would put beyond Cori Elena. Ambitious, conniving, plying her sex to get what she wanted—lying could easily fall into her repertoire. While I was genuinely fond of her daughter, Quinta, I had little use for the woman who had brought her into the world. But as long as Martín was enamored of her, I knew better than to get in the middle of it.

"Martín, this is really serious. If Cori Elena has the

Orantez money, or even if these people think she does, then we could all be in deep *caca*."

"I know."

"Quinta, your father, me, you. These people will stop at nothing."

Martín looked miserable.

"You have the right to know that." He nodded at the clipping. "But Cori Elena doesn't have his money."

"How can you be so sure?"

"I just know, *chiquita*, that's all."

Briefly, I wondered how he could have that kind of trust in Cori Elena. Why would she tell him if she had the money? This was the same woman who only a few short months before had never even told him he had fathered a daughter, then when she'd been found out, had fabricated a huge story about the girl being brain dead. With Cori Elena, every day was a surprise. Unfortunately I would not put murder and embezzlement—even if the money was dirty—past her.

"She can't go back to Mexico," Martín said.

I didn't have to ponder this. We'd already been through it many times before. Since the Mexican authorities were only interested in questioning Cori Elena, she was in no danger of extradition. But the minute she stepped across the border she'd be nailed and more than likely be thrown into jail. Definitely not a good place to be.

"You're sure she's not in contact with anyone down there?" I asked. When I had agreed to let Cori Elena stay at the ranch, my one condition had been that she not tell anyone where she was living. Her father, Alberto, who was retired and still living at the Double A Drag Ranch up in Oracle, was the only member of her family who knew where she was. While she'd been to Mesa a few times to visit her sisters, they only communicated with her through their father. I was fairly sure the bad guys could cut out Alberto's tongue and he would never divulge that his youngest daughter was living at the Vaca Grande.

Martín stood up, as did I. I handed him back the newspaper clipping and he gave me a hard hug. "This is a heads-up, *chiquita*, that's all."

As I watched him walk out, I prayed he was right.

3

"WE'D LOVE TO, BUT WE'RE LEAVING FOR A HORSEBACK TRIP Friday morning," Abby said, declining my invitation for them to join us for the weekend roundup. "J.B.'s starting another school next week, so he promised me this trip before he gets tied down with all of that."

"Sounds fun." I cradled the telephone against my shoulder and thumbed through the mail. "Where you headed?"

"Some place called the Baboquivaris." She butchered the name of the mountain range southwest of Tucson. "We're taking the horses and this will give me a chance to really ride hard, Trade. J.B. says we'll be doing at least ten miles a day!"

Thinking June an odd time for a camping trip and that ten miles on horseback wasn't really all that far, I wisely kept my mouth shut. "Just be sure he doesn't ride you hard and put you away wet," I cracked a weak honeymoon joke.

Abby laughed. "Oh, I'm counting on it."

By the time we hung up, I was convinced that Abby thought that this camping trip was the magic elixir that would turn her into a real cowgirl. Ah, if it were that easy. Still, a few more days in the saddle could only improve her riding skills.

By Saturday morning we'd gathered the rest of the cattle into the holding pasture. We'd spent the rest of Saturday & Sunday ear-tagging the heifers, cutting the young bulls, and earmarking and inoculating all the calves. Since I like to gather my cattle throughout the year, spring roundup isn't quite as wild as it is on some outfits. My calves have seen people on horseback before and aren't too concerned when someone other than their mama asks them to move.

The other nice thing about spring roundup is that after our work is done, other than the calves we may have missed, most of the mother-calf pairs get to be turned back out on pasture. Unlike fall, there's no bawling of the cows as they walk the fence lines searching for their calves.

By sundown Sunday the holding pasture and corrals were empty and the ranch was quiet once again.

It was late Monday morning and I was working in my office at the old stage stop a mile from the ranch house when Jake Hatcher's pickup pulled in. Hatcher, our local brand inspector, has been hanging around the Vaca Grande a lot lately, so while I wasn't particularly surprised to see him, I was startled that he stopped to see me.

Although Jake was old enough to be her father, he and Cori Elena had become good friends. He had dated her aunt years ago, so Martín's girlfriend had known him since childhood. But now that relationship had every indication of blossoming into something more. If Martín had noticed anything fishy, he hadn't said anything. As for me, I saw the whole thing as a keg of dynamite waiting for someone to light the fuse.

When I left my evaporative-cooled office, the dry, hot June air smacked me in the face. Although I was wearing nothing more than a T-shirt and shorts, I was sweating before I reached Jake's pickup.

He stepped out of his truck and tipped his Stetson in my direction. "Morning, Trade."

"Jake, what brings you out this way?"

"Have you heard about the accident?"

My stomach sank. Accident is never a good word.

"Abigail Van Thiessen was found dead yesterday morning."

"Dead?" Jesus, had she fallen off her horse again?

"Drowned. They found her in some stock tank south of town."

"The Baboquivaris."

"Say, that's right. She and J.B. were on some kind of camp deal down there. Apparently they whooped it up pretty good Saturday night and J.B. woke up Sunday morning and found her in the tank."

"And she drowned?" With the difference in their ages and bank accounts, it didn't take a Sherlock Holmes to think the obvious.

"Well, that's what they're calling it so far. The medical examiner's doing an autopsy. That's required you know, on all accidental deaths."

I nodded. I knew a little about autopsies. While most of my private investigation business is the boring stuff—skip traces, domestic squabbles, insurance investigation, workman's comp—I did know about autopsies. The A word had reared its ugly head before. So far, thankfully, I've not had to watch one being done.

"How's J.B.?"

"Haven't seen him. Can't say."

We talked a while longer and then Jake took off. I wasn't surprised to see him turn left toward ranch head-quarters instead of heading back out to the highway.

I tried to go back to work after that, but my mind kept drifting to Abigail Van Thiessen and her young cowboy husband. I'd just seen them both last week and she'd seemed so happy. And J.B. had been very solicitous of her. Yet how in the hell could a person drown in a stock tank? I'd heard it happen to animals but never to a person.

Finally I decided that sending out client bills could wait another day and I left the office.

I stopped at home only long enough to throw on a skirt and retrieve a poppyseed cake from the freezer on the screened porch. Then I headed up to the Brave Bull Ranch.

Passing through our little burg of La Cienega I headed up Highway 77 to Oracle. I turned off the highway and dropped my speed through the business district before hanging a right on the old Mt. Lemmon Road. Past the Environmental Research Center I hung another right onto dirt. I passed the American Flag Ranch, which was now a trailhead for a segment of the Arizona Trail, and drove for another mile or so before finding the huge wrought iron sign with a silhouette of a bull rider making a ride. Underneath in huge block wrought iron lettering were the words THE BRAVE BULL.

Scrub oaks lined the driveway and as I drove in I could tell that I wasn't the first to hear the news of Abigail's death. Mercedeses, Cadillacs and shiny new Lexuses mingled with battered pickup trucks in the paved parking lot. Obviously both Abby's and J.B.'s friends were paying their respects to the bereaved husband.

When I stepped out of Priscilla, my beloved Dodge diesel pickup, the desert air blasted me again. Although Oracle is higher than La Cienega, it was still hot. Damn, but how I dislike June. Absolutely my least favorite month in the desert. The heat is just relentless with no hint of rain. Everything seems to come to a standstill and even the animals don't move around much, unless it's at night.

By the time I got to the front door, I was damp and clutching the frozen cake to my bosom in an effort to cool myself down.

A maid, dressed in loose cotton pants and a purple polo shirt embroidered with "The Brave Bull" and the same bucking bull logo I'd seen at the entrance, let me into the refrigerated comfort of the huge remodeled adobe house. I handed off the poppyseed cake to her and passed through the foyer into the great room.

It was incredible. A massive stone fireplace was at one end and over it was what I was sure was an original oil painting by Kenneth Riley. If it had been my house, I would have found a safer place for the expensive oil than a site where it would be threatened by fireplace soot.

The walls were peppered with more original art, all of it Western-themed, ranging from the stock two cow ponies tied in front of the little adobe with smoking fireplace, to Plains Indians on buffalo hunts. There was also a huge mounted Brahma bull head, and on the wall next to the dining area, a formal portrait of Abigail Van Thiessen in her earlier life.

The furniture, like the room, was oversized with a good deal of Molesworth, lots of leather and studs and even a giant chair made of antlers.

There were probably twenty people in the room, most of them looking as though they'd come from Abby's walk of life, and I didn't know any of them.

One man stood out, as easily as did the Riley painting. A huge black man, built like a linebacker, with short salt-and-pepper hair. He was wearing a long white robe and had a large diamond earring in his left ear and a heavy gold chain with an immense gold crucifix hanging around his neck.

Choco-Willie candy was very much in evidence, as bowls of the foil-wrapped chocolate-covered caramel clowns graced several of the tables.

A small gray-haired Mexican man with a tiny puff of a mustache came by with a tray of soft drinks. I took a Diet Coke.

"Hey, Trade."

I turned to see Lolly MacKenzie. Lolly came from a ranching family in Sonoita, Arizona, and my cousin Bea and I had known her since we were children, although she was quite a bit older than we were. Her father, like mine, had come from the East years ago. Although hers had come with a ton more money. Some said that his fortune was somehow connected to that of Engine Charley Wilson of General Motors fame. Besides ranching, Lolly and I had something else in common. We were both orphans.

"Isn't this a terrible thing?" Lolly asked.

"Totally unexpected," I agreed. "They were just down at the ranch gathering cattle last week."

"And Abby and I were supposed to go to the Miraval spa for a day of beauty this week. During J.B.'s bull thing, you know."

The way she said it I could tell that Lolly didn't think much of J.B.'s bull riding school.

"Oh right, that was starting this week." My eyes scanned the room, but there was no sign of J.B. Calendar, or anyone resembling a real cowboy. "Where is he, do you know?"

"Haven't seen him."

We made small talk for a while longer. When someone diverted Lolly's attention, I slipped across the room toward the dining end, figuring that the kitchen couldn't be far behind. My whole point in coming here was to pay my respects to J.B. and I needed to do that and then get back to work.

My instincts were right and I slipped through the swinging doors and found myself in a massive French country kitchen. A small squat woman with Brillo pad gray hair was spreading what looked like ham salad on tiny pieces of bread. She was wearing a long black broomstick skirt with a Brave Bull polo shirt and thin cotton gloves that were stained with the sandwich spread. She looked startled to see me.

"Can I get out through there?" I pointed to a door.

She smiled. "Sure."

That was the extent of our conversation as I slipped out of Abigail Van Thiessen's house and back into the June inferno.

4

I WALKED PAST SEVERAL GUEST HOUSES TUCKED INTO THE scrub oaks and manzanita.

It didn't take an investigator to figure out where I'd find J.B. By the time I got to Double Indemnity's pipe corral I was damp with sweat. I found Calendar and two other cowboys—one a full head shorter than J.B.—standing under a large oak tree. Although there was a nice rectangular wrought iron patio table with six chairs nestled under the oak, each cowboy had a leg propped up on the pipe, their butts to me as they studied the Brahma bull. J.B. and the tall cowboy sported perfectly round white circles on the right cheek pockets of their Wrangler's; permanent imprints left by their Copenhagen cans.

Double Indemnity, oblivious to either the cowboys or the hordes of flies that buzzed about his massive body, stood sleeping in the far corner of the pen.

I walked up just as the tall cowboy spit a thin stream of brown tobacco juice into the dust.

Taking a place on the far side of Calendar I draped my arms over the rail and placed a sandaled foot on the bottom pipe. He turned to look at me, but it was impossible to see his eyes behind his mirrored sunglasses.

"Thanks for coming, hon." He squeezed my arm.

"I'm really sorry." I felt like a dolt. But then I always do when someone dies. I mean, what could I say? It was for the best? God's will? I hope she left you in her will? I've learned over the years that a simple "I'm sorry" is best. No sense philosophizing or preaching or trying to make sense out of death.

"In a fucking stock tank," J.B. said.

I kept quiet. I knew he would rerun the events of the weekend over and over again, both aloud and in the dark hours of the night when he struggled with sleep.

"Funny thing is she swam like a fish. Like a god-damned fish."

The tall cowboy spit another stream out, an inch or so from his earlier deposit. Briefly, I wondered if he was aiming. "God's will, it was just God's will, J.B." The spitting philosopher offered what I would not.

We stood there, staring into the corral at the stupid Brahma bull that ignored us. It was almost as though we were meditating or something and I suppose in a way we were. It was the cowboy way to stare off at stock or the horizon, or draw circles in the dirt while contemplating the affairs of life.

"She really wanted to go on a camping trip, Trade. She'd never slept out under the stars before." There was a catch in his voice and when I glanced over at him I saw a thin trail of tears slip out from underneath his shades. "Friday night was perfect, just perfect."

I wasn't surprised. According to Jake Hatcher, Abby had probably died sometime between Saturday night and Sunday morning. Briefly, I wondered what they had done Saturday night.

"We had a great ride on Saturday, cooked steaks. But Sunday . . ." He shook his head. "I woke up—" J.B. was having a hard time talking. "And she wasn't there. I mean she just disappeared. I thought maybe she'd gone for a walk or something." He wiped his wet face with his sleeve. "The horses were still on the picket line, so I knew she hadn't gone for a ride or anything like that."

I stared at Double Indemnity, who was now awake and nipping at his flank in an effort to dislodge the flies gathered there. Funny how flies don't seem to mind the blazing sun.

"I yelled and whistled for her and when she didn't answer, I started to get worried. The thought occurred to me that maybe the Indians had taken her."

Indians? J.B. had a great imagination. While the eastern slope of the Baboquivaris was government and private property, the west end belonged to the Tohono O'odham nation. Baboquivari Peak is sacred to them, for it is here that I'itoi brought the People into this world. Legend suggests that after he had created the animals and the People, and raised a little hell, that he'd retired back into a cave deep below the peak. Some of the People still believe that I'itoi lives in the cave and when he's needed he'll come out again and mingle with the common folk.

As far as I knew though, in spite of their reverence for their mountain, the Tohono O'odham have never kidnapped anyone, and even the most egregious trespasser has gotten off with only a citation and a fine.

"Were you on the reservation?" I asked gently.

J.B. looked at me like I'd lost my mind. "Hell, no. Do I look that stupid to you?"

I let it pass.

He retrieved the Copenhagen from his rear pocket, opened the lid and pinched a big wad, which he then crammed into his cheek. His tongue lolled around in his mouth for a minute packing the tobacco before he continued speaking.

"We were camped about a quarter mile from the stock tank."

This admission didn't surprise me. It was the code of the West. If you camped near a water hole you made sure you were at least a quarter of a mile away. On public lands, the Game and Fish Department demanded this buffer. The reasoning was that cattle and wildlife would be spooked from getting water if people were camped too close.

"So I threw a bridle on one of the horses and went looking for Abby. I don't know why I didn't think of checking that damned tank first."

I reached under my blouse and pressed my palm against my cold, wet belly, marveling, not for the first time, about the efficiency of the human evaporative cooling system.

"And that's how I found out what happened to Abby, when I rode up on that goddamned tank." J.B. was really crying now.

I patted him on the back and found the middle cowboy's hand also there. We glanced at each other over J.B.'s spine.

"I pushed that pony into the water and got to her and jumped off him and she was just there floating, face down." J.B. was trying to talk between the gulps of air he was sucking in. "I swam as hard as I could with her in my arms and took her to the bank."

Oblivious to our arms around him, he reached into his back pocket for a blue-patterned handkerchief. Removing his sunglasses, he wiped his tears first and then blew his nose into the rag.

"I knew right away she was gone. She was kind of stiff and her eyes looked cloudy. She just kept staring at me, begging me to do something, but there wasn't a goddamned thing I could do."

"Easy, buddy." The middle man pulled him close. He looked vaguely familiar to me. "You did everything you could."

"Why would she go there?" J.B. mused and put his sunglasses back on. He turned back to me. I stared at myself looking back from the mirrored lenses. "Trade, why would she go out in the middle of the night and go swimming in a stock tank by herself?"

"I don't know, J.B. Maybe she was hot and trying to

cool off." I swatted at a fly that was buzzing my face, thinking that a swim didn't sound like all that bad an idea.

"In a filthy stock tank?"

I knew what he was talking about. Most of the dirt dugouts are ringed in mud that the cattle have traipsed through in order to get to the water, which is never blue like in the movies. It's usually a murky green with flies, water bugs and scum floating on top.

"It makes no sense." J.B. shot a stream of tobacco juice into the corral.

"You said she swam?" The Cowboy Spitter, who up to this point had been silent, chipped in.

"You see that pool out there?" J.B. waved his hand back in the direction of the house. "It was done before the house was even finished. She swam every day, to keep fit."

"Well, she was that," the middle cowboy offered.

"But swimming doesn't make sense," J.B. said. "She usually skinny-dipped. In fact all the help knew that when she was swimming they were to stay away from the pool."

"And?" I asked.

"She had all her clothes on when I found her. Seems like if she was goin' swimming, she'd have taken them off."

That made sense to me too, but I kept quiet.

We were all silent for a few minutes, letting this new piece of information sink in.

"Mind if I join you?"

We all turned at the sound of the new voice. A tall, thin, gorgeous woman with short sculpted auburn hair walked up. In spite of the heat she was wearing Rocky Mountain jeans, Stewart boots and a black T-shirt.

"This is Jodie Austin," J.B, said, neglecting to offer our names to her. "She came for the school."

Jodie smiled brightly. "Actually my second time around. I was here in April."

"You've been to the bull school twice?" I asked in amazement.

"Glutton for punishment I guess."

She couldn't have been more than twenty-five or so and she looked more like a New York model than a bull rider.

"Hey, Jodie," the short cowboy said.

"Bevo."

I looked at the middle cowboy and knew then how I knew him. His name was Bevo Bailey and I'd seen him in action many times at Tucson's Fiesta de Los Vaqueros rodeo. Like most professional rodeo clowns, Bailey was athletic and bold. His job required him to get in between a rider and a bull after the cowboy was dumped. Bevo was brilliant at what he did and a minor Tucson celebrity.

"You really ride those things?" I nodded in Double Indemnity's direction.

"Try to," she laughed and her whole face became even more beautiful, if that was possible.

I was pretty impressed. There are a lot of Buckle Bunnies who hang out around rodeo cowboys, but this one actually wanted to compete.

"Jodie here's a model," Bevo said. "You may have seen her in those Wrangler jeans ads or the Bud Light ones."

"I'm afraid I don't watch much TV," I said.

"Just as well," the girl said.

Bevo slapped J.B. on the back.

"Well, pardner, I got to get going."

That seemed like a good cue so I took it. I gave J.B. a big hug and told him if there was anything I could do, to just call. With all the help they had around this place, I knew he'd never take me up on it.

I left Jodie Austin, the spitter and J.B. hanging on the fence as I walked out with Bevo Bailey. As I glanced back over my shoulder I got a good look at the back of Jodie

Austin's T-shirt. It read "Bull Riders Will Ride Anything Horny."

"He's really broke up," Bevo said.

"Seems to be."

"You know folks around here always thought it was funny that J.B.'d marry her, what with that big age difference and all."

I said nothing, thinking that $200 million could do a lot to evaporate any queasiness J.B. might have had about sleeping with a woman almost twice his age. If he hadn't been up to the task, I was pretty sure there would have been a long string of cowboys ready to ante up.

"But he really cared for her," Bevo said. "He loved her as much as J.B. could love anyone."

"You've known him a long time then."

"Twenty years or so. We used to rodeo together. I've been helping out here a bit with his school. Tell the students about bull riding from the clown's viewpoint. Things like how to help me save their butts from annihilation."

"Well, those are good things," I agreed.

When we reached the parking lot there were a lot more cars parked there. The news about Abby's death was spreading quickly.

"Nice meeting you, Bevo," I said as I headed for my truck.

On the drive back to La Cienega I couldn't shake the image of the elegant Abigail Van Thiessen floating face down in a dirty Arizona stock tank with water bugs using her as a raft.

5

WE WERE LOW ON SALT FOR THE CATTLE SO I STOPPED IN AT Curly's Feed Store in La Cienega on the way home. As I pulled in, I saw my neighbor Sanders's Ford pickup. Before I went in, I told one of Curly's hands what I needed in the way of salt blocks.

Curly and Sanders were at the counter sifting through an assortment of Chicago screws when I walked in.

"Lotta money," Curly was saying. I knew he wasn't talking about the hardware on the counter.

"You hear the news, Trade?" Sanders asked. A cowboy, and probably the best-looking man in the county, he lives on a small ranch next to mine, called the Quarter Circle Running N. One of my closest friends, he runs his shorthorns in with my Brahmas and had spent the weekend with us rounding up cattle.

"I just came from the Brave Bull. It's not going to be a secret for long."

"How's he doing?" Curly asked. J.B. had been a local fixture for a while and I suspected that in addition to trading at Guyton's Feed in Oracle, he and Abby had thrown some business Curly's way.

"He'll be okay."

"Guess he was having that thing this week." Sanders pointed to a bright green flyer advertising J.B.'s bull riding school that had been posted on the back of Curly's door. I'd always thought that the local postings were courtesy only since most of his students came from out of state with just an occasional one from Tucson or Phoenix.

"There's at least one student up there already," I offered, thinking of Jodie Austin.

"Well, I reckon this'll take some slack out of his rope."

"Break a headstall?" Eager to change the subject, which would drift into a lot of unnecessary speculation, I pointed to the pile of screws on the counter.

Sanders nodded. He used the Chicago screws on his gear. I didn't. Unless they were sealed with Loc-Tite or clear nail polish, they had the unfortunate habit of coming undone at the most inconvenient times. He made his selection, paid and left the store.

"Say, that load of hay's coming later this week," Curly said. He'd found us a deal on alfalfa in Yuma. I was low on hay, but had held off until Curly had checked with his suppliers. We were long past first cutting, which I refuse to buy, and I was eager to fill the barn before the summer monsoons came. Of course with the drought, that was optimistic thinking.

"Lots of stem, right?"

"Yup."

I was one of his few customers who liked stemmy hay. If it's leafy it's often too rich and falls apart when you feed it. To me, that's like sprinkling money on the ground. Besides, over the years, a lot of horses have been seriously hurt by well-intentioned owners feeding them too well.

The man outside was still loading my salt blocks so I strolled through the store, always a dangerous task, for I frequently buy things that I don't need. I grabbed a box of dog cookies for Mrs. Fierce and Blue and then remembered that I was almost out of food for my potbellied pig, Petunia. I say "my," but she really belongs to my cousin Bea. The pig's just visiting us for a while until Bea realizes how much she misses her.

I was writing out my check when Curly said, "It really is a terrible thing about that murder."

"Murder? Who said it was murder?"

"Cripes, Trade, who drowns in a stock tank?"

"That doesn't mean it was murder. Besides, who'd want to murder her?"

He grinned.

"That's not very charitable, Curly."

"Just kidding. You're right, she probably drowned."

Poor J.B. No matter what way this was sliced, he'd always be under a cloud of suspicion because he was a poor cowboy married to a filthy-rich older woman.

6

Wednesday morning I picked up the *Arizona Daily Star* at the long string of mailboxes at the end of the lane and returned to my office. After turning on the cooler and pouring myself a glass of John Wayne iced tea—half lemonade and half iced tea—for it was too hot to drink coffee, I glanced at the newspaper.

The headline in the Metro section jumped out at me: "Van Thiessen Death Suspicious." According to the newspaper, the Pima County medical examiner had determined that Abigail Van Thiessen had indeed drowned, but the sheriff's department was reporting suspicious circumstances in connection with her death.

I mulled this over for a few minutes and then succumbed to my curiosity. Picking up the phone I dialed the sheriff's department and asked to be put through to Detective Charles Borden.

He picked up on the second ring.

"Morning, Uncle C." Borden is married to my aunt Josie.

"Trade, what a nice surprise. How'd the roundup go? Bea said she had a ball."

I smiled, although he couldn't see it. Uncle C is also father to my cousins Top Dog, a triathlete and Geronimo

Hotshot firefighter, and Bea, a Channel 4 anchorwoman. Bea had spent a few days gathering cattle with us, and also an afternoon helping out with the corral work, painting the fresh brands with oil.

"We got it done," I said.

After asking about Josie and Top Dog, I got down to business. "Say, is there anything you can tell me about the Van Thiessen thing?"

Uncle C groaned. "Shit, are you working on that deal?"

While he'd never been particularly happy about my becoming a private investigator, especially since I had dropped out of the police academy years ago, he was less so now that my work frequently intersected his.

"No, no, nothing like that," I assured him. "It's just that I know Abby and J.B. Knew Abby," I corrected myself. "In fact they were here gathering with us last week and the whole thing just seems so weird."

"Not too weird, Trade. Not with that kind of dough."

As we talked, an old red Mustang roared by the stage stop. It was going fast, too fast for our dusty ranch road and open range cattle. Since there was only a woman driver in the small car, my antenna didn't go up, just my curiosity. I watched the dust settle again on the road.

"I read in the paper where the autopsy says she really did drown," I said.

"Drowning's tough. It can't be proven by an autopsy."

"But the paper says—"

"Forget it. It's an exclusionary diagnosis. Kind of like what she didn't die of."

"But drowning's on her death certificate, right?"

Uncle C gave a heavy sigh. He was used to my questions. "With drowning it's almost impossible to figure out whether it was an accident or murder, although most of them are accidental. Cause of death is still pending. The ME's office is running some routine toxicology tests and they won't be in until later this week."

"Booze?" I asked.

"That and drugs."

"She was doing drugs?" While I'd heard that J.B. was a heavy drinker, I knew nothing about Abby's habits. And I'd never heard anyone even speculate on whether the pair used drugs. "I guess suicide's out, then?"

"Very rare. And we're pretty sure this one wasn't that. Although she was clothed."

Mentally I agreed. Abigail Van Thiessen had seemed very happy last week. I'd seen no sign of depression or anxiety in her. "Why is that important?"

"Most people don't want to be found dead naked."

While that made sense to me, I thought of all Abby's surgeries and suspected she might have been the exception.

"So, I'm back to square one. What suspicious circumstances?"

"Trade, look, I really can't talk about the case, you know that."

"Uncle C, just a little?" I pleaded. "My lips are sealed, I swear."

There was another sigh. "There's just a few things that are a little suspicious, okay?"

"Like?"

"Well she had a few old bruises on her that the ME suspected might have been from abuse."

I thought about this a minute. "She fell off her horse last week and I don't think that was the first time. That could account for something."

"Yeah. That's what the young husband said. We were going to ask you about it."

"Well, he isn't lying about that. She got dumped right in front of me. Martín saw it too."

"Then there's the crime scene. God, what a mess."

"It's a stock tank, Uncle C. What'd you expect?"

"It wasn't the cows. That dumb cowboy rode his horse all around, then backtracked over his own tracks and then backtracked again."

"He told me he had to ride in to pull her out."

"I thought you weren't working on this," he said suspiciously.

"I'm not. I went up Monday to pay my respects and I talked to J.B., that's all."

"He managed to obliterate any evidence we might have found."

"Well, he was probably pretty shook up."

"What are you, his echo? He said the horse kept spooking and running away from the body."

Thinking of my own horses' aversion to dead things, I didn't find this too surprising.

I took a long sip of my drink. "So, are you arresting J.B. Calendar?"

"No use paying the sheriff's hot bologna bill until we're sure we've got the son-of-a-bitch nailed."

"Damn." I sighed. While I didn't know J.B. well, I liked him and I didn't want to think of him as a murderer.

After hanging up, I stared at the mess in front of me on the rolltop desk. I'd been working on a medical malpractice case for Garrison Wright, a personal injury attorney in Tucson. The results of last week's work were spread in front of me—handwritten notes of personal interviews and telephone calls.

Since my private investigation business is a one-woman operation, I find myself managing my cases, as well as working them. While there are times when I've thought about hiring someone else to help with the workload, it still gets back to my being able to take cases or turn them away. If my work starts stressing me, I have no problem saying no. So far, the system's worked out pretty well.

The downside is filing my weekly reports. I'd refused to take typing in high school and although I'm pretty fast with the three fingers I use, white-out tape is still my best friend.

Doing anything to avoid the work at hand, I picked

up the phone and made yet another call. In the middle of my dialing, the old schoolhouse clock chimed ten. Good. Late enough.

Charley Bell, my information broker, picked up the telephone on the third ring. "Bell here."

"Hey, it's Trade."

"Ellis, how are ya?"

"Good, Charley. Listen I was just here thinking." I closed my eyes and imagined Charley in his doublewide surrounded with all of his electronic equipment. "You know I use that old IBM Selectric."

"Dinosaur, Ellis. Dinosaur."

"I know." Although Charley had been trying to get me computer literate for years, I had remained something of a Luddite. Some days it was all I could do to retrieve my phone messages from my answering machine when I was in town. "I've been thinking about computers. What would I have to spend?"

"Well, that depends. What are you going to use it for?"

"Reports to my clients." I used Charley almost exclusively for my electronic information gathering and I wasn't about to change that. He buys all the latest software and subscribes to all the databases so he can locate the information at a much lower cost than I ever could. Plus his expertise is priceless.

"I could probably put something together for you," he said. I could almost see the gleam in his blue eyes. Computers are Charley's life and putting one together from components would undoubtedly keep him busy for a day or two. "We could probably do it for under a thou."

I winced. Spending a thousand dollars was never easy, but then I thought of all the damned white-out tape I bought and what a pain it was to use, and about the missing "o" on the Selectric and decided that it was a legitimate business expense. Besides, I could probably use the damned thing for some of the ranch records.

"You know, if you had one I could download a lot of the stuff you ask for."

"Download?"

He knew he was taxing me. "Never mind."

"Well, if you really think you could do it for that . . ."

"It's a done deal, Ellis. Trust me. Say, do you know what they're calling condoms in Sun City?"

I smiled. Sun City was a large retirement community south of La Cienega.

"I give up."

"Software!" Charley started chuckling. He loves his own jokes.

And we hung up on that cheery note.

7

WHEN I DROVE BACK TO RANCH HEADQUARTERS JUST AFTER noon the red Mustang I'd seen earlier was parked in front of the bunkhouse where Martín and Cori Elena lived. It was wearing Sonora, Mexico, plates. Damn! Had someone come up from Mexico looking for Cori Elena? Instantly, I thought of the newspaper picture of the slaughter in Juárez.

Martín's pickup was nowhere in sight and the only hopeful sign I saw was that Mrs. Fierce, Petunia and Blue were sleeping in the shade of the cottonwoods near the pond. Surely if there was a slaughter or a kidnapping going on, the dogs would be raising some kind of ruckus. Besides, I'd only seen one woman in the car, and although Cori Elena was little, she could be a real spitfire. I had no doubt that she could hold her own against most women.

Still, it needed to be checked out.

Outside the bunkhouse I stopped and listened. The evaporative cooler was running and that, plus the Mexican music Cori Elena was playing, made eavesdropping impossible. Finally, I knocked on the door.

Cori Elena opened it almost immediately. She was

barefoot and wearing a red tank top and very short white shorts, which only set off her flawless brown legs. Whatever bras Cori Elena had weren't getting much use, for she'd stopped wearing them around the time Jake Hatcher came sniffing around.

"Are you okay?" I asked.

"*Sí*, Trade. *Pórqué*?"

"I saw the car drive in . . ." I was beginning to feel a bit foolish. "The plates . . ."

Beyond Cori Elena I could see the woman from the Mustang sitting at the table. Dark-haired with a wide blond streak running up her right temple, she reminded me a bit of a skunk. Her silk blouse was wrinkled from the heat and she was wearing long black pants. The light from the open door hit her legs just right and I could see the sheen of her nylons. Definitely not from around here, I thought. Draped in gold necklaces and big hoop earrings, the woman was staring back at me.

"It's my *amiga*, Carmen Orduño," Cori Elena said with a wave of her manicured hand. This morning I saw that she had miniature boots and cowboy hats lacquered on each fake fingernail. Probably a concession to her new life as a ranch woman.

I nodded at Carmen, not eager to stay now that I knew that everything was all right. I quickly said good-bye and headed to my own house.

While I love knowing the temperature year round, it's never more important to me than in the summer. For this reason I have thermometers scattered all around the ranch, so it was no trick checking the one next to the screened porch: 105 degrees. And that was in the shade.

As I walked in I found a basket of fresh vegetables that Juan Ortiz had gathered from the garden. After rinsing the produce, I pulled a chilled bowl of leftover gazpacho from the fridge, threw a couple of croutons and some chopped celery and avocado on top and called it lunch. It was just too damned hot to think about eating anything heavier than a bowl of cold soup. Of course

Twinkies don't count, so I chased the gazpacho with a couple of my cellophane-wrapped darlings.

Martín and I had talked about tackling the hay barn this afternoon in anticipation of tomorrow's big hay delivery. By the time I got to the corrals, I found my foreman and his daughter hard at it.

"*Floja*," Martín said. He was teasing me, for we both knew that I was not lazy. There was nothing lazy about Quinta either. Like all the Ortizes she had a healthy regard for hard work. Although she'd only been at the ranch for a short time, she'd already snagged a job as a fill-in bartender at the Riata Bar.

She looked like an Ortiz with her gold-flecked brown eyes, pleasant face and perfectly aligned teeth. Like her grandfather Juan, she wore a perpetual smile. While this may have been aggravating to some people, it was very becoming on the Ortizes, since I knew the happy faces were sincere.

Where Martín was tall and lean, his daughter was petite, like her mother, only rounder. Quinta was dressed in frayed, cutoff Levi's, and one of Martín's old work shirts hugged her plump, lush body with sweat.

"Hi, Trade," she grinned at me and went back to raking the fallen hay that littered the barn floor.

We all set to work shoveling the discarded alfalfa into Martín's battered pickup. Later, he'd drive the truck out into the pastures and dump the hay for the cows, a treat since we never supplement them. That's one of the good things about raising cattle in southern Arizona. While it takes a good deal more land to support a cow here—sixteen cows to the section in our area of the county, and that's one of the higher allotments—it's not like the colder climes where the cattle need hay to see them through the winter. The only time my cows get extra goodies is when they're in the holding pastures for roundup.

We talked for a while about Abby's death, for Martín and Quinta had both heard the news from Juan, who had heard it at the Circle K in La Cienega. News, both kinds, travels quickly in a small town.

Finally I asked what I was dying to know.

"So, who's Carmen?"

Quinta wrinkled her nose. "A friend of Cori Elena's. Yuck."

"Yuck?"

"She's a real pain. But she loves her."

In her months with us, I'd noticed that Quinta only called her mother "Cori Elena" or "she." Never anything more personal that that. As far as I knew, she was barely talking to her, the end result of Cori Elena having hid the truth of Quinta's paternity for twenty-two years.

"Where's she from?" I tried to sound casual, but the Sonoran license plate was still bugging me.

"Magdalena."

Martín and I stole a worried glance at one another. I knew he was thinking the same thing I was. How in the hell had a woman from Magdalena found Cori Elena? There was only one explanation. Cori Elena had been in contact with her. Shit! Who else had she called or written, and who had Carmen told?

"What's she do?" I asked while Martín continued loading the hay.

"Do?" Quinta seemed genuinely puzzled.

"Do. Like does she work? Or does she have a husband, that kind of thing."

"She's married to a real *cabrón*."

"*Mihijita*," Martín warned.

"Sorry, Dad. But the guy's a jerk. He has a nightclub in Magdalena."

The coincidences were getting to me. Lázaro Orantez, Cori Elena's husband, had also had a nightclub in Magdalena. And now he was dead.

Martín's groan caught us both by surprise. Turning, I saw he had managed to step on the side of a fallen hay hook, and like a devil's claw it was wrapped around his ankle.

"I wondered where that was," he mused as he disentangled himself from the metal hook.

"You're lucky you didn't step on it, "I said, placing it back on a nail on one of the wooden posts. The hay hooks were indispensable when we were moving hay bales around. You could hook a bale and drag it almost anywhere using the handy tools. "Where's the knife?"

Martín reached up on a bale of hay and retrieved the survival knife that we use to cut open the alfalfa. This had been one of Juan's finds at the county dump. It used to be that the hay was baled with heavy wire that had to be popped open with pliers or wire cutters, but now since most of the growers are baling with colorful twine the knife has replaced the pliers.

We'd run a long string through a hole in one end of the rubber haft and the knife was usually left hanging near the hay hooks. Sometimes, though, like the hooks, it had been known to get lost in the loose hay. I replaced it on the wooden post and went on about my work.

When Quinta left to go get us all Diet Cokes, I turned to Martín. "What do two heads-up make?"

"Nothing we want to tangle with, *chiquita*."

8

By mid-afternoon, Carmen Orduño's car was gone. I'd given Priscilla, my truck, to Martín to put out the salt so he wouldn't have to move it from my pickup to his. He'd been gone about twenty minutes when I decided to go talk to Cori Elena.

I was halfway to the bunkhouse before I heard her music, just like always. The peace and quiet of the ranch had definitely been affected by Cori Elena's arrival, for she required that her audio entertainment be at a decibel level that even old Juan Ortiz could hear. But I'd kept my mouth shut, understanding that since I'd been adamant about her living here in relative seclusion her music could be her solace. With the appearance of Carmen Orduño however, Cori Elena had clearly breached her part of our treaty.

The bunkhouse door was open and I could see Cori Elena dancing by herself to the music on the other side of the screen door, her short bobbed hair, like the rest of her body, bouncing in time with the music. When she saw me, she boogied up to the screen and opened it.

"I need to talk to you," I hollered, stepping into the room.

"*Qué*?" She cupped a hand to her ear.

"Turn off the damned music!" I hollered, pantomiming the turning of a dial with my hand.

She must have gotten the charade, for she danced over to the kitchen counter and turned the radio off. Instantly the house was quiet, but for the hum of the swamp cooler.

"I need to talk to you," I repeated.

"You want some lemonade or something?"

I shook my head. There was no way I wanted her to think this was a social call so I cut to the chase. "How did Carmen Orduño know where to find you?"

Cori Elena shrugged. "*No sé*." She batted her big brown eyes at me in the little girl way she had perfected over the years. While it might turn Martín into hot nacho dip, it did nothing for me. Not for the first time did I wonder what he saw in this conniving bit of fluff.

"You have no idea how she got to the Vaca Grande?"

"Well, maybe one of my sisters told her."

"I thought your father was the only one who knew you were here."

"*Mierda*, Trade! I can't live here like some kind of prisoner or something."

"No," I agreed. "You could live in Mexico like some kind of prisoner."

By the look on her face, I knew I had scored.

"Mexico?" She gasped. "I can't go back to Mexico."

"And you can't have Mexico come here. Do you have any idea how serious this is?"

She studied her hands. "*Sí*. Carmen sent that clipping to my father. She wanted me to know about Rafael Félix."

"Alberto would never tell anyone where you are."

She nodded her head in agreement. "No, I called her to talk about Félix."

"You called her," I repeated, having trouble believing she was that stupid. "And told her where you were?"

She nodded, but would not look at me.

"Cori Elena, let me see if I understand this correctly. You called a woman whose husband is in the nightclub business in the same city where *your* husband was in the nightclub business and where, just coincidentally, your husband happened to get his throat slit. Now, have I got that right?"

This was really incredible. Martín was convinced that she hadn't been talking to anyone in Sonora. Hell, she hadn't even had the clipping a week before she called her good buddy Carmen.

She stared at the floor.

"I'm not an international business expert, or anything, but let me just guess here. Could some of Señor Orduño's business associates *possibly* be the same as Lázaro's?"

This time when she looked me full in the face the defiant spark was missing from her eyes. "*Es posible.* But we are *comadres.* Carmen's the best friend I have. She wouldn't tell anyone where I was."

Her faith in Carmen Orduño was stronger than mine. For one thing, I didn't trust anyone who wore pantyhose in June. Besides, Carmen's arrival could have been a fishing expedition by Rafael Félix.

"And I suppose you want to tell me again that you don't have your husband's money."

"I already tole you I don't."

"Well, for all of our sakes, Cori Elena, I hope that's the truth."

"*Es la verdad.*" Her big brown eyes were trained on my face. "*Tengo miedo,* Trade. I'm scared."

This time I believed her. After all, she had every right to be terrified. The Mexican Mafia, like our own, doesn't take kindly to people they suspect of having ripped them off of large sums of money.

"She swore to me on Our Lady that she told no one she was coming to see me."

If it came down to wits, I was betting that Carmen Orduño would be little match for the bad guys. I was sure that they also knew that she and Cori Elena were best friends. I wondered how many men it had taken to tail her to the Vaca Grande.

"You've put us all at great risk," I said. "These people will stop at nothing to get to you if they think you have Lázaro's money."

"Trade, I swear . . ." She clasped her hands in prayer.

"Stop!" I didn't want to hear it. I didn't trust her and saw no need to hear her mantra yet another time. Even the cool air blowing on my face was doing little to calm me. This little bitch had thrown any security she had out the window by calling her friend. And now we were all in serious danger. The newspaper clipping that Martín had shown me wasn't the first one I'd seen. The local papers were full of drug-related Mexican killings.

"Are you going to turn me in?" she asked.

"I don't know," I said. In reality, I did. Turn her in for what? Because the Mexican authorities wanted to question her? There was no extradition treaty on questioning. Even if I told what I suspected, that some of Félix's men might be up to southern Arizona to pay a call on the lovely Corazón Elena Figueroa de la Fuente Orantez, the DEA would just laugh at me. They had too many fish to fry and while they might love to get their hands on Félix, they'd know he'd send a couple of his flunkies for the job and he'd stay deep in Mexico were they could never get at him.

Surveillance? Protection? Ha. Cori Elena was a very small fish in a huge pond and the rest of us weren't even blips on the radar screen. If there was any protecting to be done, we'd all have to do it for ourselves. The problem was if they were coming, they'd come when we'd least expect it.

I was on my way out the door when Cori Elena said, "I'm sorry, *chiquita*."

I spun on her like a mad dog. "Don't you ever," I held up a threatening finger, "ever call me *chiquita*."

"But, Martín—"

"*Silencio!* Martín is the only one who calls me that. Ever!"

And with that, I stomped out.

9

IT WAS CLOSE TO EIGHT THE NEXT MORNING WHEN I SADDLED Gray. While some may think this late for a ride in the Arizona desert in June, I've learned over the years that this time of day, plus late afternoon, is the best time to ride. For years I'd head out at five A.M. hoping to beat the heat. The problem with this plan is that in June there really is no way to beat the heat. Hot and dry, that's the forecast, day after endless day, and there's no escape.

When I rode that early I discovered that although the temperature might be a little lower than it would be a few hours later, there was also the dead calm of early morning. The only thing stirring was the animals, for there was never so much as a hint of a breeze. As for clouds, they were nonexistent and would be until much later in the month. But nine-fifteen or so there's usually a slight breeze that comes up, which in turn dries the sweating horse and rider.

I'd left the dogs at home this morning, for it was just too hot for them. The horse and I could sweat in an effort to keep cool, but Mrs. Fierce and Blue were not equipped with this cooling mechanism and would be panting hard in an effort to cool themselves off. Besides, the two liters of water I was carrying would have gone to the dogs at the risk of my own dehydration. Gray would water at the cattle tanks.

I rode out across the dry creek. The Cañada del Oro, Sutherland and all the smaller washes would remain dusty and dry now until the rains came next month. The animals had given up digging in the dry streambeds in what would have been a hopeless search for water. There just wasn't any to be had. Our last rain was two months ago and the monsoon season was yet a month away. Even the jackrabbits and ground squirrels were few this morning, preferring to hunker down in their burrows until late afternoon. I didn't blame them. When the air temperature's 100 degrees, it can be another 40 to 50 degrees higher on the ground.

Gray climbed slowly this morning and I didn't push him. His neck was shiny with sweat and I appreciated his effort.

I rode part of the holding pasture fence line, and just as I suspected, there were no cows hanging around. There was no reason for them to be there since they all had been turned out with their babies.

As I rode out of the pasture I noticed the full mesquite trees, their limbs heavy with green beans. That was a good sign, for the mesquite beans when they turn yellow, dry and drop, make a fine feed for the cattle. While ranchers in other parts of the country spend a lot of time and money trying to eradicate the mesquite tree from their pastures, mesquite is just a fact of life out here in the desert. I feel no such enmity for the plant since it sustains my cattle when there is no grass.

Shiwóyé, my Apache grandmother who is also a medicine woman, had instilled a healthy respect for the tree in me. It's virtually a desert pharmacy. While many Indians still grind the beans into mesquite flour that they use in cooking, the gum of the tree can also be boiled and the liquid used for chapped lips, wounds, sore eyes, sunburn and even as a treatment for VD. All this and it's a sore throat gargle too. Mesquite leaf tea can be used to soothe headaches and upset stomachs. The bees make a wonderful honey from its flowers and the wood makes a fine fire. Unfortunately, New Yorkers have also discovered the excellent grilling qualities of mesquite, and now we're seeing a lot of our trees harvested, and the wood sent east.

I rode down to the cottonwoods and dismounted for a few minutes, letting Gray graze on the old dry grass there. Just a few short months ago this area had been lush and green, and would be again once the rains began, but for now it was parched and unappealing. Gray, filling his mouth with the dry feed, obviously disagreed with me.

As I took a long drink of water I thought about J.B. and Abby. What in the hell had happened out there in the Baboquivaris? Had Abby really been killed? While it didn't surprise me that J.B. was a suspect, I couldn't really imagine his killing anyone.

I heard a loud, rasping noise overhead and looked up above the tree line of the cottonwoods. There on the morning currents was a family of Harris hawks hunting together. Mom, Pop and a colleague were looking for something yummy this morning—a mouse, lizard or small bird would serve as breakfast. This is a pretty handy arrangement and the Harris hawk is one of only two hawk species in the world where the husband and wife have a helper. The third bird, usually an older son of the pair, hangs out with them and helps them hunt and defend their hatchlings.

As I watched the birds, I couldn't help but wonder if Abby had really been killed, could it have been a team effort? Did the killer, if there was one, have someone to help him or her? But what help would be needed to drown a woman out in a remote stock pond? Seems like all that would require were opportunity and one person stronger than the other, and unfortunately, J.B. met both criteria.

I remounted and headed toward the north tanks using an old cow trail. The cows had trenched several paths through here, for they each had their own favorite routes to water. The Brahmas are tough cattle and I think a good choice for this country. Unlike a lot of the English cattle—the shorthorns and Herefords—these cows are good about browsing and can make do with just about anything they can find. They're also camel-like in that they seem to thrive in the desert heat without taking on much water. Some times of the year, they may only go to the tanks every few days.

Heat was radiating from the rocks and the desert was quiet but for the buzzing of an occasional fly. Even the white-winged doves, chatty under the hottest of circumstances, remained silent. I guess it just took too much effort to open their mouths.

Two hours later I was riding through the back gate. A squeeze was shuttling hay back and forth from the semi truck, which I knew must be parked up on the road. Martín was overseeing the stacking and placing of the tons of hay when I rode in.

"Company." He nodded to the shade of the tack room porch. There sitting on the weathered pine bench was J.B. Calendar. "He drove in right after you left. I'll take your horse."

I handed him Gray's reins and walked over to the tack room.

"Morning, J.B. What's up?"

"Trade, I'm sorry to bother you, but I've got a problem." J.B. looked nervously over his shoulder toward the hay barn.

"Well, maybe we better go in the house and talk about it, then." Of course I knew what his problem was. Being the number one suspect in your wife's murder could indeed be classified as a problem.

As we walked toward the house the thought occurred to me that maybe I was being premature in thinking J.B. incapable of murder.

After all, I really didn't know him all that well.

10

"I DIDN'T DO IT," J.B. SAID.

We'd been sitting at the kitchen table sipping our drinks for a few minutes, making small talk, before he got down to it.

I said nothing. Waiting.

"I loved her. I know people think I just married Abby for her money, but it really wasn't like that at all. There was more to it than that, a helluva lot more."

At least J.B. wasn't negating the money angle.

"But the cops don't believe me. I can tell."

"Do you have a lawyer?"

"Jim Carstensen handled most of Abby's stuff. He's helping me out with this. He went with me to the sheriff's department substation."

I shook my head. "A criminal lawyer, J.B."

"Shit, I don't know any criminal lawyers."

I found that encouraging as I went to the pantry and retrieved the phone book and looked up María López Zepeda's phone number. She was one of the hottest defense lawyers in Tucson. I'd done a lot of work for her and knew just how good she really was. I jotted her name and number on a scrap of paper and handed it to him.

"I don't know how busy María is right now, but tell her I sent you."

J.B. didn't bother looking at the paper as he pushed it into his Western shirt and snapped the pocket closed.

"Do you do this kind of work?"

"Well, I do investigations, if that's what you mean."

"Do you think you could find out who murdered her?"

Jesus, but he was simple.

"Then you think she was murdered?"

He looked like a deer caught in my headlights. "No, yes, I mean, I don't know. How would I know?"

"But you think she drowned."

"Shit, that's what it looked like to me. Look, if we have a deal, is there a confidentiality thing or something?"

I mulled this over. Of course there was a confidentiality thing, but what I was really wondering was whether J.B. was going to blurt out that he'd killed her. There was no way I wanted to be saddled with that.

But confidentiality is a given in my business. Most people who hire you don't want anyone to know that they have done so. "If you become my client then, yes, we have a confidentiality thing. What that means is that your business stays right here."

"How soon do we have a deal?"

"A deal?"

"Do you need a check or something from me for you to be my investigator?"

"No, I'll have you sign a contract at the office." I'd thought about transplanting our conversation to the old stage stop, but J.B. seemed to be talking freely here at the old kitchen table and I didn't want to disrupt the mood with relocation. "If you like, you can officially be my client right now."

His face was washed in relief, making me feel guilty. I wasn't sure that I was going to be able to help him out at all, and was only taking the case because I was intrigued by it. The Van Thiessen money coupled with the dirty shirt cowboy and a murder at a remote stock pond had TV movie written all over it. Scandalous, tantalizing, all the things a PI hopes every case will bring to the table.

"Okay, then, I didn't tell the cops the truth."

I suppressed a groan.

"Let me get a pen and paper. I think you'd better start at the top," I said, grabbing an old yellow legal pad from one of the kitchen drawers. Briefly, I wondered if Charley built me a computer if I'd ever use the damned thing for interviewing clients. I seriously doubted it.

Since I knew J.B., this wasn't the same as taking on a new client. I felt he was of a sound mind and I had a good expectation of getting paid. Unlike my legal and corporate clients, individuals are usually one-shot deals where my assessment of a client's ability to pay is paramount. Good intentions don't buy hay or heifers.

In this case, I was reasonably sure that even if Abby had cut him out completely, he would have access to some money to pay me.

After we got through the usual stuff—his name, age, date and place of birth—we got down to that night in the Baboquivaris.

According to J.B. they had driven in late Friday. They'd set up camp about a quarter mile from the stock tank where Abby was eventually found. Although they'd taken a tent, they didn't set it up, preferring to camp out under the stars in the double sleeping bag that Bevo Bailey had given them as a wedding present.

Saturday morning they were up early for a long ride. They went as high as they could up in the Baboquivaris, turning back when they reached the Tohono O'odham reservation boundary. Then they rode to the north and back to camp. "We rode hard," J.B. said. "And it was hotter than hell."

"Not too many people take overnight horse trips in

June in southern Arizona," I said, knowing it was something the police would eventually ask him about anyway.

"It's cooler down there. Besides, it was Abby's idea. Sure, I knew it would be hot and uncomfortable, but I figured if she was game, so was I. With the bull school coming up this week, we didn't have time to get up north to the White Mountains."

I thought it was funny that they'd been married six months and she'd waited until the hottest, driest time of the year to request an overnight horseback trip, but I said nothing.

"Anyway, there was a little breeze down there so it wasn't too terrible. And we rested the horses a lot. But Abby really wanted to ride. She thought that the more hours she spent in the saddle, the better a rider she was gonna be."

"Did you see anyone that day?"

"Lots of people, but I'm getting to that."

After dinner at camp that night, they decided to drive into Arivaca and have a few drinks. Although the small town was miles away, Abby was getting bored with the camping routine and wanted to add a little spice to their trip.

They ended up at the La Gitana Bar in Arivaca. Saturday night it was packed. J.B. and Abby drank with a few of the locals. When I questioned him about this he said he couldn't remember any of their names and that no one in particular had paid them special attention. They shot a few games of pool, danced to a couple of slow country tunes from the jukebox, and then left.

"Whoa, J.B. What time did you get there and when did you leave?"

He scratched his curly head. "Oh, I guess we got there about seven-thirty. It was still light out I remember that. And we stayed until, um . . ."

"Yes?"

"Oh, I guess about closing time?"

"You guess or was it closing time?"

He sighed. "Closing time."

"And you were drinking all that time?"

He looked in his lap as though he could find the answer there.

"Yep. We were both pretty soused when we left. Fact is, I was probably too drunk to drive."

"But you made it back to your camp all right?"

"Oh yeah. That wasn't a problem."

"Was there anything strange when you returned? Any sign that anyone had been there?"

"No."

"Could someone have followed you from the bar?"

"I don't think so. That was a pretty black night and that road's pretty empty. Even though I was shit-faced I think I would have noticed if there'd been headlights in my rearview mirror.

"When we got back, I checked on the horses and refilled their water buckets. We had a nightcap and then we went to bed." His voice was beginning to crack. I jumped up and refilled his glass with water and brought it back to the table. He put it to his lips and drained it.

"Did anything happen that night? Do you remember anything, any little detail at all?"

He shook his head. "I was pretty out of it."

This didn't surprise me, since Martín had told me that J.B. had been drinking a lot lately, but even without that knowledge, he was a bull rider. Professional bull riders live close to the edge. They like the rush. As for partying, there's no one that does that better than cowboys, except really drunk cowboys.

"Abby was out of it too. We unzipped the sleeping bag and fell in. Hell, we didn't even get our clothes off. We just kinda collapsed."

"And then what?" I asked softly.

He jumped up and went to the kitchen sink where he refilled his water glass.

"I don't remember anything from the time my head

hit that sleeping bag. I was out like a light. The world could've come to an end and I wouldn'tna known it. Hell, I guess it did.

"I woke up late. The sun was well up and when I rolled over I was surprised that Abby wasn't there, but I figured she was off draining her radiator or something."

I smiled at his cowboy euphemism for going to the bathroom.

"I was pretty hungover so it took me a minute to figure out where the Russian army was in my head. When I finally sat up and looked at my watch it was about eight-thirty."

I jotted the time down on my pad, wondering what time the sun had come up that day. A little after five, I'd guess. And even at that time of morning, the temperature would have been climbing. Flies. Pretty hot and sunny for a guy to still be sleeping. That must have been one helluva hangover.

"I could see both of the horses were still on the picket line, so I knew she hadn't gone for a ride. Not that she would have without me. She didn't ride bareback and I always saddled her horse. Anyway, I started yelling for her, but there wasn't any answer."

"And nothing looked any different from the day before?"

He shook his head.

"There weren't any car tracks or anything near your truck?"

"Well, I didn't think to look right then, but I did later and I sure didn't see anything. Maybe the sheriffs did though. They went over everything."

"So then what?"

"I threw a bridle on Lucky and went looking for her."

Not surprising since cowboys rarely walk when they can ride.

"At first, I just rode in a wide circle around camp, hollering. Then I thought about the stock tank. When I got there, that's when I found her."

"Floating on top of the water."

"Right. We're getting to the part where I lied," he said, running his hands through his thick hair. "I told the cops that Lucky wouldn't go into that tank, that I had to force him to do it. But that's not true." Beads of sweat broke out on J.B.'s forehead as he started rubbing his knuckles. "Fact is, *I* didn't want to do it. I was a chicken-shit. I didn't want to go in there with a dead body."

"How did you know she was dead?"

He looked at me like I was crazy. "It didn't take a rocket scientist to know she was. Hell, Trade, she wasn't moving and her head was underwater."

"Right."

"So I worked the bank, back and forth with Lucky, trying to screw up my courage and go in and do what had to be done."

"And what was that, J.B.?"

"Well, get her out of the goddamned stock tank. What did you think?"

"And in the process, you made it impossible for the police to read any sign near the bank."

"I know, I know. They told me that. That I really screwed things up."

He then went into his litany about dragging Abby out. When I asked if he'd tried mouth-to-mouth or CPR he looked at me as though I'd clearly lost my mind. "She was fucking dead, Trade. I ain't no vampire and I couldn't bring her back to life!"

In reality, I knew that if he'd had trouble even going in after the body, he probably wouldn't have wanted to touch the dead Abby any more than he'd have to. Some people just can't handle death, and it was looking like J.B. was one of them. The irony of this rough, tough bull rider not wanting to handle his dead wife was not lost on me.

When we finally got to the subject of Abby's money, J.B. was uncharacteristically reticent. He swore he didn't know the details of her will, or have any idea if he was in it and said that he'd tell her lawyer it would be all right for him to talk to me. I got the distinct impression that Calendar was not happy talking about his wife's money.

When I asked for detailed directions to the Baboquivari campsite and to the stock tank, he said he'd get a map to me.

My interview with him was finished an hour later. I'd filled four pages of the yellow pad with notes, dates and names of people that I'd have to check out.

Before he left, J.B. asked me to come to Abby's private service the next afternoon at the Brave Bull. He said it would give me a good chance to meet Abby's friends and staff, and that her brother, Peter, would also be at the ranch.

As he walked out, I wondered if the lie about lacking courage was the only one he'd told.

11

FRIDAY AFTERNOON FOUND ME ONCE AGAIN IN THE GREAT room at the Brave Bull Ranch with soft canned classical music played over the sound system.

Abby's service had been a tidy one. The black white-robed giant I had seen here earlier had given a brief glowing eulogy. Checking my memorial folder I saw that he was the Reverend Lateef Wise of the Church of Brotherly Love. He was followed by Peter Van Thiessen, Abby's brother, who thanked the congregants for their service and friendship to Abby. Now we were all in that God-aren't-we-glad-that's-all-behind-us phase drinking mimosas and nibbling on finger sandwiches.

For a small, private memorial the room was packed. J.B. had told me to make myself at home, assuring me that he had already told the principal players—Abby's brother and staff—that he had retained me to look into Abby's death. Protocol, of course, demanded that I keep my mouth shut and avoid any discussion of my new case at least until this affair was over.

That was protocol. Practically, I welcomed this chance to zero in on the people who had been close to Abby. One of the burdens of being rich was the constant stream of people: staff, the accountants, attorneys, investment brokers, personal trainers and general hangers-on.

I'd found a quiet corner and was watching Lateef Wise move smoothly through the crowd. While he seemed to know many of the people, the ones he didn't, he made a point of introducing himself to. Most of them gushed over his lovely service, and how he had done such a terrific job of capturing the essence of Abby.

"He's doing a pretty good job of working the room, isn't he?" A voice at my elbow startled me. I looked up into the hazel eyes of Abby's brother.

"He'd put a politician to shame," I agreed.

"Peter Van Thiessen," he said, extending a tanned hand.

He had a nice firm handshake, not one of the wimpy ones that some men reserve for women.

"I'm—"

"Trade Ellis," he said. "J.B. told me you were coming."

Where Abigail Van Thiessen had been petite and blond, her brother was well over six feet tall, gaunt, with a nicely weathered face and startling hazel, almost green eyes.

But it was his cheekbones that caught my attention. They were the highest, most angular ones I'd ever seen; including those of models who'd had their teeth pulled to achieve the look.

A glistening silver crew cut capped off Van Thiessen's generally healthy look. J.B. had told me that his brother-in-law was a serious runner, and he looked it.

I couldn't help but wonder if someone hadn't slipped into the gene pool when the lifeguard wasn't watching. Then again, lots of families were comprised of half- and step-siblings. Maybe Peter fell into one of those categories.

"So what did you think of Dr. Jesus?"

"Who?"

He nodded in the minister's direction. "My sister's guru."

"I thought he gave a nice service," I said, figuring my remarks were fairly innocuous.

"He's a charlatan who milked her for everything he could get."

"Then I take it you're not enamored with the Reverend Wise?" Never that fond of orange juice, I sipped my mimosa anyway. I noticed Peter wasn't drinking anything.

Van Thiessen laughed. "You could say that. He used to play football, you know, before he took up religion. Bobby Bangs, 49ers."

I vaguely remembered hearing about Bobby Bangs. He'd gotten into some kind of trouble while playing pro ball, had gone into rehabilitation and when he came out he'd turned his back on the pigskin. I wondered about the epiphany that had brought about that renunciation.

"Drop-kick me, Jesus, through the goalposts of life?" I asked, reciting the title of a country song.

"Something like that. So now he's got the Church of What's Happening Now and my sister was his primo worshipper. And I do mean was. Since she married J.B. she hadn't been going all that often."

"Did her checks quit going to church too?" The minute I said it I was sorry. I'd promised myself to lie low here today, and was quickly breaking my vow.

"That would be something to check out, wouldn't it?"

"I imagine I'll be checking out a lot of things."

The small, Brillo pad woman I'd seen on my last visit came up with a trayful of tiny sandwiches. She nodded at one end of the tray. "No mayonnaise on those."

Peter took one of the dry sandwiches. "Thanks, Gloria."

"Isn't she the cook?" I asked. Eventually I'd get all the players, but I really saw nothing wrong with a head start.

"Gloria Covarrubias. She's married to José." He nodded in the direction of the small gray-haired Mexican man with the cotton ball mustache I'd seen on my earlier visit. "Gloria cooks and José mostly drives, although he was available for other chores as my sister needed him."

"They've been with her a long time?"

"A long time." He spoke with the authority of someone who'd had hired help around all his life.

"Are you from here?"

He shook his head and licked bread crumbs off his fingers. "Key West. I was at a marathon in Silver City, New Mexico, when I got the call."

"You run?"

"As often as I can." He cocked his head, as if he was listening to the music. Amazingly, I recognized the tune, a favorite of mine. It was "Somewhere, my love"—Lara's theme—from *Doctor Zhivago*.

"I'd like to talk to you before you go back."

He looked like he was concentrating on the music, not me. When he didn't answer, I repeated my request.

"That won't be a problem. I'm the personal representative for the estate and there's a lot to take care of, even with the lawyers. I'll be staying in Oracle for some time."

"Where can I reach you?"

"Here at the house. It looks like my brother-in-law and I will be roommates for a while."

As if on cue, J.B. walked up and gave me a quick hug. "Trade, thanks for coming. I see you've met Peter."

"Good choice, J.B. She's already asking questions."

"Sorry," I said, although I'd detected no hint of malice in his tone.

"No, I mean it. We're all eager to get this behind us. If something dastardly happened out there, we need to find out about it, don't we, J.B.?"

Calendar looked away, to the fireplace, as though he were in another world. I wondered if he was on tranquilizers to get through this.

"I guess, Peter, we do."

"Did you talk to that lawyer I recommended?" Van Thiessen asked.

"Yeah, but I think I'm going with María López Zepeda."

"J.B.'s had to hire a defense lawyer to deal with all of this."

Of course I knew that, since I'd been the one to mention María López Zepeda to him, but I kept my mouth shut.

"Nice meeting you, Trade," Peter said, again shaking my hand. "Give me a call if you have any questions."

"Thanks. I'll be in touch," I said as he walked away.

"Let's go outside," J.B. said, steering me toward a set of French doors that opened onto a covered veranda. As he held the door open and I walked through, I was hit with a fine spray. The porch had been equipped with misters in an effort to keep the temperature bearable. Below us was a perfectly manicured green lawn, rimmed with bright petunias, salvia and blooming roses.

"We can park over there." J.B. nodded to a couple of *equipale* chairs on the porch. As we walked over to them, he took off his Western-cut jacket and tossed it over the back of an empty chair.

After we settled into the pigskin furniture, he pulled his can of Copenhagen out of a hip pocket of his ironed black Wrangler's. Dipping into the snuff, he pinched a good wad and stuffed it into his cheek.

"I talked to Jim Carstensen, Abby's lawyer, and asked him to talk to you. He's got motions Monday morning, but he can see you around eleven."

Reaching into his jacket pocket, he handed me two sheets of paper. The first was the detailed map I'd asked for of his camp site in the Baboquivaris. I unfolded the second piece of paper and saw it was a list of names, addresses and telephone numbers.

"That's the list of the help and most of Abby's

friends. I'm sure I'll be adding to it as I think of more people."

I studied the list for a moment. Abby's staff, in addition to the Covarrubiases, included the maid, Ramona Miller, her assistant, Laurette Le Blanc, and Rabbit Carter, Abby's personal trainer.

I raised an eyebrow when I came to one of the names, Lonnie Victor. His home address was a post office box in San Carlos. I was familiar with San Carlos, it was the hub of the reservation, and the small town where both my grandmother Shiwóyé and my cousin Top Dog lived. I also knew an Apache man with the same name.

"This Lonnie Victor from San Carlos. Is he a tall skinny guy with a bad complexion and a gold front tooth?"

"Yeah. Why, do you know him?"

"I've seen him around. It says here he was a gardener." I'd never heard of Lonnie growing anything other than an occasional pot plant.

"He did a lot of the weeding, mowing, that kind of thing. Abby used professional growers for putting in all the landscaping. Lonnie just kind of kept it up. And he helped me with the bull school too."

I'd forgotten that Lonnie Victor had been a bull rider of sorts. He usually participated in a few of the local rodeos, whenever he could scrounge up enough money for the entry fee. "Surely he doesn't commute from San Carlos?" I asked. It was a two-hour trip.

"No, he lives, lived, in a little travel trailer Abby had pulled onto the property."

"He isn't here now?"

"He quit the day after she died."

"Did he give a reason?"

J.B. shook his head. "Said his relatives needed him at home, something like that."

I'd never thought of Lonnie as a particularly doting family man. Why had he cut and run just because his employer had died? He was bright enough to figure out that

J.B. would still need someone to clean up the rose petals and trim the trees.

"Does Laurette Le Blanc live here too?"

"No. She's inside." J.B. looked over his shoulder through the glass window and then leaned over and whispered, "She's standing next to the fireplace."

I looked over his shoulder. A tall, thin, gorgeous young woman, with a soft taupe color and black corn-rowed hair, was talking to Peter Van Thiessen.

I looked on the sheet and saw her home address and telephone number.

Her name was followed by Abby's accountant and, of course, Jim Carstensen, her personal attorney. I imagined that he was also somewhere in the big room, but had no desire to speak to him today. Monday would be soon enough. These names were followed by a list of Abby's closest friends. I was surprised to see my old friend Lolly MacKenzie listed. Abby's husband had done a good job of giving me a thumbnail sketch of each person, but there was a major omission.

"I'll need your close friends too, J.B."

"Mine?" He looked startled, like he was choking on his chew. "Why do you have to talk to my guys?"

"If I'm investigating, then I need to look at everything. Your friends might know something pertinent to the case."

"I doubt it, but yeah, I'll get that list together too." He didn't look too happy about it.

As I walked out, I took a last look at the beautiful lawn. It was really hard to imagine that Lonnie Victor had had anything at all to do with it.

12

I DROVE INTO SANDERS'S RANCH ON MY WAY HOME. I FOUND him out in his garden gathering ripe summer tomatoes.

"I've got a new case," I began. "J.B.'s hired me to look into Abby's death."

Sanders never said much and today was no exception.

"Anyway, I'd like to take a drive out to the Baboquivaris tomorrow and take a look around and wondered if you'd be interested in going with me." My offer wasn't entirely without guile, and we both knew it. Sanders, before his retirement, was the best tracker the Border Patrol ever had.

"What's it been, five, six days?"

"Last Sunday."

He threw a bird-pecked tomato over his garden fence. "We best go early in the morning. The light will be good then."

"We'll take the horses," I said, not eager to hike when I could ride.

When I finally got home to the Vaca Grande, I noticed Jake Hatcher's pickup parked in front of the bunkhouse. It looked like Cori Elena was becoming the

Pearl Mesta of La Cienega with all the entertaining she'd been doing lately.

I was backing up to my horse trailer when Martín suddenly appeared behind the pickup, guiding me onto the trailer hitch. I jumped out of the truck to finish hooking up.

"Jake's here, huh?" I wanted to add *again*, but thought better of it.

"He brought some *chiltepins* for Cori Elena."

I winced. I'd had an experience once with the hot chiles and it wasn't pleasant. Some people, though, could eat them with impunity.

"He's got to go up to Oracle and Cori Elena's going to ride along and spend the night with her father."

"I just got back from there," I grunted. Most of my energy was going to the trailer jack as I cranked the hitch down onto the ball attached to the truck. "I could have dropped her off at Alberto's."

He shrugged. "She didn't want to go this morning. Now she does."

I'll bet she does, I thought. Especially if Jake's driving. Maybe it wasn't her father she'd be spending the night with after all.

By the time I walked back to my house, I noticed that Jake's truck was pulling out. Cori Elena was in the passenger seat. While she hadn't even come out to say goodbye to Martín, it didn't seem to bother him any.

Having the alarm jar you awake at three-thirty in the morning is not like awakening to the gentle greeting of the rising sun. I stumbled out of bed, threw my clothes on and grabbed a quick bagel and decaf before loading Dream.

Forty-five minutes later Sanders and I were on our way to the Baboquivaris. When we got to Robles Junction, also known as Three Points since three roads come together here, we turned left heading into the Altar Valley. This road not only would keep us off the Tohono

O'odham Indian Reservation, but it was also the same one that J.B. and Abby had traveled last week.

Baboquivari Peak, over seven thousand feet tall, dominated the skyline of the mountains bearing the same name. Even with the higher elevations in this part of the county the desert grasses were as thirsty as those on the Vaca Grande. I noticed that the leaves on the mesquite trees were even shriveled.

Consulting the map that J.B. had given me, we drove past the Anvil and Elkhorn ranches and finally turned off on a faint dirt road. Sanders got out of the truck and opened the barbed wire gate and I drove through. We didn't drive far before we started seeing some crossbred cattle.

The road was rough, but we took it slow and Priscilla and the horse trailer lurched over the single, weed-studded lane. Finally arriving at the end where a bulldozer long ago had bladed a broad parking swath, I wondered with all of the terrific places in southern Arizona that J.B. could have picked, why he would have chosen this particular one.

It wasn't the most beautiful camp site I'd ever seen. When I stepped out of the truck, I could see that the area had been used heavily lately. A crazy quilt of striated tire tracks marked the dry earth. Not surprising considering that this would have been the command post for the initial investigation into Abby's death.

When the horses were unloaded, their chests and necks were dark with sweat. Sanders poured some of the water we had brought with us into a black rubber bucket and gave them both a drink. Then we tied them to the trailer and started checking out the camp site.

It didn't take Sanders's tracking skills to figure out where J.B. had made his camp. There was only one smooth raked area that would have been a logical site for their sleeping bags. Everything else was rock-studded.

Sanders walked to an old fire ring close by and knelt down. He grabbed a piece of dried cholla and poked around in the dead ashes, finally retrieving a charred lump of something. He rolled it in the dirt a minute, studying it intently.

"Steak." He said. "The fat."

Interesting, but not all that pertinent to Abby's death, I suspected. With the blistering temperatures I was surprised that J.B. had even wanted to start a campfire. He must have wanted that steak awfully bad.

Sanders walked slowly and quietly around the camp site, making an ever larger circle. I'm not much of a tracker, but it looked to me as though the ground had been tramped over pretty thoroughly. Even without the hordes, the desert is tough on tracks. Especially in June. The deformities in and around an animal's track that are left by the release of pressure as the living thing lifts its foot are dried out by the piercing sun.

Tracks were on top of other tracks and, of course, the tracks on top were the most recent, and the ones least likely to be of interest to Sanders. After all, we were looking for a sign that someone other than J.B. and Abby had been at the camp site the night before she had been found in the stock tank. The problem was all those law enforcement somebodies that had come last Sunday morning.

While I was supposed to be the detective, this time Sanders took the role. He was the one with the expertise in tracking, and tracking requires detective analysis.

I was quiet, for I knew it was important to keep sound at a minimum while Sanders was taking things in. While there is certainly a scientific basis to tracking, I've noticed that much of it is also intuitive.

Sanders said nothing as he continued checking the camp site. He was working his way back in now, finally ending up again next to the raked place where I assumed Abby and J.B. had bedded down for the night.

He walked toward the back part of the raked area, on the far side of the fire ring, and squatted down near where I was standing. He was looking at a track on the ground for a long time. It was wide and splayed, and looked like the track of a sizable bull to me, not unlike my own Brahmas.

Sanders carefully pinched what was left of the sides of the pressure wall of the print. Then he stood and studied the ground. Finding a similar track, he stepped to it, then repeated the process. He didn't need a tracking stick for what he was doing, which was measuring stride. For some as yet unexplained reason, Sanders seemed very interested in the track of this particular bull. What did a bull have to do with Abby's drowning?

I looked at the ground, trying to find a hint. Everything on the earth meant something and was a track of some sort, a signature by something that came before. Every dislodged rock, crushed weed, depression, and earth upheaval held its own story. But where it was an open book to Sanders, the ground kept most of its secrets from me.

"How far is that tank?" Sanders asked as he began following the track of the bull.

"J.B. said it was about a quarter of a mile." I pointed northwest.

"Think we'd better walk."

That was my first real clue that Sanders was on to something. Like me, he never walked when he could ride. But he'd obviously seen something in that bull track that made him want to follow it on foot, where he could be down close and personal with it.

I glanced at the horses, who were both asleep, each with a cocked back foot. They wouldn't miss us.

I walked slowly behind Sanders as we set off across the desert. It seemed to me that we were only following the lone bull.

We'd gone a few hundred yards when Sanders stopped abruptly. He squatted once again, his tanned hands passing over the air above the ground. He was definitely using his intuition now.

I squatted with him, hoping to pick up something

through osmosis. There was another print just behind
the bull's track. It was very faint and almost gone, but it
definitely looked like a small human print of some sort.
Could it be Abby's? But it was soft and smudged and
didn't look like it had been left by any kind of shoe. I
couldn't make out toe prints either.

"What's that?" I asked. I couldn't stand it anymore.

"Socks."

"Socks? Who in the hell would wear socks out here?"

Sanders said nothing as he glanced around the bull
print. He was still reading his story.

"Someone who didn't plan on walking, I guess," he
said.

"Abby?" It was half a question. Who else would have
walked to the tank?

Sanders didn't answer me.

There were a few more of the blurred human prints
and then they abruptly disappeared again. We continued
with the bull's track, stopping every now and then when
Sanders picked up another sock print.

That was our routine until we finally arrived at the
pond. We stopped at the crest of a small hill where I
made out a faint bull track and nothing in the sock department.

Sanders pointed to an almost undistinguishable dis-
turbance of the earth that I'd overlooked.

"That's not the bull," I said, barely making out the by
now familiar smudge.

We stood on the hill for a few minutes as Sanders
studied the pond.

"She made it this far," he said.

"Abby?"

He nodded.

"So Abby walked over here from the camp site?"

"Nope."

I love it when he does this. This man can say more
with fewer words than anyone I've ever met.

"Okay, so we have the bull and we have the socks." I

squatted and studied the ground as though I knew what I was doing and pointed to both prints. "And a great big puzzle. Why would she follow the bull over here?"

"She didn't."

I thought about this a minute and then asked, "Well, then, why would the bull follow her over here?"

"He didn't."

"Shit, Sanders, I give up. I just don't get it." I stood and threw my hands up in the air. "She sure as hell didn't ride the bull over here."

"Yep."

"Yep? You think she *rode* the bull?" God, that made no sense at all. I didn't know any bull you could ride where you wanted it to go. Even J.B. with his bull riding school and former pro career couldn't get one of the recalcitrant creatures to go off on a trail ride.

"She rode the bull over here."

"Rode the bull," I repeated. This really was crazy.

"Yep. But it only had two legs."

"Abigail Van Thiessen *rode* a two-legged bull over to this tank," I said, and then I finally got it. "There's no such thing as a two-legged bull."

Sanders broke out in a wide grin as though I'd just won the national spelling bee. He dropped back down to the ground and studied the bull prints once again. "Look at this."

He had a small twig in his hands now and pointed to the pressure releases of the bull's track. "There's no life there. No twists or clenches."

I nodded although I could not in all honesty see what he was talking about.

"It's dead. Dead as a can of corned beef."

"And not made by a bull," I said brilliantly.

He nodded. "There's not enough weight here for a bull. It's a stamp strapped to a man's foot. He carried her piggyback over here from where they camped."

That explained the smudged prints behind the pseudo bull's track. Whoever had carried Abby away from camp had had to rest periodically. And whoever that was hadn't wanted anyone to pick up his actual footprint.

"If she was riding piggyback, she would have had to be awake." I was thinking out loud. "Or he wouldn't have been able to get her to hang on. Why didn't she just walk?"

"Didn't you say something about some drug test?"

I made a mental note to call my friend Emily Rose in the medical examiner's office once I got home. It looked like I was going to need those toxicology results.

When we got down to the pond, Sanders again started working slowly from the bank, finally ending up at the water's edge. While the damp borders of the stock tank had probably done a good job of preserving last week's story, it was a very populated manuscript. There were a lot of tracks here—horse, cattle and human, stories on top of stories.

Judging from the horse tracks, J.B. hadn't been lying about his hesitation about going in after Abby's body. The horseshoe prints were everywhere. Sanders studied these for a while and then walked over to a mélange of cattle tracks.

While the mud had exaggerated the prints, I thought I spotted those of the "bull" we had followed over from the camp site. "That's him again, isn't it?"

Sanders nodded and pointed to smaller tracks that were clustered near the fatter, wider print. "That's the crossbreds we saw."

Looking at the two different kinds of tracks, one made by the smaller cattle and the big stamp print, it was obvious that the stamp print would have jumped out at any seasoned tracker. There was that much difference between them.

"I wonder if the police picked this up?"

Sanders shrugged. "What do those boys know about cattle?"

He had a point. The sheriff's department wouldn't,

in all probability, have been casting a suspicious eye at the cattle tracks.

It seemed to me that whoever had made the fake prints if he was smart enough to try and pull off a murder should have been smart enough to make a stamp at least the same size of the cattle that were in the area.

13

I WAITED UNTIL A DECENT HOUR THE NEXT MORNING BEFORE I called Emily Rose at home. Em is a good friend. We team-pen together often, although now that the days were so hot, most of our penning was done at night, which meant that we didn't get home until midnight or so. Since roundup had taken up a lot of my time, we hadn't penned for several weeks, but I was eager to get back to it before the monsoon season hit. Here it was sweltering June with no hint of rain and I couldn't stop thinking about the monsoons.

After catching up on some gossip I finally got around to the Abigail Van Thiessen death.

"That was a strange one," Em agreed. "Looks like a homicide, but those drowning things are always tough." After thirteen years in the county medical examiner's office not much gets past Em.

"I heard that there may have been alcohol or drugs involved," I said.

"We're running the average screen, heroin, cocaine, morphine, the prescription drugs."

"Are the results back?"

"Don't think so. Oh, I get it," she said.

"Get what?"

"She was married to that bull rider."

"J.B. Calendar."

"Do I need a crystal ball?"

"Probably not," I said with a sigh. "Listen, Em, when you do get something, will you let me know?"

She assured me that she would and we hung up.

I called J.B. next and asked when I could interview Abby's staff. He told me this morning was good since the Covarrubiases were there. I told him nothing about my trip into the Baboquivaris, preferring to keep the information about the fake bull prints under wraps until I knew something more definite.

I was just walking out the door when the telephone rang.

"Ellis, I caught you."

"Morning, Charley." Even if he wasn't the only person in the universe who called me by my last name, it would be difficult not to recognize Charley Bell's cheery voice. "You're up awfully early."

"Do you know what you call a smart blonde?"

I had to confess I didn't.

"A golden retriever!" He chortled. "Say, I got your new baby ready."

My stomach lurched. Shit. I'd forgotten about the computer. It wasn't so much the huge check I'd be writing to Charley as it was the fact of the damned thing that was making me queasy. Was I smart enough to figure out a computer? Suddenly the reports I'd been doing on the old typewriter didn't seem that bad. My clients could surely live with a missing "o." Still, he'd gone to a lot of trouble to put the machine together for me, so I really couldn't back out of the deal now.

"That's great," I lied.

"So, when do you want me to come by and set this up?"

"Well, Sundays are probably bad for you. Maybe later in the week?" The longer I was going to put this off, the better it was going to make me feel.

"Sundays? Schmondays, Mondays, they're all the same to me. How's 'bout I come down this afternoon?"

Crap.

"All right," I said, hoping he wouldn't pick up on the fear in my voice. After all, since I'd been stupid enough to give him the go-ahead, the inevitable was at hand. "I've got to run an errand but I should be back by mid-afternoon."

"Great. I'll see you about three-thirty then."

And with that my techno geek friend hung up the phone.

I arrived at the Brave Bull just after ten. Parking in front of the house was no problem, for the hordes of cars that had been there on my previous visits were missing this morning.

When Gloria Covarrubias answered the door I was assaulted with the wonderful smell of something baking. A cinnamon something.

The round little woman was wearing an old denim apron dusted with flour over the perky Brave Bull polo shirt and cotton cooking gloves. I wondered what her thing for gloves was. She was also wearing a nice smudge of the same staple on her right cheek.

"May I help you?" If she remembered our previous kitchen encounter, she showed no sign of it.

"I'm Trade Ellis. J.B. has asked me to look into Abby's death."

"Oh yes, he mentioned that you'd be coming by. Why don't you come on back?"

She let me in and I followed her back to the kitchen. Once again my investigative skills were right on. A large crock pot, with its lid steamed up, sat on a sleek granite counter, next to baking sheets filled with plump, uncooked cinnamon rolls. It sure seemed like a lot of cooking was in progress for the three people that I'd figured were in permanent residence.

"Is Peter here?" I asked, thinking I could also talk to him as long as I was up here.

"No, he went for a run on Mt. Lemmon. Left early this morning."

"And Laurette Le Blanc?"

Was it my imagination or did Gloria's eyes narrow at the mention of Abby's assistant?

"She left last night for the Caribbean."

"Really? Seems like odd timing for a vacation."

"It wasn't one. Her mother had a heart attack."

"I'm sorry to hear that. When's the funeral?"

"Oh, she's alive," she said. "Laurette won't be back for a while, though. She's gone to help with her recovery."

What rotten timing. Had Le Blanc's mother really had a heart attack? Or was it just convenient for Abby's personal assistant to disappear for a while? I made a mental note to check it out.

"Would you like a lemonade or a soda?"

I declined both and jumped right into the interview. After confirming that Gloria was married to José Covarrubias I asked how long they'd been working for Abby.

"Eleven years."

I was surprised. Judging from Peter's comment about their being with his sister for a long time, I'd expected the Covarrubiases had been with her at least twenty years. But then, maybe eleven years was a long time in the working-for-rich-people business.

Then I began asking about Abby's private life.

"Did she have boyfriends before J.B.?" This was a path I felt I needed to explore briefly, although I had a gut feeling that if in fact her death had been a murder, it would have been connected to someone in her recent present, rather than an old beau. If one of her old boyfriends was going to get upset about her marrying J.B., it seemed as though he would have taken umbrage to the idea long before now.

"Well sure. Abby was a beautiful woman. She had men friends."

"Do you think you could get together a list of names and addresses for me?"

She gave me a shocked look. "Why no, I wouldn't have access to that kind of information."

I continued asking her questions about the routines of the household, other people who worked there, and whether Abby had had any recent arguments with anyone. When none of Gloria Covarrubias's answers shed any light on the case, I headed down another avenue.

"How about Abby and J.B.'s relationship. Did they get along well?"

She continued rolling out the pastry dough on a slab of marble, but did not look up at me. "Yes. They got along well."

"So, as far as you could tell, they didn't have any arguments, any fights or disagreements, anything like that."

"I didn't say that." She picked up her dough, floured the marble and slapped the floury paste back down.

"What does that mean?"

"It means," she said, "that they got along like any husband and wife. They had their disagreements."

"What did they argue about?"

"The usual. Money. Friends. Whether or not one or the other of them wanted to go somewhere."

"Did Abby want to go on that camping trip?"

"Oh yes. She was really looking forward to it. She had me fix some of J.B.'s favorite things to take along. It was going to be like a long picnic ride for her."

"Let's get back to the money. You said they fought about money."

"Well," she hesitated, clearly concerned that she might be divulging damaging information about a man who was now her sole employer. "Not like when José and I fight about money, or like when you and your husband fight about money."

I didn't correct her assumption. I had no husband.

"I mean it wasn't like they argued about running out of money, or spending too much on things."

"No, I don't imagine it would have been," I said, having no idea what it would be like to have $200 million to spend.

"And they used to argue about it a lot more."

"Well, if it wasn't about spending too much money, then what were the arguments about?"

"He said he felt like a gig, gig something."

"Gigolo?"

"Yes, that's it. I'd never heard the word before."

"It usually means a man who is supported by a woman in return for his attention."

She smiled. "Well, I guess that's what Mr. Calendar was then."

I saw no distaste flicker across her face and guessed she was just stating a fact as she saw it.

"So J.B. told Abby that he felt like he was a kept man?" She looked puzzled.

"Like she was paying him to stay here? To marry her?" I prodded.

"Uh huh. But that was quite a while ago, right after they first got married."

"So they stopped arguing about that then?"

"Hmm, for the most part."

"What else did they fight about?"

"I didn't say fight."

While Gloria Covarrubias had been fairly forthcoming, I realized that I needed to be more careful with my word selection. "What else did they disagree about?"

"Well . . ." She went to one of the double ovens and retrieved a tray of golden cinnamon rolls. God, they looked good. "Mrs. Van Thiessen was older than J.B., you know."

Uh huh. As if anyone who saw them didn't know that.

"And she was a little sensitive."

"It bothered her."

A black look crossed Covarrubias's face again. "I didn't say that."

Cripes, I was going to have to stop trying to put words into this woman's mouth. Clearly she was having none of it.

"Sometimes, she got a little jealous about J.B., about other women, that kind of thing."

She put a fresh tray of rolls into the oven, and when her back was turned I jotted a quick note on my pad. The possibility of another woman, or women, had already occurred to me.

"Was there a particular woman?" I asked, almost holding my breath to see if I'd offend her with this question.

"Not that I'd know about," she said.

And that was about all I could get out of her.

14

IT TURNED OUT THAT JOSÉ COVARRUBIAS WAS NOT AT THE Brave Bull. Gloria said he'd gone into town to run a few errands. When I'd asked about J.B. she told me he was down at the bull pens so I headed down there next.

As I walked past some of the guest houses, I was surprised to see various vehicles in front of them, including several rental cars. Maybe some out-of-town friends were staying on, which also explained Mrs. Covarrubias's cooking frenzy.

As I rounded the last bungalow, I almost ran into Jodie Austin. The model was wearing Wrangler's and another bull riding T-shirt. This one said "Feel the *Rush*."

"Hi, Jodie."

I'd startled her and I could see that she was searching her memory banks for where she knew me.

"I'm Trade Ellis. I was here the other day for Abby's service."

"Oh right, yeah, of course."

"You decided to stay on for a while?"

"Stay on? Oh no, no, I'm here for the school."

"J.B.'s doing the school now?" I couldn't believe it. His wife had been dead a week and here he was going on with business as usual.

"Well, yeah. He had to cancel it last week you know." She punctuated her words with popping gum.

I walked with Jodie down to the bull pens where we found four other wannable bull riders sitting with J.B. in the wrought iron under the oak tree outside Double Indemnity's corral. Calendar was lecturing his rapt students. The huge Brahma was ignoring him.

While J.B. nodded in my direction, he was not going to take a break until he was ready. A huge orange Gott cooler rested on a wooden table close by so I reached for a paper cup and filled it, brushing flies away as I drank from it. That's one of the problems of being around livestock in the summer. There are always a lot of flies around.

"You got to remember," J.B. said, "that when you're riding that bull you're also riding the opinion of those two judges, plus the guy in the chute."

A slim young man raised his hand. "But I thought you just stayed on for the eight seconds." His New York accent grated through the dry desert air.

Jesus. The kid probably had never even seen bull riding, but here he'd plunked down two thousand bucks for a week to learn how to do it.

"Well."—J.B. spit a stream of tobacco in the dust—"that's one of the criteria. What are some of the others?"

A fat, bald guy, who looked to be at least fifty, said, "You can't touch the son-of-a-bitch with your free hand."

"Bingo, Fred." J.B. pointed a finger at him.

"Speed, drop and whip," said a young Hispanic cowboy, who sounded like he just might know what he was talking about.

"Very good," J.B. said. "Remember, that bull is your dance partner, and you want to cha-cha-cha as fast as you can. Best-case scenario is that your partner will swoop, buck, drop, spin and change direction, all in eight seconds while you stay with him like flies on shit."

That sounded like a pretty shitty dance partner to me, but then I've never been one to follow well, which

means that when I do get asked to dance, they usuall
don't come back for seconds.

"That's eight seconds with the bull rope," Jodi
added.

The men turned to look at us.

"Right," J.B. agreed. "The clock's still running, even
you are up in the air, not even touching the bull, as lon
as you still have that bull rope in your hand and haven
touched the bull with your free hand."

"Wow, you mean like you could be out in space an
still make the buzzer?" the kid from New York asked.

"Yup. Of course, you might not score as well as th
guy who's with the bull all the way," J.B. added. "Let
take a break."

He walked over to me, recognizing the recess as m
opportunity to further grill him.

"José Covarrubias isn't here, huh?" I asked, trying t
keep the irritation out of my voice. After all, I'd driven u
here hoping to do at least two interviews.

"I would have called you, but I didn't know he wa
leaving until I saw his truck drive out."

"Did he know I was coming?"

"I thought so. I talked to Gloria this morning abou
it."

It seemed unusual that an employee would pu
posely duck an appointment his employer had made fo
him. Was there a reason Covarrubias didn't want to tal
with me?

"I forgot to mention that I'd like to take a look a
Abby's calendar, or Day Planner, also look through he
papers, her desk stuff."

"No problem. I'll intercom Gloria and tell her to le
you go whole-hog up there." He nodded in the directio
of the main house.

Finally I got down to what was bothering me at th
moment. "J.B., why in the hell are you doing the bull rid
ing school this week?"

"I know, I know. It doesn't look that good, wha

vith Abby being dead just a short time and all. But,
rankly, Trade, I don't know how this whole thing is go-
1g to shake out, and I might need the money."

If ten thousand dollars was going to make a major
ifference in his current lifestyle, then J.B. really was in
eep *caca*. My fees could be too.

"Besides, I had to cancel the school last week, and
ome of the students had already made their plans."

"Like Jodie Austin."

He gave me a funny look. "Like Jodie Austin. Memo
1ores took a week off from the mines, that guy from
Jew York took a two-week vacation from his ad agency
guring he'd see some of the West." He pointed to a tall,
ood-looking young man, the only one who hadn't spo-
en during the part of J.B.'s lecture that I'd heard. "Paulo
Aoraes there came all the way from Brazil. People made
lans."

"And Abby's death interrupted that." It was hard to
eep the sarcasm out of my voice.

"Whatever. Look, Trade, it's done. Maybe I should
ave called you before I decided to go ahead with it, but
hired you to be my private investigator, not my con-
cience."

Ouch. The cowboy was getting uppity on me.

15

AN HOUR LATER I WAS SITTING AT ABBY'S FRENCH PROVINCIAL desk feeling like a voyeur. At least I was rummaging through her papers, and not her cosmetics, for that would have been far too personal.

I flipped through her Day Planner for the weeks before she died, but I didn't notice anything too jarring. She'd placed the minutiae of her daily life on these pages and written her appointments and engagements down in pencil.

There were a lot of erasure marks where she'd either eliminated engagements, or preempted them with something else. I'd read somewhere that when Donald and Ivana Trump were married they'd also gone the pencil route since their schedules frequently collided. Ah, the busy rich. I was lucky to write an appointment down on the back of an old feed store receipt.

I checked the dates of Abby's ill-fated camping trip. She'd marked through the days with a yellow Hi-Lite and in the margin of that week were general directions to the camp site in the Baboquivaris. Interesting that she'd left these notes. Why? In case of an emergency? Seeing them written in her Day Planner meant that anyone who checked it would have known exactly where to find Abby and J.B.

There was really too much to absorb from her appointment book in one sitting, so I placed it to one side, intending to take it with me.

Her address book was another matter. I compared some of the names and addresses in it to the names on the list that J.B. had supplied. I knew I couldn't take this one, for it was likely that there would be people Calendar would want to contact about Abby's death.

I found her personal checkbook in the right-hand desk drawer. It was one of those big, oversized jobs with three checks to the page. I noticed that the signatory on the account was Abigail Van Thiessen. Period. I rummaged through the desk drawers looking for a joint checking account, but found none.

As I glanced through her check stubs I learned a lot about Abby's charitable giving. While she generously supported the Humane Society, the Christian Children's Fund, the Sierra Club, the Nature Conservancy and the Girls Clubs of America, her largest contributions went to the Church of Brotherly Love. I knew whose church that was. One Lateef Wise, formerly Bobby Bangs of the San Francisco 49ers. The Reverend Wise had managed to garner almost fifteen thousand dollars from Abby since March. That averaged out to about five thousand dollars a month. Not a bad tithe, not bad at all.

Noticeably absent from the check register were any checks written to J.B. Calendar. Yet Gloria Covarrubias had mentioned that Abby and her husband had fought about money in the early months of their marriage. J.B. had to have money. Where was it coming from? Was there a separate joint account somewhere or a personal account for J.B.? I jotted a note on my pad to check it out.

If Abby kept any correspondence, either written by her or received from others, it was not in her desk. Other

than the address book, Day Planner and checkbook register, there wasn't much to pique my curiosity here.

There was a picture of Abby and Peter in a silver
frame. I studied it for a minute or two. I might need a
picture of Abby, I thought as I flipped it over, pushed
aside the clamps and took it out of the frame and slipped
it into my pocket. Fortunately, underneath was one of
those "pretend" pictures so I positioned this one face out.
To a casual observer, it wouldn't appear that a picture
had been taken. Of course I could just have easily told
Peter or J.B. what I'd done, but at this point I didn't know
who the players were so I decided to keep the photo
theft a secret.

A large telephone that showed three different telephone lines sat on one corner of the desk. I jotted down
the numbers and then turned to the side console where
there was another phone, this one in pink to match the
burgundy and blush room decor. An answering machine
connected to it sat quietly on the desk. There were no
blinking lights. I wondered about the significance of the
single phone. Was this Abby's personal line? And why
would she need a separate line if she had three others?

I debated for a minute and then punched the message button on the answering machine. There were two
old telephone messages on the tape. One from her
brother, Peter, and the other from someone named
Clarice who left a telephone number for a man named
Hornisher and suggested that Abby call him about collagen implants. It didn't sound like she knew the guy she
was recommending. I jotted both names down on my
pad, bundled up the Day Planner and quietly made my
way out.

The revelation I'd been hoping for wasn't there so
there was really nothing left for me to do but to get
down to some serious detective work.

I was in my office trying to figure out my attack plan
on the list of names that J.B. had given me when Charley

Bell drove up. My ordering a computer still didn't seem like such a hot idea. But there was no stopping Charley. I watched him struggle with a huge carton, feverishly wishing that I could recall my order. At this juncture, that was impossible, so I did the next best thing. I walked out and helped him bring in the equipment.

A half hour later my office was a wreck. There were boxes and cables strewn everywhere with Charley happily in the middle of it.

"You're gonna love this, Ellis," he said.

I doubted it, but said nothing.

"Say, did you hear about the chicken and the egg in bed?" he asked.

I shook my head.

"The chicken's lying there smoking a cigarette with a big smile on his face. The egg, on the other hand, is frowning and looking put out. Finally the egg mutters to no one in particular, 'Well, I guess we answered *that* question!' "

I laughed and began stuffing bubble wrap back in the cardboard boxes.

When Charley finally had everything set up, we agreed on placing the new computer on a long conference table that I used when I spread out paperwork. After wrestling everything up there, Charley then turned the equipment on.

"This is your power button," he explained.

Encouraged that I at least understood that part, I sat through his patient instructions, all the while knowing I would be hopelessly lost once he left the Vaca Grande.

"This is your cursor," he said, demonstrating a little schizophrenic gizmo that alternated between being a line and being an arrow. "Your friend."

Anything called a cursor was sure to be okay in my book.

We concentrated on the word processing program, since that was the one that I would be using for my reports to clients. After showing me the wonders of the computer, including something called cut and paste, Charley had me sit at the keyboard. I was amazed at how light the keys felt compared to my old typewriter. Leaning over my shoulder he'd alternate between the delete and backspace keys to clean up my mistakes.

While it was fun, I had to admit that I was frustrated every time a typo popped up. Why couldn't my white-out work with this stupid machine?

Finally Charley moved the funny-looking line thing and shut down the program. The next thing that popped up on the screen was a deck of cards.

"Solitaire. I want you to play a lot of Solitaire."

"Charley, I don't have time to be playing games."

"It's not a game, Ellis. Think of it as a tutorial."

"A game of Solitaire is going to tutor me? I don't think so."

"Absolutely. This is one of the best ways to get familiar with your keyboard."

Although I offered to help Charley clean up the mess, he insisted that I continue playing Solitaire. On my sixth game I finally won and was rewarded with a house of cards doing a roller-coaster act across my screen.

"I won! I won!" I screamed, genuinely pleased that my first effort with my new computer had been so successful. As I turned to gloat, I was stunned to see Charley with the IBM Selectric cradled in his arms.

"Wait, what are you doing with that?"

"Gotta go, Ellis. You'll never learn as long as you have this dinosaur around."

"But, but, it's not a dinosaur, it's my typewriter."

"Righto," he said as he walked out the door with the machine.

I was not a particularly happy camper by the time I left my stage stop office and drove home. I'd spent a couple of hours on the new computer and had a single paragraph to show for it, and that production was rife with typos.

The good news was I was met by my fan club—Mrs. Fierce, Blue and Petunia the potbellied pig. They greeted me warmly and we all went to the corral to feed Dream and Gray, with a stop for the dogs to take a dip in the pond to cool off. Petunia, whose previous experience with swimming had not gone well, decided to forgo the afternoon dip.

Although it was well after six o'clock, it was still hot. The thermometer at the barn read 97 and it looked like it was going to be another hot, dry night. The horses, the very same ones who in winter would come racing up with their long tails flipped over their backs, now walked in, plodding one foot after the other, stubbing their feet in the dust.

We'd fed the last of the loose hay, so I grabbed the survival knife from the hook and sliced easily through the three lines of baling twine. Although the barn floor had just been cleaned, it was starting to get littered with fallen alfalfa once again.

I had just finished feeding when Quinta walked up.

"Hey kiddo, what's up?"

She gave me the Ortiz megawatt smile. "I just wanted to report in on my tata." She'd given her grandfather this affectionate Mexican nickname shortly after her arrival.

"Is he all right?" I hadn't seen Juan in a few days, but as far as I knew he'd been healthy.

"Oh, sure. We went dancing last night. He was great!"

I smiled at the image of Juan Ortiz, well into his eighties and very hard of hearing, dancing. His granddaughter was definitely breathing new life into him.

"Where'd you go?"

"The Riata, where else?" Quinta, who did not drink, got all of her soda pop for free from her employer. Juan, who liked his *cerveza*, would not have fared as well. "Guess who was there? Alberto."

"Alberto?" I was surprised. When I'd seen Martín

yesterday he'd told me that Jake Hatcher was dropping Cori Elena off to spend time with her father. Why would he leave Oracle and come to La Cienega without his daughter?

"My mother wasn't with him," Quinta said, with a touch of disgust in her voice, which told me that she'd heard of her mother's overnight plans. "Surprise."

Shit. Cori Elena had probably had a sleep-over with the brand inspector.

"Does Martín know?"

"I'm not getting in the middle of that one. Neither is Grandpa."

As I walked back to the house, I found the idea of strangling Cori Elena very appealing.

16

I'D BEEN SITTING ALONE IN JIM CARSTENSEN'S OFFICE FOR AT least fifteen minutes. Like most professional inner sanctums, there was nothing to read, unless I was interested in the *Arizona Revised Statutes* or old copies of the *State Bar Journal*.

When Carstensen finally came in, he got right down to business.

"Mr. Calendar has suggested that I cooperate with you. You're following the money, I presume." He looked at me over the little half glasses that perched on his bulbous nose.

"That's certainly one of the things I'm looking at."

"Well there was a pile of it. It will take the tax attorneys years to get this all sorted out."

"That complicated, huh?"

He nodded.

"Primary beneficiary?"

"Not that easy." He held up a hand and thumbed through some papers in a manila folder. Finally finding the one he wanted, he withdrew it and handed it to me. "I had my secretary prepare this for you, because I thought it might be helpful."

Indeed it was. The sheet in front of me listed Abby's

beneficiaries. While I would study it in depth later, a quick glance told me that J.B. Calendar stood to inherit $60 million. With that kind of money, he'd never have to sponsor a bull riding school again if he didn't want to.

Another $60 million was bequeathed to something called the Happy Clown Foundation with Abby's brother, Peter, as the executive director.

"What's this clown thing?"

Carstensen looked up from cleaning his glasses. "It's a charitable foundation established by Abby and Peter through their New York attorneys a few years ago. As you probably already know, both of the Van Thiessens are childless. Both are, were in Abigail's case, extremely wealthy." He held his glasses up to the light of the window and examined them. "So they formed the foundation with each bequeathing $60 million at the time of their deaths."

"And Peter's the executive director?"

"In name, and I suppose in principle. They have a New York staff that actually runs the organization."

"Theoretically, could Peter have access to foundation funds?"

Carstensen replaced his glasses on his nose. "While the foundation is outside my area of legal expertise, I don't believe so. It was not the intent of either Van Thiessen to leave a large sum of money to the surviving sibling. They were in agreement on that. There were, of course, some personal items that each stipulated the other should have."

Interesting. Abby's brother would not get a penny from Abby's estate.

"You are aware, I suppose, that Peter Van Thiessen is an extremely wealthy man in his own right?"

I nodded and returned to the list that Carstensen had given me.

Lateef Wise was a bit lower on the food chain, but still a heavy hitter, batting in with an escalated deal that could eventually garner him a cool $5 million. After the top three contenders, the amounts tapered off significantly with bequests to many of the same charities I'd seen in Abby's checkbook register.

Her bequests to her employees only covered the Covarrubiases and Laurette Le Blanc and weren't overly generous. She'd left nothing to her hairdressers, manicurist, personal trainer, accountant, maids, gardeners and the crew of people I knew had to be on the periphery of her life. Apparently she was big on giving money to organizations, not individuals.

I noticed she'd left José Covarrubias $17,000 and Gloria $41,000.

"Why the disparate amounts to the Covarrubiases?" I asked.

Carstensen consulted a sheet in front of him that I assumed was a duplicate of the one I was holding. He tapped a finger beside his nose as though he was lost in thought. "You know, I don't recall her saying why she wanted it done that way."

"But normally you'd lump them together, wouldn't you? I mean you'd have $58,000 to Gloria and José Covarrubias." What was Abby's logic in doing the bequest to the couple separately? Was there trouble between the Covarrubiases? Is that why she had given them each a specific amount rather than designate a lump sum for the two of them? And, if that was the case, could it possibly have anything to do with her death?

"Well I would have if Abigail had wanted it done that way. Obviously she didn't, preferring to give Mrs. Covarrubias more money. She must have had a reason, but I just can't recall what it was offhand."

Although I thought I knew the answer, I asked anyway, "Those funds would be separate property then, wouldn't they?"

"Each gift would retain its separate character until the party involved commingled them in a joint account. At that time, the commingled funds would then become community property."

"And if the other partner chose not to commingle?"

"Then his or her property would remain separate."

I glanced at the list again.

"I understand that Laurette Le Blanc was Abby's personal assistant. I'm surprised she only left her $5,000."

"Ms. LeBlanc has only been with Abigail since December," Carstensen said.

I did some quick mental math. Interesting. Laurette Le Blanc had been hired shortly before Abby and J.B. had married. Could there be a connection? And did that have anything to do with Laurette's returning to the Caribbean?

After leaving Jim Carstensen's office I headed east on Broadway and then turned south on Park, past the interior design type stores Rustica, *Aquí Está* and the Magellan Trading Company. Finally I hung a U-turn and parked in front of Tooley's Café, "home of the outrageously delicious turkey taco."

While I hadn't been to Tooley's for some time, nothing had changed: the glass windows, the colorful yellow walls with turtles, coyotes and snakes painted on them, and the low, midget-sized wooden counter were still there.

I wrestled with the menu for a few minutes. While the Tooley's mole is legendary, I prefer my chocolate straight so I wasn't even tempted. I actually considered ordering the Killer Mailman Burrito; the same one that the menu swears killed the Park Avenue mailman. Finally common sense, and the heat, overruled me and I opted instead for a taco salad with grilled turkey.

As I waited I reread an old framed ad that swore, "More doctors smoke Camels than any other cigarette."

My food finally came on an old chipped plate that looked like it came from the Value Village thrift store. Appropriately, it was accompanied by dull, mismatched silverware.

As I ate, I pulled out the list of names that J.B. had

given me and went over it. I decided to drop in on Rabbit Carter, Abby's personal trainer, since the address was close by. According to my list, she or he—for J.B. hadn't given me Rabbit's gender—lived in an apartment near the University of Arizona.

Fifteen minutes later I was wilting outside 15B waiting for someone to open the door. After knocking several times, I finally gave it up. As I was walking down the stairs, a tall, shaved-head kid leaned over the railing from above.

"Hey! You looking for Rabbit?"

"Yeah, do you know where I can find him?" I made a wild guess, figuring I had a 50 percent chance of getting it right.

"Her, Rabbit's definitely a her," he said with a grin.

Well, at least we had that settled.

"You don't know when she'll be home, do you?"

He looked at his watch. "She should be at the Bear Canyon Gardens. She works there afternoons."

"Do you have any idea where that is?"

He shrugged. "You might try the phone book."

As I walked across the parking lot, I saw two kids frying eggs on the asphalt. This sounds like a story, I know, but it really is that hot in Tucson in June. You don't need a skillet. Just throw those puppies on the pavement and presto! Fried eggs. And perfectly edible as long as you're not too fussy.

Digging in my toolbox, I fished out the Tucson telephone book and then dove back into the air-conditioned comfort of my truck to look for the Bear Canyon Gardens. The telephone number was listed, but the address just read Tucson, which wasn't too helpful.

It didn't take me long to find a pay phone, for the university area is loaded with them. As I stepped back out into the grueling heat, I thought, not for the first time, about the wisdom of getting a cell phone. Since I had just spent $1,051 on a new computer, another new toy—make that tool—was probably not in my immediate future.

"Bear Canyon Gardens, this is Lisa, how may I help you?"

When I asked for a street address, there was a long pause. Finally Lisa asked, "May I ask what this is regarding?"

"I have business with one of your employees."

"And who would that be?" She asked in a still pleasant voice.

I hesitated. It really was none of her business, but on the other hand, I needed to have the address before I could drop in on Rabbit Carter. I gave her Rabbit's name.

"She's in the pool right now," she said. "May I have her return your call?"

Sounded to me like Rabbit had a pretty cushy job if she was allowed in a swimming pool during the course of her workday. "I'm sorry, but I'm only in town for a short time," I said. It wasn't such a big lie, since I was planning on returning to the Vaca Grande later this afternoon, and after all, that was at least thirty minutes outside Tucson. "And I'll be in my car. I don't have a cell phone. It's really important that I meet with Rabbit."

Lisa was pretty good at hesitating and she did so again before finally relenting. "Well, okay, this is fairly irregular, but since you know her . . ." She paused and I didn't correct her assumption that since I was asking to see Rabbit that I automatically knew her. With that she finally gave me the directions to Bear Canyon Gardens.

Driving across Tucson in the middle of the afternoon in June is a fairly bloodless task. Although our traffic used to thin out considerably in the summer, this is no longer the case. As more and more retirees come to call the Tucson area their permanent home, our traffic has increased substantially. Frankly our last good traffic year was 1994, and we didn't even recognize that until the hordes hit the following year.

Thirty-five minutes later I found myself looking for

the address off Bear Canyon Road. I found the numbers Lisa had given me etched in a couple of granite boulders. As I turned onto the long, graveled driveway, I discovered why the Bear Canyon Gardens address was not listed in the Tucson telephone directory.

ATTENTION NUDIST COLONY AHEAD

I was driving through a thick mesquite *bosque*. While southern Arizona is not known for its good cover, a mesquite forest was as good a natural landscaping as one could hope for. A few hundred yards later I was again cautioned:

ATTENTION BEYOND THIS POINT YOU MAY
ENCOUNTER NUDE GUESTS

And finally, before I reached the main parking lot:
BEAR CANYON AU NATUREL GARDENS

I parked under the shade of a huge mesquite and hit the electric buttons on the windows so the air could come in, ventilate and hopefully cool Priscilla's cab.

As I walked up to the lobby, the thought occurred to me that not only had I never been to a nudist colony before, but I also had no idea of what the etiquette was. Inside, would I really find naked people? If so, would I be able to divert my eyes from the obvious lower realms? And, even more importantly, would they expect me to take off my own clothes?

17

THE LOBBY WAS A COOL SANCTUARY WITH HUGE TINTED windows overlooking a manicured Tiff Green lawn. Overhead wooden ceiling fans, natural rattan chairs and sofas, and oversized palm trees in thick terra-cotta pots contributed to the overall feeling of peace and tranquillity.

Whatever fears I'd had about opening the lobby door and being met by a band of naked hedonists were quickly laid to rest. A beautiful black woman, not more than twenty-five, was talking on the telephone behind the front desk. While I couldn't see below her waistline, her top half was clad in what appeared to be a loose white cotton dress.

She nodded to me and held up a finger indicating that she would be with me in a minute. A plastic sign on her desk confirmed that Bear Canyon Gardens was affiliated with the American Association for Nude Recreation.

She was quoting membership rates to the caller on the other end of the line as I strolled over to a display of local brochures touting the Pima Air Museum, Colossal Cave, Nogales and the Arizona Desert Museum. I picked up a pamphlet for the Shangri-La Nudist Colony in New

River, Arizona. This one touted an equestrian trail and I found myself wondering if nude riders wore spurs.

I was pretending to study a leaflet from Old Tucson, a movie set west of town, when a voice interrupted me.

"May I help you?"

I turned to find the receptionist standing behind me and was relieved to see that in fact she was wearing a dress and it did indeed go below her waist.

"Hi, Lisa." A quick glance at her name tag verified what I already suspected. "I called for Rabbit Carter."

"Oh, right," she said. After consulting her watch she continued, "She's still in the pool."

"Oh Lord, I really need to talk to her," I said. "It's about a death in the family." While I doubted that Rabbit was related to Abigail Van Thiessen, she had worked for her so this didn't seem to be too much of a stretch. I neglected to mention that Abby had been dead a week and that Rabbit probably was already aware of that fact.

Lisa's cheery face fell. "I'm so sorry. Oh, that's terrible. I mean, she doesn't know, right?"

"Well, I really need to talk to her."

Lisa consulted her watch again. "She should be out in about seven minutes. The intercom's broken down there so I can't call her." She thought for a minute. "Maybe it's better if you go on down to the pool and wait until she's done with her class."

She walked over to a set of French doors and pointed down a shaded garden path. "You go out these doors and after that big mesquite tree you'll come to a fork in the path, you'll go left, it's marked, and then follow that down to the pool. You can't miss it."

"That will be all right?" I looked down at my clothes. "I mean, I'm okay like this?"

Lisa looked at me and chuckled. "We have a dressing room, if you'd prefer going *au naturel*, but it really isn't required, unless you're planning on going in the pool or the spa."

"Oh no," I said, perhaps too quickly.

She smiled. "We have a lot of textiled visitors, delivery and service people, and then, of course, there are our visitors' guests."

"Great," I said, feeling only a tiny bit disappointed in missing a great opportunity to skip and go naked.

As I walked out the French doors, another thought occurred to me. I turned back and asked Lisa, "Will your guests mind, I mean . . ."

"You'll be the fish out of water," she told me.

I did as she directed and headed back out into the miserable heat. Turning off at the left fork, I followed the path to the swimming pool.

Lisa had sure been right about the fish-out-of-water thing. Once I opened the heavy wrought iron gate I discovered that I was the only one wearing any semblance of clothing. The jazzy strains of Olivia Newton-John's "Let's Get Physical" blared out of the patio speakers as a group at the far end of the pool bobbed up and down in the water in time to the music.

A foursome, two men and two women, sat under an umbrella table near the deep end, playing cards. Their upper torsos were nude, and it didn't take Superman's X-ray vision to see that the game was honest. Not only was there was no place to hide a card, but they'd all be in big trouble if they dropped a cup of hot coffee on their laps.

While one of the male card players looked up and nodded as I walked by, it was apparent that I was more interested in them than they were in me.

I was walking close to the edge of the deep end when an overweight young man did a swan dive off the diving board, collecting himself just in time to shield his private parts from slapping the water. While it was an interesting variation on the popular dive, he still left a very small splash as his feet entered the pool.

I couldn't say the same for the group in the shallow end. Their dancing to Olivia had a churning effect on the pool water and small waves lapped the sides of the tile.

A tall young Nordic goddess was next to the steps, leading the group in their water aerobics. I did a few leaps in logic and figured her to be Rabbit Carter. As she performed her jumping jacks in the pool, her firm bare breasts tried to bounce in time to the music, but nothing jiggled. While they may have been willing, the enhancements she'd obviously had prevented any real movement of her boobs.

The shaded ramada looked inviting, but there was an elderly couple already there. He was bald, smoking a stogie and reading the *Wall Street Journal*. The woman, who I presumed was his wife, had her chair nestled next to his. The clacking of her knitting needles seemed oddly in tune with the music. Sweet little domestic scene, but for the fact that they were both naked as jaybirds.

I avoided looking at them and instead studied the Coke machine.

"Fifty cents," the *Journal* reader said. "Takes fifty cents and then sometimes you have to hit the side with your fist."

"Oh, I'm just looking."

He stood up. "Here, I'll help you with it."

"No!" I insisted. "I don't want a soda." Actually I did, but I sure didn't need a naked man pounding on the side of the machine to get it for me.

"Well, okay," he said, settling back down in his chaise lounge.

Relieved, I grabbed the closest lawn chair and plopped in it. Was that stupid song ever going to end?

It was awkward, since I really didn't know where to look. While I had a pretty good idea of where not to look, the fact that everyone was naked confused me.

I wasn't a prude or anything. After all, I'd even untied my own bathing suit top while catching rays, but truthfully, all this was a bit overwhelming. After all, what good was a tan if you had no tan lines? That was always the best part, seeing not how tan you were, but how white your white was against your tan or against someone else's white. Somehow, I didn't think that was a diversion for these guys.

So I settled for staring over the heads of everyone in the water aerobics class.

Finally, blissfully, it was over and the nudists began emerging from the pool. I picked at my fingernails, hunting for flecks of dirt to flick out, anything to avoid looking.

The Nordic goddess retrieved a towel from a chaise lounge and began drying herself. Bending over, she fluffed the water out of her white blond wet hair. Once done, she headed for the ramada.

"Rabbit Carter?" I stood and tried to concentrate on her eyes, which seemed to be at least a foot taller than my own.

"Yeah."

Up close, she was in her twenties too, just like my pal Lisa in the front office.

"I'm Trade Ellis. J.B. hired me to look into Abigail Van Thiessen's death." I handed her a card.

If she was surprised, she didn't show it. She examined the front of the card, then flipped it over and back again.

"I was wondering if I might talk to you for a few minutes."

Two of the women from the class were hovering; either in hopes of overhearing our conversation or of having a private word themselves with Rabbit.

"Sure." She wrapped the towel around her body. "Let's go inside. It will be cooler there."

I followed her into the pool house where she headed to a small refrigerator behind the bar.

"Want a kefir?" she asked.

I shook my head. I'd never been that fond of fermented milk.

"There's a Coke machine outside."

"I know, I'm fine." A vision of the naked financier banging on the machine clouded my thoughts.

We settled into a couple of chairs overlooking the pool area.

"So, what's this all about?"

"Abby's death. I'm exploring a few things."

"You think J.B. killed her?"

Rabbit obviously didn't pull any punches.

"Why would you say that?"

"Well, it makes some sense, doesn't it, if he hired you to investigate things."

"I understand you were her personal trainer."

"Uh huh."

We talked for a few minutes about her tenure with Abby. She'd worked for her for two years.

"You must have been with her before?" I asked.

"In New York. She asked me to come out here when she moved to Tucson. I liked the climate." She shrugged. "I drove out to the ranch three times a week. It was easy work for great pay."

She assured me that Abby had pursued her regimen alone on the remaining days of the week in the weight and workout room she'd built at the ranch.

"Did she seem all right to you?" I asked.

"All right? In what way?"

"Was she depressed, or preoccupied, or anything like that recently?"

Rabbit sipped her kefir. "Recently?"

"Say in the past six months."

She sighed heavily. "Look, I really don't know anything."

The way she said it made me think she did.

"Really." Now she was staring at the slate floor, ignoring any eye contact with me.

"Rabbit, if there's any possibility that Abby didn't drown, then a lot of questions are going to be asked."

"By the police?"

"Yes, and insurance investigators. There's a lot of money involved here."

She nodded.

"So I'm probably just the first of many that you're going to see."

She thought about this for a minute.

"They fought."

"Abby and J.B.?"

"Yeah."

"What'd they fight about?"

"Women. Abby didn't trust him. She was a lot older, you know."

What was it with these people? Didn't they think I had eyes? Abby looked good, damned good, for her age, but she sure as hell wasn't thirty-six and no amount of drinking on J.B.'s behalf would ever have evened that score.

"She was in incredible shape and really worked hard."

"You mentioned women. Was there a certain one?"

"Look, things were cool at first. When she started dating him, he never looked at another woman, and she never accused him of doing so."

"But . . ."

"But then during his last bull school, there was a woman who came out from New York and Abby was very jealous of her."

"Jodie Austin?" I remembered her saying that this was her second bull riding school and made a wild guess.

"You know about her?"

"She's up there now, enrolled in the new session."

Rabbit rolled her eyes.

"Anyway, one afternoon we quit early since Abby had a headache. Jodie was staying in number 12, which is right near the workout studio. As we were leaving, J.B. walked out of number 12."

"Did Abby see him?"

"Oh yeah. Big time."

I remembered Jodie's T-shirt, "Bull Riders Will Ride Anything Horny." Had that included J.B.?

"Was there a scene?"

"Not then. She pulled me back in the studio and waited for him to leave. It was kind of like high school. We were peeking out from the blinds, trying to see what was going on."

"Was anything?"

"He left, and then Abby sent me over. She wanted me to ask Jodie if she was interested in working out. It was just an excuse."

"So you went over there."

"Uh huh. When Jodie answered the door, she was buttoning up her blouse."

"Did you tell Abby that?"

"I didn't have to. She was still peeking out the blind. She and J.B. got into a major fight later, I heard."

"Someone told you about it?"

"Ramona, the maid. She's not all there, but she said they went round and round over Jodie Austin."

"So do you think something was going on between the two of them?"

Rabbit shrugged.

"Did he ever hit on you?"

"No." She laughed and flexed her biceps. "I think I was too much for that little squirt."

The young man who had done the swan dive walked in the pool house and approached our table. "Rabbit, you think you could help me with my bench presses later?"

He was standing next to us and since we were seated, that put the things I was not supposed to be looking at right in my face. This was just too tempting, and I found myself cheating and looking whenever I thought I could get away with it.

"Sure, Reuben, how about four?"

"Great, thanks."

And with that the plump diver was off.

My sneak peeks had not gone unnoticed by Rabbit.

"Do you know who the most popular guy at a nudist colony is?"

I shook my head.

"The one who can carry a dozen donuts with no hands."

Reuben, as near as I could tell, was not going to be breaking donut records any time soon.

When I finished my interview with Rabbit Carter she had shed no new light on my investigation. What had made the drive across town worthwhile was the information she had given me about a possible tryst between J.B. Calendar and the New York model, Jodie Austin.

While jealousy could be a powerful motive, it could also induce people to take action. Could Abby have been thinking about divorcing J.B.? And just because her young husband cheated on her, did that make him a murderer?

As I drove out the thought occurred to me that I had forgotten to ask Rabbit about her name.

Then again, maybe some stones were better left unturned.

18

I HAD A THREE O'CLOCK APPOINTMENT WITH CLARICE Martínez and found her in the patio aviary of her spacious Catalina Foothills home, spraying her birds with water. She was a tiny little thing with dyed red hair cut pixie style and a gap between her oversized front teeth. Her khaki shorts and Nature Conservancy T-shirt were good camouflage for the fortune behind them.

I'd done some homework on her and knew that she had been born a Mellon, married a Vanderbilt and had ended up with Pepe Martínez, a local rags-to-riches story who had founded Pepe's Auto Parts, a chain of seventeen stores spread around the state.

"Mommy's birdies are hot. Sweet little chirpies," she cooed and made kissing noises to what looked like a flock of nervous finches. From their flight patterns, I suspected that they really were not enjoying their afternoon shower all that much.

"Mrs. Martínez?" I peered through the wire of the cage. Clarice Martínez looked pretty well preserved, and I suspected, like Abby, she'd had quite a bit of surgery done.

"Oh, you must be the detective. How exciting!" She coiled the hose, exited the coop and extended a wet freckled hand. "Clarice, call me Clarice, honey, everyone does."

"Okay, Clarice."

"Now I know you want to know all about Abby, so let's go inside. Goodbye my lovelies." She threw a kiss to her birds as I followed her into the house.

Without asking, she poured two tumblersfull of iced tea, handed me one and motioned to the glass top table in her breakfast nook, which overlooked the swimming pool and the birdcage.

"Just love those birds, love 'em." Her eyes were that clear, sparkly blue that give some people a mystical look. Suddenly she jumped back up, disappeared around the corner and returned a minute later and handed me a photograph. It was of her and Abby. Both of them were wearing biker's black leather jackets and straddling a Harley. Clarice, the smaller of the two small women, was in the driver's seat, Abby behind. Both women wore black pants and high heels.

"She was my best friend."

She was on J.B.'s list of Abby's closest friends.

"I knew her forever. Our nannies were friends and they used to push us in our strollers together in Central Park when we were babies. It was always just the two of us, at least until Peter came along."

"Peter's younger then."

"By three years. He's actually her half brother. Her mother remarried when Abby was five."

"And she took the Van Thiessen name?"

Clarice nodded. "Her own father had died in a boating accident, so it wasn't a problem."

"Were there other sisters or brothers?"

"Nope. Just the two of them. They were tighter than ticks though, because of that mother they had. Madeleine." Clarice let wind whistle through the gap in her front teeth. "She was a real basket case and made dysfunctional look normal."

"In what way?"

"Oh the usual Oprah stuff. Abused them. Beat them. Tied them up. She had a special closet she'd throw them in when she really wanted to punish them. She called it the Cave and did that pretty regularly. For rich kids, they had it pretty rough."

Jesus. She had all that money. Couldn't she have just sent them to the zoo with a nanny? I remembered Uncle C's talking about the bruises on Abby's body, suggesting they might have been from spousal abuse. If she'd been abused as a child, would that have made it more likely that she would have hooked up with a man that would mistreat her? I had no idea.

"So, where was Peter's father when all of this was happening?"

"When he wasn't at the candy factory, which was most of the time, he was too drunk to much care about how Madeleine was spending her days. He'd come home, drink his fill and pass out, ignoring his wife. In fact I used to think that was the reason Madeleine was so mean to Peter and Abby. I thought she was taking her anger toward him out on them, but then I figured out she was just naturally wicked. Some people are, you know."

I nodded, for I'd seen my share of wicked.

"Peter's father died of cirrhosis when we were all in college."

Clarice stared out the window. I suspected she was admiring her birds. And then she continued my Van Thiessen history lesson.

"And she was crazy. One year Abby said she wanted to marry Peter. That's what she wanted for her birthday. Do you believe it?"

"Peter, her brother?"

"The same. You have to remember we were really into playing house back then. Anyway Mad Madeleine sent out invitations, had her dressmaker make the bridesmaids' dresses, and even ordered a wedding cake."

I rolled my eyes. "They didn't really have a wedding?"

"The whole nine yards."

I wondered how many years of therapy it would take to work through that one. If ever.

"And then the following week there was a very quiet divorce. There was no Cave that time. She locked them in separate closets for five days."

"Pretty sick. So what's the story on Peter? Does he have a family?"

"Oh, he's a confirmed bachelor. Never married. Honey, it's been so long now he doesn't even appear on those most eligible lists anymore. Everyone's given up on him."

I raised an eyebrow.

"Oh no." She laughed. "He's always had lots of girl-friends."

"I didn't mean . . ." But of course I did.

"While I understand why they were so close, fact is I was always a little jealous of Peter. I'd had Abby to my-self until he came along. But then we went to a girl's boarding school and then on to Vassar, which was all girls back in those days. We were there until I dropped out to find myself. And we've gone through seven hus-bands together."

"Seven?"

"Well, five of them were mine," she said with a wist-ful smile. "Pepe's my husband *du jour*."

I laughed at what I hoped was a joke.

"God, I can't believe she's gone. And to drown? She was a great swimmer, just great. We used to go to the Caymans skin diving all the time."

"Well, the police are looking into that."

She didn't look surprised. "I imagine they are. How deep was that pond anyway?"

"I don't know." It had been one of the questions I'd intended on asking Uncle C, but I was waiting for Emily Rose's call on the toxicology reports, figuring I might as well lump together all my questions for him.

"How's J.B. doing?"

"He'll be all right," I said.

"For the record, honey, I do believe that boy loved her."

Interesting choice of words. Boy.

"And she was nutso about him. Old John Wilson hadn't been planted three months and she fell head over heels with that cute little cowboy."

"Who was John Wilson?" I asked, suddenly realizing I knew very little about Abigail Van Thiessen.

"Her husband. Wilson Made Fabrics."

"The textile company?"

She nodded. "She met him when she was in New York working for Choco-Willie Candy, her stepfather's company. He was quite a bit older than she was. She was twenty-three. I was her maid of honor."

I did some quick math. "They must have been married about forty-five years."

"Just short of. He was in Costa Rica skin diving with some friends and had a massive heart attack. Never made it out of the water alive. She was devastated."

"But then J.B. came along," I said, prompting her.

"Poor Abby, that was one thing about her, she always had to have a man around."

It seemed to me that anyone who'd had five husbands might also fit into that category.

"And the sex!" Clarice fanned herself with a newspaper. "I guess the cowboy was really something in that department. Jeepers, Abby used to say he was so good, she wanted to share him with her friends. Not that she ever did, of course."

"Then she wasn't jealous about J.B., I mean, what with the age difference and all."

"Jealous? Hell, yes, she was jealous. I was very careful when I was around the two of them. She had a green streak a mile wide."

"Did she ever say anything about other women?"

"Sure. She thought he was having an affair with someone."

"Did she say who it was?"

"Which time?"

"My God, they'd only been married six months
How much screwing around was he doing?"

"In reality or in her mind? Realistically, maybe not a
all. In Abby's mind, he couldn't be trusted in that depart
ment and she didn't like that, didn't like it at all. She wa
a Scorpio, did you know that?"

I shook my head.

"Jealous as hell, all of them. They'll pull out tha
stinger and zap!" Her fingernail dug into my arm, star
tling me. "You're gone."

"Are you saying that you think she was getting read
to dump J.B.?"

She sipped her tea and thought about my questior
"Now I can't really say that for sure, but she was sur
trying to slow him down. Right before that trip sh
called me, furious since she'd just found out that bul
riding woman was coming back."

"She thought there was something going on?"

"She didn't like her hanging around. She was
model, you know, and everything on her looked real."

"What's that mean?"

"Honey, Abby worshipped at the altar of the plasti
surgeon." She brushed back her hair and I could see
faint line. "Hell, we've used some of the same *artistes*, bu
with her it was an obsession. Eyelids, lips, boobies, nose
she'd had them all rearranged. She thought liposuctio
was like having her hair done."

"She did look good."

"Still mutton dressed as lamb. It was deeper tha
that, though." Clarice looked beyond me to the finches,
faraway look in her eyes. "She was truly terrified o
growing old, of being incapacitated in any way and get
ting ugly. I guess she doesn't have to worry about tha
now."

"No."

"We were thirteen when Abby's mother died. Sh
had cancer in her jaw. It was terrible. Madeleine ha

een a beautiful woman, but they just kept cutting up
er face. Of course, they never did get it all."

"Cancer's tough," I agreed.

"Poor Peter and Abby didn't know whether to cele-
rate or cry. That's the funny thing about all of that. A
woman can do terrible, brutal things to her babies and
hey'll still love her. It was the first funeral any of us had
ver been to, and it was pretty scary."

"I can imagine."

"Where were we?" Clarice asked, pulling herself out
f her melancholy. "Oh, the plastic surgery. Abby had a
great body for a sixty-eight-year-old woman. But that
model was in her twenties and tough competition. She
old J.B. to call her and tell her she couldn't come out
again."

"I guess that didn't turn out the way she wanted."

"Basically he told Abby to butt out of his business."

Pretty ballsy for a guy who hadn't had a pot to piss
n before his marriage.

"What can you tell me about Laurette Le Blanc?"
While Jodie Austin was drop-dead gorgeous, Laurette
was no slacker in the looks department. The thought oc-
urred to me that if J.B. fancied himself as a ladies' man,
Laurette might have been high on his hit list.

"As far as I know, J.B. never had a thing for Laurette,
although who could blame him if he did? Half the men I
now would pay to put their pee-pee in that woman.
No, she was all business. I don't think Laurette even had
boyfriend."

"She hadn't worked for Abby very long," I said, fish-
ng.

"You don't know that story?" Clarice gave me a dis-
elieving look. "They brought her back with them from
heir honeymoon!"

"Brought her back?"

"You know, like you might go to Italy and bring back
ome nice pottery, or Ireland and bring back Waterford,
hey went to St. Martin and brought back Laurette

LeBlanc. She was working in L'Anse Margot in Nett
Bay and Abby thought she'd make a great secretary."

What was the wisdom of bringing such a gorgeou
young woman into your household? Especially if yo
had a much younger husband with a straying eye? Ha
Laurette Le Blanc been a test for J.B.?

"And Abby wasn't jealous of her?"

"She never said anything. But frankly, it probabl
never occurred to Abby that J.B. would fool around wit
Laurette because of her color."

What a stupid attitude.

"You have to understand that Abby loved collectin
beautiful things. Of course you wouldn't know it by th
cowboy house she remodeled up there, but if you wer
in some of her other homes, you'd see what I mean."

"That must have been quite a honeymoon."

"J.B. paid for the whole thing himself, he did. Ever
dime. Abby was really proud of that."

I wondered where J.B. had gotten the dough.

"I've heard that they used to argue about money,"
said, feeling slightly guilty. After all, I was being paid b
J.B. to investigate Abby's death, but so far most of my in
vestigating had to do with pointing questions in his d
rection.

"Well, they did fight about it, but only that firs
month or so they were married."

I thought about the bruises the medical examine
had found on Abby's body. "Did she ever say anything t
you about J.B. abusing her?"

"You mean like hitting her?"

I nodded.

"Absolutely not. Listen, honey, Abby would neve
have put up with that. Not for a moment. She'd suffere
enough abuse at the hands of her mother."

I knew abuse could be a perpetual thing and won
dered how Clarice could be so sure of Abby's resistanc
to it, but let the subject drop.

"Anyway, as I was saying, they fought that first month about money, but then Abby got smart and decided to give him some of his own so he wouldn't have to ask her for any, or have to sit there, humiliated, in restaurants and stores while she fished out her credit card."

"So she gave him his own checking account?" I picked up my iced tea.

"Checking account, hell. She gave him a million dollars."

My tumbler almost crashed against the glass top table.

"A million dollars," I repeated. "Abby forked over a million dollars to a guy she'd only known for a few months?"

"Not just a guy, honey. He was her husband."

"No strings attached. I mean, she just gave him the money and he could do whatever he wanted with it?"

"As far as I know."

Wow. J.B. really had hit the jackpot. If what Clarice was telling me was true, J.B. was a millionaire, his money secure. Even under the worst-case scenario, if Abby had decided to divorce him, he'd still have the money.

My suspicion meter dropped a few points in his favor. He didn't strike me as particularly materialistic so why would he be greedy and kill her for the rest? Still, a million dollars was about $59 million short of what he was scheduled to inherit. I had to wonder, would he have been so cocky about Jodie Austin if he hadn't had the money? And why had he told me that his reason for running the bull school so soon after Abby's death was because he was worried about money?

We talked for a while longer but Clarice Martínez dropped no more bombs.

19

Martín and Quinta were pushing a few cows and a lame bull up the lane when I drove into the Vaca Grande. The cows were just along for the ride since it's usually easier to push a bull around if he's got company.

I stopped the truck and shut down the diesel so we could talk as Martín reined his horse in. Quinta continued driving the cattle down toward the corrals.

"Old Faded H has a hitch in his getalong, huh?" I said, for I recognized the Hereford bull. His ear tag had faded out a long time ago and we had resorted to calling him Faded H.

"I thought I'd bring him in and see what's going on with that foot," Martín offered.

I was encouraged to see the Hereford with girl friends, for he was very fond of another bull and hadn't been paying too much attention to the cows lately. Hanging out with the boys was definitely not the job he'd been hired to do.

"Maybe he's just sore-footed from all those dates," Martín said, grinning.

"Well, we can only hope and pray." I was dying to hear if he knew that Alberto had been up at the Riata, which meant that Cori Elena had not spent the night with her father. From his cheery manner I doubted whether he had heard the news and I sure wasn't going to share it with him.

"I'm taking salt out early tomorrow, *chiquita*. Want to come?"

Ah, there it was. Something was definitely up. As kids we'd often gone out together to drop salt blocks in the pastures. While some of the salt could be dumped from a truck, a lot of the higher pastures were only accessible by horseback. Over the years, Martín and I had spent a lot of time together setting out salt, checking on cattle and riding fence. It was the one time we had where each of us gave our uninterrupted attention to the other. Was that what Martín was looking for?

"I'll have to check my schedule, I've got a new case I'm working on. Let me make a few calls, and I'll let you know."

"J.B.'s keeping you pretty busy, huh?"

While I had said nothing to Martín about my new client, news on the small town telegraph travels fast.

"We'll talk, Martín," I said as I started up Priscilla.

I stopped at the stagecoach office and checked my answering machine. There was a message from Peter Van Thiessen returning my call as to when we could get together, one from Charley Bell wanting to know how I was getting along with my new computer, and one from Emily Rose. The old schoolhouse clock read 4:48 so I returned Em's call first.

Sharon Roberts answered the phone.

"Hey, what are you doing?" Sharon was a filing clerk and not usually the one to answer the telephone. "Roberta's out sick. Guess you want Emily, huh?"

Without waiting for my answer the call was transferred.

"Do I have to guess what color your hair is this morning?" I asked. It was a running joke because Emily Rose was always screwing around with her crowning glory. It drove her husband nuts and amused the rest of us.

"Don't believe that business about rather being dead than red," she said. "That's a hint."

She hadn't been a redhead for at least a year, but I guess that had changed. Suddenly my world was getting full of them—Jodie Austin, Clarice and now Emily Rose.

"The Van Thiessen toxicology report is in. Thought you'd like to know."

"Don't keep me in suspense."

"They found a blood alcohol of .15." She snapped her gum in my ear.

"Wow, she must have been pretty tanked."

"Bad pun," Em said. "It's here somewhere. I know you'll want the specifics."

I heard the rustling of paper.

"We had a little Prozac."

Prozac? She was rich, thin, beautiful and a newly-wed. Why in the hell would she have been on Prozac?

"And then it got interesting. We had an anonymous tip."

"What kind of a tip?"

"The caller suggested we run a screen for ketamine."

"What in the hell is that?"

"It's a veterinary thing."

"Used for what?"

"It's one of a class of drugs known as dissociative agents and a distant cousin to PCP. Definitely hallucino-genic."

While I'd never heard of ketamine, I knew PCP was weird stuff. From what I'd read, after taking Angel Dust even the puniest grandmother had a good chance of dis-abling an entire SWAT team.

"Dissociative?"

"Users report that when they're on it, it feels as though their mind is separated from the body. It's also an anesthetic, so they don't feel pain. Date rape ring a bell?"

"That's the drug they use?"

"One of them. Turns you into a zombie. You can be alert, but you can't move."

Suddenly I thought of the fake bull tracks that Sanders and I had seen and the places where we'd also spotted smudged sock prints near the fake bull. At the time I'd said that Abby would have had to have been awake to be carried piggyback over to the pond. From the sounds of the toxicology results she could have been awake, but in a zombie state, unable to walk on her own or to defend herself against whoever was carrying her off.

"Abby never struck me as a user, J.B. either. I knew they drank a bit, but drugs . . ."

"We don't think she was a user either. It was in her stomach."

"And?" I had no idea what that implicated.

"Special K is a very versatile little number. It can be injected, or taken orally. But—and this is an important distinction—most users get the powder and snort it."

"So if you found it in her stomach, then she would have had to have eaten it."

"Or drunk it. Probably disguised in something else since it's pretty nasty-tasting stuff. While we've got her stomach contents, there's no way of telling if the ketamine went in with the steak, or the alcohol."

"So she couldn't have taken it deliberately that way?"

"Operative word is wouldn't. Highly unlikely. They were out in the toolies, just the two of them. If they were steady users they would have had the powder, and she would have snuffed that."

"How easy would it have been to get?"

"On the streets, a breeze. Or from a cooperating veterinarian."

"I've never heard of it."

"It's primarily used as an anesthetic for immobilizing cats and monkeys."

No wonder I wasn't familiar with the drug. There weren't many monkeys on the Vaca Grande.

"What in the hell was she doing with that?" I asked, thinking out loud.

"Funny, that's the same question the docs down here are asking. The detectives were in a while ago conferencing with them."

Shit. If a veterinary drug had anything to do with Abby's death, J.B. was going to be in an even bigger pile of *caca*. The detectives were already looking for a murder and they would be asking the same classic questions I was. Who had the desire, the opportunity and the motive to kill Abigail Van Thiessen?

Clearly, J.B. had the opportunity and the motive, for money was always a strong contender in the motive department. Desire was what I was wrestling with. Did J.B. want to kill his wife? And had he? He'd been around animals all his life and getting a veterinary drug would have been easy.

Too easy, my brain whispered.

20

I THOUGHT ABOUT THE KETAMINE ON AND OFF AS MARTÍN and I rode the next morning. As we started climbing into the higher elevations, it was a relief to be leaving the parched Sonoran desert behind.

The brittlebush and ocotillo had gone dormant, leaving their leaves on the desert floor in an effort to conserve what little water they could suck up. The prickly pear cactus was now as flat as thin battered pancakes and the giant saguaros looked like they'd been fasting. The animals weren't doing much better. Other than the tanks and few natural springs, all the arroyos and water holes had dried up. With the humidity hovering around 7 percent and the nighttime temperatures refusing to plunge below 80 degrees, everything had been sucked out of the desert. Some of the birds had flown to cooler climates and the remaining animals were forced to scavenge for water at night, and hunker down in their burrows during the day.

We talked very little as we rode, mostly about the lame bull. Martín, after doctoring his sore foot, had turned him out in the holding pasture where he could keep an eye on him.

We'd watered the horses and pack mule at two tanks

on the ride up, and Martín and I were also drinking lots of water this morning. While the desert animals have adapted to drought conditions, we aren't as versatile. If we lose 6 percent of our weight to dehydration we're distressed, 10 percent we're confused and unable to help ourselves. Fifteen percent? Forget it. We shut down entirely and have to count on a fairy godmother to save us.

A Gambel's quail, on the other hand, can lose a full 50 percent of its body weight without ill effects, which gives it the gold medal for vertebrates in terms of dehydration tolerance.

Thinking of such physiological things as dehydration brought me back to thinking about the date rape drug, ketamine. How much would it take to turn someone into a zombie? Em had said that it was nasty-tasting stuff, so how would you disguise it? And, more importantly, who wanted Abby dead and why? While I wouldn't find any of my answers out here, it was as good a place as any to mull over the possibilities.

The problem with being as rich as Abigail Van Thiessen is that someone would always benefit from your death. In her case there were a lot of someones— J.B., Lateef Wise, José and Gloria Covarrubias, Laurette Le Blanc. While the temptation was to go to the guys who would inherit the most, I had to also consider that the combined $58,000 the Covarrubiases would inherit could also be a strong motive. Why had José decided to go to town when he knew I wanted to talk to him? Did he have something to hide? And the five grand that had been bequeathed to Laurette Le Blanc could stretch a ways on the local St. Martin economy. After what I'd learned from Clarice Martínez I couldn't overlook Jodie Austin either.

Halfway up the mountain Martín and I unloaded the salt blocks from the panniers that Old Hadley, the ranch pack mule and escape artist of the Vaca Grande, was carrying. All of us—horses and mule included—were dripping with sweat as the Arizona sun beat down upon us.

Dream, Martín's horse, Chapo, and the mule were moving more slowly now as they began their climb to 5,500 feet. Just before nine, after scrambling through manzanita, scrub oak and juniper we finally hit Samaniego Springs.

The Catalina Mountains still towered ahead of us and La Cienega was spread out below. On the western horizon, I could just make out Picacho Peak.

We tied the horses under a couple of alligator juniper trees, letting them cool off before we'd offer them water. Old Hadley was hobbled and nibbling at what was left of the dry, brown grass.

Martín and I sat on a log in front of an old fire ring. Samaniego Springs, used by hunters for years, had been set up as a utilitarian camp. Various corroded pots and pans hung from trees, a ratty blue tarp used for shelter was rolled and tucked under a large boulder, and a wooden-lidded box was partially hidden behind a huge stand of oaks. From my previous visits I knew that the box contained provisions—canned peaches, beans, tomato sauce, even toothpaste. As long as we'd been coming up here no one had ever destroyed anything. Occasionally the canned goods would change, I imagine replaced by whoever had used them.

It had almost been too hot to talk all morning and what chitchat we'd done had been idle; nothing serious had floated to the surface of our conversation. Maybe I'd been wrong about Martín's wanting to talk. Perhaps he'd just wanted company on the ride.

Even at the higher elevation it was really too hot to even think about eating, but we ended up splitting a granola bar.

Finally Martín began talking.

"I have some bad news, *chiquita*," he began.

While I'd thought he was going to tell me about Cori Elena's not spending the night with her father in Oracle, what he said next absolutely stunned me.

"Carmen Orduño is missing."

I felt as though someone had just kicked me in the belly. Suddenly the day had taken a dark turn. The disappearance of Cori Elena's best friend from Magdalena could only mean trouble for all of us.

"What do you mean she's missing?"

"She got home and disappeared the next day. Her husband's looking everywhere."

"How'd you find out?"

"He called Alberto looking for her. He told Cori Elena and Cori Elena told me."

"Maybe she left him," I offered, not really believing it myself.

Martín shook his head. "Cori Elena says she was happily married."

"Shit."

"If Rafael Félix went after Carmen to find Cori Elena . . ." Martín picked at his granola bar, tossing pieces of it into the brush.

It seemed a hell of a time to tell me that evil goons might assault his girlfriend and my ranch when I was miles from it. But then, Martín, while predictable in some ways, was a loose cannon in others. Besides, if they came for Cori Elena, they'd probably do it at night. Or when the cavalry wasn't home. Like this morning.

"She would have told her husband about Cori, wouldn't she?" I asked, trying to put together the pieces.

"Cori Elena says no. She said that Carmen would never have given her up."

"So what gives her that much faith in her *comadre*?"

Martin stared off at the horizon. "She had an affair in Magdalena."

"Cori Elena?"

"No, Carmen. Cori Elena covered for her. If Orduño had ever found out, he'd have killed her."

"Maybe he did."

"I don't think this is about that. But it was insurance that Carmen wouldn't tell about Cori Elena."

"Because if she was found she would have told about Carmen?"

"Exactamente."

Great friendship. Sell me out and I'll rat on you. Seemed like a precarious relationship at best.

"Martín, *does* she have the money?" I asked for the umpteenth time.

"No."

"You're sure? Because if she does, maybe we can get it back to Félix and he'll forget about killing her." I didn't really believe it. Those drug guys always liked to make examples of people who stiffed them so others wouldn't.

"She swears she doesn't have it. I believe her. So, *chiquita*, I think the stakes have gone up." There was a catch in Martín's voice. "And we're going to have to leave for a while."

"Leave? What are you talking about?"

"I'm taking Cori Elena and Quinta off the Vaca Grande. We may even leave Arizona. We need to get far enough away that Rafael Félix won't find her."

Tears welled in my eyes at the thought of losing Martín. He was the closest thing I'd ever had to a brother and now because of that little slut, who most probably was sleeping with the brand inspector, he was leaving his home. I thought why in the hell couldn't Cori Elena go to California with Jake Hatcher? I was sure he'd be more than happy to take her to Disneyland, but of course I said nothing.

As I sat there trying to get control of myself, the more practical consequences came creeping into my brain. I'd have to get another foreman, but who would I find that was as good or as trustworthy as Martín? And what of poor old Juan Ortiz? How would he take their leaving?

Unfortunately it made sense. With Carmen Orduño missing, it was more than likely that Cori Elena's hiding place had been revealed to a man who wanted his money back and probably wanted her dead.

"How soon?" I stammered, still fighting the tears.

"As soon as I can get things together here. I want to find someone else for you too."

Ah, Martín. Always so willing to jump in for me, to see that I was taken care of. Now, in the midst of his personal crisis he was going to find his own replacement.

"Don't worry about it, Martín. We'll find someone. Just do what you have to do."

"Thanks."

"You must love her an awful lot."

He was quiet for a long minute. Finally he said, "She's the mother of my daughter, *chiquita*, and I can't stand by and let her go to slaughter like some feedlot steer."

On the way down the mountain I found we had very little to say to one another.

21

At one-thirty I was standing outside the Church of Brotherly Love in Oro Valley. It was a very simple rammed earth structure with a giant sculpted concrete cross listing at a 45 degree angle to the earth. What was that supposed to mean? Rising sinners or fallen righteous?

The grounds were filled with gray Texas Ranger blooming small lavender flowers, orange and yellow Mexican bird of paradise and similar drought-resistant plants blanketed with coarse pink gravel—what we used to call pea gravel—interspersed with winding aggregate concrete paths. The offerings of the communal plate obviously weren't being used for much in the way of landscaping services.

While sickened with the thought of Martin's leaving the ranch, I doubted whether I was going to find any comfort in Lateef Wise's church, but then I wasn't here for solace. I had a job to do for J.B. Calendar and interviewing Wise was just one of the grunt steps in the process.

As I stepped into the church's entry, a skinny teenage girl wearing a mouthful of metal and a Final Four U of A basketball T-shirt greeted me.

"May I help you?" She asked in an entirely too perky voice, giving away what I suspected was her first summer job.

"I have an appointment with Reverend Wise," I said.

"Oh, right. I'll tell him you're here."

Wise, who seemed even larger than he had when I'd seen him at Abby's service, quickly appeared. The white robe was missing this afternoon and he wore tan Dockers and a white T-shirt that looked like it had been ironed. The tight shirt showed off his muscular forearms and his pecs bulged under a small purple cross over his heart. With his pro football career in the rearview mirror, was Bobby Bangs still working out? Even if he wasn't, he'd easily be strong enough to lift a little thing like Abigail Van Thiessen and carry her a quarter of a mile.

Lateef led me back to his office. Like the church itself, it was spare. A large wooden desk set out from a wall of books. Two mission style wooden chairs faced the desk. Behind them was a large picture window looking out onto a small courtyard filled with desert plants.

The walls were similarly unadorned. There were a couple of framed certificates, which I assumed were the good reverend's credentials. While I would have liked to have studied them to see where Wise had gotten his theological training, the timing didn't seem right, so I slipped into one of the mission chairs instead. As I did so, I chuckled to myself. Some kind of missionary position.

From this vantage point I had a better look at the desk and decided that my original assessment of austerity was wrong, for I recognized the highly polished wood as mesquite. Definitely not cheap. Some of the Fourth Avenue artisans I knew were hauling in five to seven thousand dollars for similar handcrafted mesquite furniture. Why would a man of the cloth want or need such a luxurious desk and who had paid for it?

My look had not gone unnoticed by Wise.

"This was a gift," he said softly as his hands ran over the smooth top of the desk, caressing it. "From Abigail."

"Nice present."

"She said it was in appreciation for all the time we spent together."

I raised an eyebrow.

"Counseling, Miss Ellis. We were very close." His hooded dark brown eyes were almost reptilian. And bloodshot. Had he been working late? Staying up nights with a guilty conscience?

"Was Abby having problems?" It was a throwaway question, for I knew that his relationship with her would have been a confidential one, much like that of attorney and client, priest and confessor.

"We all have problems, don't we?" His soft voice was offputting caged in such a gigantic body.

"Would you mind telling me a little about your relationship with her?"

He spread his immense hands out, palms up in a gesture that I suspected had been practiced in front of the mirror many times. "An angel, a true ray of light. Abigail Van Thiessen was one of those people who come into our lives at just the right time."

"And when was that, Reverend Wise?"

"It was back in the late '80s. I'd come from a church in Salem, Massachusetts, back to San Francisco and had some savings from a former career and was eager to start my own mission."

So Bobby Bangs, former 49er, had managed to save some money. I waited for him to allude again to his pro football career, but he didn't.

"I'd found an old warehouse down near the wharf and started a church for the street people. I was working with some of the local community service programs and through the Food Bank I met a woman named Gretchen Pignelli who became a good friend. Her husband had made a lot of money in Silicon Valley and Gretchen traveled in some very wealthy circles. She brought Abigail to church one Sunday."

Interesting. Even back then Abby was cavorting with

the downtrodden. The street people then, bull riders now.

"Well, I must say, we just hit it off. Splendidly. Abigail felt very blessed by her good fortune and, like Gretchen, wanted to spread the wealth, as they say."

Remembering the donations from her checkbook register, I wasn't at all surprised by Abby's generosity.

"She gave me a check for a thousand dollars that first Sunday. And I must tell you, preaching in that old cavernous, drafty warehouse, that check was like a blessing from God. And that was the beginning of our relationship."

"She's supported your churches over the years?"

"I prefer to think that she's supported God's children," he said with a smile that seemed sincere.

"Was she a regular churchgoer?" I asked, remembering Peter Van Thiessen's reference to his sister's not seeing as much of Wise since her marriage to J.B.

"She used to be." He shook his head. "But not as much since she married Mr. Calendar. I'd hoped, of course, to perform their ceremony, but they preferred to go off to Las Vegas."

The light from the window behind me cast a golden glow, not unlike an angel's halo, around his head. I wasn't fooled though. What *was* that problem he'd had that sent him out of the NFL? Something to do with the police, I recalled. I scribbled *Bangs's problem?* on my yellow pad.

"You know she left you five million dollars?" I watched him very carefully, but his eyes never wavered or left my face.

He shook his head again. "She left me nothing. The church is her beneficiary."

Very slick. How was the church structured? Surely Lateef Wise had a church board to govern such bequests. But how easy would it be for him to pull the money out? Could it be done?

"Of course," I agreed. "I understand there are some escalation clauses in conjunction with the gift."

"Fairly standard. Most of them are tied into number of congregants, programs, that kind of thing. However, an immediate two million dollars is to go directly to capital improvements. We'll be putting in a day care center once the estate is settled."

He showed no signs of being shy about receiving money from the dead heiress.

"Do you have any idea who would want Abby dead?" I asked, abruptly changing my tack.

"I read that article about suspicious circumstances surrounding her death. A double tragedy."

"Double in what way?"

"Well, I mean she's passed on, and then to have it be a deliberate vicious act, that just compounds the loss in some ways, don't you think?"

I ignored the question. "You were her confidant. Did she ever indicate to you that she was worried that someone was angry with her, angry enough to kill her?"

"Any conversations I had with her would be confidential."

"Of course, but I believe the confidentiality issue might be moot once your client has died."

He studied a thick gold and diamond Super Bowl ring on his right hand. While it looked huge from where I sat I doubted that it was even close to the size 23 that I'd read that the "Refrigerator" wore.

"I've already talked to the police. They were here earlier this week."

I waited.

"And I will share with you what I told them because of who you are working for. Abigail came to me several weeks ago quite distressed." Wise turned the gold ring round and round his finger, took a deep breath and then continued. "She was concerned that her husband was having an adulterous relationship with another woman."

"Did she mention anyone in particular?"

"No. She was quite sensitive about the issue, told me that she felt rather foolish about marrying someone so much younger than she. Apparently her brother had warned her about that and she didn't want to discuss her husband's infidelities with him."

"Because of the 'I told you so' factor?"

"Perhaps. At any rate, she felt that she really had no one to talk to so she came to me."

"Had she talked to J.B. about it?"

"Oh, yes. They'd had several conversations, but Mr. Calendar denied everything. When I suggested marriage counseling, Abigail said that he was dead set against it, wouldn't even consider it."

"Do you think she was considering divorcing him?"

He gave me a hard look. "She was more concerned about keeping her marriage together, of honoring the sanctity of her wedding vows."

I continued fishing for any details that would further damn J.B., but got nowhere. Either Lateef Wise really didn't know anything, or he was too cagey to share information. The thought occurred to me that he might want to stay on J.B.'s good side, at least until his $5 million was in the bank.

When I couldn't think of anything else to ask him, he walked me to the front of the church and shook my hand.

"We're a fairly liberal church here. You might want to drop by some Sunday and try us out."

"Thanks, Reverend, I'll consider that."

"By the way, I perhaps neglected to mention that I was in the Bay Area when Abigail died. If I can be of further assistance, Miss Ellis, please don't hesitate to call."

As I pulled out of the parking lot I had already determined that I didn't think much of Lateef Wise. He was too quick and too slick with his answers to my questions. He struck me as a man with something to hide. But what was it?

While I was hot and frustrated when I left the church parking lot and would have preferred to go back to the

Vaca Grande, I still had a lot of work to do and hanging out at the ranch wasn't going to get it done. I headed down Oracle Road instead.

J.B. had listed one of his best friends as Dusty Lord, a weekend bronc rider who also filled in as a salesman at Western Warehouse. I headed there next.

I found Dusty surrounded by boxes of Tony Lama and Justin boots, his full attention on a pale, overweight, gray-haired woman who I suspected had just moved to town. She was standing up, with a boot half on her foot as she tried to wiggle her way into it.

"This is too tight," she insisted.

"Ma'am, there's a little ledge there near the heel, if you just sort of wiggle your way down in it, your foot will seat right into the boot and it will fit just right." Dusty Lord was somewhere in his thirties with a receding hairline and a farmer's tan.

The woman leaned over, pulled the boot up by its ears and stomped on one leg in an effort to get the footwear on.

"There! I've got it!" she said with a broad smile covering her face. "Harold!" She yelled to a man who was trying on straw cowboy hats. "Harold, I've got it. Ooh, give me the other one," she said, reaching for the boot that Dusty was holding out.

I waited, pretending to look at boots, shooing the other salesmen away saying I was waiting for Dusty. Lord heard me and gave me a puzzled look since we had never met.

The woman had just made a lap around the carpet in her new boots when she plopped back down in the chair and tried to wiggle out of them.

"Ma'am, let me help you with those," Dusty said.

He had the first boot off when I heard, "Excuse me?"

I continued looking at boots.

"Excuse me." Louder.

I turned. "Are you talking to me?"

"Yes." She pointed to my feet. "What kind of boots are those?"

I didn't have to look down to know what I was wearing. "Ariats."

"Oh, they lace up, don't they?"

Duh. Good call since the hooks were clearly visible.

"So you don't have that stupid ledge thing."

"No, you just lace them up."

"Do you have those?" She asked, pointing at my boots.

Dusty Lord gave me a look to kill.

"Sorry," I said, smiling.

Twenty minutes later he was finally done with the woman and then turned to me. "Now, what can I show you?"

I introduced myself and handed him a card.

"Oh. This is about J.B., right? He said you might call."

I wondered if Calendar had called his friends as a courtesy or if he was running interference. Either way I wished he hadn't.

"Yes. I was wondering if we could talk."

Dusty wandered to an end cap of boots toward the back and then proceeded to tell me that J.B. Calendar was the best friend he had ever ever had. He and his wife had seen a lot of J.B. and Abby, thought they were happy and knew of no enemies she might have. He also knew about J.B.'s million. Screw around? Nope, not old J.B. Never. Not my pal.

I was just getting ready to leave when I got a jewel.

"You might check with Tommy Renner out at the auction barn," Dusty offered. "He and J.B. used to be best friends."

Tommy Renner. Curious. He wasn't on J.B.'s list.

I noticed that while Dusty wore no ring, there was a telltale white skin band, set off by his tan, around his left ring finger. He probably didn't screw around either.

As long as I was on a roll with J.B.'s friends, I decided to try to reach Bevo Bailey. After leaving Western

Warehouse I stopped at a pay phone and tried the number I had for him. I got a recording telling me that Bevo was out, but if I could leave my name and number, he'd get back to me. I did.

I tried Tommy Renner at the Marana Stockyards and was told he was in and out, but would definitely be there Friday morning for the sale. I doubted that I'd have much luck reaching him if I made the drive out. Tommy could wait.

Since most of the day was shot now anyway, I decided to head back to La Cienega.

All the business with J.B.'s and Abby's friends still hadn't been enough to take my mind off the thing that was really eating at my guts.

Martín Ortiz was leaving the Vaca Grande.

22

I STOPPED AT THE EEGEE'S ON NORTH ORACLE ROAD, PARKED Priscilla and went in. I was in luck. Sherry Kibble, Emily Rose's sixteen-year-old daughter, was working. After ordering a lemon eegee's, only the best frosted drink in the entire world, I asked to use the phone, figuring the refrigerated restaurant was a much better choice than melting into the pavement outside using the pay phone.

After dialing my number and punching in the remote code, I accessed my answering machine. The first message was from Charley Bell, again asking how I was getting along with my new computer. A feeling of embarrassment washed over me since I really hadn't had time to get acquainted with the damned thing. The second message was from Peter Van Thiessen, who said that he'd be at the Brave Bull all afternoon and if I wanted to come up any time before eight this evening, he'd be there.

I grabbed my drink off the counter and headed out the door.

We sat in the great room sipping ginger ale and for the last few minutes had been making small talk, over the soft music that was playing. Peter was wearing a short-sleeved purple Brave Bull polo shirt and white shorts that set off his smooth, tanned legs. In fact they were so smooth that I wondered if he shaved them. I knew that swimmers did that, but did marathon runners do it too?

Outside the window I could see José Covarrubias brushing down the walls of the swimming pool with a long-handled metal pole.

"Looks like you've been getting some sun," I said.

"I've been running like a madman. Taking advantage of the dry heat." He smiled.

I wondered if he'd ever been running in the Baboquivaris. The lawyer and Clarice Martínez had both assured me that Peter was a very wealthy man in his own right. Plus he didn't stand to inherit any money from his half-sister. So why would he want to kill her? While I couldn't discount the possibility, I saw no need to bait him.

"I visited Lateef Wise this afternoon at the Church of Brotherly Love."

"Church of Brotherly Rip-Off, you mean." Van Thiessen snorted.

"He seems to have been genuinely fond of your sister."

"Why not? She was his ATM machine."

"It sounds like you suspect him."

"It's certainly within the realm of possibility, don't you think?"

I nodded. "Do you have any other candidates for me?"

"You mean, I presume, other than the obvious?"

"The obvious?"

"Come on." He was smiling, but it was a hard smile.

"I'm thinking." I wasn't going to say it and I was right, I didn't have long to wait.

"J.B."

"You think J.B. killed Abby?"

"Like Dr. Jesus, I think there's a distinct possibility."

"You don't think much of him, then?"

"Think? Sure I think about him a lot. I see a down-and-out cowboy who charmed the socks off a woman who was thirty-two years his senior. That boy hit the mother lode."

"But that doesn't make him a murderer."

"Don't worry, I haven't forgotten who your client is."

"It's no secret that J.B. has retained me, but that retainer doesn't preclude me from disclosing the truth, whatever that may be."

"That preclusion would still be your choice."

"Yes."

"And if you found he was implicated?"

"As you said, my choice." I smiled and drained my ginger ale. "But in order to move on, I've got to ask some hard questions first." I hesitated a moment to let this sink in. "Like, did Abby do drugs?"

He laughed. "You didn't know my sister well, did you?"

He was right about that. I shook my head.

"She considered her body a temple, a violated one to be sure, all that business with the liposuction, the face lifts—three that I knew of—the tummy tucks and eyelid nips. The only drugs she took were vitamins. Fistsful."

My mind flashed to the yummy cinnamon rolls that Gloria Covarrubias had been baking and to the lump of fat that Sanders had found in the campfire. Apparently J.B. hadn't shared his wife's diet.

"Your sister drank?"

"Sure she drank. But not excessively. She'd have one or two cocktails in an evening and she did like her Baileys before bed."

"And J.B.?"

He cocked his head, listening to the music. I felt that maybe he was lost in it, instead of paying attention to our conversation.

"What?"

"And J.B.?"

"Well sure, he drank too."

"Moderately?"

"As far as I know."

I returned to the drugs. "Did she ever take Prozac that you knew of?"

"The antidepressant?" He looked startled.

"I'm sure the police will be contacting you." I was surprised that they hadn't already called. "But they found Prozac."

While I was willing to give up the Prozac, I kept my mouth shut about the ketamine. Until the police approached him I couldn't volunteer it. Em had given me the ketamine information confidentially. If the police were truly interested in it, they'd have to find probable cause to get a search warrant and that could take time. In the meantime if I tipped their hand, Em could lose her job and I could lose my license and the case could lose its implicating drug.

"I don't get it." He looked genuinely puzzled. "Why would Abby take Prozac? What was she depressed about?"

"I was hoping you could tell me."

"We didn't talk all that often, Trade. I think the last time was a couple of weeks before her . . . death. But she didn't mention anything being wrong and didn't seem upset at all. And she sure didn't mention anything about taking Prozac."

"Do you mind if we take a look?"

"Not at all."

As we got up I saw José walk away from the pool.

I followed Peter through a long series of hallways into the back of the house. We passed through Abby's sitting room, past her French provincial desk and into a cavernous marble bathroom. The top wall above her marbled vanity was all mirror with no sign of a medicine cabinet anywhere.

Peter was opening the vanity drawers when Ramona, the maid, came in.

"May . . . I . . . help . . . you . . . sir?" Her speech was very slow, deliberate and not quite right.

"Oh, Ramona. Abby's medicines, where are they?"

"Med . . . i . . . cines," the girl repeated. It was obvious to me that she was slow. She thought about this for a long minute and then her face lit up. "Oh!"

She reached for a lacquered Japanese cabinet on top of the sink and opened the top like a wooden basket. Inside were nestled a horde of vitamin pills—E, C, selenium, B complex, calcium, D, zinc, ginkgo biloba, kelp lecithin, shark cartilage and one amber plastic bottle with a white label. Peter handed it to me.

There were two pills inside. The label identified the contents as Prozac and indicated that the prescription was available for a refill. The doctor's name was Samuel Mullon.

I copied the name and phone number on my pad.

We continued searching the bathroom, but other than a myriad amount of skin toners, tighteners, retin A, cosmetics, masks, lotions and oils we found no other drugs. Certainly nothing resembling the veterinary drug ketamine.

Back downstairs we settled back into our chairs. I noticed that our soda glasses had been refilled in our absence.

"I wonder what she was depressed about," Peter mused. "It couldn't have been money."

"Were your sister and J.B. getting along?"

"She didn't confide her marital issues in me."

"But as far as you knew, there weren't any problems there?"

"Unfortunately not." Peter made no bones about not liking the match his sister had made.

I didn't mention the bruising that had shown up in the autopsy report. He'd find out soon enough and if he wanted to jump to conclusions about J.B.'s relationship with his sister he could do so then.

"Her health was good?"

"Yes. She was always on top of that."

Money. Marriage. Health. The Big Three that usually drove people to depression, or worse. While Clarice had already told me about Abby's suspicions of J.B.'s fidelity, I wasn't going to share that with Abby's brother either. At least not yet.

On my way out of the house, I purposely went through the kitchen in the hope that I would find Gloria Covarrubias. I wasn't disappointed.

Her wedding ring and gloves sat on the sink as she buried her hands in a huge bowl of ground beef mixed with what looked like egg, cracker crumbs and spices. As her hands kneaded the mixture I was struck at how easily they blended in with the pink hamburger. I guessed meat loaf or meatballs for supper.

"Hello, Gloria," I said as I placed my empty ginger ale glass on the counter.

"Afternoon."

"Do you know where I can find José?"

She gave me a dark glance, thought a minute and then nodded her head in the direction of the back door. "He's finished with the pool and is probably doing one of the cars."

I thanked her and continued out, wondering if she knew everyone's schedule as precisely as she knew her husband's.

I found José Covarrubias on a paved patch of driveway near the adobe four-car garage, a chamois cloth in one hand, a jar of Simonize in the other. The object of his attention, a silver Lexus muddy from the wax application, sat between us.

"I'm sorry I missed you the other day."

He offered nothing, gave no excuse for standing me up.

"I'm investigating Abigail Van Thiessen's death," I

said, after introducing myself. He continued buffing the car.

"Yes, my wife told me."

"The police suspect that she may have been murdered."

"I don't know nothing about that," he said, his eyes cast downward as he rubbed the Lexus.

"I'm wondering if you noticed anything unusual about Abby recently, anything at all."

"Unusual?"

"You know, did she seem depressed about anything, down in the dumps? Did her routine change?"

"No." Where José's wife had accused me of putting words in her mouth, her husband seemed reluctant to put any in his own. Still, I had to wonder why he had disappeared before my last visit when we were supposed to meet. Had there been a reason?

"Maybe she had a health problem?" I prodded.

My inquiry was met with silence.

A shadow fell across the car and we both looked up to find the maid, Ramona Miller.

"Hello, José," she said, her eyes glittering with excitement.

"Ramona."

I waited but the maid said nothing, nor did the chauffeur, so I continued my questions.

"So there were no health problems that you know of?"

"No."

"Drop . . . things." Ramona said.

"What?"

"She . . . drop things," she repeated.

José kept polishing, seemingly oblivious to the maid's revelation.

"Ramona, I don't understand. What do you mean she dropped things? Was she canceling appointments?"

She picked up the lid to the can of wax and dropped it onto the hot asphalt. "Drop things."

"Abigail was dropping things?" I asked, not quite getting it. "What kind of things?"

"Glass . . ." She pointed to her empty earlobe. "Ear . . . ring."

"So Abby was dropping glasses and earrings?"

The girl nodded enthusiastically.

"José, did you notice Abby dropping things?"

"No."

He was a real chatterbox, this one.

"No glasses, earrings?"

"No."

"And there wasn't anything different about her?"

"No."

"She was happy as far as you knew?"

"Happy?" He looked puzzled. "I guess so."

"Ramona?"

The girl nodded. "Happy."

"And J.B. was happy?"

They looked at one another then and while Ramona nodded, José shrugged his shoulders.

"You don't think that J.B. was happy?" I asked Covarrubias.

He shrugged again. "It's not for me to say."

"Was there a problem of some kind?" I zeroed in for the kill.

"She was an old woman, he was a young man." Since I'd pegged Gloria to be about fifteen years younger than her husband, clearly José did not understand the attraction that J.B. had for Abby. Briefly, I wondered if the words two hundred million dollars meant anything to him.

I continued on in this vein, asking more pointed questions about J.B. and Abby, but got nowhere. Ramona, who had started out very chatty, leaned against the Lexus and twirled strands of her hair around her fingers. José reverted to his Silent Sam routine.

"Ramona, will you show me to the corrals?"

"Show corrals," she repeated and trotted ahead of me.

When we got to the corral path she started to turn back to the house when I stopped her.

"I understand that you overheard an argument between J.B. and Abby, is that right?"

"That right."

"What were they fighting about, can you tell me?" I was speaking very slowly, hoping that she would be able to understand my words.

Her hands went up chatting in pantomime motion as her lips moved silently. Then she took a fist and pounded her heart.

"One of them hit the other one?" I guessed.

She shook her head. "Hot . . . broken."

I thought about this a minute.

"Abby said that J.B. was breaking her heart?"

She grinned and nodded.

"Ramona, this is important. Do you know why Abby thought he was breaking her heart?"

"Joe . . . Tee."

With this confirmation I left her.

As I walked down to the corrals I found myself wondering why Abby was dropping things. Did it mean anything?

23

At the arena there was a lot of action going on. The sun was low on the horizon and the temperatures were getting cooler, probably somewhere in the 80s with the higher Oracle elevation. J.B. had taken advantage of the cool of the day to buck out some of his bulls.

The ground had just been disked and I could see that there was a lot of sand mixed with the dirt, a good shock absorber for the students, most of whom would eventually bite the dust.

Bevo Bailey, dressed out in full clown regalia—white makeup around his eyes and mouth, tattered shirt, wild polka dot suspenders holding up his patched Wrangler's, striped socks and running shoes—was inside the arena, waiting. His padded barrel was rolled on its side, ready to receive him in a moment's notice.

In the chutes I could see J.B. leaning over a bull, adjusting the rigging. Just in front of the gate was a cowboy I recognized as the spitter I'd seen the day after Abby died.

I walked along the outside of the arena fence until I got to Bailey.

"Looks like they're riding today," I said in a flash of brilliance.

Bevo grinned. "Well, sort of. Treble Trouble's in th
chute."

"Sounds mean."

He shook his head. "Double Indemnity's the star c
this show, the rest are all cupcakes."

"Cupcakes?"

"Sweetie pies. Heck, that little old bull don't weig
twelve hundred pounds. And there aren't any rhythr
eliminators here except for the big boy."

I didn't have to ask for an explanation. A rhythr
eliminator made sense. Once a bull rider got into the bull'
rhythm, it was a lot easier to ride him. Most bucking bull
had patterns. Some just bucked in one direction, other
bucked both left and right. The good ones had some spi
to them, which all the top riders agreed was important.

Of course the spinning could differ too. There wer
flat spins and then there were the punishing spins tha
whiplashed the rider. While most spinners would try t
drop the rider to the outside, others tried to plant him t
the inside of the spin into the well, the area inside th
curve of the bucking bull.

"It's got to be hard to ride the bigger ones," I said.

Bevo spat a stream of tobacco into the dust. I won
dered if he ever worried about choking on his chev
while he was bull fighting.

"In real life—not this here—none of it's easy. Th
bigger bulls are usually slower, but they're a lot stronge
Those are the ones that can plumb jerk you over thei
heads and pay for your dentist's Harley. The little guy
are more athletic, faster with quicker direction changes
The thing that's the same is that when you climb on on
of those suckers you know they want you off. The onl
thing that's different is how he's gonna do it."

"I left a message for you a little while ago. I'd like t
talk to you sometime."

"Sorry, but I don't talk about my friends," Bevo said
spitting again in the dust. He grinned. "That's just a rid
that takes you nowhere."

In the chutes I could see the slim New Yorker put on a leather riding glove. Even from this distance his chest looked a little bulky and I suspected he was wearing a protective vest. Most of the professional bull riders did. I figured that providing them was probably a requirement of J.B.'s insurance company.

Briefly, I wondered if I could convince Bevo to talk. I doubted it.

New York was all business as he ran a rosin chip over his bull riding rope and then scraped his glove with it too. This would make his equipment sticky, and hopefully easier to hold on to. How much rosin to apply depended on the weather.

Bevo left me and took up his position in the arena, not far from the chutes.

Finally, the student slipped onto the bull. J.B. leaned over and said something to him.

The young wannabe gulped hard, grabbed his rope with his right hand and nodded, the universal cowboy signal to open the chutes.

The gate flew open as the bull, a small Black Angus named Treble Trouble, trotted out. About fifteen feet from the chutes the humpless, hornless creature—a "muley" to the bull riders—jumped into action and began bucking and slowly spinning to the right. While I haven't seen all that much professional bull riding, this one really didn't seem to be putting his heart into it. Still, I knew that the cowboy on top of him had to be sweating bullets on his first bull ride. On the third buck, his brushed felt cowboy hat sailed off.

I watched in fascination. The New Yorker tried to stay with the complacent bull, while taking care not to touch him with his free hand.

"Ride him," J.B. hollered. "Climb that son-of-a bitch's shoulders."

New York was yanking on his rope in an effort to stay on the bull, but muscling the Angus wouldn't do the trick, and it was as if the bull knew it. He spun to the

right hard and his rider began flailing him with his free
hand—automatic disqualification if this had been a real
event. I could clearly see that the New Yorker was seriously off balance, hanging on to the left side of the bull at
an angle that would have made Pythagoras cry.

Finally, it was over. The rider lay face down in the
dusty arena as the bull kicked out, narrowly missing the
young man's head with his hooves.

Bevo moved in immediately, flashing a red rag in
front of the Angus, who snorted in disgust, ignored the
clown's bait, and trotted off to the far end of the arena
where he would be put in a pen. There was no fooling
this bull, he knew what was expected of him and gave
just that. Barely.

New York rolled over onto his side, got to his knees
and then to his feet. As he stood and dusted off his
chaps, a broad grin spread across his face, showing his
dirt-encrusted teeth. "Man!" He slapped his chaps with
his gloved hand. "Man!"

"Congratulations." J.B. was in the arena, extending
his hand. "You're now a full-fledged bull rider."

"Man!" he repeated, and I was beginning to wonder
if his first bull ride had turned him into an idiot. "That's
like the best roller coaster I've ever been on."

J.B. chuckled.

"Fred!" he yelled. "You're up."

The fat baldheaded fifty-year-old I'd seen earlier
walked woodenly across the arena.

"You better get ready, you're next," J.B. said.

While it was hot, it wasn't hot enough to warrant
the pebbling of sweat that marched across the man's
forehead.

"I, I . . . don't think I can do it, J.B."

J.B. slapped him on the back. "Sure you can, Fred.
We're gonna put you on old Daisy Clipper there and it's
gonna be a piece of cake."

Fred's hands were shaking and his voice was cracking, the way it does when people are really scared and the moisture's sucked out of their mouth.

"Honest to God, J.B. I . . . I don't think I can do it. I'm an accountant, for Chrissake, not some bull rider."

"Fred, take a deep breath, don't go hyperventilating on me now. Everything's gonna be fine. You're gonna get up there and climb on that little cupcake and have the time of your life."

As he talked, he was walking to the chutes with his hand still on Fred's shoulders. I couldn't tell if he was dragging him along or if the accountant was willing to be led to his own slaughter.

Within minutes, Fred, wearing a protective helmet, was hovering above the bull. I stepped closer to the chutes so I could eavesdrop on J.B.'s pep talk.

"Now you just talk to old D.C. there and you tell him that you're the meanest son-of-a-bitch that's ever crossed his path. You are flat gonna ride his ass. He knows his job, now your job is to remember those drills we've been working on, all that subconscious stuff, right?"

Fred, looking somewhat cheerier, but still terrorized, managed to nod. It was a lot easier I suspected, when it wasn't *the* nod, the one that set all hell loose.

"Don't go getting cerebral on me, Fred, just let your subconscious do what we've programmed it to do. You're just along for the ride."

J.B. reached for Fred's arm and gently pulled him onto the bull. The accountant, who looked a little like Elmer Fudd, was stiff with tension as J.B. helped with his rope and glove. Calendar, to his credit, kept up a steady stream of chatter in an effort to distract Fred from his fear.

"Remember, you are one tough son-of-a-bitch and this poor little piece of hamburger just doesn't stand a chance."

Fred looked as though he would have cried had he had anything left in him to give.

"You just let us know when you're ready."

The bull, a Charolais-looking thing from what could see of it through the wooden planks of the chute stood patiently. So did J.B.

Time passed.

Finally J.B. said, "Fred, we ain't got all day here."

Fred nodded in agreement and then realized his mistake as the chute flew open and Daisy Clipper stumbled out.

D.C. was a large bull, weighing in I guessed a around eighteen hundred pounds. While he probably had the power to be one of the mean ones that Bailey had told me about, this one seemed a cousin to Ferdinand a he humped his massive back in a halfhearted buck.

Fred stayed with the first one and D.C. trotted a bit and then humped up again. It was as though I wa watching it in slow motion, for there was no speed to this bull. Although I was no judge of such things, i seemed to me that if D.C. was a legitimate bucking bull then Treble Trouble, in spite of his failings, was rea National Finals Rodeo quality.

Fred was doing a good job of hanging on to his rope as his left hand flailed the sky. So far, his free hand had come nowhere close to the bull. I could see the stiffness in his body as his legs tried to grip the bull's broad barrel Now the accountant looked like Elmer Fudd on a missio to eradicate Daffy Duck. His face was screwed up in intense concentration as his pudgy body bounced along the bull's back.

"Move with him!" J.B. hollered.

Fred showed no sign of having heard as D.C. went into a slow spin. It was enough to dump his rider. The accountant landed on his feet, stumbled, fell to his knees and miraculously regained his footing.

D.C. now decided to really pour it on as he bucked away from his fallen rider. Bevo left him alone, the mark of a good clown who knows the importance of staying out of the way, yet has the instinct of when to jump in.

Fred swiped his hand across his face and patted his body, as though to insure that all the parts were still there. He was ripping off his helmet when J.B. arrived to congratulate him, but Fred was having none of it.

He handed J.B. the helmet.

"That scared the shit out of me."

J.B. grinned. "So join the club."

"No, I mean it, J.B. You can have it."

"Ah, Fred, you did a good job of riding old D.C. here. Hell, another couple of seconds and you woulda made the buzzer."

"Fuck the buzzer, J.B. I'm done." Fred was unbuckling his chaps and handed them to Calendar. "I have looked death in the eye and it sucks."

"You're just decelerating right now. You had a good ride, you're in one piece." J.B. slapped him on the shoulder. "Now cowboy up."

"Fuck cowboy up, fuck the bulls and fuck you!" Fred said as he stomped off.

J.B. laughed as he watched him walk across the arena.

I couldn't resist asking, "Another happy camper?"

"That's the first one I've had. Guess he blames me for his being stupid enough to climb on the back of a bucking bull," he said with a wink in my direction.

"Where's Jodie?" I asked, for she was nowhere in sight.

"Migraine. She's taking the afternoon off."

Paulo Moraes, the Brazilian, was the last to ride. He not only rode a tough Brahma with the unlikely name of Charley Horse, but he was also able to use his dull rowled spurs in a great effort that didn't hurt the bull. This one was tougher than the others I'd seen this afternoon and Paulo was relaxed as he made his ride. He also made his eight seconds. I knew that a lot of Brazilians were doing very well in the Professional Bull Riders standings, and from what I'd seen, Paulo Moraes could soon be joining their ranks.

After congratulating Paulo and dismissing the clas
J.B. stepped into his office and retrieved a couple o
Cokes out of his refrigerator. He handed one to m
popped the tab on the other and took a healthy pull o
the can.

Then he stepped over to his desk, opened a botto
drawer and retrieved a fifth of Jack Daniel's and a funne
Placing the mouth of the funnel into the can's slot h
poured some of the whiskey in, replacing the Coke he'
drained from it. The operation went smoothly and I su
pected that he'd had a lot of practice doing it.

While I knew that bull riders were known for the
flashy dress, big spending, heavy gambling and har
drinking, it seemed to me that J.B. was overdoing th
drinking part. I wondered if this was his first doctore
Coke of the day.

He held the bottle up to me with a questioning lool
I shook my head.

"Well then, let's walk," he said.

Neither of us said anything as we walked up th
graveled path.

We finally ended up at Double Indemnity's corr
and settled onto the wrought iron chairs with the mes
table between us.

"We'll have more privacy here. It's quiet," J.B. said.

"I've been talking to a few people," I said. "I haven
typed up your weekly report yet." I neglected to mentio
my terror at the thought of tackling my new computer.

"No rush."

"Well, it's my office policy to give clients a weekl
written report. Yours is just a little late, that's all."

"Trade, I don't give a goddamn about any written re
port. I hired you to find out what happened to Abby an
to clear me."

"Easy, J.B., I know." Why was he so testy? "Have th
police been back?"

"No. And I've already paid María López Zepeda
small fortune in case I need her."

"Money well spent."

"Do you know something?" He gave me a wild look and ran his fingers through his lush dark hair.

"Not about that. I've been talking to a few people, though, and I've got some tough questions for you."

"Shoot." He took a deep slug of his Coke.

"Were you having an affair with Jodie Austin?" I hit him with one of the big ones first, but he didn't flinch.

"Not exactly an affair."

"What does that mean?"

"Well, I wasn't in love with her, or anything like that."

"But you're sleeping with her."

"Slept."

"You slept with her?"

"I just said that, didn't I?"

"And Abby found out about it?"

"Yep." He was staring off in Double Indemnity's direction.

"J.B., it would be helpful if you could elaborate a little more on these answers."

When he turned back to me I was surprised to see that his eyes were damp.

"Trade, I ain't no angel. Never have been and I told Abby that before we were married." He turned the Coke can round and round in his rough hands. "Yeah, Jodie and I tumbled around a bit, but I loved Abby, and that's the God's truth."

He swiped at his nose, and I suspected that it was running.

"Was she going to leave you, J.B.?"

"Leave me?" He looked at me as though I'd lost my mind. "No, she wasn't going to leave me."

"But she was a very jealous woman."

He smiled. "Passionate."

"And you fought about it."

"A little. But that was over before Jodie left the first time."

"I was told that Abby didn't want her to return."

"No, she didn't. And we did have a big fight over that. It was over between us, though. But Abby still didn't want her back. To me Jodie was just another student with big bucks to spend on lessons. I've never lived with hen tracks on my back and I wasn't about to start."

I was disgusted with his choice of words, but hid it.

While I really wanted to get into the ketamine, I couldn't for the same reasons that I hadn't brought it up in my conversation with Peter Van Thiessen. Emily Rose gives me information knowing that I will never betray her, and in spite of J.B.'s having hired me, in spite of my wanting to get at the truth, there was no way I could say the K word. Until it was public knowledge, or at least until the police had braced J.B. with it, I had to keep silent, so I went in another direction.

I took a deep breath and then asked, "Did you ever hit Abby?"

He gave me a startled look, and then drained his Coke.

"No."

"You never laid a hand on her, never even pushed her accidentally?" I was giving him a nice way around the question.

"Never. The police asked me that when they first questioned me. I know about the autopsy."

Not all of it, I thought.

"The bruises. Hell, she fell off her horse with great regularity," he said.

"Did she in the Baboquivaris?" This was a test question, for I knew that the bruises were old.

"No." He chuckled. "We rode hard, but mostly only walked and climbed and she somehow managed to stay on." He stood up, threw his can to the ground and stomped it flat with his cowboy boot, then picked it up. "Let's go back to the office."

I figured he was after some more of his medicinal Coke so we walked quietly back.

Inside, he went straight to the desk drawer, brought out the bottle, put it to his lips and took another healthy swig of booze. I guess he was tired of Coke. Finished, he brushed flecks of the golden liquor off of his dark handlebar mustache.

"I was talking to José earlier and Ramona mentioned that Abby was dropping things."

"Ramona's an idiot," J.B. said, tapping his head.

"So you didn't notice that Abby was dropping things?"

He shrugged. "Not to where I thought it was a problem if that's what you mean. Sure, she dropped a drink glass occasionally, or her mascara, stuff like that, but I didn't think anything about it."

I did. I couldn't remember the last time I'd dropped a drink glass or my mascara.

"So she wasn't dropping things excessively?"

"Not that I noticed."

While I couldn't bring up the ketamine, I could waltz around it. "You and Abby ate dinner both nights at the camp, right?"

He settled into his chair and nodded as I perched on the corner of his desk.

"Where'd that food come from?"

"What do you mean?"

"Did you stop at the grocery store on the way down, or bring it from home? Where'd it come from?"

"Gloria packed it for us. Abby gave her a list of what we needed and then right before the trip I picked up the cardboard boxes and ice chests in the kitchen and packed them in the truck."

"So Gloria Covarrubias packed all the food?"

"Hell, it wasn't all that much, Trade. We were only planning on being out for two nights."

"Did you eat anything at that place in Arivaca?"

"La Gitana? Nah. Maybe a handful of popcorn, but we had those steaks before we left camp."

"But you drank at La Gitana?" I was going over old ground, but kept at it.

"Oh yeah."

"Did you have any booze in camp?"

He gave me a suspicious look.

"Look, J.B.," I explained. "I really don't care how much you drink. What I do need to know is what you guys ate and drank and where you ate and drank it."

"You know something."

"No," I lied. "I'm just building a diary here, a record of what happened in the days before Abby died. It may or may not be important."

He nodded and kicked the desk drawer with the toe of his boot. "We took a couple of bottles from the bar here. Some red wine, a bottle of Jack and Baileys."

"You drank Baileys?"

He made a face. "God, no. That stuff is pig swill. Abby liked it though, said it made her sleep better."

"You mentioned that when you got back from Arivaca you were both so tired that you fell into bed with your clothes on."

"That's right."

"But you took your boots off?"

"Hell, sure, I wasn't that drunk."

"Did Abby take hers off?"

"Yeah. She didn't have them on when I found her."

"But she kept her socks on?"

J.B.'s forehead furrowed as though he was trying hard to think up the correct answer. "Yeah, she had her socks on."

We talked for a while longer and then he began hitting the Jack Daniel's again.

As I said my goodbyes, he offered to walk me to the car, but I left him alone with his demons and his Jack.

24

I WAS SURPRISED TO SEE JODIE AUSTIN STANDING BY MY pickup when I got back to the parking lot. Her eyes were red, as though she'd been crying, and her cheeks were blotchy. She didn't look quite as glamorous as she had on my earlier visits.

"Is your migraine better?"

"I've got to talk to you." She clasped a hand over her mouth as though she was going to throw up.

"Okay."

"I'm really scared."

"About what?"

"What you're gonna find out." She chewed on her cuticle for a moment, took a deep breath and then said, "I slept with J.B."

"I know."

"But I'm not sleeping with him now, I swear it."

"That's what I heard."

"God, Trade." She grabbed my arm. "You've got to believe me. I'm not sleeping with him now."

"It's okay, Jodie, I believe you."

"If my fiancé finds out about this, I don't know what he'll do."

Fiancé? Jodie Austin slept with J.B., but she had a fiancé? Things were definitely getting interesting.

"He's a lawyer in New York. With Sullivan and Cromwell. We're supposed to get married next May. I don't know why I did it. God." She burst into tears. "J.B. doesn't mean a thing to me. Charles can't find out, he just can't."

After finding out about their affair, Jodie had been on my list. Admittedly, not in a very high position, since there were so many ahead of her that stood to gain real money. In order for Jodie to do that she'd have to marry J.B. once the smoke cleared. A possibility, but almost too obvious to seriously consider.

The sun was down by the time I pulled into the Vaca Grande. I was surprised to see my cousin Top Dog's old green pickup with the rusted camper shell sitting near the pond. As far as I knew he was still on the San Carlos Reservation.

As I stepped out of Priscilla I heard a car running, or at least trying to, the engine punctuated by a terrible knocking noise.

Mrs. Fierce, Blue and Petunia the pig were all overjoyed to see me. I suspected partly because they had not yet been fed.

The horses had. When I walked out to the corral Dream and Gray had their heads buried in their feed bins, munching their alfalfa. Chapo, Martín's roan horse, was doing the same in one of the pipe corrals. I was surprised to see his right rear leg bandaged with fluorescent pink Vet Wrap.

It didn't take a brilliant detective to figure out where the noise was coming from. Martín's battered old Dodge was sitting under the barn light, hood up, with Top Dog and Martín hunkered under it. Under normal circumstances this would not have been good news, but the way I felt about Martín's leaving, I viewed it as no less than a sign from God.

I walked over to the car. "Everything okay?" I asked, trying to keep enthusiasm out of my voice.

"Hey, Trade." Top Dog ducked out from under the hood long enough to give me a quick hug.

"Rod," Martín said.

"You threw a rod?" We sure weren't having much luck in the rod department. Just a few months ago Martín had replaced all of them on the old tractor.

"Sounds that way," Top Dog offered.

"That sounds expensive."

Martín shrugged and wiped his greasy hands on a dirty towel.

"At least it didn't go through the block," Top Dog said.

"Hey." Martín slapped my cousin playfully with the greasy towel. "Do I look like a *tonto*? I'm just old, not deaf, I heard the *pinche*."

"How'd you get home?" I asked.

"Curly towed me."

"Can you fix it?"

He shook his head. "I don't have the tools."

"You'll probably want to pull the block, maybe get a new one." Top Dog was full of helpful information. A pulled block, how long could that take?

Martín slammed the hood of the truck down. "I'll see if I can get Prego," he said.

"What's with Chapo?" I nodded toward the corral.

"He came in from the pasture with a nasty cut on that leg."

"And no clue, I'll bet." If there was a way for one of the horses to get hurt, they'd usually find it and leave us with the mystery of how they did it.

"None at all, *chiquita*," Martín said as he walked off.

I turned to Top Dog. "So how long does it take to put in a new block?"

"Couple of days. You've got to get one first."

I crossed my fingers that Prego, a guy we all went to

high school with who was now a mechanic working out of his home in La Cienega, would be overworked and unable to get to Martín's truck for a while.

We were walking back to the house when I asked, "What are you doing down here? Aren't you at the height of your season?"

Top Dog, in addition to being a triathlete, is also a member of the Geronimo Hotshots, an elite Apache fire-fighting unit based in San Carlos. Arizona is hell for firefighters since June can be brutal when it comes to wildfires.

"Someone had to come to town for supplies. I volunteered."

"Let's go get some dinner."

Since a lot of our fair-weather friends, the snowbirds, had cleared out, we didn't have to wait for a table at Rainbow's. Rainbow Dancer herself—formerly Rebecca Liebowitz from New York—waited on us.

We both ordered hamburgers and then got caught up on the family news. Top Dog had seen Aunt Josie and talked to Cousin Bea this trip, but his father had been tied up on a homicide case.

"Was it the Van Thiessen thing?" I asked.

"Who? Oh that rich lady that got killed?"

I nodded.

"Nah, he didn't say."

I'd have to call Uncle C. I'd like to know if they were going to bust J.B. Calendar for murdering his wife.

"Lonnie Victor used to work for her," I said.

"Lonnie Victor? No shit?"

"He helped out around the place, did some gardening, and I think helped J.B. a little with the bull riding school."

"Gardening?"

"Doesn't sound like the Lonnie we knew, does it?"

Rainbow came and put the hamburgers down. Top

Dog flipped his bun back and poked his patty with a knife. "Come on, Rainbow," he said, "I wanted it rare."

"Doesn't matter," she said. "It's all well done nowadays. Can't afford to take chances."

I groaned. I knew what she was talking about. It was an epidemic that was taking over the country, begun a few years ago when everyone started getting prissy about letting people ride mules into the Grand Canyon. That segued into caveats on water sports and skiing. Now it was our food. I'd been to a wedding reception a while back at the Arizona Inn and asked the bartender for a Ramos Gin Fizz and was told they couldn't serve me one because they weren't allowed to put egg whites in the drinks. Something about salmonella. The cover your ass syndrome was epidemic thanks to trial lawyers everywhere.

"Well, why'd you ask me how I wanted it then?" He asked good-naturedly.

"Makes you feel better, as though you're part of the process," Rainbow said, patting him on the back as she drifted off to another table.

"I come here because I don't want to be part of cooking my food!" I yelled to her back.

We ate in silence for a few minutes and then I came back to Lonnie Victor. "He left the Brave Bull right after Abby was killed. He may have gone back to San Carlos."

"Haven't seen him, but that doesn't mean he's not there."

"Do you have any idea where he might be living?"

Top Dog squirted a healthy dollop of catsup on his fries. "Probably under a rock somewhere."

"Oh come on, he must have family." Everyone in San Carlos had family, or was somehow related.

"I'll ask around if you want me to. But offhand I'd say that if Lonnie was working for some rich woman, he's probably reached the peak of his career."

"He must have friends."

"Slugs, rodents, snakes." In spite of his beef being too
well done, Top Dog was wasting no time attacking it.

"Glad to hear you're so fond of him."

Top Dog grunted and continued eating.

We had finished and I was paying the bill when my
cousin remembered something.

"You know, Lonnie used to ride bulls, maybe he still
does."

I'd neglected the paperwork on the Van Thiessen
case too long so the next morning found me in my stage
stop office, my rolltop desk littered with paper.

Abby's appointment book was in front of me. This
one was just for the current year so I only had six months
of penciled entries and erasure marks to sift through. Of
course there was a good chance there might be clues in
the preceding years, but for now, my headlights were on
January to the date of her death, June 6.

Van Thiessen had been a good diarist, recording all
sorts of information—everything from having a cold to
traveling to New York City. Sandwiched in between
were the minutiae of her daily life—the tooth cleanings,
benefit dinners for the Nature Conservancy and the Girls
Clubs of America, meetings with staff, dancing with J.B.
at the Riata. It was all there.

I noticed an appointment with Dr. Samuel Mullon
that coincided with the date on the Prozac bottle and
made a note of that on my yellow pad. Again I wondered, what precipitated the need for an antidepressant?
Was she that discouraged about J.B.'s tomcatting around?
Had Abby really been significantly dropping things the
way Ramona had said? Could there be a connection between that and Abby's Prozac prescription? If so, what
was it? What made you drop things?

My mind was thinking faster than my hand could
write. I glanced at the new computer, sitting silently on
the conference table, and felt guilty. I still hadn't returned
Charley's telephone call asking me how I was getting

along with my new wonder machine. Problem was now I needed to call him to check on some things for me and I didn't dare tell him I hadn't even turned the damned thing on since he'd left.

Then it hit me. Charley had taken my old reliable Selectric. I was stranded. While J.B. hadn't been at all concerned with my late weekly report, it sure was bugging me. I like to have a routine with my cases, and I was getting pretty sloppy with this one. Besides, I needed to aggregate my notes. Reluctantly, I turned the new computer on. It whirred and blinked red and green eyes at me before the screen finally lit up.

A few wrong turns later I seemed to be into my word processing program. I started with my name. Easy enough, although misspelled. How in the hell did you erase on this thing? I pushed the little blinking line thing close to the letter I wanted to eliminate, then spotted the Dele key, pressed it, kept my finger on it too long and managed to eradicate my entire last name. Great work.

After playing around for a few minutes I decided to try and get the gist of my notes onto the thing. I'd worry about cleaning up the material later, or call Charley and ask for help.

I turned back to Abby's Day Planner, paying particular attention to the weeks before her death. A couple of things stood out. She'd penciled in an appointment with her lawyer, Jim Carstensen, the week before and then crossed it out. What had that been about? Why was it crossed out and not erased as so many of her engagements had been? Had she kept the appointment or had it really been canceled? Rescheduled? Had Carstensen known about the appointment, and if so, why hadn't he mentioned it?

I dialed the lawyer's number and sat on hold for a few minutes. When he finally came on the line he said he knew she'd canceled her appointment, but that she hadn't said what it was about. I hung up wishing that all of my questions could be answered so easily.

I turned back to the computer and started typing. Never a typist, I found that using three fingers across the swift keyboard was still a lot faster than my pinching things out in longhand. Maybe I was going to like this after all.

Abby had also had lunch with Clarice Martínez two days before her fateful camping trip. Clarice had suggested that Abby was unhappy with J.B., suspected him of having an affair, yet she hadn't mentioned having lunch with her so soon before her death. Why not? Was that an innocent oversight or had something more ominous been going on? What had Abby told her at that lunch? I struggled, but again managed to somehow get the information entered into the computer.

There was nothing else that really jumped out at me from the appointment book so I turned back to my yellow pad and, starting from the beginning, began rereading my notes, keying them in as I went along.

When I got to my visit with Carstensen, the disparate amounts Abby left to the Covarrubiases again jumped out. Why $41,000 to Gloria and only $17,000 to José? If she'd disliked José, it would seem logical to leave him nothing, but instead she'd chosen to leave him $24,000 *less* than the amount she'd given his wife. Why? I made a note to ask Gloria about it. Typing fairly quickly I hit a few wrong keys and then went back to try and retype and, to my horror, all of the words ahead of the blinking line disappeared. Shit! What had I done?

The ringing phone interrupted my angst. I snatched it up.

"Ellis?"

"Hi, Charley."

"Have you heard the one—"

"No, and I've got a crisis here. I'm working on this stupid machine and my words are all disappearing, almost as fast as I can type them."

"Easy, Ellis. We can fix that. On the bottom of your

screen do you see something called ovr appearing in bold letters?"

I looked. Sure enough there it was. "Yeah."

"Okay, do you see those keys to the right of the keyboard? Press the one marked insert."

I did and miraculously the boldfaced ovr on the screen disappeared. "So what's that mean?"

He chuckled. "It overwrites what you've written, which means it will replace the words ahead of you as you type."

"Oh." Would I ever get this right?

"And Ellis, you can't hurt the machine."

He read my mind. I was trying hard not to be paranoid, but the thought had occurred to me that I might punch a key and blow the whole thing up.

"They put kindergartners on them," he said reassuringly.

My breathing slowed. "I was just about to call you. I need some information on a few things."

"Shoot."

"Peter Van Thiessen, Abigail's brother. I need to find out what you can on him. Also a woman named Laurette LeBlanc. She's from St. Martin and has only been here since December so that one may be tough. Supposedly her mother just had a heart attack and she's returned to the Caribbean to help her out. I'd like that checked out and anything you can find on José and Gloria Covarrubias." I spelled out all the names for him.

"Also run by J.B. Calendar. I'd especially like to know if you can dig up any previous connection between him and Laurette Le Blanc." This was a long shot, as I doubted whether he'd find much, if anything, on the itinerant cowboy. Since Laurette Le Blanc had come back from St. Martin with J.B. and Abby, I couldn't help but wonder if there had been a relationship between Laurette and J.B. *before* his honeymoon with Abby. Especially since, by his own admission, he was a pretty good ass bandit.

"And there's a former pro ball player, Bobby Bangs . . ."

"Forty-niners," Charley said.

"Right. Also known as Lateef Wise. Run both names. Anything you can find on either. He left the NFL for some reason, got into some kind of trouble, I'd like to know what it was."

"Righto, Ellis."

"Now, Charley, why were you calling me?"

"Just checking to see how you like the new machine."

After we hung up I felt a little bad that I'd cut off his joke.

When I finished putting my notes into the computer I reread them and noticed something I was about to overlook. When I'd checked Abby's answering machine, Clarice Martínez had left a message for her to call someone named Hornisher for collagen implants. While it sounded like plastic surgery stuff, could it possibly have anything to do with Abby's dropping things? I started to pick up the telephone to call Clarice and then decided not to. The next time I was in town, I'd drop in on her and ask her in person.

Sometimes, you get better information that way.

25

HAD TURNED OFF THE SWAMP COOLER AND THE LIGHTS IN the stage stop and was just getting in my truck when Martín rode in. He looked exhausted, as though he hadn't slept all night. Judging from the sweat on Shorty, the ranch horse he was riding since Chapo was laid up, he'd also been riding a while.

"I turned that bull out," he said. "Pushed him up to the north tanks."

"Is he moving any better?"

Martín shrugged. "At least it's not anything serious."

"Did you get hold of Prego?"

"I finally got his mother early this morning. He's fishing up at Big Lake and won't be home until Sunday night."

Yes! If Prego didn't get home until Sunday night there was no way he could even touch Martín's truck until Monday at the earliest. While this didn't seem like a very sophisticated way to delay the inevitable—Martín's leaving—I'd take it.

"Is there anyone else?"

"Sure, but you know Prego's prices."

Of course I did. Prego was cheap, dirt-cheap. That's why we all used him.

"Chi Chi Tapia offered to help out while I'm gone," he said.

"The chickenshit cowboy?" God, we all knew Chi Chi. He was a standing joke—a cowboy who was scared to death of cows. This guy would be working in the pens and if a cow looked cross-eyed at him, he'd climb the fence and anyone in his way to get out. He was a tentative and lousy roper. On the ground he never stayed close enough to the cattle to get a decent brand on them. He didn't ride very well either. Overall he had a rotten report card and the only reason any of the ranchers put up with him was because his wife was an excellent roundup cook.

"He overheard me talking to some of the guys and volunteered," Martín said with a grin.

"You just want to make sure you'll have your old job back." As the words came out, the sick feeling was back in my stomach. How would I ever manage without Martín? It wasn't all the work he did—which was tremendous—as much as I'd miss his company. The thought of his leaving was not dissimilar to the thought of losing one of my own body parts. "Don't worry about it, Sanders will help out," I said.

"Another thing. Quinta doesn't want to go."

"Well, she's over twenty-one."

"Yeah, that's what she tells me. But she won't be any safer here than she was in Mexico as long as they're looking for her mother. I was wondering if you'd talk to her."

Now that was a pickle. I didn't want any of them leaving, well not entirely true. Cori Elena could hit the road anytime and I wouldn't shed any tears. "I'll see what I can do."

He nodded. "If you wouldn't mind."

"You look pretty tired."

"I'm not sleeping too good."

"Has Cori Elena heard any more about Carmen?"

"Nothing. But I still jump up and look out windows."

I knew what he meant. The whole business with Rafael Félix had me fairly jumpy too. I was sleeping with my .38 on top of the bedside table instead of leaving it nestled safely in the drawer.

"I guess another week won't kill us," he said.

I shuddered at his choice of words. "You know, Martín, if they were coming after Cori Elena, it seems to me that they would have already done it."

"You never know with those guys, *chiquita*. You just never know."

With that he rode off toward headquarters and I drove into town.

Dr. Samuel Mullon's office was in an old medical complex off Tucson Boulevard not far from the Arizona Inn. The room was empty when I walked in and I wondered what kind of a practice he had that his patients weren't stacked up to see him.

So far I saw nothing but a few dying plants and a receptionist who looked almost as old as the building. Her eyes were rimmed in red and the crepey skin around them was blotchy, as though she'd been crying. She was nonplussed when I handed her my card.

"I've been hired by Mr. Calendar," I said, "to investigate Abigail Van Thiessen's death."

"Oh yes, I read about that in the newspapers," she said. "It was a terrible thing. She was one of our patients, you know."

"That's why I'm here. I'm wondering if I might have a quick moment with Dr. Mullon."

"Oh dear, I'm afraid that's not possible, not possible at all."

"He's not in?"

"I guess you didn't see it in the paper?"

Sometimes, I must confess, I only glance at the morning newspaper. I've even been known not to read it at all.

"See what?"

"Dr. Mullon's been killed. It was a terrible thing. Shot to death just outside his house in his carport."

I did remember reading about someone who had been shot and the ensuing neighborhood panic that incident had incurred. Since the name Mullon hadn't meant anything to me at the time, I hadn't stored the information.

"*That* was Samuel Mullon?"

The receptionist grabbed a fistful of tissues and blew her nose heartily into them. "Yes. He was a lovely man. I don't know why anyone would want to take his life."

"When did he die?"

"June 6th. Sometime after midnight."

I pondered this for a minute. Dr. Mullon, Abby's doctor, had been killed the same night as she had. That was too close for coincidence. What in the hell was going on? Had someone murdered Abby and then taken out her doctor? And if that had really happened, why? I tried to collect my thoughts.

"Have they arrested anyone?"

She shook her head and swiped at her eyes with the same Kleenex she'd used to blow her nose.

I stayed silent for a minute trying to figure out a way I could frame what I was going to ask her next.

"I'm sure he was well loved," I began. "I know Abby thought an awful lot of him." So it was a lie. It was a harmless one and it might even cheer her up.

"Oh yes," she sobbed.

"He helped her when she was so depressed, when she went through that awful time."

She kept quiet.

"I mean he gave her that medicine and all."

She barely nodded.

"And it did wonders for her, it really did."

Shit, where could I go with this?

"Of course, when your husband's cheating on you . . ."

She was now giving me an interested look.

"I mean J.B., you know."

She picked up the card and looked at me suspiciously. "I thought you were working for Mr. Calendar."

"Oh, I am. But you have to uncover every stone, know what I mean?" I gave her a wan smile.

She stiffened. "I don't know what you're talking about."

"The other woman, you know . . ."

She shook her head. "Anything that Mrs. Van Thiessen told Dr. Mullon would have been in complete and total confidence and I will not disclose anything, anything at all, even if I knew what specifically you wanted to know."

Damn nobility.

"So I suppose that the chances of glancing at Abby's chart are out of the question?"

She gave me a horrified look and waggled her finger at me. "Not very funny, miss."

"Even if it meant saving an innocent man from going to jail?"

"Hah. What man is ever innocent?"

I tried a while longer, but if the receptionist knew anything about why Abigail Van Thiessen was taking an antidepressant, she wasn't talking.

As I left the medical complex I knew the pressure on the case had ratcheted up a few notches. Now there were two people who had known each other who had been murdered. Who was going to be next?

Finding Uncle C wasn't hard, since I knew he had Wednesdays and Thursdays off. After going through the requisite catch-up with Aunt Josie, I trotted through their backyard to the converted garage. I let myself into the light-filled studio.

My uncle, the bad-ass homicide detective, was hunched over a drafting table, rendering a fine pen and ink drawing. His sketches of some of his cases had started out as a hobby, but now he was selling some of his work in a downtown gallery. While Uncle C must have heard the door open, he completed a few strokes before looking up.

"Hey, Trade, what brings you out?"

"The usual."

"I don't know nuthin' 'bout no murder," he said in a mock imitation of Prissy in *Gone With the Wind*.

"Right."

"But, if I was you, this is hypothetical of course, I'd be sure some of my accounts were paid up pronto." He snapped his fingers, then grabbed a rag and rubbed at the ink stains on his right index finger. "Hypothetically."

"Well, hypothetically, I've wondered if the police could ever make a mistake and arrest an innocent man," I said with a bravado I did not feel. I had no evidence, one way or the other, that J.B. had not killed his wife. What I *was* getting was a lot of heads-up on him.

"My lips are sealed, sweetie."

"Well let's not talk about that one, then." I picked up a jar of his India ink and studied the label. "Let's talk about Sam Mullon."

"Who?" He feigned ignorance.

"The internist."

"Oh that doc that got whacked at home. *That* Samuel Mullon."

"Abigail Van Thiessen's doctor, one and the same."

"We know."

"Hell of a coincidence, isn't it?"

"We're looking into it, Sherlock." My uncle has never been all that fond of my chosen profession. He loves me, but has admitted on numerous occasions that I can be a real pain in the ass when it comes to this murder stuff.

"Any leads?" I swirled the ink around in the jar.

"The guys are working on it. They've canvassed the neighborhood, are interviewing his friends and family, going through the motions."

"And patients?"

"Some of them. Others, as you've pointed out, ain't feeling so hot. There was a guy who was pretty unhappy because his wife died and Mullon was her doc. He was on a camping trip, but could have driven into town, boom, boom!" He pretended he was firing a gun. "And then headed back out to the sticks."

I rocked the India ink back and forth in the bottle.

"Couple of days before the trip he and the missus went to a movie and then caught a late steak at McMahon's Steak House."

"So? Is there a law against that?"

"Ah, I love your optimism." He leaned over and looked at his sketch. "Aren't you gonna ask me?"

"Ask you what?"

"Which missus?"

Shit. What was he talking about? "Abigail."

"Bzzzz. Play again."

"Not Abigail?"

"Ding, ding, ding, correct. Not *the* missus, but *a* missus."

"He was out with someone else's wife?"

"Nope. His own. His former wife."

Jesus Christ. I didn't have to look at J.B.'s list to know that there was no mention of a former wife on it. "He was married before?"

"Right. To a cute little thing who used to dance at T.D.'s."

I knew the place. I'd seen the ads in the paper. *Nudes! Live Girls!* As if anyone would pay to see dead ones. The former Mrs. J.B. Calendar had been a topless dancer.

"At least she used to dance there when she could. When she wasn't too bruised to perform."

I was afraid I knew what was coming next.

"Your boy's a real charmer, sweetie. He likes to beat the shit out of women."

I sank into a chair next to the drafting table. "Shit."

"We're thinking maybe Mrs. Van Thiessen didn't fall off her horse all that often."

"But nothing was fresh, right?"

He gave me an incredulous look, as though how could I side with such a scumbag?

"Not that weekend, if that's what you mean, but

Jackie Doo Dahs told the investigating officer that Calendar did hit her."

"Jackie Doo Dahs?"

"That was her stage name. She took it back after they got divorced."

"Which was?"

"About a year ago, right before he came into the victim's life."

"But he was still seeing Jackie?" This was getting hard to assimilate. First there was Jodie Austin, now Jackie Doo Dahs. How many more were there? Could I hope that J.B.'s philandering was just limited to women whose names began with J?

"Nah. She was squeezing him. She's been trying to get alimony out of him ever since she discovered he married Mrs. Candy Bar."

"So you think there's a connection between Mullon's death and Abby's?"

"Hell, I don't know what to think. I've been in this business long enough to know there's rarely a rational rhyme or reason to murder. Kids whack other kids for their Chicago Bulls jackets or Nike tennies, people stab each other over parking spaces and recipes, and sometimes people just put holes in each other's heads for $43.12."

"Maybe Mullon knew something about Abby's murder."

"Maybe we'll find a connection, maybe not."

I replaced the bottle of ink on the drafting table.

"Why was she depressed?" I asked my question carefully, not wanting to mention either the Prozac or the ketamine.

He gave me a strange look. "Who said she was depressed?"

I smiled. "Okay, so maybe I'm wrong."

I thought, briefly, about mentioning what Ramona Miller had told me. That Abby was dropping things. But then I decided not to. Ramona clearly had some developmental problems and so far I hadn't been able to substantiate what she had told me, so maybe it was just a red herring. I'd wait. I wasn't going to mention the bull tracks that Sanders had found either.

We talked a while longer, but neither of us were willing to just come out and say what we were thinking, so it turned out to be a polite waltz, nothing more.

As I left, I was furious with J.B. Calendar, not only for letting me get blindsided by my uncle on the issue of his former wife, but also for withholding such vital information from me. Did he think I was so inept that I wouldn't find out that he'd been married before? That he used to beat his first wife?

There was also the immediacy of the whole thing. He'd had dinner with Jackie a few nights before his camping trip with Abby. Why didn't he think that would be uncovered? Hadn't he seen enough TV cop shows? Didn't he know that they'd resurrect his life and certainly the week or two before his wife's death?

I was really beyond furious. I was super-pissed. And as I thought about everything, I realized that I was also really angry with myself. Why had I trusted J.B. so completely? Was it because he'd hired me? Or was it because his world and mine weren't that far apart? We were part of the same tribe and he had let me down. I should have seen it coming. First with his not telling me about the million bucks Abby'd given him. Then he'd neglected to tell me he'd slept with Jodie Austin. And now, conveniently, he'd forgotten to tell me about a little thing like an ex-wife. What a great client I had.

Not only was I too trusting, but I also wasn't digging hard enough or deep enough. Shit. What kind of private eye was I?

One thing was for sure. There was a lot more to J.B. Calendar than I'd first thought.

And like peeling an onion, I was about to get deeper into his layers.

26

As long as I was in town anyway, I decided that an impromptu call on Clarice Martínez was in order. I wanted to ask her about that business with Abby dropping things and also thought that maybe she could clarify who Hornisher was and why she'd left his number for Abby to call him.

Forty minutes later found me standing outside the Martínezes' front door, my entrance blocked by the cleaning lady.

"She no here." She said in broken English as she twirled her dust rag in my direction.

"What time do you expect her?"

She shrugged.

"Lupita? *Quién es?*"

The woman stepped aside as a huge Hispanic man, the size of a small upright freezer with gray curly hair and a friendly face, filled the doorway. While I don't watch much TV, I recognized him from all of the Pepe's Auto Parts ads as well as his billboards.

"Hi!" he said. "I'm Pepe."

I introduced myself and he smiled again, showing me a mouthful of fluoride-stained teeth. "Clarice told me about you. Do you want to come in?" He opened the carved Mexican doors wide.

"Well, I have a few more questions for your wife, but I understand she's not home."

"No, she's volunteering down at the Botanical Gardens this morning. Is this important?"

"Oh, it can probably wait."

"Well it wouldn't be a problem, if you want to run down there. I'm sure she's just potting plants or something and would be happy to talk to you."

I thanked him and headed back down to the center of town.

The Tucson Botanical Gardens is a lovely, peaceful enclave in the middle of town. Spread out over ten acres, the property was the former Porter home and gardens and now hosts wedding receptions, fund-raisers and private parties as well as the general public.

I sweet-talked my way past the front desk, loath to paying an admission fee if I didn't have to. The woman there was kind and let me slip in after I promised her that I wouldn't look at the plants nor smell the roses, that I just wanted to talk with one of her volunteers.

I found Clarice in a back patio hand-watering herbs. She wasn't at all surprised to see me, a mystery that was cleared up when she reached into her gardening apron and pulled out a cellular phone. "Pepe."

"I won't take up much of your time."

"So what if you do? Honey, they're not going to dock my pay," she said, the pixie grin spreading across her small face.

I smiled. "I was out at the Brave Bull yesterday talking to some of Abby's staff and Ramona Miller mentioned that Abby was dropping things. Did you ever notice that?"

She hesitated as though she hadn't understood me. "You mean party invitations, that kind of stuff?"

Same thought I'd had when Ramona had told me, al
though Clarice's timing seemed just a bit off.

"No. Drink glasses and earrings. Maybe other things
too."

"Never noticed it. Why would she drop things?"
Clarice was studying me intently.

"I don't know that she was. So far Ramona's the only
one who's mentioned it."

"Well, Ramona's, you know . . ." She was flooding
the basil.

"I've been going through Abby's Day Planner and I
noticed that you had lunch with her a couple of days be
fore they went on the camping trip."

"I guess that's right. We had lunch a lot."

"Would you mind telling me about that one?"

"Well, let me think. We went to the Blue Willow, I
remember that because I wanted one of their great bean
tostadas. It was too hot to sit outside, in spite of the mis
ters, so we were indoors."

"What did you talk about?"

"The usual. Girl stuff." She wiped the bridge of her
nose with her index finger, leaving it wet.

"J.B.?"

"Sure. I told you that before. That she was upset be
cause she thought that he was cheating on her."

"So she was pretty upset?"

"More like furious."

"She was mad about the lady bull rider?"

"Among others."

Others. Why hadn't she mentioned that before
when I'd visited her at her house?

"What others?"

"Look, I didn't want to say anything before, because
I just figured what would it matter. Abby had asked me
not to say a word to anyone and since she's dead, I
thought why take J.B. down with her. But then I was
talking to Pepe and we decided that maybe I should tell
you what I know about him."

"I'd appreciate that."

"The day before we had lunch, Abby had just found out that J.B. had been married before."

"She didn't know that?" I was feeling better. Maybe I wasn't the last person in the universe to discover J.B.'s former marital status after all.

"He neglected to tell her that small point. When she found out she was livid."

"How'd she find out?"

"She found a large check that he'd written on his own account to this woman named Jackie. When she finally cornered J.B. he admitted it."

"Why didn't he tell her before, did she say?"

"Sure. Said he'd intended to all along, but then they got serious so quickly that he didn't know how to tell her, then too much time went by and he felt as though he couldn't. Said it had been hanging over his head the whole time. He told her he was relieved that it was finally out in the open."

Yeah, I'll bet.

"But if you ask me, personally, I think there was more to it than that."

"What do you think was going on?"

"Do you know what his ex-wife did?"

"You're talking about the stripping?"

She nodded. "I think he conveniently neglected to share his former marriage with Abby since the ex was younger and made her living taking off her clothes. I'm betting that he thought that Abby couldn't have handled that. Bless her heart."

"Could she?"

Clarice shrugged and sprayed the oregano with water. "She wouldn't have been happy about it, that's for sure. But probably more from the social standpoint than anything else. I mean how'd you like to follow a stripper? Here's my new husband, his former wife did table dances. But he has his health certificate. I don't think that would have gone over well with her."

"I asked you before about whether you thought Abby was thinking of leaving him."

"And you're asking me again?"

I nodded.

"I can't say that she ever actually said that."

"But you think she was?"

"Honey, I don't know. I honestly don't. Abby liked being married. Hell, she was married to old John Wilson forever. It was important to her to have a man around. There was a defenseless side to Abby, a side that wanted to be protected. John Wilson gave her that and I think she was hoping that J.B. would too."

I thought back to how solicitous J.B. had been when Abby had gotten dumped during roundup. He had taken care of her, so there was probably some truth to what Clarice Martínez was telling me.

We talked for a while longer and right before I left I remembered the other thing I'd wanted to ask her.

"When I was going over my records I found a note I'd made when I listened to Abby's answering machine. You'd left a call for her, something about a man named Hornisher."

"Hornisher," she repeated. As she wiped her wet hands on her apron they seemed to be shaking a bit. Could she have Parkinson's? "I did?"

"You left his number and told Abby to call him," I nudged.

She shook her head. "It probably wasn't anything or I'd remember."

"So the name Hornisher doesn't ring a bell?"

She thought for a minute. "Oh, of course. Hornisher. He's a lip guy."

"A lip guy?"

She brushed her wet hands across her own pouty-looking lips. When she replied, she wasn't looking at me though. Her eyes drifted upward and to the right. "Enhancements, collagen implants. Does great work.

Abby was thinking about having it done and I left her his name. He's in Phoenix."

As I walked back through the Botanical Gardens I had the distinct impression that maybe Clarice Martínez wasn't telling me everything.

It had been my experience that people who suddenly look up and to the right when you're interrogating them were telling you something.

They were lying.

27

J.B. CALENDAR WAS ARRESTED FOR THE MURDER OF HIS WIFE, Abigail Van Thiessen, Thursday morning.

By the time I got back to my office, there was a message from Jodie Austin waiting to tell me of this calamity. I figured María López Zepeda, the defense attorney J.B. had hired, would get around to calling me when things settled down and she had either sprung J.B. or had figured out how to mitigate his circumstances.

I called the number Jodie left, listening to the phone ring as I gazed out my window admiring my grazing Brahma cows. I love these girls. Even in the drought years they manage to keep looking good. Their browsing does that for them, for they're not all that picky about what they'll eat, unlike the fussy English cattle.

When Jodie finally answered, I asked, "What happened?"

"The police came in early this morning with a warrant." The way she said it sounded like war ant, probably not too far off base.

"They were here all morning searching, looking, tearing things apart. They covered everything."

"Did they find anything?"

"I think so. There was a lot of commotion down at the barn."

The barn. A logical place to keep a veterinary drug, like ketamine.

"Then they arrested J.B."

"The sheriff's office?"

"I think so."

"Who else was there?"

"Only the police."

"No, I mean the staff."

"Oh. Ramona had the day off, but the Covarrubiases were here, and of course the rest of the students."

"And Peter?"

"He left to go running early this morning, before the police came. That man's a running maniac."

Briefly I wondered about the cow stamp, the padding that had been made to look like cow prints. Had the police found the stamp at the barn too? If so, had they figured out that there were fake prints in the Baboquivaris?

Once again it hit me. Even if J.B.'s brains had been a bit scrambled by all of his bull rides or too much booze, he wasn't stupid. He knew about cows. And he sure as hell would have known the difference between a smaller-footed crossbred and a big-footed Brahma.

He also would have known that ranchers typically graze the same general kind of cow together. The fake bull print I'd seen with Sanders had stood out from all of the other tracks, both across the desert, and at the wet edges of the stock tank. J.B. flat would have known better. If he was going to plant a fake print, at least he would have made it the right kind.

Although I had a lot to talk to J.B. Calendar about, including his former bride, Jackie Doo Dahs, I suddenly felt a lot better about my client.

I asked Jodie to leave a message for Peter to call me and hung up the phone. Then I went ahead and left a message for María López Zepeda.

Although J.B. was in jail, his weekly report was still hanging over my head. I spent the next hour figuring out how to clean up all the typos. Of course it wouldn't be really done until I printed the damn thing out.

I struggled with the printer for a while, hitting all sorts of buttons and finally got it turned on. It made some chattering noises at me and, feeling somewhat confident, I put a wad of paper in the tray.

After hitting a few buttons, trial and error really, the paper started feeding through the machine and within minutes J.B.'s report miraculously appeared in my hands.

I felt like the Cheshire cat as I grinned at the neatly typed pages in front of me. This was a lot better looking than anything I could have produced on the old Selectric. Maybe this computer business wasn't going to be so bad after all.

I put a copy of the report into my files. Then I slipped J.B.'s copy into a manila envelope and sealed it.

Before leaving the office I looked up Samuel Mullon in the Tucson telephone book and was amazed to find his home address listed. I scribbled it on a scrap of paper and headed out the door.

Although I'd wound down the windows in Priscilla and parked her under a mesquite tree at the stage stop, the interior of the white truck was still as hot as Hades when I got in. My shorts and cotton T-shirt kept me cooler than Levi's would have, but I was still roasting. The air conditioner wouldn't cool the truck off on the mile drive to the house, so I left the windows down and didn't bother to turn it on.

Jake Hatcher's truck was at the bunkhouse when I pulled into the drive. He was definitely a regular around here. It bugged me a lot that he was probably fooling around with Martín's girlfriend, but then they'd all be gone in a few days and I wouldn't have to worry about it anymore. One thing was for sure. Martín didn't seem to be losing sleep over it.

I had just stepped out of the truck when Martín came up.

"We're having lunch. Want to join us?"

I didn't really, but I nodded. The way things were going, I probably wouldn't have that many more opportunities to talk to Martín.

The swamp cooler hit me full in the face when I walked into the bunkhouse and the room reeked with that fishy smell evaporative coolers sometimes get.

The radio, tuned to a Mexican station, hummed quietly in sharp contrast to Cori Elena's usual high-decibel levels. A couple of cardboard boxes sat in the middle of the kitchen floor and I could see that they were partially filled with newspaper-wrapped dishes. My heart sank.

Cori Elena was dressed in the shortest cutoffs I'd ever seen and a tank top with oversized armholes. She stood at the sink, slicing jicama into a bowlful of lettuce, tomatoes and onions. As she bent over, her tank top slid forward, giving me a good profile shot of her left breast. With her in heat, no wonder Jake Hatcher was hanging around like a stud dog.

"Trade!" she said. "You're going to join us."

"Yeah, thanks. Hi, Jake."

"Hey, Trade." Jake Hatcher sat at the table in the seat that I knew was Martín's and that pissed me off. He'd probably been here enough times to know where the head of the family sat, but even if that wasn't the case, he still had no business sitting there. Or even breathing, for that matter.

"Martín, fix her something cool to drink," she said, reaching for another fork and paper napkin that she handed to me.

Martín grabbed a glass from the cupboard, some ice from the refrigerator and poured me a glass of iced tea. It was the premade stuff, loaded with sugar, but I still managed to suck it down.

Cori Elena handed me the salad to throw on the table and then she brought over a platter of bean burros wrapped in tinfoil. They were just lukewarm, which was fine since we were all too parched to even think about eating a hot meal. I suspected she'd made them earlier that morning and had reheated them in the microwave, then wrapped them in the tinfoil to keep them warm. In the summer, a lot of us avoid turning on our ovens. It just adds heat to heat and doesn't make much sense.

We ate quietly for a few minutes. Finally I couldn't stand it.

"So, Jake, what brings you out our way?" I asked. I avoided looking at him, taking care to concentrate on what was left of my burro.

"I heard that Martín's truck was on the fritz, so I thought I'd stop by and see if they needed anything."

Sure.

"I told Jake that we were goin' to be taking a trip," Cori Elena offered.

Jesus, how stupid could she be? Nothing like advertising that they were leaving so the bad guys could come in and nail her before she left. Great thought process this one had, although in truth the brand inspector would have been blind not to have noticed the moving boxes, especially the tall stack in the corner of the room.

"Prego's out of town," Jake said.

"Right."

"*Chiquita*, I forgot to tell you. That screech owl has her babies again."

"Down along the creek? In the fork?" I asked. It seemed late, but with the drought, that wasn't all that unusual. Some animals weren't having babies at all.

Martín and I had watched this particular owl for years. While many screech owls carved out holes in the saguaros, she always threw a few twigs together—something owls rarely do, as they prefer to take over nests built by other birds—in the fork of a mesquite tree. Usually it worked out, but last year she'd lost her one baby when it fell out of the mesquite and broke its neck.

He nodded. "She's got two this year."

"I'll check it out." God, I was going to miss this. Martín and I had been watching wildlife together all our lives, marveling at the animals, their nests and dens and habits and babies. While Sanders and I also shared the same interest, my history with Martín was longer. We could even talk about the things we'd seen together as kids. "I'm going to ride this afternoon, interested?"

He shook his head. "I've got too much to do."

I didn't press it.

We were halfway through lunch when the phone rang. Cori Elena jumped up to answer it.

While she said "hello," she quickly reverted to Spanish. She was speaking so rapidly and so quietly that I couldn't make out her words.

Judging from the worried look on Martín's face, though, he knew there was a problem.

Cori Elena took the long cord and disappeared with the phone into the bedroom, leaving the three of us to finish our lunch.

Late that afternoon I caught Dream. He stood, half asleep from the heat, as the flies buzzed us while I saddled him. I put my canteens on my saddle and then rode out through the back gate, across the dry creek. I'd been worrying on and off about what the drought was doing to the water table, but there was no way, short of pulling the well, to see how much it was actually dropping.

We climbed slowly up through the saddle and Dream was wet with sweat before we even cleared the crest. I took it slowly with him, saying to myself, *but it's a dry heat*. He probably knew the difference too, for when the temperature and the humidity are both high, that's when a horse can get into trouble. His air-conditioning system, designed to make him wet, never gets a chance to dry off in high humidity. This can seriously overheat a horse.

As I rode, I wondered about the telephone call that Cori Elena had taken. After she answered the phone, we didn't see her again. I figured the call probably had something to do with Carmen Orduño, but after lunch I'd left along with Jake Hatcher. I knew I'd get the story later, and while I suspected that he would too, we played the charade, pretended nothing was wrong, and left the bunkhouse together.

As I rode across the mesa I was struck by the extreme fire danger. Some of the national forests had already been closed to horses, for fear that sparks from their metal shoes would start a fire.

It wouldn't take much to incinerate the entire desert, as dry as it was. While the cattle had chewed a lot of the grass down, there was still plenty to spark a brushfire. Worrying about it wasn't very productive though. We did what we could around the ranch, keeping the weeds down and the grass clipped along the perimeters. In a pinch, a helicopter with a bucket could pull water out of the pond—they'd done it before. Still, in a severe drought, the brushfires could rage out of control for days. In Mexico, some had already been burning for months, spewing their smoke across the border.

My one consolation was that Catalina State Park, which adjoined my grazing leases to the south, had placed a moratorium on campfires. Of course, that didn't discount all the happy campers with cigarettes or the mavericks who would go ahead and light a fire anyway.

I headed toward the Coronado National Forest, running into a few groups of Brahmas with their calves. They were still bedded down in the shade under the mesquite trees, waiting for the temperature to drop lower before they headed off for water. The babies I saw were all branded and the heifers ear-tagged, so it looked like we hadn't missed too many of the calves on roundup.

I also ran across a few groups of dries—cows that hadn't calved—and I stopped long enough to place their ear tag numbers in my leather tally book. My calf percentages were taking a hit with the drought, and many of my reliable cows, the ones that never missed having a calf a year, were now in the dry group.

An hour or so later I made my turn south, heading to the fence line and then riding through a few canyons before dropping back into the Cañada del Oro. I had just hit the creek and was crossing it when I spotted Sanders riding up from the park.

"Hey, what are you doing out here?" I hollered.

"They called, said my shorthorns were down there at the campgrounds again."

"Didn't find them, huh?" It was obvious since he wasn't pushing any cows. Sanders ran some shorthorns in with the Vaca Grande herd, and losing cattle in the park was a problem for both of us. For years the park fence had been down and the cows had the run of the place. When the new fence went up, people cut it and left gates open. It didn't take the cattle long to find the breaks and they'd end up in the park where the grass was always greener—at least in their minds.

"I'll try again in the morning."

"Martín says that screech owl's kids hatched out. I'm heading there now." I took a long drink of water from my canteen and then, since I was so close to the ranch, let some of the cold water trickle over Dream's neck, hoping it would help cool him off.

We rode up a small sandy tributary and found the little brown ear tufted screech owl sitting on a limb beside her decrepit nest, which was rider level in the fork of an old mesquite tree. She was small, like most desert screech owls. In another of Mother Nature's grand plans, these owls are usually smaller than their northern counterparts, since their heat loss increases with the decrease in size. Two white, fuzzy hatchlings with enormous dark eyes stared at us, unblinking, while their momma snapped her mandibles together making a noisy clicking sound, clearly unhappy at our attention.

We were sitting quietly on our horses, silently admiring the owlets when all of a sudden something swift and fast flew close to our heads, buzzing us and startling the horses.

"Poppa," I said, although I really couldn't tell. Sometimes even owls have trouble telling themselves apart. Still, it was a reasonable assumption as we watched another small brown owl fly up to a high limb across from the nest where he studied us with big angry eyes. We left.

We hadn't ridden very far when Dream suddenly shied and ducked away from a mesquite tree on my right.

"Snakes," I said to Sanders, an unnecessary warning since he had also pulled his horse up.

The two Mohave rattlesnakes underneath the tree had their coontails entwined. The Mohave is one of the most lethal snakes in North America. Its venom can be almost twenty times as toxic as that of the Western diamondback. The good news is that it only zaps you with about a sixth of the venom that the average diamondback will. You do the math.

It didn't take a Dr. Ruth to figure out what was happening. They were blatantly involved in a sexual act. Of the thirteen species of rattlesnakes found in the United States, we have eleven of them right here in Arizona. Which translates into the possibility of finding some of them going at it from the middle of March to the end of October, so it's not all that unusual to catch them en flagrante delicto. Although it was a bit late for the Mohaves.

"Wonder how long they been doing it," Sanders said.

I laughed. We both knew about that. Rattlesnakes rarely make love for less than an hour or two and usually it's longer—like six to twelve hours. Some have them have even been known to go at it for twenty-four, which probably results in a lot of rattlesnake headaches.

We sat on the horses and watched the snakes for a few minutes. They were oblivious to us, so intent were they on their lovemaking.

I looked at my watch for effect. "I think they've been at this for, oh, about sixteen and a half hours." Of course I had no way of telling that, which Sanders knew.

"I've been wondering what I wanted to come back as," he said with a chuckle as we rode off.

"You'll have to grow another one," I suggested, for the rattler has two penises, known as hemipenes and located in the tail, although only one is used at a time.

Seeing the snakes made me think of Abby and J.B. out on their romantic tryst in the Baboquivaris. If he'd wanted to kill her, couldn't he have found a place closer to home? Then I immediately dismissed the speculation, since the Baboquivaris, from a killer's standpoint, were ideal. Far enough away that no one from the Brave Bull or La Cienega would see them and remote enough that the chances of encountering a stranger would be rare.

Hell, a killer could have taken all night to kill Abby if he'd wanted to. But then that brought me back to J.B. If someone had killed Abby other than her husband, where was J.B. when it was going on? Why hadn't he saved her? Had he really been that drunk, or had he also been drugged?

I wondered if that had happened how long the drug would stay in his system and made a mental note to myself to check it out.

28

THE SUN WAS JUST GOING DOWN WHEN I RODE THROUGH THE back gate. Blue, Mrs. Fierce and Petunia all greeted me. Their duty done, the dogs proceeded to play their favorite game, Hump Dog, while Petunia rooted around in the dirt.

Dream, still a bit unsure of the pig, cast a wary eye on her as she wandered in and out of his legs, looking for nonexistent truffles.

After unsaddling the Arabian, I led him over to the hose and began squirting him so his wet sweat wouldn't dry and leave patches of salt on his hide. I paid particular attention to his hind legs above his hocks, a natural settling place for body salts. If this area isn't hosed off, the salt can actually scald the horse, causing him to eventually lose his hair.

While I can't say that the gelding was thrilled with his bath, he put up with it. Once I finished with his body, I took a wet sponge and wiped his face and behind his ears and then reached for the flat metal sweat scraper. Running it first across his rounded sides, I moved on to his neck, rump and legs as the water slid into the metal groove and then off the horse and onto the dry, thirsty ground.

Once I'd finished with these ablutions, I turned Dream loose in the pasture with Gray. He wasted no time in trotting off a ways, then dropping and rolling in the soft sand. He stood and shook, resembling something out of a military school mud roll. When he dried, he wouldn't look like he'd been ridden at all.

I quickly threw alfalfa to the horses, then scattered scratch for the ducks and dumped dry dog food in the dogs' pans. I whistled softly for Petunia and let her onto the screened porch, where I reached into a plastic garbage can, scooped up her pig chow and filled her bowl.

I had poured my canteens half full of water and was putting them in the outside freezer so they would form into solid ice chunks for my next ride, when Martín appeared at the screened porch door.

"Bad time?" he asked.

"Nope." I closed the freezer door. "I was just going to get a beer. You want one?"

He nodded and I stepped into the kitchen, opened the refrigerator and retrieved two cold Coronas, a lime and a couple of chilled Mountain Oyster Club pewter mugs. I opened the bottles and carefully poured the beer into the frosty steins and then carved up the lime, squeezing a healthy dose into each mug before finally throwing the rinds in for good measure. Petunia was nudging my leg, telling me it was time for her to go back outside and join her girlfriends.

I handed a cold mug to Martín and we stepped back into the porch. I opened the door and watched Petunia trot out, wiggling her rear end in gleeful anticipation of rejoining Blue and Mrs. Fierce. Maybe she was just saying, "Goody, goody, guess what I got and you didn't?" The dogs had never shown any true interest in her food, which is not to say that they would not have been interested in her *as* food had she been roasted. Which, I suppose, is an indictment of a lot of friendships.

Although the sun was fading, it was still hot, so I

flipped the overhead fan to high as we settled into th
pigskin chairs. The breeze from the fan rolled over u.
shrouding us in lukewarm air. At least it kept us dry.

"So, what's up?" I asked.

"She's dead."

I knew he was talking about Carmen Orduño.

"I kind of thought that she might be," I said. The firs
sip of iced beer from the cold mug was heaven. "Tha
was the call?"

He nodded and drank his beer.

"She was found in an old dump outside of Mag
dalena."

I waited.

"Shot."

I still waited.

He took a deep breath. "A couple of her fingers wer
broken."

We sat quietly for a few minutes, both knowin
what that meant. Someone had wanted to get informa
tion out of Carmen Orduño. That someone was proba
bly Rafael Félix and the information most likely had t
do with Félix's missing money. Money he somehow a
tributed to Lázaro Orantez's widow, who was no doul
at this moment bebopping around the bunkhouse. Was
being too unkind? She might have been shattered wit
the news of her friend's death. After all, she hadn't com
out of the bedroom after receiving the call.

"Maybe you better move to town until the truck
fixed," I said. "In a motel or something. I can run you a
in tonight."

"No. I've got too much to do here."

"Martín, for God's sake, those people could kill you

His strong brown fingers caressed the raised M(
symbol—the behind of a well-hung bull—on the side (
his beer mug. "If I went to town, how would they know
They could still come here, and then you and Dad woul
be here alone."

Frankly, that thought had occurred to me. I was (

he opinion that the more people around, the merrier.
Hell, Jake Hatcher was even beginning to look good.
Now I knew how Bowie and Crockett and the boys felt
when new blood rode through the gates of the Alamo.
Then I remembered the fat lot of good that did them and
I didn't feel all that encouraged. "You'll be leaving any-
way, what difference does it make?"

"Don't think I don't feel bad about that."

"I know you do."

He took a long pull on his Corona.

"They say she'd been dead awhile."

Like many things, I imagined that forensics in
Mexico was not quite as up-to-date as ours. It would
probably take longer to post the body than it would in
our country.

"So if she gave them any information, they would
have had it for some time."

"Exactamente."

We finished our beer and I jumped up and got two
more bottles from the fridge. Popped the caps off and
poured them into the mugs. As I settled back into my
chair, the only sound between us was the hum of the
ceiling fan. That was one of the things I was going to
miss when Martín left. The silences. Silences that only
blossomed when you were either very uncomfortable
with someone or very, very comfortable with him.

Damn, but I was going to miss him.

I didn't sleep very well that night. I kept expecting
Félix and his men to come storming the Vaca Grande in
their quest for Cori Elena. When I wasn't up prowling
the house, peeking out windows, I tried to go back to
sleep. But that didn't work either, for I kept thinking
about Abby being drowned in the stock tank and her
doctor getting slaughtered in his own carport. It seemed
like danger was everywhere, floating around me like
some inexplicable aura. Just before three in the morning I
was so exhausted that I finally fell asleep.

♦   ♦   ♦

The old Pueblo Stockyards runs an auction every
Friday morning. I'd come before it started in the hopes of
being able to talk to J.B.'s friend Tommy Renner, but the
large volume of consigned cattle made that impossible.
About as close as I'd been able to get to him was to see
his straw cowboy hat floating above the pens as he went
about the business of moving and sorting cattle.

It was sobering to see all of the consignments, since
it was as good an indication as any that the drought was
taking its toll. These were ranchers, just like me, selling
off their cattle because their range could not support
them without water. If things didn't change quickly, I
could easily find myself in the same situation. Not a
pretty thought. Not pretty at all.

The Wilson boys, after their national calf roping ca-
reers, had built a million-dollar state-of-the-art auction
and stockyards facility out in Marana. Just off I-10, it was
convenient to the freeway, and far enough out in the
country that no one was going to complain about a little
cow manure, or a string of pickup trucks and stock trailers filled with horses, heifers, steers, cows and bulls dis-
rupting neighborhood traffic patterns. The fact that the
owners, Jeb and Cody, were salt-of-the-earth, good old-
fashioned American boys, didn't hurt their business either.

The thing about ranching is that in a world gone
crazy with lawsuits and broken contracts, you can still
find people in our world whose word is golden. Who,
when they say they'll do something, do it. Who, when
you need help, give it without being asked. Whose word
you can take to the bank. The Wilson boys were no exception.

Add to that that ranching has become high-tech for a
lot of these folks and the Wilson family does everything
they can to help the rancher determine when the best
time is to sell his stock. The commodities exchange is
checked several times every day for the price of beef. Jeb

and Cody will also happily tell you how many chicken and fish places have been replaced with steakhouses.

While some auction-goers like to be close and lean against the red pipe ring, I prefer a higher position in the tiered stands where I can look down on the computerized electronic scale. I also like the higher elevations so I can see who's there without turning around. The other reason is that in the hot weather it puts you closer to the cool air being pumped out of the side-mounted draft evaporative coolers. I sat in line with the bigger of the two cooler vents.

They ran the horses through first, and there were a number of them. Many were scrawny, underfed things that had been turned out on the sparse Indian reservations. Then there were the well-broke, older ranch horses, being sent through since they were perhaps beginning to stumble, or not go about their daily work with the same alacrity as they had when they were youngsters. They'd still make good riding horses for people who weren't going to ride them at breakneck speeds through cactus-studded desert in pursuit of rogue cows.

The number of horses was yet another barometer of our drought. One thing was for sure, I'd never give up Dream or Gray. Not willingly.

Perhaps some of the consignments were from ranchers spooked by the Fortunada's recent loss of fourteen head of horses after they had eaten too much burro weed.

The horse part of the auction used to be a lot more fun when they were ridden in the ring. Then you could get an idea of how the horse worked, although truthfully, they all looked like they reined pretty good when they were ridden in the small area. When a cowboy put spurs to them and rolled them around, there really wasn't any place they could go, but to turn over their hocks and execute a nice rollback.

They don't do that anymore. Now the auctioneer reads a script that is provided by the horse's owner. From this piece of paper you learn that the horse is gentle, has been used to gather cattle, whatever.

What usually isn't provided is if the horse has reared up and fallen over backward and killed someone, which is why buying a horse at auction is tricky. A guy I know who is in the dude ranch business and really knows his stuff, tells me they're lucky if 60 percent of the horses they buy at auction work out. For the rest of the buyers, those with a lot less horse sense than my friend, the percentages are much lower; the mistakes more costly if you count the broken equipment, busted limbs and shattered vertebrae.

There are some scrupulous owners who will consign a horse who has a bad attitude or is crippled and stipulate that the horse must go for dog food. Sometimes though an unscrupulous owner says nothing. It's the Wilson's policy to deny their sale to anyone who has ever lied about a consigned horse.

If no history is provided on the animal, the auctioneer might volunteer information such as "He's got iron downstairs," which you can then use to make the jump in logic to the fact that if the horse has shoes on they must have been put there so he could be ridden, ergo he must be a saddle horse.

Most of the horses went for dog food prices, which was unfortunately probably their destination. With the drought, no one I knew was looking to take on more mouths to feed or water.

The cattle sales took a couple of hours. I'm always amused at the body language on sale days. Some bidders start out bold, waving their hands or cards and then become more subtle when the auctioneer knows they're in the game. The regular buyers raise a finger, wink or barely nod their heads. A few latecomers walked up the steps with their backs to the ring and twitched their cards or made a fist, both actions that were readily picked up by the bid spotters. Cell phones have also invaded the auction barn as the buyers stay in close contact with their clients.

The music of the auction barn played—the snap of the whip to encourage the cattle to move out of the ring, bored kids kicking the back of the wooden seats, the buzz of the flies, the lowing of the cattle, the constant clanging of the heavy metal gates and above it all, the singsong of the auctioneer's patter.

When a group of scrawny uncut Indian cattle came through, they were "all frame, boys." A calf, blind in one eye, was "Look at that! A miracle on his way to town."

Cody's wife sat next to the auctioneer, recording the information on each sale into the computer. As I sat there watching the cattle move through the arena I was amazed, as I always am, by the sheer volume of money that was changing hands, most of it by wire transfer. Conservatively at least a half million dollars a week goes through the old Pueblo Stockyards. That's a lot of beef.

Finally it was over and I found Tommy. He was tall and lean, anorexic almost. His blue work shirt was splattered with the remains of the day, his Wrangler's were stained with something suspiciously brown and held up with a carved leather belt and a badly scratched calf-roping buckle. A cigarette dangled from his blistered lips, its long ash marching dangerously close to his mouth. His shapeless straw cowboy hat had seen better days as a wide band of sweat stained the crown where it attached to the brim. When he gave me a thin smile, I noticed that he was missing one of his front teeth.

We went back inside to the air-conditioned comfort of the café, which was now relatively empty since most of the ranchers had headed home, although many of their brands remained here, painted on the brown cement floor. There was no mistaking this as anything other than a cowboy café with the walls of photographs of old roundups, calf ropings, rodeos and cutting contests, interspersed with ancient canteens, cracked leather harnesses and discarded chaps.

When Tommy removed his hat, it turned out that he was like a lot of cowboys. Bald.

We ordered hamburgers and waited for our lunch to arrive. He'd known J.B. Calendar on and off for years and detailed highlights of the times their lives had commingled, many of which seemed to be centered on alcohol.

"Is J.B. drinking a lot these days?" I asked.

"Compared to what?"

"I don't know. I guess compared to usual."

He laughed, a snort really. "J.B. always drinks a lot. Maybe he's gotta live up to his name or something."

I gave him a puzzled look.

"His dad died drunk, but before he did he named his kid after his best friend."

I thought about this a minute.

"Jim Beam?"

He nodded.

Probably not good news. From what Martín had been telling me and from the drinking I'd seen J.B. do up at the Brave Bull, it sounded as though he was headed down the same grim path as his father. Interesting that he and Abby had both had abusive parents. Had that been part of their attraction for one another? And if so, had they left the abuse behind them or had they repeated with each other that which they'd learned as children?

Our hamburgers arrived and we were busy for a minute or two slathering mayonnaise and mustard on them. One of the great perks about eating at the Marana Stockyards café is that the beef is always excellent and our lunch was no exception. After I had my burger under control, I continued my questions.

"I hear that J.B. and Abby had quite a honeymoon."

Tommy was burying his French fries in salt. "J.B. hocked everything he had for that and when that wasn't enough he started borrowing money from his friends."

"Including you?"

"Yeah, he got me for a hundred bucks. But hey, he paid it back, with interest."

It sounded like Abby had paid for her own honeymoon after all since I imagined the money to pay back his friends had come from J.B.'s new bank account.

"Well, he probably doesn't have to worry much about money these days," I said. It was a fishing trip to see if Renner knew about J.B.'s million bucks.

"Don't imagine."

It didn't sound as though Tommy knew about J.B.'s windfall.

"You knew Jackie Doo Dahs?" I abruptly changed the subject.

"Knew her?" He smiled, once again showing me the space where one of his front teeth used to live. "I used to date her."

"When?" It was hard for me to imagine that a woman who had been married to J.B., who at least got points for being relatively cute, would also date Tommy Renner. Where J.B. had a healthy cowboy outdoor look to him, there was something consumptive about Tommy.

"Before she married J.B. And after their divorce," he said. "And before she married J.B., and after their divorce."

He didn't look like a parrot, but hadn't I just heard him repeat himself? "You said that twice."

"Well, they were married twice."

"J.B. and Jackie were married twice?" Now, who was the parrot?

"Yep. And divorced twice. Me and Jackie go back a ways. After that last time, that's why J.B. don't talk to me."

Not only had my client not told me about his ex-wife, but he had also somehow neglected to mention that he had married the same woman twice. Great guy. No wonder Tommy Renner's name had not appeared on his list. He knew too much. Interesting that Uncle C hadn't mentioned J.B.'s two marriages to Jackie either. Maybe he didn't know.

"When'd they get divorced?"

"The last time?" Tommy was talking with his mouth full and mayonnaise was dribbling out as I looked for something else to focus on. The sign warning NO DANCING ON TABLES WITH SPURS would have to do.

I nodded.

"Oh, 'bout a year before he married the rich one."

At least that part jibed with what Uncle C had told me. It also coincided with the time that J.B. had started dating Abby. I wondered if he'd dumped Jackie for her.

"I guess she came back into J.B.'s life after he married Abby," I said. "Something about wanting more alimony."

"Alimony?"

"You don't think she was after more money?"

"Jackie? Nah. She wanted J.B., that's what she wanted."

A cold chill went up my spine. How badly had she wanted him? Enough to kill?

"You think she wanted to have an affair with him?"

He shook his head and bit into a handful of French fries that crunched when he talked. "Oh no, she wanted him back. All of him. Permanent like."

"You're telling me that she wanted him to divorce his wife?"

"Yeah, that's what she told me. She was working on him to do it too."

My mind was spinning. The fact that Jackie and J.B. had been married twice was probably a pretty good indication of some kind of strong attraction between the two of them. What had Clarice told me when we were talking about sex *I guess the cowboy was really something in that department. Jeepers, Abby used to say he was so good, she wanted to share him with her friends.* Was that the attraction J.B. had for Jackie?

But the money may have been an even stronger lure. Abby had given J.B. a million dollars, which had probably looked pretty good to his former wife. Had she somehow known about the $60 million he was going to inherit now that Abigail Van Thiessen was dead? If Jackie Doo Dahs could pull off a third marriage to J.B. Calendar she'd be in tall cotton. Suddenly, I had another strong suspect in my already crowded field.

"Are you dating Jackie now?" I was betting that most of Tommy's appeal could be found below his scratched calf-roping buckle.

"Nah. She only has eyes for him. As far as I'm concerned she might as well be a nun."

My eyebrows shot up with the image of Sister Doo Dahs in her habit.

Tommy took another giant bite out of his hamburger. "But anyway, she's got another cause now instead of sex and J.B." He had the good grace to finish most of his bite before continuing. "She's into animals."

"Really?" I'd heard that some exotic dancers used animals in their acts. Was Jackie one of those?

"Yeah. That was a problem her and J.B. had. Her and me too. She didn't like rodeo, said it was mean to the animals. Hell, most of them only have to work eight seconds a week, what's mean about that?"

"Well, some people don't like it," I said.

"And then them lab people with the mice and dogs and stuff."

I knew what he was talking about. The University of Arizona was using some lab animals and had been picketed by some of the local activists.

"So she's involved in the animal rights movement?"

"Yeah. Big time. She's even got this sandhill crane costume that she wears."

"She dresses up like a sandhill crane?"

"Only sometimes. When she's protesting."

I ate for a minute and then asked, "Do you know if J.B. ever abused her?"

He choked on his hamburger. "You mean like hit her?"

"Yeah."

"A couple of times that I knew of."

Damn. There was that trust thing again. J.B. had lied about that too. Had he told me the truth about anything?

"But it was after she hit him."

"What do you mean?"

"Jackie's got a pretty good temper." He stopped eating long enough to roll up his dirty shirtsleeve. He pointed to a crescent-shaped scar on the inside of his forearm. "That's one of Jackie's brands."

"She did that to you?" It looked like a pretty healthy scar to me.

"She threw a bottle at me and it hit the counter, broke and I got the ricochet."

"Jackie do that kind of stuff to J.B. too?"

"A couple of times they got into some knock-down drag-outs. Hell, when she was with me I had to shove her around a bit. Self-defense. He had to do the same thing. She can get kinda wild."

I let the subject drop. While I wasn't keen on J.B.'s pounding on women, it sounded like Jackie Doo Dahs may have been stepping over the line a bit. One thing was for sure in any event: I needed to check out his ex-wife.

After I paid the bill we headed back out into the sweltering heat.

"Where can I find Jackie, do you know?"

Tommy was lighting a cigarette and although he had no problem talking with his mouth full of food, I had to wait until he got it lit before he answered.

"You mean like now?"

"Yeah."

"That's an easy one. The circus is in town. That's where I'd try. Look for a stacked lion or something."

And with that he was back to the pens.

29

IT WAS WELL AFTER TWO WHEN I HIT I-10 AND DROVE DOWN-town. I'd called María López Zepeda before leaving the Old Pueblo Stockyards and she had agreed to give me a few minutes as long as I could get to her office before three-thirty.

Parking can be a bear when you're driving a big pickup, and it's never more troublesome than when you are trying to park in one of those big overhead garages. I drove slowly since I always think the concrete ceiling is going to crunch the top of the cab and cave it in on my head. While it felt close, I probably had feet to spare. Still, not one of my favorite things to do.

López Zepeda's office was on the seventh floor of the Arizona Bank Building. I gave my name to the receptionist and sat on a soft brown leather couch admiring the view and the Michael Chiago painting of a group of Tohono O'odham people gathering saguaro fruit. Seeing that for some reason reminded me of the old Apache words for June, before we started using the English language. While I don't speak the language, I remembered the translation—face painted red with cactus fruit—a reference to the saguaro fruit. In the background of the painting was a large mountain peak that I recognized as

Baboquivari. Interesting coincidence given the scene of Abby's death.

María, along with her two partners, had built a healthy defense practice, stoked in large part by their defense of a lot of drug dealers. The senior partner, Oscar Horowitz, had teethed on defending guys like Joe Bonano and Peter Licavoli, Mafia kingpins who years ago had made Tucson their home.

Three minutes later I was in María's office. After she thanked me for referring J.B. to her, I asked, "Did you get him out?"

"Can't. He's not bailable."

"So he's been charged with murder one?"

She nodded. "And the county attorney's concerned that he may skip town."

"The itinerant cowboy business I suppose." I was sure J.B.'s former lifestyle probably had something to do with it.

"He's got access to money and he could flee."

"It's a pretty good can of worms, isn't it?"

She nodded again. "Are you getting anywhere?"

Since J.B. had made it clear from the beginning that I could share anything I learned with his defense attorney, I brought her up-to-date on what I'd learned, which really wasn't all that much. When I got to the part about Jackie Doo Dahs, María was clearly upset.

"Another wife? He never said anything about that."

"That makes us both surprised."

"*¡Hijuela!*"

"I'll see if I can track her down. Apparently she wanted J.B. back."

"I'm not surprised," María said. "He probably looks pretty good to her with his saddlebagsful of money."

"That's one of the problems with this case." I stood and walked over to her window and looked out. Below, miniature people scurried along the sidewalks and jaywalked across the streets. "With Abby dead, everyone stands to gain—J.B., Lateef Wise, Abby's staff, the charities."

"Not to mention the peripherals."

"Right. So now I've added Jackie Doo Dahs to the list." I turned back to the desk.

"I'd be interested in what she has to say." María twirled a pen with her long slim fingers. It was like watching a kaleidoscope as the gold of her many rings sparkled and flashed with each turn. "I've advised him to take the Fifth."

I let this sink in. While I'm not a lawyer, I do know a little about the Fifth Amendment of the Constitution. The part we were talking about here had to do with a defendant not being compelled to be a witness against himself.

"What in the hell is he afraid of?"

"Not him. Me. I'm not willing to let even the smallest part of the case be made against him by his own words."

"So you think he knows something?"

She shook her head. "Not necessarily. But he was in the neighborhood of the scene of the crime and he's been arrested for it. If he admits he knew the victim or was wearing a blue shirt, any little detail at all could be used to help convict him."

While I knew this was a strategy used by a lot of defense lawyers, it seemed a lot more suspicious when the person doing it was *my* client. I always thought the guilty guys were the ones taking the Fifth.

"I guess it's a good thing that he came to see you first then," I said.

"We talked about it last week, so when they read him his Mirandas, he chose to remain silent and, as far as I know, has remained so. We do have another problem though. He wants to take a lie detector test."

"Oh, God."

"Definitely not a good idea. They're unreliable and there's a chance he'd fail."

"I didn't think they were admissible in court."

"They're not. But he has this idea in his head that if he takes one and passes, that will make him look good and the police will start looking for the real murderer."

"Is that true?"

She nodded her head. "Usually it means they'll look elsewhere, saving valuable time they might have wasted on the suspect. That's why cops love them. But even if I let him take the test, and even if he passed, that's not going to happen here. Not with the drugs they found."

"Ketamine," I guessed.

She wasn't surprised I knew about the veterinary drug.

"It's been placed in evidence."

"What's J.B. say about it?"

"That he's never seen it before. Claims he didn't even know there was such a drug. Unfortunately the detectives found it among his bull riding paraphernalia." She gathered up a stack of manila folders on her desk and put them in a slim leather briefcase. "Trade, I've got to run. I'm late for a deposition. Keep in touch."

The next morning the elephant poop on my tennis shoes was driving me crazy. I'd accidentally stepped in it looking for Jackie Doo Dahs. Thank God I hadn't worn my sandals.

I finally found Jackie, or what I thought was Jackie, anchored to a chain link fence near the Tucson Community Center. There were four of them, waving protest signs saying things like CIRCUS IS CRUEL TO ANIMALS and WOULD YOU WANT TO PERFORM WITH THE FLU?

Since two of the protesters were men, I immediately discounted them. The third, a heavyset woman, was also probably out unless Jackie had gained a lot of weight that Tommy hadn't mentioned.

My target was a tiger mask with giant tears painted below its feline eyes. This was a schizophrenic beast, judging from its downstairs, which was clad in a very skimpy, barely-cover-the-butt Zena warrior princess costume. The strapless top did an excellent job of showcasing a huge set of Doo Dahs. The Tiger Woman was waving a placard that read, BORN FREE, LEAVE ME BE.

Catching the tiger's eye was impossible since I had no idea where to look in the giant mask. Finally I just marched up to the cat face. Now that I was closer I could see that it was pretty raggedy. The thing looked like it was molting with large bare hairless patches scattered across its oversized cheeks. "Are you Jackie Doo Dahs?"

Something that sounded like a muffled "yes" came back.

I placed one of my cards in her hand, relieved that it wasn't a paw.

"I'm Trade Ellis. J.B.'s been arrested and he's hired me to check out Abby's murder." While this wasn't the exact sequence of events, it was close enough.

A mumbled "I know."

"I'd like to talk to you about it."

"Busy," she muttered.

While I couldn't see her face because of the mask I thought she was probably surprised to see me. I imagined that J.B. had told her that he wasn't giving her name out.

I was cranky with the heat, the drought, the price of cattle and my reeking tennis shoe so I grabbed her arm, the one carrying the sign, and pinched it just a little.

"Jackie, we've got some serious stuff going down here and I need your help if J.B.'s ever gonna get out of jail."

She hit me with her chained hand and the metal hit my wrist bone hard, causing me to immediately release her arm. I'd been warned about her temper and probably shouldn't have provoked her. Provoke her? Hell, now I was ready to kill her.

There was a long pause. Finally her hands went up to the cat's neck and she began tugging on the huge furry mask. She was having a tough time with it, but my wrist was red and hurting and I saw no reason to help her out.

When she was finally unveiled, our Lady of the Perpetual Protest had black hair sticking out all over from the static electricity generated by the cat's head. She had buggy brown eyes, the kind that look like they don't fit in their sockets, and thin-arced penciled lines for eyebrows. Her lipstick had gotten a little smeared and ran off the side of her uneven lips.

"What's with the chain?" I asked, rubbing my sore wrist.

She rattled her arm, the one that was still attached to the fence. "That's in case they try to arrest us. Makes them work harder."

The way she said it made me think she'd done this before. Maybe her cop relations weren't all associated with animal protest. Could Jackie Doo Dahs have a police record? If she did, I was sure Uncle C and his gang would find it. "Good for self-defense too," I suggested.

"Hey, you asked for it. So what's the deal with J.B.?"

"He's in jail and won't be out any time soon. I just came from seeing his attorney."

"Bummer."

"I understand you had dinner with him a few weeks ago."

"Is there a crime against that?"

"No. Just a bit unusual since he was married."

She rolled her bug eyes. "We used to be married."

"I know. Twice."

"So we were just good friends."

"That's not what I hear."

She glared at me and then dropped her eyes. "Look, I'll come clean with you. I wanted him back."

"The dog and the bone thing."

"Huh?"

"A dog has a bone, loses interest in it and another dog comes along and picks up the bone causing the first dog to go crazy because it's *his* bone and he wants it back, even though he threw it away."

She thought about this for a minute. "Are you saying Abby was a bitch?"

"God, no. I'm just giving you a discourse on human nature. You just said you wanted J.B. back."

"I was sure trying." She smiled briefly. "But he wasn't interested. He'd found Mrs. Got Rocks and didn't want to upset that apple cart."

"Well you got him to dinner. Sounds like that may have been a start."

She laughed. "I had to lie to get him there. Said I'd had some bad news from my doctor."

"I'll bet that sold well." I was having no trouble feeding her lines.

"He was pretty mad." Some early circus goers were walking by and Jackie waved her placard in their faces, earning her a healthy scowl from a mother who pulled her small child closer to her.

"So how long were you blackmailing him?" I guessed.

"Blackmail? I wasn't blackmailing him. It was more like a loan. I was gonna pay it back."

"Then you never threatened to tell his wife that you and J.B. had been married?"

She grinned again. "Well as my mother used to say, nothing ventured, nothing gained. But it wasn't really blackmail."

"Did J.B. ever hit you?"

"Maybe once or twice. No big deal."

The way she said it really did sound like no big deal, something I could never relate to. If a man laid a finger in anger on me it'd be the last time he ever had the chance. "So you wouldn't call him abusive?"

"I thought you said you were working for J.B.," she said suspiciously.

"Oh, I am. I just need to know what's going on, what his past married history was, that kind of thing. You told the cops that he abused you."

"Did I?" She seemed confused and I wondered if she was a drinker, like J.B.

"So they say." I was stretching the truth a bit. Uncle C had said that Jackie had missed work because of her bruises, that was all.

"Well, he didn't *really* abuse me. He's a nice guy. A real nice guy. Yeah, we had our problems, what married couple doesn't? Maybe I mentioned the bruises to the cops, but he's not a wife beater or anything like that."

We talked a while longer and then when I was pretty sure I had her off guard, I hit her with the big one. "Where were you when Abby was killed?"

She glared at me. She was quicksilver, this one. Furious one minute, beguiling the next. And she wasn't falling for my trick. "Home in bed. Reading."

I'll bet. What? *Honey Bunch at Snow Top*?

As I drove out of the community center parking lot I couldn't help but think of J.B.'s wives.

What would the elegant Abigail Van Thiessen have thought of the woman dressed up in the ratty cat mask?

30

WHILE I NEEDED TO VISIT J.B. IN JAIL, I WASN'T EAGER TO head right over. I wanted some time to help me cool off about the business with Jackie Doo Dahs. I was still feeling very betrayed and stupid. I was stupid to have trusted what J.B. Calendar told me. I should have taken what he told me with a grain of salt. And I didn't.

Besides, how in the hell could J.B. expect me to do my job if he wasn't willing to come clean with his past? The thought crossed my mind that maybe I was his smoke screen. That by hiring me he'd deflect attention from himself. Did he do it? Probably not too far a stretch since I had had clients in the past who had done just that—hired me even though they'd done the thing they'd hired me to investigate. I was their insurance policy, the radar detector that would let them know when the evidence against them was stacking up and when the police were getting close.

My private eye work brings me into town a lot more frequently than I like. Since I always have a long list of errands to run, I decided to knock off some of them.

By noon I was starving. I headed to Rosa's Mexican food at Campbell and Ft. Lowell. During the week

there's usually a wait, but I lucked out, perhaps becaus
it was Saturday, and was immediately seated. I ordere
an avocado enchilada and I nibbled on chips and sals
while I admired—not for the first time—the great Fran
Franklin murals. After spreading my computer-generate
notes out on the tile table I began rereading them.

When I got to the part about Dr. Mullon's death,
circled his home address. It was in the university area
not far from where I was sitting.

I paid my bill and headed back out into the heat. A
long as I was this close, why not check out Mullon'
house?

I wasn't really expecting to discover anything when
arrived at the compact mission style home on Thir
Street half a block east of Campbell Avenue. This is on
of Tucson's major bicycle routes and in spite of the heat
few bicyclists were cruising by.

As I pulled up I noticed that Mullon's lawn was dr
and overgrown, his marigolds shriveled and brown. Eve
his palm trees looked stressed by the heat. It looked a
though no one was taking care of the place.

As I walked up to the front door I could see that th
draperies were pulled so there was no way to look in
side, even if I wanted to, which, of course, I did. I ran
the doorbell, but there was no answer.

I walked around the side of the house to the carpor
and was greeted with a dark, suspicious stain on th
concrete. God, was that his blood? I shuddered in spit
of the heat. There's just something about being wher
you know someone has been killed that's downrigh
creepy.

Other than the blood, the carport was tidy with
long workbench against the far wall, paint cans neatl
lined up on it, gardening tools hung on racks along with
set of jumper cables. When a startled neighborhood ca
leaped out from behind one of the paint cans I jumpe
and stumbled backward, my heart racing. After al

omeone had killed Abby and someone had killed Dr. Mullon. If the murders were connected, I could be putting myself in serious danger just by snooping around.

A small walkway aligned itself with an adobe patio wall west of the carport. In the dark it wouldn't have been much of a trick to stand on the walkway flush against the back patio wall and wait, undetected, for Mullon to come home.

I followed the footpath back to the alley where there were two battle-weary garbage cans. Looking west I could see the high-volume traffic on Campbell whiz by. Access to the target—Mullon—would have been a snap, and as far as a getaway was concerned, anyone could have used the alley and then pulled out on Campbell or driven up it east to Tucson Boulevard to make his escape. By using the back street, the killer would have most likely escaped the attention of any neighbor that may have heard the gunshots.

As I walked back to my pickup, the only thing I'd earned after checking out Samuel Mullon's residence was that it would have been relatively easy for someone to pull a trigger and then walk away.

I couldn't help but wonder: who was next?

My last errand was at Southwest Animal Health, where I picked up some horseshoes, nails and salve for Chapo's leg. Also some parvo vaccine for the dogs. The owner, Bobby, put the vaccine in a bag with a couple of cold sacks and once I got to Priscilla, I slipped them into the cooler I had brought from the ranch. If I kept the truck windows down when I made my stops, the medicine would probably be okay until I got home.

The Pima County jail is out on Silverlake Road. I parked in the lot and headed to the maximum security area.

I crossed the lobby and showed my PI identification to a woman behind the front counter. After filling out the inmate visitation form, I handed my purse to the woman, who placed it in a locker. She then handed me a yellow pass with a large V on it, indicating that I was a visitor. After clipping it to my shirt, I walked through the magnetometer and then through the sally ports.

It's always chilling to hear the heavy iron doors shut behind you, knowing that you are as much a prisoner as the inmates, at least until someone decides to open the doors and let you out. I'm claustrophobic and the clang of the doors bothered me. I tried not to think about it.

When I got to the professional visitation area I handed the officers J.B.'s card. They noted it with 4D, his housing unit, and then called for him.

Looking through the glass window above the command center I could see that there were only two prisoners visiting on this side of the area. Inmates are required to sit facing the center aisleway. In this way, an officer can look through the glass at any time and verify that all heads are accounted for.

I waited for my client in one of the small individual rooms and took my assigned seat, a blue plastic chair that was closest to the unlocked door.

A few minutes later J.B. Calendar strolled into the room in his orange jumpsuit and rubber sandals, the dress code favored by the Pima County sheriff's department. He didn't appear at all surprised to see me.

J.B. looked haggard and unsteady as he took his seat in a beige plastic chair across the narrow table from me. Was he feeling alcohol withdrawal?

"We've got to quit meeting like this," he said with a shaky grin.

"Right. How are you doing?"

"All right, but they don't let you chew in here. Guess I'm gonna be here a while, huh?"

"That's what I hear. Finding that ketamine in your stuff didn't help."

He looked nervously around the room.

"It's okay, these rooms aren't monitored."

"God, Trade, I have no idea where that shit came from. I've never seen it before."

"You never used it on any of the animals, maybe a horse or bull?"

"I swear." He held up a trembling hand as though he was pledging his allegiance to the flag.

"Well, I guess that's what we're going to have to find out, how it got there," I said with a confidence I didn't feel.

"You know Abby gave a lot of money to her preacher. Have you found out anything about him?"

"I'm checking him out. Nothing yet. Tell me about the Covarubbiases. What was Abby's relationship with them?"

"She never said much to José, he doesn't talk much. She was pretty close to Gloria though. I think that's why she gave her more money than José."

"Fifty-eight thousand dollars could be a pretty good motive."

"Yeah, well, that's what they're saying about $60 million," he said with a dry laugh.

"You want to tell me about Jackie Doo Dahs?" I studied his face carefully.

"Shit. I should have told you about that."

"You sorry son-of-a-bitch! You sure should have. I should throw this case in your face and let you rot in here!" I didn't feel good about losing my temper, but I was still hurting from the trust issue and pissed because he'd taken advantage of me. Why had I let that happen anyway?

"Look, I'm sorry. I really am. I should have told you, I know that, but I didn't want to get her involved. Not because I'm playing around with her or anything like that." He glanced through the glass to the inmate in the next room. "It's just that I knew that she'd be a suspect and that people would think there was some kind of conspiracy or something between the two of us."

"Was there?"

He gave me a hurt look. "No. It wasn't anything like that. Not like that at all."

"But you never told Abby about her. Or me. Or María. What was she, your little private secret?" Maybe I was hitting below the belt, with his being in jail and all, but I was still pretty upset about this major omission.

He exhaled deeply. "Okay, so I was stupid, real stupid. But that's not a crime. I didn't kill her, Trade. And neither did Jackie."

"How can you be so sure? She's pretty violent from what I hear."

"Who have you been talking to, Renner?"

I didn't answer his question.

"Was she blackmailing you, J.B.?"

"We never called it that. I gave her a little money and prayed she'd keep her mouth shut, but Abby eventually found out about it anyway."

"And there wasn't any more to it than that?"

Another big sigh. "Okay, this is a tough one for me to admit and I know you're gonna think less of me for saying it . . ."

I waited.

"I'm betting you've already talked to Jackie, right?"

I nodded.

"You've seen her?" he pressed.

"Yes."

"Well, she's just not the kind of person that Abby ran around with, you know what I mean? It's like I was afraid if she knew about her early on that she wouldn't think I was good enough for her. I can't explain it, but I guess I was"—he hesitated and then forged ahead— "ashamed of Jackie. Ashamed that I'd married her not once, but twice."

I let this sink in. While it didn't give J.B. a lot of character points, it did make sense. Jackie, although she'd given up her exotic dancing career in favor of animal rights, still had a very hard edge to her. I glanced at my wrist, which was sporting the beginnings of a bruise where she'd clobbered me with the chain.

"All right." I was willing to let the subject drop for the time being. "Tell me again about that night in the Baboquivaris."

The story he told me in jail was pretty much right on with the one that he'd been telling all along.

"You drank before you went to La Gitana and at the bar?"

"Yep."

"And you were both pretty drunk?"

"Well, let me put it this way, I never knew I had a twin brother until I looked in that mirror behind the bar."

"Did you eat or drink anything after you got back to camp?"

"I had a Jack Daniel's and Abby had a couple of Baileys before we went to bed."

"You weren't drinking the same stuff?" I already knew the answer, but pressed the point anyway.

"That shit's too sweet for me."

"You didn't buy the bottles at La Gitana and bring them back?"

"No. Gloria sent them with us. I already told you that. She packed all of our food and booze."

The obvious came back to me. With Abby and J.B. drinking different whiskey, it would have been easy to selectively doctor each bottle. Abby could have gotten the ketamine, and J.B. something else that would have only put him in Nighty Night Land.

"Did you drink Friday night?"

"We drank a couple of those little airline bottles on the way down. By the time we got there, got the horses settled and camp set up we were exhausted and just fell into bed."

If there had been something in their drinks, how could the murderer have known they wouldn't drink the booze Friday night?

"Were they new bottles?"

He thought for a minute. "No, they were both open. I remember that because Abby was asking what would happen if we got stopped by a cop with an opened bottle in the truck."

Now my scavenger list had two bottles of booze on it.

"Okay, on Saturday night, did you feel normal before you drank at your camp when you got back from La Gitana?"

He thought for a moment. "Normal drunk."

"And then you had a Jack Daniel's and Abby had a Baileys, right?"

"More than one. For both of us," he admitted.

"What did you do after you had the nightcaps?"

"Not what you're thinking." He laughed, but it wasn't what I was thinking at all. "We talked for a while and then crashed. I've told you all of this."

"Yeah, well we're going over it again. Was anything different that night from a normal drunk?"

"Well, it was a doozy, like I told you. I was drunker than a Baptist preacher out of town. Really out of it, so was Abby."

"How about the next day. Anything odd about the hangover?"

"Well, I never sleep in like that. And I felt like shit all day, but then after what happened, who wouldn't? You think something was in my booze?"

"It's a possibility. A drug would have taken both of you out of the picture long enough for someone to take Abby over to the pond and drown her. Since you have no recollection of what happened that night, I don't think you were dosed with the ketamine. We know she got some in her system somewhere."

We talked for a while longer and then both got up. J.B. walked with me up to the door.

He retrieved his identification card from the office there and then started back down the hallway, to go out the door he'd come in. Halfway down, he stopped and then turned back to me.

"Trade, you've got to believe me. I swear to God I had nothing to do with it."

And with that, I headed out the door that would take me back to freedom.

He didn't.

31

It was after I turned off at the Cow Palace onto Arivaca Road later that night when I finally got serious with Quinta. Martín had asked me to talk to her about leaving with him and Cori Elena and I knew now was as good a time as any. In her short time with us, she hadn't talked about her mother much and was obviously still very angry with her. Confined in the cab of the truck, at least she couldn't walk away if she didn't want to talk about it.

"You know your mom and dad are thinking of leaving the Vaca Grande for a while," I began.

"Yeah, he told me."

"You know why?"

"Sure." She gave a sarcastic laugh. "Because of Carmen."

"It's probably the best thing to do," I said. "Since those men may come looking for your mother."

"I'll miss my dad."

"Maybe you ought to go with them."

I saw her looking at me out of the corner of my eye. "Why would I want to do that?"

"Seems to me that there was a problem in Magdalena when your father got you out," I said, thinking of the time months ago when Martín had first come home with Quinta. He'd been a bit black-and-blue and had told me that some people had argued about his taking his daughter out of Mexico. Even then, Félix's men had had Cori Elena's daughter under surveillance, hoping her mother would return. What they hadn't counted on was her father's courage and doggedness.

"That was then. Now they know where my mother is." There was a coldness in her voice that, in spite of the hot desert evening air, chilled me. "I'll be fine."

"Your father doesn't think so."

"Well, he's wrong. I've got my job. Besides, who'd take Tata dancing if I left?"

I kept my eyes on the narrow two-lane road, mindful of the raccoons and deer that liked to cross at night.

"You wouldn't consider going, just for a week or two?"

Even in the darkness and without looking directly at her I knew that she was shaking her head. "Not even. The thought of being in the truck with my mother for that long makes me sick."

"You hate her that much?"

"No, Trade, I'm that angry with her," she admitted as she placed her forehead against the window glass and stared out into the dark night.

There was nothing dark about La Gitana when we finally pulled in shortly after ten. A brightly lit Cerveza Pacifico neon sign greeted us—"Welcome to the Oldest Bar in the Oldest Continuously Inhabited Townsite in Arizona." The parking spaces in front of the large sign were full of pickups, a couple of sport utility vehicles and a battered old woody station wagon. I slammed Priscilla into reverse and edged into a tight space on the east side of the building.

Not looking for trouble—after all, it was late and we *were* two women alone—I reached into the glove compartment and pulled out my .38. Checking the cylinder to make sure five bullets were chambered, I then unbuckled my leather belt and threaded the holstered pistol through it. When I pulled out my shirt, the .38 was concealed. It was definitely illegal to carry a weapon into a bar in Arizona, in spite of my concealed weapon permit. This infraction didn't bother me a bit since I'd rather be judged by twelve than carried by six anytime.

We stepped over an ancient sleeping Australian shepherd dog and into a room filled with smoke, the cacophony of drunken conversation and Patsy Cline wailing about walking after midnight. While Arivaca is known for having a lot of inhabitants with questionable reputations, I was still surprised at the rough trade in La Gitana. It was packed with bikers and men who looked like the kind of guys who lived in caves and blew things up.

Our entrance had not gone unnoticed by a lot of the patrons. There were no free tables so Quinta and I sidled up to the bar. I was aware of more than one man undressing us with his eyes.

If the bartender was any clue, it looked like as safe a place to be in the crowded rough bar on a Saturday night as any. He was enormous, well over six and a half feet tall, with huge forearms that looked like ham hocks, a full head of curly brown hair and a wisp of a goatee. With him on board, the management probably never needed a bouncer.

We ordered two Coronas, squeezed a couple of limes into the bottles and then dumped them in on top of the beer. For some reason, sitting on the bar stools drinking beer with Martín's daughter after drinking with him just a day or two ago made me very sad.

We watched a couple of young, drunk cowboys attempt to shoot a game of pool on one of the two tables. It was taking more of a licking than either one of them as they scratched time after time, letting the pool cues skip and skid across the scarred green felt. A chalkboard on the wall held the names of several challengers, and I suspected that the next games would go very quickly since so far neither of the young studs had managed to come anywhere near a pool ball. Solids and stripes alike sat with impunity on the table.

As I sat there drinking I tried to take in as much as I could. I'd deliberately picked this time to come since it was a Saturday night, and approximately the same time that J.B. and Abby would have been in the bar two weeks earlier. There was a good possibility that many of the same people that were here now would have been here then. Not to mention the help.

When it finally slowed down a bit and it looked as though the bartender had things under control, I introduced myself and asked him about J.B. and Abby.

"The deputies have already been in here," he said as he wiped the thick mesquite counter, which didn't look as though it needed it. "I told them I remember those two because they didn't look like they fit in around here. Especially her." He eyed Quinta and me, and I wondered if he thought we fit in.

"Did anyone talk to them?"

"Sure. I did. The barmaid did, maybe a few of the regulars. But no one spent any time with them if that's what you mean. They were pretty wrapped up in each other."

I sipped the Corona. "And they didn't buy any take-out."

"Nope. But to be honest with you, they didn't look like they needed any more to drink. I probably shouldn't admit that," he said, winking at me.

"How long did they stay?"

"Closing. I do remember that because she wanted to stay and dance some more. She was doing a kind of hoochie koochie thing out there, all by herself. She'd been dancing with the pool sticks, the broom, whatever she could find." He nodded to a bare patch of cement on the far side of the pool tables that I assumed was what they called the dance floor.

Abby must have been soused. I'd never seen her do

anything close to that. "What, no one would dance with her?"

"Sure, she danced with a few of the guys earlier in the evening, but mostly with her old man."

"There wasn't any trouble though?" I knew from experience sometimes things could get out of hand when you danced with a cowboy's woman. Cowboys liked to flirt with danger and with whiskey, and oftentimes the two met in the middle and had a hell of a row.

"Nah. Most of these guys"—he flicked his bar rag in a wide arc—"are regulars. We don't get much trouble in here. They look like shit, but they really stick to themselves. Fact is, other than Squeezy McNeil wiping out on his motorcycle on the way to Round Hill a few years ago, I don't remember anyone ever going from here to the Happy Hunting Ground."

"Did they leave with anyone?"

"Now that I can't say. Right before closing she was dancing with a bottle of booze in her hand and she dropped it. It made a helluva mess and I was busy cleaning that up when we closed."

There it was again. The drop. Abby dropped a bottle of booze while she was dancing. Did it mean anything? Or was she just so drunk that hanging on to things had been a problem that particular night?

While some of the regulars were delighted to talk to us, they scattered like wanted felons when I got around to asking about J.B. and Abby. We were strangers in their midst, and their behavior was not all that surprising since this is frequently the norm in small towns. No one wants to share dirty laundry or juicy gossip until they're sure you're one of them—something I couldn't convince them of in the scant hour we'd been in the bar.

I left with not a lot more information than I had when I went in. Mostly confirmations of what J.B. had already told me, other than the dropped, shattered bottle.

◆　　　◆　　　◆

After leaving La Gitana, I took the back road and headed west. Arivaca Creek, banked with its lush green trees, paralleled the road for a while and the moon was just coming up. Even with its soft glow I could barely make out the San Luis Mountains to the south. While the winding, curving road was paved, it was desolate. Except for a couple of rattlesnakes stretched out on the warm asphalt, we didn't see another soul or car until we hit the Sasabe road. This was the same route that J.B. and Abby would have taken on that fateful night. Had someone followed them from the bar? At the stop sign I checked my rearview mirror, but there were no headlights in it.

Briefly, I debated about turning south and heading into Sasabe. There wasn't much there, and at no time in his recitation of the night's events had J.B. mentioned a trip to the border town, so I headed north instead, toward his camp site.

The foothills were dark, in spite of the mailboxes we passed on the road. Like country people everywhere, the people of the Baboquivaris appeared to be early-to-bedders.

I was driving more slowly now, fearful of missing the road into J.B. and Abby's camp site. Finally I found the turnoff.

Quinta had the Ortiz courage for she never questioned the wisdom of our being out in the middle of nowhere late at night. Eager for an adventure, she jumped out of Priscilla and opened the barbed wire gate and waited while I drove through before she closed it and bounced back into the pickup.

"This must be the place, huh?" she asked.

"Part of the place," I explained. "She actually drowned at a cattle tank a quarter of a mile from here."

The road hadn't gotten any better, but I could drive a little faster over the single, weed-clogged lane since I wasn't pulling a horse trailer this time. The brush at the end of the track had been packed down with all the county vehicles that had come in after Abby's body had been found.

I turned the truck around, facing it toward the road in the event we'd have to get out of there in a hurry. When I shut the engine down, the night took on an eerie silence.

Although the .38 was still on my hip, I grabbed a speed loader from the glove compartment for my pocket.

"Now that's gonna scare the *caca* out of the coyotes," Quinta said with a wide grin.

While I really wasn't expecting any trouble, I sure didn't want to be unprepared. There was no reason that anyone would be out here at all, but there is still something very spooky about being in an area where you know someone has been killed in the dark of night. I was feeling the same things I felt in Mullon's carport earlier in the day. I can't really explain it except to say that it had the hairs on my arms standing up, and all my senses on hyper-alert.

I retrieved a big Mag-Lite from the center console, and then turned off the interior light before opening the door. There wasn't any reason to silhouette ourselves against the light if we didn't have to.

The night air was as cool as it had been in days, as the desert gave its heat back to the sky. It felt good.

In the darkness I knew I wasn't going to find anything that Sanders and I and the police hadn't noticed in broad daylight. Stopping here had really just been an afterthought from our visit to La Gitana.

I'd come more for an impression than anything else. I wanted to feel the scene in the night, the same way that Abby and J.B. had felt it on the night of her death. Well, not exactly the same way, since I was a liter or so short of the booze the two of them had consumed.

I swept the flashlight over the ground, and as near as I could tell, there were no fresh tracks. The drought was taking its toll even on the ones that had been left by all the emergency vehicles, as they melded into the dry, dusty desert floor.

We walked slowly around the camp site, listening to a coyote concerto of mournful songs. Somewhere off in the distance, a cow was calling for her calf. Moths fluttered around the lens of the flashlight, attracted to its bright glow. Silly things, using the light for their flight orientation. Unfortunately it was a lot closer than the moon, and many of them were crashing into the lens.

After circling the camp site with the light, we returned to the truck. I dropped the tailgate and Quinta and I sat on it as I turned the Mag-Lite off.

Although I hadn't told her what I was doing, she must have known, for she sat quietly with me. I closed my eyes, again trying to get some idea of what had gone on two weeks earlier.

I don't know what kind of epiphany I was looking for, but none came. After sitting there for ten minutes or so, I was done. The only thing I had determined was that it was indeed quiet out here.

I was closing the tailgate of the truck when I had another idea. Dropping it once again, I stepped up on the bumper and then stood in the bed of the Dodge. From up here, my view was better and as I looked off in the direction of the stock tank, I saw the bright twinkle of a campfire.

It had been unusual enough for J.B. to pick this spot in June for a camp out, but who in the hell else was that crazy? Most of the people I knew with camping in mind were up in the White Mountains or somewhere up in Colorado. While this was not an unknown route for people coming into the country illegally, coyotes—those who charged to bring them in—didn't usually build campfires that would announce their presence.

I whispered—ridiculous really, since the campfire was a good distance away—for Quinta to get my binoculars out of the console. She handed them up to me and I scoped the darkness with the glasses, concentrating on the flickering light to the north. While they brought the fire in a little closer, I couldn't make out any activity there. Either it had been left unattended—a dangerous possibility given the dry drought conditions—or the fire builders had already gone to bed. Of course then there was the worst-case scenario—they had seen our headlights when we'd driven in and were coming for us. At the thought, I dropped one hand from the binoculars and unsnapped my holster so I could get my gun out quickly if I needed to.

"Are we going there next?" Quinta whispered excitedly in my ear, unaware of my fear.

"No," I answered, taking the binoculars from my face. "Not tonight."

Adventure was one thing, but going into a stranger's camp well past midnight was something entirely different. I was praying that whoever was camped across the desert from us felt the same way.

This one would have to wait until first light.

32

"THIS IS IT, HUH?" QUINTA SAID WITH CHARACTERISTIC GOOD humor.

"I'm afraid so."

The guys at La Gitana had probably spooked me more than I was willing to admit for I found myself preoccupied with thinking about our neighbors coming over in the dark to check us out. While I have nothing against camping out—like it in fact—maybe doing so here, in the same spot where Abigal Van Thiessen had met her death, wasn't such a hot idea.

I entertained the thought of going home and coming back in the morning to investigate the campfire people, but it really didn't make a whole lot of sense. We were at least fifty miles from the Vaca Grande, it was now close to one in the morning, and I figured if we could just make it through the next few hours, daylight would come and the camper mystery would be solved.

Besides, realistically, there was probably no connection between the people camped to the northwest and Abby's death, or to the patrons of La Gitana for that matter.

I fished around in the toolbox and finally found an old, faded serape that I keep handy for spur-of-the-moment picnics. It was one of the thick cotton ones and as I spread it over the bed of the pickup, it gave some cushion against the hard ridges of the bed liner. I found a couple of old red Dodge windbreakers that the dealer had given me years ago when I'd bought the truck, and we wadded these up and used them as pillows.

Although the desert cools at night, this was June so we weren't going to freeze without blankets. Still, we kept all of our clothes and our boots on. I put my holstered .38 up near the wheel well and settled in for what was left of the night.

There are few things as humbling as sleeping out under an open sky. Staring up at the constellations I was struck by how much clearer and more defined they were than in Tucson, or even at the Vaca Grande. There were so few lights here—no Kmart parking lots or Cineplex Odeon theaters or Diamondback stadiums to pollute the sky. No wonder Kitt Peak Observatory had been built high up in the Baboquivaris.

The coyotes had also settled down, leaving the night quiet and still. I counted stars until I finally drifted off to sleep.

I didn't sleep very well. The bed of the truck wasn't that comfortable and I kept waking up, expecting to have undesirable company, either the people camped across the way, or our new friends from La Gitana. While I probably wouldn't have slept any better had I been in a Ramada Inn somewhere the other factors made sleep very elusive.

It was well before first light when I finally rolled over and checked my watch—4:17. I was very still, not wanting to disturb Quinta. Probably not a problem since she was snoring heartily next to me, her mouth open.

Finally nature called. I stood slowly and grabbed my binoculars off the top of the truck box. Scanning the northwest, I saw what I thought might be the dying embers of the fire I'd spotted last night. While it still seemed unlikely that the people camped there had anything to do with Abby's death, I was looking at caution over valor. After all, no one knew where Quinta and I were, so we could be missing for quite a while before anyone would find us.

Carefully I slid over the side of the truck, not wanting to risk awakening Sleeping Beauty with the sound of a dropping tailgate.

A few minutes later I was scrounging for water in the cab of the truck. Even if I'd had something to heat it in, I didn't want to risk a fire. It was too dangerous with all the dried grass. I also didn't want to be seen by the Campfire People before I had the chance to visit them.

I retrieved my revolver as Quinta rolled on her side and stared at me.

"Are we going?"

I'd just learned something else about her. She was one of those wide-awake-first-thing-in-the-morning kind of people. Just like her father. And just like me.

"In a few minutes," I said. "I want to get there before the sun comes up."

I was mentally wrestling with our approach. Priscilla was white and I knew that once the sun started making its ascent that if the people at the fire looked our way, they could probably spot the top of the cab.

As the sky began turning gray, I jumped back up in the pickup's bed, grabbed my binoculars and trained them on the spot where I'd first seen the campfire. In the dim light, I could barely make out what looked like a small blue truck. So far there weren't any people moving around.

"Damn."

"What's wrong?" Quinta asked.

"I can't figure out if we should hike over there and risk their leaving before we get there, or if we should try to find the road they drove in on. That way if they drive out, we'll be able to talk to them." Why I was talking in terms of "them" I didn't know, since I had no idea how many people were over there, except it didn't seem logical that someone would be camping alone. After all it wasn't deer or javelina season.

Quinta helped herself to a drink of water and rubbed her eyes. "That's easy. You hike over and I'll drive and try to find the turnoff."

"I hike?" I teased.

"Hey, you're the one with the *pistola*." She grinned. "Or you give me the .38 and I'll hike."

I opted for the former plan and that's the way we settled it. We agreed that we'd meet back up on the highway if she couldn't find the road into the mystery campers' site. If after an hour and a half we hadn't reconnected, I told her to drive for help. Even as I said it, my speech crackled with my dry mouth. Joining Abby in the stock tank was definitely not something on my Things to Do Today list.

I clipped my holster onto my belt and pulled my shirt out over it, threw the binoculars around my neck and grabbed a bottle of water before starting out on the trek to the stock tank.

The desert is always alive in the early morning hours of summer. The animals take advantage of the early light and coolness to hunt. I hadn't gone very far when I'd flushed out several coveys of quail and startled a red racer who slithered up a mesquite tree in his flight.

As I walked along I heard the "who-cooks-for-YOU?" call of the white-winged doves, in concert with the "cha-cha-cha" of the cactus wrens. Everyone was chatty this morning. Except me. I was just plain worried.

A lot of the desert plants that had bloomed last month were heavy with seed pods—the acacia, yucca and mesquite, although most of the lower mesquite beans had been picked off by the hungry cattle.

The sun was making its ascent now and the birds began to sing it up along with the whirring buzz of the romantic male cicadas.

I passed groups of thin cows who were picking the

leaves they could reach from the trees. Although a few of them had passed through cholla patches, they didn't seem to mind the spiny cactus stuck to their faces and lips.

Since I wasn't following tracks this time, I took a more direct route to the stock tank. As I did so, the thought occurred to me that whoever had carried Abby off from her camp site hadn't really known exactly where the tank was. If he had, he would have gone as the crow flies as I was doing, not on the circuitous path that Sanders and I had followed over a week ago. While this wasn't particularly helpful since I didn't think that a Baboquivari local had killed Abby, it had to mean something, but what?

There were a few saguaros here and I noticed that in spite of the drought a few of them had converted last month's waxy white flowers into ripe red fruit. Greedy doves were perched on their crowns, picking at the edible pulpy mass. Eventually what was left would fall to the desert floor and provide fodder for the animals down below—ants, mice, even coyotes loved the succulent fruit.

The terrain was rolling and while I tried to keep my eyes on the blue truck, I lost it every time I dropped down into a small arroyo. I found myself spinning around a lot, sure that I was being followed by someone. Yet every time I spun, of course no one was there.

I kept to the trees as much as I could, not eager to be discovered any sooner than necessary. To the east the sky glowed, and I knew it wouldn't be long before the sun crept above the horizon.

Finally I came up on the south side of the tank, the side where the dirt embankment corraled the water. I used it as cover as I sat down in the dirt and took a good drink of water and then stashed the bottle in the waistband of my jeans.

On hands and knees I crawled to the top of the earthen dam and peeked over. Now that I was this close,

I could see that the blue truck was parked some distance from the stock tank. That told me that the campers knew what they were doing—these were no neophytes who would park close to the animals' source of water.

I scrambled to the far side of the embankment where I hovered behind a hackberry bush for cover. The sun was to my back, which was good. Hopefully it wouldn't hit the binocular lenses and give me away. I focused the glasses on the camp site and saw a woman sipping something as she tended a large pot on the fire. For some reason that made me feel better. A woman cooking breakfast couldn't be all that bad, could she?

Just beyond her under a mesquite tree were what looked like a couple of cots. One was clearly empty, but the other had a huge lump in it. Could that be another person? Judging from the size of the lump, I suspected it was a large man.

I glassed the scene for a while longer, but the lump didn't move and the woman kept to the fire.

The sky was light now.

I hit a dirt road that ran alongside the tank and then headed northwest. I could see the tire tracks in the dust and there was a lot of night sign over them—the skitterings of night beetles, ants and a light dusting of tiny mesquite leaves—so I was pretty sure that the blue truck had not had company yet this morning.

I walked up the road for a short distance, and then dropped into a small arroyo to the north. This would give me cover until I got to the camp. Now that I was getting closer this seemed like a really crappy idea. What was I doing playing Girl Spy out here in the desert? I should just give it up. Those people, whoever they were, probably didn't have a thing to do with J.B. or Abby.

I tried to corral my imagination but it started annoying me again. Maybe the campers were involved in some really big dope deal and the desert was about to come alive with nasty drug smugglers. Interrupting those transactions is never good, unless of course you're a cop. The

Tucson papers are full of bodies found buried in shallow arroyos.

Still, I'd been hired by J.B. to do a job. In spite of my misgivings, I felt that I had to check out the people in the blue truck.

Reaching under my shirt, I unsnapped the holster and practiced pulling the .38 out quickly. This, like dry shooting people on TV, is one of the things I suppose I should practice more often, but never think to do. Real-life PI work, for the most part, is pretty boring. It's only on occasions like this morning that even thinking about having to use my gun ever crosses my mind.

I told myself that I was overreacting, that the campers were harmless, and rationally, I knew that was probably true. I was light on the rational side, however, since I was alone out here, with no quick escape until Quinta arrived.

I trudged through the thick sand of the wash until I heard a woman's voice speaking what sounded like the Tohono O'odham language. I froze. Who in the hell was she talking to? I waited, listening for the voice of her companion, but nothing came. Was the lump still in bed? Or was he out here, stalking me? My head swiveled around, looking for him, but there was no sign of him.

Figuring I was just below where the truck was parked, I took a deep breath and began climbing the small hillock. Right before the top I dropped to my knees and peered over, not eager to show myself any sooner than I had to. I wanted to get the lay of the land before I was spotted.

I had a clear view of the truck. It was an older Nissan, its paint faded and chipped, its windshield cracked, and it was missing its grille. A front bumper sticker read TOO MANY SNOWBIRDS, TOO LITTLE FREEZER SPACE.

The camp was a mess, littered with pots and jars and cooking utensils. I was right about the beds being cots and both had rumpled bedding. My eyes skimmed them quickly—both were now empty. There was nothing or either that would suggest a big lump. What had made that lump and where in the hell was it?

I rolled around on the hill, checking my back, but there was nothing there.

Finally I stood up and approached the camp.

The woman's back was to me as she bent over the campfire, stirring the pot. Her long black ponytail was slipped through the back of a baseball cap.

"Excuse me."

The Indian woman jumped and turned, dropping her wooden spoon into the dirt as she did so. Her eyes bore into me.

She was wearing loose cotton pants, a white T-shirt splattered with red stains, unlaced dirty tennis shoes and a heavy silver bracelet on one arm. She looked like she was forty-five or so.

"I'm sorry." I held my hands open so she'd know I wasn't a threat. I hoped the same was true of her and her unseen companion. My heart was doing aerobics in my chest.

The woman spoke loudly, rattling something off in Tohono O'odham.

I walked slowly up to her. "Excuse me, do you speak English?"

Now that I was close I could see that cement blocks on three sides cradled the campfire I'd seen. Nesting on a grate on top of them was a coffeepot and a huge aluminum pot with something red and bubbly in it. The two steaming tin mugs of coffee resting on the concrete blocks confirmed my conclusions about the lump. My eyes scanned the landscape. Where in the hell was he or she?

The woman said something in Tohono O'odham. Again loudly. And then she snapped, "Of course I speak English. I teach English." She reached for the wooden spoon in the dirt, wiped it with a stained dish towel and returned it to the bubbling pot as she stirred her brew.

Leaning against the dented tailgate of the blue truck

were a couple of poles, two saguaro ribs lashed together
with baling wire and crossed at the top with a piece of
ironwood. In the shade of a mesquite were three of five-
gallon white plastic buckets, each partially filled with red
saguaro fruit.

I felt better knowing that I had stumbled into a
saguaro camp and the woman and her invisible friend
were harvesting and collecting the cactus fruit. In spite of
the missing person, I probably wasn't in any real danger.
Many times the Tohono O'odham worked in pairs while
harvesting, one to knock the fruit off the saguaro; the
other to catch it before it hit the ground. Allowed to free-
fall, the fruit would burst when it hit the desert floor and
would invariably pick up small stones, which are impossible to get out.

"I was camping over there." I waved my hand in the
general direction from which I had come. "And saw your
truck."

She gave me a suspicious look, which was war-
ranted, considering I didn't have any equipment with
me.

"A friend is driving in," I explained, nodding toward
the road.

She said nothing.

I reached slowly into my shirt pocket and retrieved a
card and handed it to her, knowing full well that she
probably wouldn't keep it and was taking it just to be polite. "I'm Trade Ellis."

She studied the card and then slipped it into a pocket
of her loose cotton pants. "Stella Ahil."

"A woman, a friend of mine, died at this stock tank a
few weeks ago and I'm looking for anyone who may
have seen anything."

Her hooded black eyes revealed nothing.

"Have you camped here long?" I knew that the few
Tohono O'odham who were still harvesting the saguaro
fruit frequently camped out for weeks at a time in the
same location.

"Here?" She asked.

I nodded.

She shook her head. "Not exactly here. We've been moving around a lot. Many of the old places have no fruit this year."

"How about a couple of weeks ago?"

"Not here." She was volunteering nothing.

Damn. I thought I might have stumbled on to something.

I stared at the extra coffee mug. "You have a friend helping you gather?"

She bent over the bubbling saguaro pulp and said nothing.

I waited for a moment before continuing. "Are many people using this area for harvest?"

"Hmm, not that I know of. My cousin Jimmy told me about these." She pointed to the few saguaros around her camp, all of which were missing their fruited crowns. "With the drought we've had to go where we could to get them. This isn't where we usually come."

"So you weren't in the area a few weeks ago?" I asked again, trying to keep the disappointment out of my voice.

"Not in this area," she repeated.

Why did I have the feeling she was holding back? Was it just because she didn't want to talk, or was there really more to tell?

I mumbled something in Apache, one of the few phrases I knew, under my breath, but purposely loud enough for her to hear.

She gave me a startled look. "Are you . . . ?"

"Part Apache," I said, hoping that our Indian kinship might engender some trust. "Do you speak Apache?"

She shook her head. I was relieved since I wasn't eager to confess that I didn't speak much of my ancestors' language. After all, my grandmother was a full-blooded Apache. But then, my English didn't have a trace of a Scottish accent either and my maternal grandfather,

Shiwóyé's husband, had been Duncan MacGregor from the Highlands.

Stella Ahil pulled the pot off the stove and strained the juice into another pot.

"Do you know of any other People that may have used this area a few weeks ago?" I persisted.

"No." She had the saguaro pulp in a big metal bowl and I followed her as she spread it out to dry. "I told you, this is not usually one of the places we go."

Priscilla's roar could now be heard over the low hhhooo-hoooo-hoo-hoooo of the heat-resistant white-winged doves. Stella Ahil gave me a questioning look.

"My friend," I explained.

A few minutes later Quinta came driving in. She shut off Priscilla's engine and reached for a pad of paper on the dashboard.

As I walked up to the open window I saw that she was writing something down.

"913 . . ." I said softly.

". . . BAS," her whisper completed my sentence. I was impressed. Quinta had already thought to write down the license number of the old blue pickup.

"Did you see anyone?" I asked in a low voice.

She shook her head.

I turned back to Stella Ahil. "If you think of anything, or run into anyone who may have been out here, I'd sure appreciate a call."

"Sure," she said as she continued spreading her cactus pulp out on waxed paper, anchored by rocks.

As we drove off I wasn't counting on getting that call.

33

WE PULLED INTO THE VACA GRANDE JUST BEFORE SEVEN. JUAN Ortiz was out watering the garden and his face lit up like a Christmas tree when he saw us drive in. I was used to coming and going as I pleased. We had a long understanding that neither Martín nor Juan was to worry excessively about me if I didn't show up. That was one of the things about my work. I never knew where it would take me, or if I'd have to unexpectedly overnight somewhere other than home.

I'd been thoughtless this time, though, since Quinta was with me. Of course her father and grandfather would have been concerned when we didn't come home.

He wasn't the only one. Mrs. Fierce, Blue and Petunia did a wild Maypole dance around us as Martín came around the barn, with a horseshoe in one hand, wearing his short leather shoeing chaps. "Where have you been?" he asked as he hugged his daughter.

"God, I'm sorry. We should have called," I said. "I just assumed you'd know she was okay since she was with me. We had to camp out unexpectedly."

"I'll go tell Tata," Quinta said as she raced off toward the garden.

"We were worried," Martín said.

"I would have called, but we were miles from a phone before I knew we were going to have to stay." I again considered getting a cell phone. But it was just one more thing to complicate my life, and I'd lived forty plus years without one. "Lose a shoe?"

"I thought I'd get the horses shod before I left."

There it was again. His leaving. Like a knife in my heart.

"Prego's not back yet, is he?"

He shook his head. "Sometime tonight. I just hope he can get to the truck right away."

And I hoped he couldn't.

There were several messages on the machine, none of them as important as the one that Top Dog had left.

"I found Lonnie. He's in San Carlos, at Billy Cassa's."

I knew Billy Cassa. He worked at the hospital and had a fifth-wheel parked out at the Bylas rodeo arena. I was also pretty sure that Billy Cassa didn't have a telephone. Besides, I wanted to talk to Lonnie Victor and my best chance of doing that might be if I came unannounced.

I took a quick shower, changed my clothes and pulled a couple of tamales out of the freezer and zapped them in the microwave. Throwing them on a paper towel, I retrieved a Diet Coke from the fridge, a fistful of Twinkies and a box of Cheez-Its from the pantry and dashed out the door with my road food.

Petunia was resting under a cottonwood close to the edge of the pond, but Mrs. Fierce and Blue must have known that I was leaving again, for they were both sleeping in the shade of the truck. As I walked up, they rolled those great soulful brown dog eyes at me.

They followed me to the barn where I told Martín where I was headed and that I hoped to be back tonight.

I was just getting in Priscilla when Mrs. Fierce wedged herself between the door and me and gave me one of those "not again" looks. I hesitated only a moment. After all, I hadn't spent much time with my girls. But I drew the line at taking the pig.

I guess they figured possession was nine tenths of opportunity for they wasted no time bounding into the cab of the pickup. By the time I passed through La Cienega they were both curled up behind the front seat, sound asleep, and I had polished off the tamales and was already on my second Twinkie.

Although it was a fairly easy drive and still midmorning, an hour later the lack of sleep I'd had was starting to get to me. There was something about the morning sun streaming into the truck that was so lulling. Fortunately by my third yawn I was just outside of Winkelman and able to stop and grab a quick cup of coffee. No decaf this morning. I'd take the shakes over sleeping at the wheel any day.

Since I hadn't seen my grandmother in a while, I drove directly to her house on the west end of San Carlos. Shiwóyé's a medicine woman, but a modern-day one. These days most of her work is counseling Apaches in trouble—those with addictions, personal problems, out of work or in prison. On Sundays it was a good bet I'd find her home so I wasn't surprised to see her little green Geo parked outside her modest cement block house.

Blue and Mrs. Fierce, delighted to be reunited with their brown San Carlos counterparts, took off in a mad game of doggy tag as I made my way to the front door.

Shiwóyé opened it before I could knock and wrapped her brown leathery arms around me. I hugged back, conscious of the fresh White Rain shampoo smell of her gray bun as her head came just under my chin.

She gave up the hug as abruptly as she had begun it and I followed her into the house, through the book-lined living room, past the wood stove, leaking over-stuffed couch and into the kitchen. *Pride and Prejudice* was on the Formica table, a long red ribbon marking her place, along with two placemats and sets of silverware.

"You're expecting company?"

"You, Pretty Horses." She called me by my Apache name, the one she had given me years ago.

"There's something to that medicine woman stuff, huh?"

She grinned, her whole face a tapestry of wrinkles and warmth, the most beautiful I'd ever seen. It made me wonder what Abigail Van Thiessen would have looked like if she'd left well enough alone.

After ladling soup into two bowls, Shiwóyé handed me a piece of folded paper. "Top Dog left you this. He thought you might be up."

I unfolded my cousin's note. *Lonnie was at Billy Cassa's as late as 4 p.m. Saturday,* I read. I looked at my watch. Almost twenty-two hours had passed. Would he still be there?

"Your cousin had a fire or he would have joined us," my grandmother explained as she set the bean and corn soup and donkey bread—a kind of thick tortilla—on the table.

We spent the next hour getting caught up. She'd seen Lonnie a few years ago when he'd been on probation for smoking dope, but had lost touch with him. She hadn't heard that he'd been working for an heiress in Oracle.

After lunch I left the dogs at Shiwóyé's and drove the few miles back through Peridot and down to Highway 70 and then turned east to Bylas. A roadside sign encouraged, CHOOSE TRADITION, NOT ADDICTION.

Passing Wildhorse and Bone Springs Canyon, then Yellowjacket road, I finally turned off for the rodeo arena, which was just off the highway.

Not much was happening this morning. Billy Cassa's old fifth-wheel trailer was parked on the far side of the arena, close to the announcer's booth. I drove slowly around and pulled in next to an elderly Yamaha motorcycle. Two new lawn chairs were sitting in front of the trailer.

As I walked up to Billy's house I could hear a cooler running and spotted a long orange electrical cord that ran up a pole next to the stand.

I knocked on the hot metal door, but there was no answer. Waited. Knocked again until my knuckles hurt. When there still was no response, I resorted to pounding on the windows. It was Billy's trailer so I concentrated my efforts on the area I assumed to be the living room, since that was probably where Lonnie was bedded down.

Finally, a curtain was pulled back and I found Lonnie Victor's pockmarked face staring at me, framed by a tangle of long black hair. "Billy's at work," he growled.

"I'm not looking for Billy."

"Whadya want?"

"Hey, Lonnie. Trade Ellis, Top Dog's cousin, April Thompson MacGregor's granddaughter." It felt funny to call Shiwóyé by her full name and I threw in the Thompson since MacGregor sure as hell wasn't an Apache last name.

He rubbed the sleep from his eyes and yawned. Not a pretty sight. "Hang on."

A minute later he opened the door and stepped out wearing nothing but a pair of faded, torn Wrangler's. A key, attached to a metal ring, hung from one of the front loops of his pants. Probably the key to the old Yamaha.

Lonnie had one of those skinny sunken-bird chests, populated with a few sparse hairs. His bare feet were long and skinny, like the rest of him. Looking like something out of an El Greco painting, he wasn't the healthiest-looking Apache I'd ever seen.

"Who are you again?" He ran his hands through his shoulder-length black hair, ignoring the crust that was collected in the corners of his eyes.

"I'm looking into Abigail Van Thiessen's murder for J.B. Calendar. I understand you were working for them."

He stepped back inside and pulled out a pack of Camels.

It was hot outside, but he hadn't asked me in, and confined with him in there was not a place I wanted to be anyway.

Lonnie grabbed one of the lawn chairs and pulled it around to the back of the fifth-wheel where there was a little shade from the announcer's stand. I did the same.

He settled into the aluminum chair, lit the Camel, took a deep drag and exhaled, blowing three small smoke rings. "Yeah, I did some gardening for them."

"You were still working there when Abby died, right?"

He was staring at the road, not looking at me. "Yeah."

"Do you have any idea who might want to kill her?"

"You gotta be kidding? With her money?"

"I know there were a few people who stood to inherit. Gloria, José, J.B. . . ." I watched him carefully, but if the mention of any of these names meant anything to him, he was doing a good job of hiding it. "That preacher."

It was one of those merciless San Carlos afternoons and I wished I'd thought to bring my water out of the truck, but I didn't want to interrupt our conversation so I continued with a dry mouth. "You got any ideas?"

"Look, I just worked there. I don't think I was ever even in the house. My stuff was all outside, so if you're looking for someone who saw something, or knew something, or something like that, you've come to the wrong place." He studied the long ash on the end of his cigarette. "Because I really don't know anything."

The chairs were too close together and I could see the sweat from his left armpit drip down his side. Thank God I had my shirt on, since mine were doing the same thing. Mother Nature's air-conditioning system can be pretty effective.

"You helped J.B. with his bulls?"

"Sometimes. When he had that school of his running, I might open a chute, or something like that."

"Ever help him doctor them?"

"Hey, do I look like a fool?"

"Did you ever see him give them any medicine, inject them with anything?"

His eyes narrowed. He was no dummy and was perfectly capable of reading between the lines. "Nope."

"So why'd you leave then right after she died?"

He exhaled hard. "Wasn't my choice."

"You were fired?"

He nodded, his long black hair swinging on both sides of his neck.

"May I ask why?"

"I saw something someone thought I shouldn' have." He was slouching in his chair now, his long legs stretched out in front of him, his cigarette down to the butt.

I waited, but Lonnie Victor needed another prod.

"So do I play 64 Questions or do you want to share that with me?"

He threw the spent cigarette toward the announcer's stand and reached for another. "Hey, I don't owe them anything. I ran into a couple of people going at it who shouldn't have been."

"J.B.," I sighed. "And Jodie Austin."

"J.B.?" Lonnie was looking at me now. "No, not J.B. That brother of hers and that black woman."

"Peter Van Thiessen and Laurette Le Blanc?"

"Yeah. Those are the ones I saw. Late one night, out by the pool. I'd left and then had to come back since couldn't remember whether I'd turned off one of the water valves. That's when I saw them. He fired me the next day."

"J.B.?"

"Nah, the brother. Said they were getting a professional landscaping service. Yeah, as though they wouldn't have to pay an arm and a leg for one to come up to Oracle."

I picked the dogs up at Shiwóyé's and headed back to La Cienega. The drive down gave me a lot to think about. As far as I knew neither Peter nor Laurette was married. So why would they worry if someone found them in a compromising position? Who'd care? But Peter had been concerned enough to can Lonnie Victor. He obviously didn't want him telling what he'd seen. But, why? Was this just a fling between Peter and Laurette or had Peter known her before and used her as a setup to get into his sister's house? And if so, why?

Whatever was happening here had just tilted my investigation. Surprises. Sometimes the tilts worked, sometimes they didn't.

Only time would tell.

34

ONE THING ABOUT JUNE IS THAT THE DAYS ARE NOT ONLY HOT but they're long. Arizona's one of the few states in the union that doesn't honor Daylight Saving Time. Thank God. With our summer heat, the last thing we need to be doing is encouraging the sun to stick around any more than is absolutely necessary.

It was still light when I drove into Charley Bell's at seven that night. His pack of dogs came running out from under his mobile home and drove Blue and Mrs. Fierce crazy. I waited until Charley came out before shutting down the engine and winding down the windows.

"Ellis! What a nice surprise!" he said. "How's that computer going?"

"Oh, great." In truth I had forgotten all about it.

"You know why e-mail is like a penis?"

I shook my head and braced myself.

"Play with it too much and you'll go blind!" he chortled.

I didn't have the heart to tell him I wasn't even sure how someone got e-mail.

"Say, you got time to come in for a drink?"

"No, I better not, Charley. It's too hot for the girls to stay in the truck."

He nodded. Along with computers, Charley also un-
erstood dogs and knew that his pack wouldn't be
rilled if the visitors got out.

I handed him a sheet of paper with Stella Ahil's
ame and license plate number on it. "More homework. I
ought I'd stop in and see if you had any luck with that
her stuff I gave you."

"Oh yeah. I dropped the paperwork off at your office
is afternoon. Stuck it in that old mailbox." He was re-
rring to one I'd put on a post for people to leave things
. "I've still got some queries out." He scratched the bald
ot on top of his head. "But there were a couple of
ings I thought you might really be interested in. That
otball player . . ."

"Bobby Bangs?"

"Yeah, that's the one. That trouble with the NFL?"

I gave him a hopeful look.

"Wife battering. Big-time. Cherry Bangs spent ten
ays in ICU in Brooklyn. Then declined to press
arges."

"Cherry's his wife?"

"Ex."

I should have been incensed, but instead I felt relief.
y client wasn't the only one with a history of abusing
omen. Although from what Tommy Renner and even
ckie Doo Dahs told me, J.B. had acted more in self-de-
nse than out of malice. But what case could be made
r a man putting his wife in intensive care for ten days?
ould Lateef Wise have turned that vile temper on
bby?

"After that, he found Jesus, left professional football
d bummed around, preaching where he could. He fi-
lly struck gold in a church out in San Francisco. It's all
the report."

"The good reverend told me he was there when
bby was killed. Can you check that out for me?"

"Okey doke. Should be easy, assuming he flew."

"Anything interesting turn up on J.B.?"

He shook his head. "Not much. Lousy credit un[til] about six months ago. Surprise. No police record or ou[t]standings. Same for that Peter guy."

"Van Thiessen." Charley, a computer wizard, som[e]times had trouble remembering people's names. [I] wouldn't expect him to have bad credit. Nothing susp[i]cious there, eh?"

"Not so far. Loaded with dough, a fine upstandi[ng] citizen, charitable giver, avid runner, does a lot [of] marathons, never married, but dates a lot. He was d[e]voted to his sister."

"So I've heard," I said, remembering my conversati[on] with Clarice Martínez. "But I think he might have ha[d] something going with that Laurette Le Blanc."

"Miss St. Martin."

"Pardon me?"

"Laurette Le Blanc was Miss St. Martin back in th[e] 80s. A fox. Comes from a good family. Dad's a doc dow[n] there. She was an honor student in high school, had [a] year of college before doing the Miss Pretty bit."

"No arrests, skeletons in her closet, anything li[ke] that?" I was still toying with the idea that Laurette ha[d] known J.B. before he and Abby hired her on their hone[y]moon. Now that Lonnie had told me that she and Pet[er] were fooling around, maybe he had known her befo[re] too. "Any evidence she may have known either J.B. [or] Peter before she came to work for Abby?"

"So far not. Her mother's heart attack checked o[ut] too. I can get the hospital records if you need them."

"I don't right now."

"Now those people who worked for the rich la[dy] have been doing all right."

"What do you mean?"

"Got into their bank account."

"Charley!" I feigned shock.

"Ssh." He held his finger to his lips. "Some pretty f[at] deposits lately."

I knew the estate was nowhere near being settled so
that wouldn't have accounted for the extra cash. "How
at?"

"Mmm, seven thousand here, five there. Somewhere
round twenty-eight thousand dollars in the past couple
f months. And I misspoke. I got into their bank account,
ut that's not where I found it."

I raised an eyebrow.

"*She* opened a separate account three months ago."

"Abby left her more money in her will." I was think-
g out loud.

"She worked for her longer. Mrs. C only married José
ven years ago."

A new wrinkle. Maybe that explained why Abby
ad left Gloria more money than José. But, if that was
e case, why hadn't Jim Carstensen, Abby's lawyer,
own it?

Suddenly Gloria Covarrubias was looking a lot more
teresting. Where had the money come from and why
as it in a separate account? Did José know about it?
ad someone paid her to do something? Like spike J.B.'s
d Abby's booze so Abby could be hauled off and
lled? If José had been involved, why the separate bank
count?

"So is that the second interesting thing?"

He shook his head. "Not the really interesting thing. I
rned up an old *New York Times* clip. Seems there was a
agic fire years ago at the Van Thiessen mansion on
ntral Park. Mrs. Van Thiessen got trapped, couldn't get
t and died in it."

"Madeleine Van Thiessen?"

"The same. Abigail's mother."

"That's strange. I could have sworn Clarice Martínez
ld me she'd died of cancer."

"Who's Clarice Martínez?"

"She was Abby's best friend."

"Well, the mother did have cancer. She was bedrid-

den at the time. That was part of the problem. Hang c
to your hat, Ellis. One of the kids was playing wit
matches in Mrs. Van Thiessen's closet."

"Abby or Peter?"

"Neither, the nanny's daughter. She was five yea
older than Peter, a year younger than Abby."

Jesus. I remembered the cave and the irony
Madeleine's perishing in a fire started in a closet did n
escape me.

"How old was she?"

"Twelve. According to the accounts I read, Pet
saved her life. You'll have to read the clip."

He didn't have to suggest that. I'd already decided
would be the first thing I'd pull out of the packet he'd le
at my office.

"Another interesting thing." Beads of sweat we
bubbling up on Charley's forehead. Although it was ge
ting cooler, it was still hot and I felt guilty about keepir
him outside talking to me. "The nanny's daughter?"

"Yeah."

"Glory Chukker."

"Let me guess . . ."

"Yep, Covarrubias, née Chukker."

Holy cow. Gloria's mother had been Abby ar
Peter's nanny. The three of them had apparently bee
raised together and yet neither Peter nor Gloria ha
mentioned it. Why not? Did that have anything to c
with the extra money Abby had left Gloria? And whe
Clarice was talking about growing up with Peter ar
Abby, why had she neglected to mention Gloria? (
the fire? Didn't that qualify as a milestone in the
childhood?

On the way into the ranch I retrieved Charley
notes from the old mailbox at the stage stop. I knew he
shared with me most of the information so I waited un
later that night, when I was curled up in the La-Z-Boy,
go over them.

The copy of the *New York Times* article was on top of the stack. There were several pictures—of a healthy-looking Madeleine Van Thiessen and of Peter's father. As I read the story there was no doubt how or where the fire had originated. Glory Chukker had been playing with matches right before all hell had broken out in the Van Thiessen closet.

Peter Van Thiessen had pulled Gloria out of the bedroom, but was unable to save his mother, who was bedridden since her cancer had already spread to her bones. In spite of the best efforts of first her nurses and staff, and then the fire department, Madeleine Van Thiessen had perished in the blaze. Her daughter, Abigail, had been at boarding school at the time.

When I flipped to the second copied page, where the story had jumped, underneath another photograph was the caption, "Boy Hero Saves Nanny's Daughter, Mother Dies in Fire."

But more interesting than the caption was the picture itself. A pretty little girl with long dark curls and intense eyes was standing behind a young Peter Van Thiessen, who was seated in a chair. The girl's arms were draped over his shoulders and it looked like both of her hands were encased in catcher's mitts, the bandages were that big.

Unfortunately Prego, the mechanic, got home from his fishing trip late Sunday night. By seven o'clock Monday morning Martín had borrowed Priscilla to tow his old Dodge up to Prego's home shop in La Cienega.

After doing a few household chores I put Petunia on the porch, and Blue, Mrs. Fierce and I walked the mile to the stage stop. We were all hot and thirsty by the time we arrived.

The dogs plopped on the cool cement floors as I threw on the evaporative cooler, cracked a few windows and refreshed their earthen crock of water. I mixed a quick pitcher of Trader Joe's lemonade, reached into the tiny refrigerator and popped a miniature tray of ice cubes and poured myself a cold drink.

I went through Charley's packet again, looking for something I might have overlooked, but there was nothing there. It wasn't like I didn't have enough to work with. Now I had almost too much information to assimilate.

Gloria's childhood connection to Abby and Peter had added another twist to the case. Charley had uncovered her new bank account and some hefty deposits. Where had the money come from, and why? Since I'd gone through Abby's checkbook at her house, I was pretty sure that the heavy deposits had not come from Gloria's employer. And why had Gloria been left more money than her husband? What did that mean? Did it have to do with her growing up with Peter and Abby, or, God forbid, did it have to with the fire?

Going over my own material, I had a hunch that I was missing something, but what was it?

I turned to my notes when I'd talked to José Covarrubias. Ramona Miller had come up when he was waxing the car. I'd underlined Ramona's comment "drop . . . things." Could Abby have been getting drugs all along? Drugs that affected her coordination? And if she really was dropping things, why had no one except the maid noticed?

Then I remembered the bartender at La Gitana. He'd said Abby had dropped a bottle of booze while she'd been dancing. Had I been too quick to write that off to her being drunk? Had something really been wrong with her?

While I could probably find what I was looking for quickly using the computer, I had no clue how to do that so I resorted to shuffling through my computer-generated pages. Finally I found the notes I had taken at Abby's desk when I was going through her Day Planner and checkbook. There it was. The old message left by

Clarice Martínez encouraging Abby to call a man named Hornisher for collagen implants.

Recalling my conversation with Clarice, it hit me. She'd said that Hornisher was a lip guy. Did implants, that sort of thing. Yet Abby had the full, pouty lips of a sexpot movie star. Hadn't they already been done? How long did that stuff last? Was it like dying your hair? Or more permanent?

I picked up the telephone and dialed the Phoenix number she'd left for the doctor.

"Barrows Neurological Institute," a matter-of-fact voice answered.

Neurological Institute? While most lips were found on heads, I didn't think there was much connection between neurology and plastic surgery. What in the hell was going on?

I asked to be connected to Dr. Hornisher.

"Dr. Hornisher's office, this is Julie."

"Julie, this is Trade Ellis from Tucson. A friend of mine, Clarice Martínez, suggested that I make an appointment with Dr. Hornisher," I lied.

"Hmmm, Clarice Martínez. Is she one of our patients?"

"I believe so," I continued the fib. "She told me that Dr. Hornisher was the best," I gushed.

"And you've been diagnosed?"

Diagnosed? What the hell for? Lips?

"Yes."

"Well, the earliest that Dr. Hornisher could see you would be September."

He must be popular with a three-month waiting list.

"Oh, I can't possibly wait that long." I tried to sound pitiful. "I'm taking a cruise in August and I'd hoped to have the work done by then."

She took the bait. "A cruise?" She sounded alarmed. "Work? I think you've been given some misinformation."

"Dr. Hornisher does lip rejuvenations, right?"

"Oh no." She sounded aghast. "He's a neurological doctor. His specialty is amyotrophic lateral sclerosis."

I tried to echo her phrase, stumbling through the words. "I . . . I'm afraid I don't understand."

"Lou Gehrig's disease. Dr. Hornisher specializes in Lou Gehrig's disease," she repeated right before she hung up.

35

I WAS HALFWAY OUT THE DOOR WHEN THE TELEPHONE RANG.

"Trade? It's María López Zepeda. I'm afraid I've got some bad news. J.B.'s insisting on the lie detector test."

"You don't think he'll pass it?"

"He's sure he will, but who knows? As I've said, they're fairly unreliable. But he's the client."

"You're not going to let him do it, are you?"

"Well . . ." I heard the hesitation in her voice. "I sure don't want him taking one of theirs, so I guess we don't have much choice if he's determined to do it. We'll use one of the private firms."

"What if he flunks?"

"The results will be confidential if we do it this way. The police will never have to know that he even took one."

The defense attorney had a lot more faith in the confidentiality thing than I did. The downtown community was pretty tight and I wasn't so sure that J.B.'s test results would remain a secret.

"I'm trying to schedule him now."

I groaned.

"He wants out of jail and the judge won't bond him

so he sees this as an out. If he passes the thing, he thinks a case can be made for setting bond."

"Do you agree?"

"Not necessarily. And I told him so, but we have a pretty stubborn client."

I liked the way she said "we." At least I wasn't in this alone.

"María, will you let me know the results when you get them?" I asked, wondering what I'd do if he flunked the damn thing.

"Sure," she promised before hanging up.

I knew finding Clarice Martínez at home was going to be a total crapshoot, but I got lucky. I found her sitting in a patio under the misters near her aviary of flitting finches. She was wearing what looked like one of her husband's white dress shirts and just under the long tails I spotted a hint of faded denim shorts. She was sitting reading and sipping an iced tea.

"Well, look who's here!" She dropped the latest copy of *Vogue* on the table as she jumped out of the heavy wrought iron patio chair and greeted me warmly. "Honey, can I get you some tea?"

"No thanks." I held up the bottled water I frequently carry with me in summer.

"Too hot? Shall we go inside?"

"This is fine," I said, settling into a patio chair.

"Well, then, how's everything going?"

"It's getting more intriguing all the time." I watched her closely. "Have you figured out why I'm here?"

"Why no." Her hands fluttered, not unlike a flight of her beloved tiny birds. "Should I?"

"I called Hornisher's telephone number," I said. "And it was very interesting." I paused for effect. "I found out he's not a plastic surgeon at all. He doesn't even do lips."

"Oh." It was as though the air had been let out of her. Tiny to begin with, she seemed even more diminutive in the heavy metal chair.

"He's a neurological specialist," I continued. "Lou Gehrig's disease. Does any of this sound familiar?"

To her credit, she didn't try to evade my question. Her big blue eyes watered as she nodded. "I promised," she whispered.

"Who did you promise?" I leaned across the table and patted her thin freckled arm. "Abby?"

She nodded, withdrew her arm and brushed the tears away with the tips of her fingers. "She didn't want anyone to know. I was stupid to leave that message on her machine, but I didn't know that she was going to die."

"No, of course you didn't," I said gently. "How could you?"

"I was hoping that you'd let it go, that you wouldn't find out about Dr. Hornisher."

"I almost didn't," I admitted, thinking of how close I'd come to ignoring the answering machine message. "But then I figured out that Abby didn't need collagen implants in her lips. I finally called Hornisher's office this morning. Do you want to tell me about it?"

"God, I promised." She lifted the tail of her long white shirt and rubbed her eyes with it.

"Clarice, Abby's dead. What you know may help me find out how and why she died."

"And who killed her?"

"Maybe."

She sighed heavily. "If I tell you, you have to swear you will not breathe a word of this to a single living soul."

"I can't do that. After I called Hornisher's office, I began putting the pieces together."

She thought about this for a moment and then began talking.

"About three months ago Abby started noticing that she wasn't feeling right. Her hands were getting stiff and cramping, stiffer than she thought they should with just the normal arthritis."

"And she began dropping things."

"You knew about that?"

I nodded.

"She felt like she was getting weaker, although there was no reason for it, and that scared the pants off her."

"Did she tell J.B.?"

"Honey, are you crazy? Abby was terrified of getting old, of getting ugly. She'd seen her mother go through a terrible, disfiguring disease, and that was the last thing she wanted for herself. And she sure didn't want to share the news with J.B. any sooner than she had to."

I let the reference to Madeleine pass for the time being.

"There was no way on earth she was going to tell that young husband of hers that she was getting weak and feeble, no way at all."

"Was she ever diagnosed?"

"Oh, sure. Her regular doctor ran a number of tests and had just come up with Lou Gehrig's right before she died. While they were running more tests, I was checking around trying to get some names for her. When I found Leland Hornisher right up the road in Phoenix, I left the message, but I had to be sneaky about it since Abby didn't want anyone knowing. That's why I mentioned the collagen."

It was a smart deception. After all, I'd almost fallen for it.

"You mentioned her regular doctor, was that Samuel Mullon?"

"Uh huh. He was going to give her some referrals too. Wasn't it freaky that he died the same night as Abby?" Now that she had confided in me about Abby's disease, it was as though a huge load had been taken off her and she was eager to talk.

"Freaky," I agreed, but in my mind I wasn't finding Mullon's death coincidental at all. Had the information he had on Abby's Lou Gehrig's killed him? Could someone have wanted to make sure he didn't pass that on? And if so, who and why? "Who else did Abby tell?"

"No one."

"Not even her brother?"

Clarice shook her head and the filtered light picked up copper highlights in her short red hair. "She was really definite about that. Said she didn't want anyone to know about it until she'd decided what to do."

"What's to do with Lou Gehrig's?" I asked. I didn't know a lot about the disease, but I knew enough to know that it was a progressive thing and that most people, once they had it, had no way out.

"Not much," Clarice agreed. "That thing is surely unkind. It kills your body but your mind still works. By what she was gonna do, I just meant that she wasn't sure who was going to treat her, or how. She was just destroyed by the news."

"That's when she went on the Prozac," I guessed.

She nodded. "It helped with her depression. Her doctor wasn't one to pull punches, and he told her what she had to look forward to. He didn't paint a pretty picture, honey."

"I don't imagine he did."

"She told me she couldn't stand the idea of being in a wheelchair, drooling and breathing through a machine. That she'd rather be dead than go through that."

"Well, it looks like she got her wish," I said. "Only it sure wasn't suicide. Clarice, have you told anybody about Abby's illness?"

"Lordy, no." She was shocked.

"Although she's dead, I think it would be a good idea if you kept this to yourself." I didn't want to scare her, but I was concerned that there was a possibility that whoever had killed Abby and Dr. Mullon might come after her.

I reached in my purse, pulled out the copy of the *New York Times* article on the Van Thiessen fire and handed it to her. It was folded back to the second page with the picture of Peter and Gloria. "Do these kids look familiar to you?"

She glanced at the clip and handed it back. "Sure. That's Peter's hero picture."

I remembered that Clarice had told me she'd known Abby since they were babies, that their nannies had been friends and had strolled together in Central Park. "And Gloria Covarrubias is also in it."

She wasn't at all surprised.

"You never mentioned that she grew up with Abby and Peter."

"Well, frankly, it really wasn't like that. Glory didn't live there or anything. She stayed with an aunt in the Bronx while her mother worked. She really wasn't involved in Abby's and Peter's lives so I guess that's why I forgot to mention it. It was only after Lala Chukker died—that was her mother—that she came to work for Abby. Maybe ten, twelve years ago."

"But you led me to believe that Madeleine Van Thiessen died of cancer."

"No." She was very definite. "Honey, I told you she had cancer in her jaw and that she died when we were thirteen. That's all I said. After the fire, none of us ever talked about that day again."

Of course she was right. I was the one who had stupidly made the assumption that the cancer had killed her.

As I drove out her driveway, I was haunted by the irony of all of it. Jackie Doo Dahs, J.B.'s ex-wife, had lured him to meet with her under the pretext of illness. Yet Abby, his wife, really was ill and hadn't shared that with him.

By the time I hit Oracle Road I'd thought a lot about Abby's disease and come to the conclusion that like many people with troubling news, she might have shared it with her minister. Since I had a little time to kill I drove out to the Church of Brotherly Love.

I found Lateef Wise standing next to a tall ladder in

he chapel. I was again struck by how absolutely huge he
was. The skinny young girl with braces was on top of
he ladder holding a wire basket with what looked like
an industrial size light bulb in it.

"You're a day late," Wise said, but he was smiling.

"And a dollar short," I said. "I thought of a few things
wanted to go over with you."

"Sure. Marly, you can come down now, we'll change
t later."

The girl climbed down from the ladder. When she
dropped from the last rung, instead of hitting the floor,
she landed on Reverend Wise's foot.

"Watch it!" He snarled in what I thought was an
overreaction. He had to have a hundred pounds on the
skinny little thing.

"Sorry," she smiled, showing a mouthful of metal.
"I'll go finish those letters now," she said as she skipped
out of the chapel.

"Doggone thing won't hold me," Wise said, nodding
at the ladder.

"Well that wouldn't be a graceful fall," I said, pleased
with my pun.

"Shall we go to my office?"

"This won't take long."

"All right." As he dropped onto the front pew the
wood creaked with his weight. He motioned for me to
join him.

"During the course of my investigation I've run
across a few things."

His hooded eyes were focused on my face, but they
gave nothing away.

"Did Abby ever mention to you that she was sick?"

"Well, I knew she was depressed about that business
with her husband, if that's what you mean."

"No. She had Lou Gehrig's disease."

One of his eyebrows shot up. "That's terrible. I had
no idea, none at all."

"I thought with you being her minister and all, that

maybe she would have talked to you about it. It's a very debilitating thing."

"Yes, I know. But as I told you last week, Abby's church attendance had fallen off lately. We weren't as close as we once were."

"But she was still sending money to the church," I said, remembering the healthy checks she'd written.

"Yes."

I wondered if her disinterest in his Sunday services had worried him. Of course if he'd killed her the giving would have stopped entirely. But what if he'd known about her will and the five million dollars before her death? Wouldn't he be concerned that if she wasn't going to church that she might change her mind about that? Five million bucks any way you cut it was a pretty good motive for anything. Even murder.

"Before she died did you know the church was in her will?"

"Yes." He was leaning on his knees and he rubbed his face with his huge hands, his gold and diamond Super Bowl ring sparkling, caught by the light from the windows. "But I didn't know the amount."

It was quiet in the chapel with only the occasional hum of the air-conditioning refrigeration as it kicked in.

"Aren't you going to ask me?" He trained those dark eyes on me once again.

"Ask you what?"

"About Cherry."

I exhaled. "Yeah, I was going to get to it."

"I supposed you would. I've been waiting for you to return. There have been some things that I have done in my past that I'm not proud of, the good Lord knows. And my treatment of my ex-wife is at the top of the list of the sins I will have to one day atone for."

Ten days in intensive care. I sure hoped he was going to have to answer to someone for that.

"I was an angry young man back then. Full of fear and hate. It was before I found the Lord."

"There haven't been any other incidents?"

"No." His head was back in his hands. "Nothing. I ave learned to channel my energies in more productive ays."

Since I'd just witnessed his overreaction to the enager's accidentally stepping on his foot a few min-tes earlier I was skeptical.

"I still attend anger management classes once a eek," he admitted before standing up. "And now, Miss llis, unless you have further questions, I believe I should et back to doing the Lord's work."

I'd called Peter Van Thiessen before leaving Clarice's nd he'd agreed to meet me for lunch at the Tohono hul Tea Room on the northwest side of Tucson. I got ere early and strolled through the gift shop.

It turned out he was late. He'd been running again up n Mt. Lemmon. It was too hot to eat in the front court-ard or the back patio so we were seated inside.

We'd just ordered when I got down to business.

"I'd like to talk to you about your sister's relationship vith Gloria and José Covarrubias," I began.

"She was fond of both of them."

"But more fond of Gloria than her husband?" I prod-ed, seeing if he would bring up the fire.

"You're looking at the extra money Abby left Gloria, ren't you?"

"That's one thing."

"She'd been working for Abby for several years be-ore she married José so my sister was closer to her. I hink that's probably why she left her more."

"Twenty-four thousand dollars more?"

"And because Laurette didn't work very long for her, he only got five thousand." He glanced at his watch.

With the mention of Laurette Le Blanc's name I was empted to delve into his relationship with her, but de-ided against it. Until I was sure who the players were, I vas going to hold my cards pretty close to my chest.

I stayed quiet as the waitress deposited our sand
wiches.

"Gloria Covarrubias opened a separate bank accoun
about three months ago."

His hands, with the sandwich in them, stoppe
inches away from his mouth. "What bank account?"

"One separate from the one she had with her hus
band. The interesting thing is that about the same time
large deposits started appearing in that account."

"Well, that's certainly surprising." His eyes nar
rowed. "How large?"

"About twenty-eight thousand dollars all togethe
So I'm wondering if there's a connection between tha
money and Abby's death."

"You think Gloria might have had something to d
with it?"

"I'm not saying that, not yet." I held up my hand.

"Maybe someone died and left her money," Peter of
fered before taking another bite of his basil, tomato an
fontina cheese sandwich.

"When that happens there's usually a large single de
posit, not money trickling in in different amounts ove
three months."

"I'm sorry, but I don't know anything about th
Covarrubiases' financial arrangements with my sister, o
any of their other sources of income. Maybe you shoul
talk to Gloria about it."

"I'll do that."

We ate quietly for a few minutes before I change
my approach.

"Peter, why didn't you tell me that Gloria's mothe
was your nanny?"

"Why would I?" He took another bite of his sand
wich, not missing a beat.

"Well, when I asked you how long Gloria ha
worked for Abby you just said a long time. I was sur
prised when I learned you that you all grew up together.

"Not hardly." He laughed, and looked at his watch

gain. "She was our nanny's daughter, that's all. We
weren't encouraged to play with her and she was rarely
round anyway."

"But you were a boy hero," I said, smiling. "From the
picture I saw it looks like Gloria suffered some pretty se-
ous burns on her hands."

"That was an awful day. I don't talk about it."

I suppose I could have prodded him, but didn't see the
eed to. At least he hadn't lied about the fire when I'd asked.
That was better than nothing, but not as good as telling me
bout it from the get-go. I switched direction again.

"Did you ever notice that Abby was sick in any way,
maybe taking medications or dropping things?"

"God, we've been through this," Peter Van Thiessen
aid, an edge to his voice. "You were with me when we
ound the Prozac. I didn't know my sister was taking that
r anything else for that matter. What's this about drop-
ing things?"

"Well, Ramona Miller mentioned that Abby was
aving trouble. Then at the bar the night before her
eath the bartender said she'd dropped a bottle." I
watched him carefully. "She was having trouble holding
n to things. Her hands were getting stiff and cramping."

"I never noticed anything like that."

"So you didn't know your sister had Lou Gehrig's
isease?"

"What?" He coughed and pieces of his sandwich flew
ut of his mouth. He wiped his lips with his napkin. "My
God, what are you talking about?"

"Lou Gehrig's. Your sister was sick."

"That's impossible. She would have told me." His
and trembled as he lifted his iced tea glass. "I would
ave known."

"According to my sources"—I used the plural to
over Clarice—"only her doctor and a few friends knew
bout it."

"Lou Gehrig's. That's the one that paralyzes you,
sn't it?"

I nodded.

"I can't believe she wouldn't have told me."

"You were close," I said, remembering my first conversation with Clarice. What had she said? *They were tighter than ticks, because of that mother they had.*

"Obviously not as close as I thought we were," he said dryly. "I guess you've talked to her doctor."

"Unfortunately not. He was killed the same weekend Abby died."

"God. How did that happen?"

"He was shot at his home."

"But you know for sure that she had this disease?"

I nodded. It was kind of a bluff, but coupling Hornisher's specialty with what Clarice had told me, I felt that I was on solid ground.

"She told one of my sources that she'd rather be dead than debilitated."

"What are you saying, Trade? Do you think she drowned herself?"

"Not likely."

"So I don't get it." His voice was harsh. "Am I supposed to feel better about my sister's murder because she was going to die anyway?"

36

After leaving Peter I drove up to Oracle and dropped in on the Covarrubiases at the Brave Bull.

It had been impossible to physically separate José and Gloria, so I'd had to ask them about Abby's disease together. Gloria had her stonewall act down cold, and her husband, never a chatterbox to begin with, also pled ignorance. I kept my mouth shut about the deposits that Gloria had been making to her private account. There was no sense tipping my hand any earlier than I had to.

"I understand your mother was Peter and Abby's nanny," I said. "That you grew up with them."

If Gloria was surprised, she didn't show it. Unlike Peter, she saw no need to clarify my assumption that they had grown up together. She said nothing.

"What can you tell me about the fire that day?"

"What's to tell? Is this what you want to see?" She jerked off one of her thin cotton gloves.

Her right hand was shriveled with a cicatrix of gnarly rivers of faint pink scars and ridges of thick, ropy scar tissue running wild. The deformities ran up her wrists, finally disappearing under the fabric of her long-sleeved shirt. I noticed webbing between her fingers and her index finger was significantly shorter than her middle one. She had no fingernails.

Gloria held her hand in front of my face. Too close. "What do you mean asking me, what happened that day? I was a little girl, playing with matches when and where I should not have been."

José Covarrubias studied his hands in his lap and said nothing.

"And God in his grace spared me."

"I understand Peter had something to do with that too." It wasn't particularly kind, but then I was no fan of Gloria's. "You must be very grateful to him."

"Grateful? And who wouldn't be? I have nothing more to say to you." With that she walked off.

"*Adiós,*" José said quietly as he followed his wife out of the room.

On the drive home I had to admit I didn't really like Gloria Covarrubias and failed to find what Abby had found so endearing in her. While that didn't necessarily make her a murderer, I couldn't overlook the fact that she was the one who had packed all of J.B. and Abby's food for their fateful camping trip, and more importantly, their whiskey. The more I thought about it, the more convinced I became that both of them had been drugged.

Of course there was the possibility that the ketamine had belonged to J.B., but even so, that would have made it accessible to Gloria. José, in his position as handyman-chauffeur, could have easily spotted the drug in the bull barn and given it to his wife.

And of course the big bombshell was that she and Abby and Peter had all known one another as children. I thought about what Gloria's childhood must have been like. It had to have been hard to have your mother work for really rich people, to be a nanny to children whose every wish was granted while you were shunted off to an aunt in the Bronx. How had she felt, deprived of her mother's company, week after week, while Lala Chukker had tended Peter and Abby? Would she have gotten the message that her mother thought the Van Thiessen children were more important than her own daughter? That she was somehow less important, less deserving?

I found myself doubting that little Gloria had intentionally set the fire that had taken Madeleine Van Thiessen's life. What was the percentage in that? Wouldn't that make the nanny's services even more in demand? The fire probably had been an accident. But again, an accident in the house that took Gloria's mother away from her day after day of her young life. And what did she have to show for it? Terribly scarred hands and arms, a big collection of soft cotton gloves and mental scar tissue that could probably never be debrided.

While I'm no psychologist, it seemed to me that such a background could foster a lot of pain, anger and resentment. How much was the question. Had she killed Abby? And was Peter next?

When I got back to the stage stop I tried the number that Charley Bell had dug up for Laurette Le Blanc in St. Martin.

I couldn't afford to overlook her. There was a lot going on there. Her suspicious hiring by either J.B. or Abby on their honeymoon, her easy access to Abby's accounts and business affairs, and her romantic involvement with Abby's brother all implicated her. Throw into the mix the womanizing J.B.—although I had no evidence of his having fooled around with her—and Laurette Le Blanc also turned up high on my suspect list.

When I finally reached her, Abby's personal assistant shed no new light on my investigation, although she did admit she knew that Abby had been taking Prozac for depression. She said she knew nothing about the Lou Gehrig's disease.

◆   ◆   ◆

I had to keep asking myself, why would anyone want Abby dead? And that question led to the Big Three. Who had the desire, the opportunity and the motive?

Unfortunately, a lot of people would profit monetarily from Abby's death. Her husband clearly had the most to gain. Then there were the Covarrubiases. Their combined inheritance of $58,000 might not mean much to a wealthy man like Peter, but to a poor family, it would seem a fortune. Perhaps enough to kill for.

And if Gloria was in it, there was a good chance that she was not alone, judging from the money that had been deposited in her separate account. Where had that additional $28,000 come from? Could Gloria or Laurette somehow have wangled it out of Abby's accounts? Or how about J.B.? Could he and Gloria have conspired to kill Abby, and the additional money to buy Gloria's silence had come from the million dollars that Abby had given her husband?

Thinking of J.B., I certainly couldn't overlook Jackie Doo Dahs. She'd convinced herself that she wanted her husband back. How badly did she really want him and his money? Enough to kill for? I stared at my bruised left wrist.

And of course, out in left wing was the not so pure Lateef Wise aka Bobby Bangs. Wife abuser, now born-again preacher who hadn't begun to strike it rich until he had met Abigail Van Thiessen. Five million dollars could definitely be a great motive.

Now I'd hit a real snag. The Lou Gehrig's. What did it mean? I was convinced that there had to be a connection between Abby's death and that of Samuel Mullon, her doctor. But what was it? Who wanted him dead? And what had he known?

If no one knew about Abby's disease, other than her doctor and Clarice Martínez, did that implicate Clarice? What would she stand to gain if Abby died? As far as I knew, Abby had left nothing to her, so why would she want to kill her? No, Clarice was not in the mix, other than I was truly worried about her. If whoever had killed Dr. Mullon did so because he knew of Abby's diagnosis, then Abby's best friend could definitely be in jeopardy.

The whole thing was like a crazy quilt of mixed patterns. None of it made much sense. But all my suspects had a common denominator. Money. If Abby'd been poor, the whole thing would probably have been a lot easier to sort out. The trouble with being rich, it seems to me, is that someone always wants you dead. Even if they like you, they might like your money better.

My head was spinning by the time I arrived home and I was in no mood for Cori Elena, who came bounding out of the bunkhouse the minute she heard the truck in the drive. I'd just shut down Priscilla when she ran up.

"Trade, I've got to talk to you." She was dressed in her short cutoff fringed Levi's and a halter top. Barefoot, she danced on the hot soil, hopping from one foot to the other. "*Por favor*, it's *importante*."

"Okay, let's go inside before your feet get cremated."

I followed her racing form back to the bunkhouse, grateful for the evaporated air that hit me in the face when I walked in. Her hot Mexican music was blaring, and to her credit she turned it down to a low murmur.

"*Cerveza?*" she asked, holding up a bottle of Dos Equis beer.

While it sounded good, I wasn't eager to prolong my time with Cori Elena any longer than I needed to so I shook my head. "What's up?"

She finished off the bottle she'd been working on, wiped her mouth and said, "Guess who was killed yesterday in Magdalena?"

"Carmen Orduño's husband?" I made a wild guess.

"*Tonta!* Rafael Félix!"

It didn't take me long to figure out that this was indeed very good news. Félix was the guy who had been in some kind of questionable business with Lázaro

Orantez, Cori Elena's husband. The reputed drug lord who had accused her of taking off with some of his money.

I breathed a sigh of relief. With Félix out of the picture Martín would be staying at the Vaca Grande. There'd be no need for him to pack up his things and head off with Cori Elena for California.

"God, that's great news," I said, feeling slightly guilty that I could revel in someone's death. How selfish was I? Still, it meant that Martín and Quinta, two people I really cared about, were no longer under any threat. Besides, all indications were that Rafael Félix had been a scumbag. "Maybe I will have that beer."

She withdrew one from the refrigerator and handed it to me. I popped the cap and drank. Dos Equis wasn't as good in my book as Corona, but it still tasted good. I held the cold bottle against my face. "What happened?"

"There was a shooting in one of the bars and Félix was killed."

"How'd you find out?"

"A friend of mine down there called me." She popped the cap on a fresh beer. "It was a drug thing."

Her admission had not gone unnoticed by me. Supposedly no one but her father knew where she was, yet not only had Carmen Orduño showed up at the Vaca Grande, but now she had just admitted that she'd also given her phone number to another friend in Magdalena. I'd never thought of Cori Elena as particularly stupid, cunning was more like it, but how could she be so blithe with her whereabouts when someone as ruthless as Félix was after her?

My anger with her was somewhat diluted by my euphoria that Martín would not be leaving, so I cut her some slack and said nothing about her slip. "That means you won't be leaving then."

She smiled and the little mole at the corner of her mouth winked at me. "I called Martín over at Prego's, they're working on the truck, and told him. Still, I think a

rip to Hollywood would be nice, so maybe we'll go for a
ouple of days anyway." She caught herself. "I mean if
hat's okay with you."

"Whatever." I was pretty sure that Hollywood was
ot on Martín's list of Top Ten Places he'd want to visit,
ut a short hop over to California for a few days
vouldn't hurt a thing. I was just so damned relieved that
élix wasn't going to be around to blow all of our heads
ff.

"That's great news." I walked over to the counter
nd placed my half-empty bottle of beer down. "Now
ou can all live happily ever after here on the Vaca
Grande," I said, trying to hide my disappointment for
aving to include her in the equation.

"Seguro," she said with a lack of enthusiasm that
choed my own.

When I finally got inside the house there were a cou-
le of messages waiting for me. The first was from María
,ópez Zepeda.

"Trade, the lie detector test is scheduled for tomor-
ow morning. I'm still against it, but J.B. won't back off.
'll let you know."

There was what sounded like a collect call from the
ail, which could only be J.B. I was sorry to have missed
hat one, since there was no way I could call him back. I
uspected that he was also calling to tell me about his
est.

The third call was from Curly at the feed store.

"Sorry to bother you, but there was a woman in here
while ago that said your north tank's got a problem.
hought you'd want to know."

Shit. We have a lot of recreational horseback riders
n the state land I lease for grazing. Occasionally one of
hem notices some cows out, or a cut fence or a broken
vater pipe and calls Martín or myself. Apparently the
ider who had noticed the north tank problem hadn't
nown us.

With Martín at Prego's there was nothing for me to

do but go fix it myself. Since I was on a roll with the bee
I grabbed a Corona and headed out the door.

Mrs. Fierce and Blue wanted to come with me, but
turned them down. There wasn't much shade at th
north tanks and they'd be cooler if they stayed home.

My trip took me twenty-five minutes over deserte
back dusty roads. I was expecting to find my Brahma
restless with thirst and was surprised to find a mud slic
and puddles of water on one side of the tank as the wate
gushed out several small holes. The few cows that wer
in the area were bedded down, looking quite conten
While I hated to see the water wasted, I was happy i
knowing that my cows hadn't been cut off. The weathe
was brutal enough on them without their being dehy
drated.

It didn't take a hydrologist to figure out the problem
Three small holes were peppered right above the botton
rim of the tank and it was from these that the wate
seeped out. Judging from their size, I guessed them to b
from a .22. Probably some bored target shooter who'
decided over the weekend to take a shot at the tank. I
was one of our fairly common problems, as near to civi
lization as the ranch was. Still, it beat the hell out c
someone target-practicing on cows, which they've als
done.

While Martín would eventually have to come ou
and weld the tank, I had a couple of options this after
noon. There was some J-B Weld in the truck box, and
could patch it with that. I didn't feel like mixing the stu
together and turning the water off for it to set, so I opte
for the easy out.

Grabbing my buck knife from the cab of the truck,
cut a thin branch from one of the mesquite tree:
Whittling this down to a small stub, I pushed it into th
hole and plugged it. I repeated the procedure two mor
times and presto! The tank was temporarily fixed. As i
filled with water, the mesquite would swell and furthe
plug the holes. There would probably be some sligh

leakage, but the whole thing should hold until we could get the welding equipment up here.

I drove out past a huge saguaro. While I'd been by this particular specimen almost all my life, the light from the late afternoon sun gave it a strange halo. I stopped the truck, jumped out and studied the cactus. It was crowned with a ring of bursting carmine fruit.

The saguaro made me think of the Michael Chiago painting in María's office, and that led me to thinking about Stella Ahil's saguaro harvesting camp.

I don't know where the epiphany came from, but I couldn't shake the feeling that none of it was coincidental. That, somehow, all of it was related to Abigail Van Thiessen's drowning in a murky stock tank in the Baboquivaris.

37

IT WAS GETTING DARK AND I HAD JUST PULLED ONTO THE LAN[E]
from the back road when I spotted Prego's beat-up ye[l]
low Land Rover coming out of the Vaca Grande. W[e]
stopped in the middle of the road for a neighborly chat.

"Hey, Trade, it's been a while. I left some fish for yo[u]
with Martín."

"Thanks, Prego. Guess they were biting, huh?"

He spread his hands a couple of feet apart and the[n]
slowly inched them back together and grinned. "It'[ll]
break up the monotony of all that beef you eat."

"How's the truck coming along?" While there proba[-]
bly wasn't any real rush on it now that Rafael Félix wa[s]
dead, being down one truck on the ranch could become [a]
serious handicap.

"We'll get 'er done, but I'm swamped this week sinc[e]
I took off fishing. I told Martín we could work on it to[-]
morrow night."

"Sounds like a plan to me," I said. "Take care."

At the ranch I fed the horses and chickens. As I sca[t]
tered scratch at the pond for the ducks, I heard a cluckin[g]
sound from the brush and a proud mallard hen trailin[g]

even little yellow balls of fluff emerged. It was Baby Duck Time again. After admiring the ducklings and congratulating the mallard, I fed Mrs. Fierce and Blue and then let Petunia in the back porch where she squealed and grunted in an effort to encourage me to fill her bowl with pig chow. From her prodding, it didn't sound as though she thought I was moving fast enough.

Juan or Quinta had left some fresh tomatoes and cucumbers from the garden on the porch table and I grabbed these and headed inside the house. In the kitchen I sliced a clove of garlic and ran it around a wooden salad bowl and then rummaged through the refrigerator. I finally came up with some old microwaved baked potatoes and a hardboiled egg, which I peeled and cut in pieces, along with the fresh cucumbers and tomatoes. I tossed the vegetables with lettuce, a few black olives and a can of tuna, and then doused the whole thing with vinegar and oil. My ersatz salad Niçoise along with a glass of cold Chardonnay made a pleasant enough dinner.

I was halfway through the salad when the telephone rang.

"Trade? It's Em. There's a new fly in your ointment."

I set the wineglass down on the Mexican tile counter and clutched the headset to my ear.

"What kind of fly?"

"The analysis is in on those bottles of booze the detectives picked up at the camp site."

"Let me guess. They'd been messed with," I said, remembering the Baileys and the Jack Daniel's that J.B. said they'd had late that night.

"That's the fly. *They* hadn't. The Baileys had."

"You're saying that the J.D. was all right? That there wasn't anything in it?"

"Just sour mash whiskey. Not a trace of drugs. The Baileys was something else. They found traces of triazolam in it, trade name Halcion."

"The sleeping pill?"

"Yep. It's a pretty sure bet that Abby was drugge[d] before the ketamine ever went in her body."

"So it wasn't actually in the booze?"

"Not the ketamine, just the triazolam. They've got [a] fresh puncture wound too. The speculation here now [is] that's how the ketamine was administered."

"Thanks, Em. You've given me a lot to think about," [I] said before hanging up.

It made sense. Someone had drugged Abby to th[e] point where she wouldn't fight a hypodermic, or som[e] one messing with her in the middle of the night. On[ce] the ketamine hit her system she'd have been in a zo[m] bielike state, unable to resist anything, including her fat[al] trek to the pond.

The rub, of course, was that J.B. had told me th[at] he'd also been out of it. If that was the case, why hadn[t] drugs been found in his Jack Daniel's? And if he wasn[t] drugged, why hadn't he noticed his wife being carrie[d] off?

Since only the Baileys had been doctored, it had [to] have been done by someone who knew J.B. and Abb[y] very well. Well enough to know that he wouldn't tou[ch] the Baileys and that she would.

Gloria Covarrubias immediately came to min[d]. She'd been the one to pack all of the food, as well as th[e] whiskey. All of that had been confiscated by the poli[ce] after Abby's death was reported, so there was no way [to] switch bottles. Unless the killer had exchanged the do[c] tored bottle of Jack Daniel's with a clean one that nig[ht] either before or after killing Abby.

I picked up the phone and called Emily Rose back.

"I know it's stupid, but those bottles were dusted f[or] prints, right?"

"As far as I know, but that's not our job."

"I know, I just thought maybe you might have hea[rd] something."

"More importantly is what I haven't heard. A[n]

hat I haven't heard is that anyone else's fingerprints
ve shown up anywhere. They're not looking too far
yond J.B. Calendar."

Discouraged, I still needed to check out implications
Abby's having Lou Gehrig's disease. I placed a quick
ll to Charley Bell asking him if he could dig up some
formation for me.

"Sure thing, Ellis, we're heading into my time of
y," he assured me.

After hanging up, I let Petunia out of the back porch
d took my glass of wine to the pond and settled into
e of the Adirondack chairs. The hot night air settled on
e like a cloak. Now that the sun was down, the cicadas
d ceased their singing. A lone coyote who sounded
e he was somewhere down along the Cañada del Oro
ash sang a sprightly solo as I stared at the still water of
e pond.

What in the hell was going on? The thought had
ssed my mind more than once that J.B. had killed
oby and had hired me to make things look good. But
as he really that stupid? Stupid enough to not doctor
s own bottle of booze if he really had killed her? Even a
azed bull rider could surely figure out the implications
his dead wife's whiskey was loaded with sedatives and
s was not. And even with the worst-ever hangover,
ouldn't a jury have trouble believing he'd actually slept
rough her abduction?

On the other hand, if he had been drugged, it was a
etty slick trick for the real killer to swap the bottles of
ck Daniel's to further implicate J.B.

Gloria, if she was the killer, could not possibly have
ted alone. Almost as wide as she was tall, she didn't
ok fit enough to walk the distance from the camp site
the stock pond. Even if she had been able to do all the
st of it, there was no way that she could have carried
oby, even taking time to rest along the way.

No, if Gloria Covarrubias was involved, as I was be-
nning to suspect she was, she had to have had an ac-

complice. But who? While her husband, José, was th
logical choice, how did that explain the extra deposi
and why Gloria opened up her own separate accoun
Was she hiding that extra money from her husband?

If the deposits were in fact related to Abby's murde
then the field of possibilities narrowed to those who ha
an extra $28,000 to throw around. J.B. could have easi
taken that out of the million that Abby had given hir
Peter would also have had no trouble coughing up th
money. Lateef Wise's church looked like it could surviv
a twenty-thousand-plus hit, and hadn't Charley Bell to
me that Laurette's father was a doctor in St. Martir
Maybe she dipped into a trust fund somewhere.

While Jackie Doo Dahs didn't look like she had tw
nickels to rub together, I still couldn't discount her. Lov
and greed were powerful motivators. Besides, J.B. ha
admitted that he'd been giving her money. I guess th
question now was, how much? Calendar had marrie
her twice, so would it have been unreasonable for her
think that if she had Abby out of the way he wou
take her to the altar again?

But I had a new twist. The Lou Gehrig's. Dr. Mullc
had known about Abby's disease and he had died
tragic death. Was that related? And what did the Lc
Gehrig's have to do with Abby's murder?

I felt a cold nose on the palm of my hand. Mrs. Fierc
had joined me.

"So what do you think, old girl. Who's our villain?"

Her response was to lick my fingers.

I leaned back and studied the night for answers.

The only thing I saw was the constellation Libr
high in the evening sky.

Somehow, seeing the scales made me think that
would eventually sort it all out.

38

WHEN I ARRIVED AT THE STAGE STOP OFFICE THE NEXT MORN-
ing the flag was up on the old mailbox. Charley had left
me a fat envelopeful of information on Lou Gehrig's disease. Now that I had a computer, I suppose I could have
tried to find the stuff myself. But I also knew that I was
never going to be very adept on the damned thing and
that I'd find a lot of dead ends on the Information
Superhighway. As far as I was concerned, Charley and I
were a team, and I wasn't going to steal his job.

As I read through Charley's notes I learned a little bit
more about the disease. The bottom line was a loss of
muscle control that would eventually lead to paralysis. If
you had Lou Gehrig's, the nerve cells controlling muscle
movements would die, and you'd eventually waste
away. Your arms, legs, torso, throat, tongue and finally
breathing muscles would progressively weaken until you
were totally dependent on life-saving machines. Among
others, the disease had recently taken another famous
baseball player, Catfish Hunter.

No wonder Abby was on Prozac.

I was studying this new information when the
phone rang. It was María López Zepeda with bad news.

"He flunked," she said.

"Shit."

"Right. But that doesn't mean he's guilty."

"Well, I'd feel better about things if he'd aced it."

"I tried to tell him this could happen, but he was insistent. He just knew he'd pass." Although María wa trying to keep the accusation out of her voice, she wasn doing a very good job of it.

"Do you think he did it?"

"I don't think in those terms," she said. "My job is see that he gets the best possible defense I can give hir Period."

"Mine isn't." My job wasn't that cut-and-drie There was nothing tying me to J.B. Calendar other tha our signed contract. Part of my deal was that I could c and run at any time. While I've never had a client befo that I *knew* was guilty of that which he or she was hirir me to investigate, supporting a murderer was anoth thing altogether.

"Just because he flunked the test doesn't mean he guilty," Maria repeated, trying to assuage the doubt sl heard in my voice. "A lot of things affect these tests—th subject's anxiety, physical or mental problems, their pe sonal discomfort. Sometimes they're excessively interr gated before the test."

"I thought these guys were pros."

"Oh, they are. I'm not saying that happened in th case, I'm just saying that it's one of the variable Indifference to a question can even affect things."

I couldn't imagine J.B. being indifferent to bein asked about his wife's murder.

"My point, Trade, is that the tests are not infallib When you're measuring blood pressure, pulse, respir tion and electrical conductivity all simultaneously, prol lems can, and do, occur."

"I think I'd better have a talk with J.B.," I said befo hanging up.

◆   ◆   ◆

An hour and a half later I was checking into the Pima County jail for the second time in a week. When J.B. appeared in the professional visitor's room this time, he looked even more haggard than he had on my earlier visit.

He walked in saying, "I didn't do it, Trade. I swear."

It was beginning to sound like a mantra.

"I should have listened to María. She told me not to do it. That it could turn out this way."

"Well, she should have figured out that anyone who was stupid enough to get on a pissed-off bull would be stupid enough to try to ride a lie detector test," I said.

My feeble attempt at humor brought a slight smile to his face. "At least I'm glad I didn't take one of theirs," he said, nodding toward the officer behind the window.

"Yeah," I agreed. "By the way, I'm sorry I missed your call the other day."

"I am too. Maybe you could have talked me out of it."

"I doubt it."

"How's the investigation coming? Have you found out anything that's gonna help me?"

While I had a lot of suspects, I couldn't in all honesty say that I had, so I just gave a slight nod. "Did you know that Abby was sick?"

He was startled. "Sick? You mean depressed? She was a little depressed a while back."

"But you don't know why?"

"I just assumed it was some woman thing."

Poor thing. Didn't he realize that his bride, thirty-two years older than he, was long past menopause or the normal female mood swings?

"She was diagnosed with Lou Gehrig's disease."

"The baseball guy? What's that?" His face wrinkled in surprise and concern. If he'd known about Abby's sickness, he was doing a great job of covering it up.

"It's a serious illness, a debilitating one that eventually kills you."

It took a minute for this to sink in.

"Christ." He wiped the back of his hand across his mouth. "Why didn't she tell me?"

"Clarice thinks she would have, she was just trying to figure out how. She was afraid that it would affect your relationship."

"Bullshit. I loved her. Why do people keep having trouble with that? Sure, she was a little older than me, but so what? If she'd been twenty-two everyone would have thought *that* was okay."

He was right about that. Unfortunately people aren't as forgiving or as understanding of the May-December thing when it swings the other way. But then, in J.B.'s case, if he'd married someone thirty-two years younger than he, he'd have had a four-year-old for a bride.

"The guy who diagnosed her was killed the same weekend as Abby," I said.

"Dr. Mullon?"

I nodded. "He was shot in his carport. There might be a connection between that and Abby and her Lou Gehrig's."

"What kind of a connection?"

I shrugged.

"How long would she have had it?"

"I don't know. Sometimes loss of hand coordination is one of the first symptoms and she was starting to do that. She was dropping little things at the house and she dropped that bottle at La Gitana."

"Yeah, but we'd had a lot to drink that night. That doesn't mean anything." He was defending her against her illness, even in death.

"Trust me, J.B., Abby had it."

With bowed head, he cradled his thick curly head in his hands. "God, I just don't get it, Trade. I don't get any of it. Why didn't she tell me? Maybe I could have helped her in some way. Didn't she trust me?"

I thought of his relationship with Jodie Austin and with his ex-wife, Jackie Doo Dahs, but said nothing.

"J.B., I need to know about the money you gave Jackie."

When he looked up, I could see that his eyes were red and tearing.

"What about it?"

"How much did you give her and when?"

He sighed deeply. "God, I don't know. Seems like after Abby and I were married I was always giving Jackie money. A couple of hundred here, a couple of hundred there."

"Out of your million?"

He looked stunned. "You know about that, too?"

Jesus. He hires an investigator and then is surprised when he finds out that I'm discovering things about him? Go figure.

"Yeah, J.B., I'm finding out about a lot of stuff. This would have been easier from the get-go if you'd come clean about a few things."

"I know, I know." He held up his hands. "I'm sorry about that. But I swear I'm not holding anything back now. I can't protect anyone anymore, not Jackie, not myself."

"So, how much, J.B.?" I had to know if Jackie Doo Dahs had had the means to pay Gloria.

I watched his index and middle finger tap the table as he thought about my question. "I don't know, maybe eight, nine thousand dollars. Why?"

"Gloria has been depositing pretty good chunks of money in a separate bank account. She opened it about three months ago."

"How much?"

"Around twenty-eight thousand dollars as near as we can tell." It was a far cry from the money he had given his twice ex-wife.

He whistled. "You think that has something to do with Abby's death?"

"I don't know," I said frankly. "I'm checking it out."

We talked for a while longer and I was about to leave

when I remembered Stella Ahil and her saguaro harvesting camp.

"J.B., I've got to ask you again, are you sure that you didn't see anyone in the Baboquivaris either when you were out riding, or Friday or Saturday night?"

"No, we didn't run into any hikers or riders or anyone like that."

"I went back to your camp site and found some people out there harvesting saguaro fruit. I was wondering if they'd been there before."

His face lit up. "God, I forgot! We were riding back to the tank on Saturday to water the horses and there was an old beat-up truck, one of those Jap jobs, parked on one of the back roads. We rode right by it and the bed was full of junk—buckets, tarps, that kind of stuff. Maybe it belonged to them."

"But you didn't see anyone?"

He shook his head. "Just a blue truck."

Suddenly I knew that I had to talk to Stella Ahil again. Maybe she or her invisible friend had seen something after all.

39

As I left the jail I caught a blurb on the front page of the morning paper in one of the machines outside. I plunked coins into the slot and retrieved the newspaper—an extravagance since my *Arizona Daily Star* was still waiting to be picked up at the end of the lane.

When I flipped to the Metro section I found Lateef Wise's face staring out at me. He was on the business end of what looked like a chrome-plated shovel, breaking ground for his new day care center. "Heiress' Gift Endows Baby Center" read the headline. Funny he hadn't mentioned the ground breaking yesterday. And during our first meeting hadn't he said he was going to put in the day care center *after* the estate was settled? Why the rush now?

There was nothing new in the story, but I had to hand it to Wise to get PR on the back of a dead woman. It seemed too soon after Abby's death to be making any press releases about what her legacy would or would not have endowed. It occurred to me that he had a lot of faith and I wondered how he was financing his construction project until the estate was settled.

A few minutes later I stopped at a pay phone at a Circle K on Mission Road and waited ten minutes for a stringy-haired young man to finish convincing what I assumed was a young woman on the other end of the line how much he loved her.

The phone book had been ripped off so I had to call Directory Assistance for the phone number of Baboquivari High School out in Sells. Since Stella Ahil had told me she taught English, I figured she was probably at either the junior high or high school.

Many of the Tucson schools have gone to a year-round schedule and I was hoping that the Sells high school had followed suit. Unfortunately this was not the case and my quarters went for naught as a recording came on the other end of the line.

I punched in Charley's number next.

"Ellis, did you hear—"

"No jokes. I'm at a pay phone melting. Did you get anything on Stella Ahil yet?"

"Yes and no."

"Great. How about the yes part?"

"You were right, she teaches English at Baboquivari High, but they're down for the summer. I've got a phone number for her."

I scribbled the number down on a corner of the newspaper.

"But I can't get a twenty on her." Charley reverted to his old CB jargon, the language he'd spoken before he'd gotten into computers. "She's listed everywhere as a Sells post office box."

I groaned.

"Wait, there's hope," he chuckled. "I ran the license plate you gave me. The truck belongs to her nephew Benny Francisco, who lives out in Topawa southeast of Sells."

"There's good news in all of this, right?"

He gave me an address and directions that he'd pulled off something called mapquest.com. He says it's not only free but will give you a map and written directions to any location in the country.

I thanked him and headed back to Priscilla.

I hung a right at Ajo and headed west, past the saguaro-dotted hillsides of the Tucson Mountain Park and past the turnoff to the Arizona-Sonora Desert Museum, past all the private airplanes at Ryan Field and past Marstellar Road where I frequently team-pen at Bishop's Arena. The saguaros quickly gave way to a grassy plain.

I finally arrived at Three Points. This time, instead of turning south toward Sasabe I kept straight and drove toward Sells.

Now the landscape boasted creosote bushes, probably the only desert plant that can survive not years, but decades of drought. The first bush to settle in the desert after the Ice Age, it's not uncommon for a creosote to live for a thousand years. Its longevity is helped, in part, by the fact that its resin does not appeal to cattle so they leave it alone.

The great white tower of the famed Kitt Peak National Observatory was ahead of me as I drove. After finally convincing the Indians that the facility and its people with the long eyes would not desecrate the sacred peak, the observatory was established in the late 1950s. Situated high in the Quinlan Mountains, it's a great landmark that can be seen from forty miles away.

The highway was dotted with roadside crosses signifying people who had been killed on the road, an old Mexican custom dating back to the eighteenth century. The crosses, or *crucitas*, usually made of iron or wood, depending upon the deceased's family members' talents, were dressed with bright plastic flowers. Many were paired with small shrines featuring tall glass religious candles bearing pictures of the Virgin Mary. There were more crosses than I'd ever seen along a single stretch of road before, and in an effort to pass the time more quickly, I began mentally counting them. I was up to ten before I passed the Coyote Convenience Store.

That I was on the Tohono O'odham Reservation became quickly apparent as I passed turnoffs to places with names like Ali Chuckson, Nawt Vaya, Pan Tak, Haivana Nakya and Chiawuli Tak.

I drove the speed limit since in spite of the fencing on both sides of the road, there were quite a few thin cattle browsing along the verge.

When I finally passed the modern Baboquivari High School I had counted thirty-three roadside crosses. A record for me.

I took the turnoff into Sells, the tribal headquarters and largest town on the Tohono O'odham Reservation. Not exactly a booming metropolis, Sells has grown from a sleepy little Papago village with one of the few reliable water supplies to a town with a modern Basha's supermarket, video rentals and a bank. Papago is still stuck in my brain since they went by that name for hundreds of years until 1986 when they decided that being known as the Bean People wasn't seemly, so the entire tribe opted for a name change to the Tohono O'odham, the Desert People.

Known for their baskets, the prices of which can range from twenty to hundreds of dollars, the twenty-four thousand Tohono O'odham are a scrappy bunch. With no permanent stream or lake on the reservation, both the people and their cattle have learned how to survive long periods of drought, interrupted only occasionally by the miracles of rain. Their huge desert reservation, encompassing almost three million acres, is second in size only to that of the Navajo.

Like many tribes, gambling has come to the Tohono O'odham. While it's certainly brought its problems, it's also helped pull the tribe out of bitter poverty. Their Desert Diamond Casino earns close to $80 million a year, some of which is distributed to each of the tribal members.

Fortunately a farsighted tribal chairman, encouraged by twenty-nine other tribes in the country who have successfully started their own community colleges, managed to earmark some of the casino revenue for such a project. In a few years, the local students won't have to make the long trek into Tucson's Pima Community College. The college will also keep them on the reservation, living comfortably in their own communities.

I studied the directions that Charley had dictated over the phone and turned left at the road fork a short way out of Sells. Now I was on tribal Highway 19 heading south for Topawa.

I drove through the small Burro Mountains and then the road became flat, the country stark and bleak, I imagine much the way it has been for thousands of years. These Indian lands are so unattractive that there was never any real threat of anyone else wanting them, so these reservation boundaries weren't even established until this century.

The people here take advantage of their vast space, and while there are dozens of tiny villages scattered about, there are still some families living in remote outlying areas. I glanced at Charley's directions again, fairly sure that I would find Stella Ahil's nephew living in the general locale of Topawa.

The vistas are long out here, with the naked eye being stretched for mile after endless mile, the flat desert plains and valleys occasionally broken up by hills and mountain ranges. As I drove, I never lost sight of the towering Baboquivari Peak to the east.

If I kept on the highway I'd eventually hit the Mexican border, marked by a barbed wire and wooden fence at the San Miguel gate. When the U.S. bought thirty thousand square miles of land from Mexico during the Gadsden Purchase of 1854, no one considered the people living here. The result was that the traditional Tohono O'odham homelands were split, with thirteen hundred of the tribe's members currently living south of the border.

It's a catch-22, for although members living in Mexico are eligible for tribal benefits—including Indian

Health Services—many of them cannot enter Arizona legally since they have no documentation of their birthplace. While tribal members work on getting Congress to authorize passport waivers, the border questioning, hassling and even deportation continue.

As I drove, I noticed that the Tohono O'odham cattle, never plump to begin with, were painfully thin. The bags, even of those few who had calves by their sides, were shriveled and looked as dry as the land. Out here in a good year, five to eight inches of rain would fall. This was not a good year. Seeing the cross-bred suffering cattle made me think of my own herd.

Twenty minutes later I was in Topawa. Besides the large new governmental complex and the tiny post office, the only other building grouping of any note here is the San Solano Mission and a few white stucco and rock buildings clustered around the old church.

Those mapquest directions were good and I turned right before the mission onto a dusty, rutted road. I drove for a mile or so and then hung another right onto the road where Benny Francisco lived. I drove slowly down the lane, past a few decrepit house trailers with junk-filled yards, rusted cars and faded clothing on the line, past a dead tree that was blooming discarded tires, past a flattened coyote and past two scrawny horses snuffling in the dirt for something to eat.

Finally I pulled up to a tired gray slump block house, its front yard adorned with a huge wooden play center with a nifty fort on top, swings and a plastic slide. There were a few scattered children's toys in the dirt yard— what looked like an old faded Fisher-Price farm barn, a bald doll missing her left arm, and child-sized Melmac plates and cups along with a huge satellite dish, one of the old kind.

I was hoping that Benny Francisco, if he was home— his wife if he was not—could tell me where I could find his aunt. She hadn't been exactly forthcoming when I'd seen her in the Baboquivaris so calling her to alert her to

ny visit was the last thing I wanted to do. Unfortunately,
his was my only hope before I'd have to make that
phone call.

I opened the ratty aluminum screen door and
knocked on the bleached, blistered wood of the front
door. All I could hear as I stood there waiting for some-
ne to answer was the steady hum of the swamp cooler.

Although my long hair was swept up in a ponytail, it
was hotter here than in Tucson or La Cienega and as I
stood there, I could feel the sweat begin to pool under
my collar. While I'd taken a good swig of water before
leaving the truck, my mouth was dry again. It really was
too damned hot to be out hunting people in Topawa,
Arizona.

The door opened slowly and as it did I was surprised
to find myself facing none other than Stella Ahil. A small
toddler-sized child with brown skin and matching eyes
was clinging to her baggy cotton shorts.

"Hello again," I said, stunned that it would be this
easy.

She squinted, as though she was trying to place me.

"Trade Ellis. I met you out in the Baboquivaris."

"Oh, right." She didn't sound all that thrilled to see
me.

"I'm wondering if I might talk to you."

Somewhere in the bowels of the house a baby cried.

"I'm baby-sitting. I don't have time." She started to
close the door but I stopped it with my hand, earning a
splinter in the process.

"It's really important, Mrs. Ahil." I had no idea if she
was married or not, but thought this a prudent form of
address. "I can't go away."

She sighed deeply and I could see the acquiescence
in her face. "All right then, come in."

The toddler gave me a wary look as I followed Stella
into the house. Then he walked over to the television
and turned up the volume before settling onto a beanbag
in front of a cartoon.

"I have to get the baby," Stella said and it sounde like a good idea to me, since the wailing infant and th television had a most unpleasant concerto going on.

She returned with a plump dark-haired baby whos screams had now diminished to whimpering status. I fo lowed Stella into the kitchen where she retrieved a bott from the refrigerator, put it in a plastic sleeve full of wa ter and popped the whole thing in the microwave, all th while jiggling the hungry child on her hip.

"I visited my client," I began saying while we waite for the microwave to finish. "And he remembers seein your truck out in the mountains."

The microwave timer went off and Stella Ab grabbed the bottle, shook it, and expertly tested it on th inside of her wrist. Satisfied that it was not too hot, sh plopped it into the delighted baby's mouth.

"He described it to a tee."

She gave me a blank look. "I don't have a truck."

"Right. I meant your nephew's truck. Benny Nissan."

She grunted.

I waited a minute before asking, "You were out ther that night, weren't you, Stella?"

A long sigh escaped her mouth and she finally no ded. "We left when we heard the sirens. When you sav me, I came back for the fruit I'd left behind."

"We?"

"A friend was with me."

"Did you park in the same place?"

She rotated the bottle in the baby's mouth. "Just u from there, on the far side of the pond."

I searched my memory banks for a visual image c the stock pond. The berm on the far side would hav prevented anyone coming in from the southeast, the d rection of J.B. and Abby's camp site, from seeing Stella saguaro camp.

"You saw something, didn't you?" It was a gu hunch.

She nodded, but would not look at me.

"You were parked close to the tank, maybe even within the quarter-mile limit. There was a full moon." I was talking to myself as much as to her. "J.B. and Abby were parked not far away. They came in from drinking, they were partying. There was no need for them to be quiet, after all no one was around."

I watched her impassive face, but it told me nothing.

"It was a still June night and we all know how sound can carry across the desert. Even if you'd been asleep"—I was remembering the cots out in the open air—"their noise could have awakened you."

She set the bottle down on the counter and threw the baby up on her shoulder where she patted its back in an effort to get a burp out of it.

"I'm pretty close, aren't I, Stella?"

She gave a slight nod of her head.

"I don't have it exactly right, though, do I?"

She disappeared with the baby and returned a minute later.

"Let's go outside where I can have a smoke," she said, opening the dirty sliding glass door to the barren backyard. She left it open so the evaporative cooler would blow out, giving us some small comfort from the day's heat.

We stepped out onto a tiny cement porch that harbored a washing machine. A cardboard box was on top of it with tiny mews coming out. I glanced inside and saw a thin gray tabby cat nursing three tiny kittens.

Stella lit her cigarette and threw the match out onto the dirt.

"My friend heard them. I slept through it. But they were too far away and he couldn't see them."

Invisible was a man. Interesting. I kept quiet.

"After a while things settled down and he went back to sleep. A little bit later a car woke him up. He said it sounded like it was coming up the road we were on. He could hear it, but there weren't any lights."

I nodded, again remembering the full moon. If some one were driving very slowly up the old dirt road, they could navigate without headlights.

"He has trouble sleeping, my friend, so after that he got up, had a cigarette, and that's when he saw it."

"Saw what?"

"The light in the desert. He saw someone with a flashlight walking through the desert toward them."

"Toward J.B. and Abby's camp site?"

She nodded.

"He was curious about what was going on so he climbed up on the tank and watched the light walk across the desert. Then he lost it."

"He was probably wondering what was going on," I said, encouraging her to continue her story.

"Yes. He said it wasn't long until he saw the light again. He waited and watched it for a long time as they made their way through the desert."

They. She'd said they.

"He thought maybe it was something to do with drugs, and that's why the car had come in without lights and why the man had walked across the desert to the other place with a flashlight."

"He saw a man?" My impatience was getting the best of me.

"I'm getting to that. As the flashlight got closer to the pond, he slipped behind the berm of the tank and took cover under a hackberry bush. The man came into the pond and he was carrying something on his back."

I was suddenly aware that I was holding my breath.

"He walked right into the pond and when the water got to his chest, he pulled the thing off his back and pushed it out in front of him and held the bundle under water."

"Did she struggle?"

She shook her head. "We didn't know it was a woman until we heard it on the radio the next day."

"What'd the man look like?"

"He couldn't tell. There was a moon, but it wasn't light enough to see his face."

"Was he huge?" I was thinking of Lateef Wise, who was almost a giant. If Stella's friend hadn't seen the face, he probably wouldn't be able to identify the carrier as a black man.

"I don't know. I didn't ask him."

"I need to talk to your friend."

She shook her head. "That's impossible."

"I have to, Stella. A woman's been murdered and he's an eyewitness to what happened."

She continued shaking her head.

"Is he married?"

"Heavens no." She was shocked that I'd consider that he'd carry on with a married man. "It's nothing like that."

"He's got to come forward and tell the police what he saw that night."

At the mention of the police her eyebrows shot up. "No police. He didn't see anything."

"Stella, look, you're an educated woman. You teach English at the high school. You must know how important this is."

She thought about this for a minute and then made her admission. "He's illegal." She gave me sad look. "You know how that would turn out."

Ah, there it was. Her invisible friend was an illegal alien, most likely a Mexican man who had come up for a better job. The last thing he'd want to do was make his presence known to the authorities. He'd be deported in no time flat. No wonder he'd been invisible in the Baboquivaris. He was ducking *La Migra*, the Border Patrol. And of course he would have been cautious, sleeping lightly, which is why he'd seen the murder.

"Cripes." My mind raced. Would the cops give him immunity on the immigration issue in exchange for his testimony about what he saw at the Baboquivari stock pond? I had no idea. It was something I'd have to explore.

As I left Stella Ahil I was simultaneously thrilled with my discovery and stumped by how in the hell I was going to exploit it.

40

WHEN I GOT BACK TO THREE POINTS I STOPPED AT THE Chevron and used the pay phone there to call María López Zepeda with my news of a possible eyewitness. She was not only thrilled, but was going to go to work immediately on the immunity issue for Stella Ahil's illegal escort.

"J.B.'s pretty down," she said.

"Well, I guess jail time will do that to you."

"This will really cheer him up. I'll call the county attorney's office right away and see what we can work out on getting the mystery man off the immigration hook."

As I hung up and walked back to Priscilla, the thought occurred to me that maybe I *could* use a cell phone.

What was I coming to? First the computer and now considering a cell phone? Still, it would beat sweating out in the heat or waiting for some starstruck teenybopper to finish his phone call to his girlfriend. I wondered how much one would cost.

By the time I got back to the Vaca Grande it was 112 degrees. Like ranchers everywhere, I'd been keenly attuned to the weather forecasts and there was no hint of

rain in sight. It was still too early. Mid-June is the worst
of the worst. The days can skyrocket as high as 115; a
necessary evil so that the thunderheads can build up into
the fierce thunderstorms that, if we're lucky, will come in
early July. This year, it was looking like we weren't going
to see much in the way of rain.

As I drove in, I spotted Quinta harvesting tomatoes,
cucumbers, peppers and squash. There was no sign of
Juan Ortiz's truck so he was probably making his rounds
in La Cienega. I parked, greeted the dogs and the pig, and
walked over to the bountiful garden.

"How's it going?"

She handed me a huge zucchini, obviously one that
had been hiding under the leaves for weeks.

"Isn't that amazing? They practically grow in your
hand," she said, wiping her sweaty face with the sleeve
of her blouse.

I laughed, my evil, celibate mind thinking of other
things.

"There was a guy who came to see you." She
dropped the squash into a five-gallon bucket that was almost overflowing with vegetables.

"Who was it?"

She reached into her shorts and pulled out a card.

Peter Van Thiessen.

That's all it said. Sort of like those old-time calling
cards that rich people used to use. Hell, maybe they still
did. A useless card that gave only the name. The kind of
card the butler was supposed to trot upstairs with to announce a visitor's presence to the lady of the house.

I put the card in my shirt pocket. "What did he
want?"

"He said it wasn't important. Just that he was in the
neighborhood and thought he'd stop in."

If being on Highway 77 driving down from Oracle to
Tucson counted as "being in the neighborhood," then
Peter would always be in the neighborhood.

"How's the truck coming?"

"Don't know," she shrugged. "Tata ran Dad up to Prego's a little while ago. They're going to work on it tonight."

Playing all the games of who dun it, coupled with the little sleep I'd been getting lately, had tired me out. When shortly before ten I found myself rereading paragraphs, I knew it was time to turn out the lights. As I drifted off to sleep, the last image I had was of Abby at roundup, dusting herself off after her fall and looking beautiful in her Thievin' Vaqueros hat.

The gunshot woke me up. And another one quickly followed it. Blue and Mrs. Fierce went apeshit, barking and snarling at the French doors of my bedroom. I leaped out of bed, shaking.

What in the hell was going on? Whatever it was, it was big-time.

I yanked the bedside table drawer open, pulled out my Smith & Wesson and then fumbled around for my glasses since there was no time for putting in contacts.

Dressed only in my thin cotton nightgown, I ran to the kitchen door and stared out at the bunkhouse. Although there were no lights on, it looked as though the front door was wide open. Shit! Why was it open?

I thought Rafael Félix was dead. Had Cori Elena been wrong about that? Had the story of his death been a setup? Had they finally come for her? Two shots. One for Cori Elena and one for Martín? I felt the tears well in my eyes and wiped them away.

I cracked the kitchen door and listened, but heard only the wail of a single coyote who sounded like he was down along the creek. There was no sound of people running or the starting of car engines.

"Stay," I hissed to the dogs as I slithered out the door, closing it behind me. Petunia grunted, but made no move to get up as I quickly crossed the screened porch.

I nudged the door open and slipped out.

Barefoot, I sprinted across the yard to the pond, trying to stay in the shadows, running a zigzag path, figuring that my white nightie would make a great target against the black night. My heart thundered in my chest. I skirted the water and stopped under one of the huge cottonwoods and listened again. Still nothing but the stupid yapping coyote. That and my own heavy breathing. Jesus, if anyone was out here, he'd know for sure I was around. I peeked around the heavy trunk of the cottonwood and saw that the bunkhouse door was still open, the lights still out.

I started across the last stretch to Martín's house, inching along in shadow, willing my bare feet to tread silently as they dug into the tiny rocks on the ground.

I was halfway there when I heard something moving alongside the bunkhouse. I ducked back, held my breath and listened as it came closer, closer. Suddenly a huge shadow started coming around the corner of the old adobe. I jumped as my breath huffed out of my mouth in fear. My right arm shot up with the .38 in my hand as I instinctively braced it with my left, prepared to take a shot.

The shadow kept coming. My God, it was enormous! Could it be Lateef Wise? I held my breath, not sure what I was looking at, but not wanting to give myself away if he had not already seen me, and not willing to take a shot until I knew for sure what my target was.

The shadow ignored me as it walked around to the front of the bunkhouse. It was only when it got in front of the opened door that I became aware of a dim light from inside. And in that light I could make out the silhouette of Old Hadley's ears.

It was the mule! He'd somehow gotten out of the corral and was taking a nighttime stroll. I breathed a sigh of relief and lowered my gun.

Still, the mule sure as hell hadn't left the bunkhouse door open or fired the two shots I'd heard.

Old Hadley was at the opened door and for a minute

I thought he was going to go inside. Instead he started nudging the wooden door with his nose, banging it loudly against the wall. If they were okay, why weren't Cori Elena and Martín coming out? Shit.

Taking advantage of the noise he was making, I dashed across the open ground. Once I hit the corner of the adobe bunkhouse, I stopped, flattening myself along the face of the building, trying to minimize myself as a target. My ear pressed to the cool adobe wall, I tried to make out sound from inside, but the thick wall was too good an insulator and nothing came through.

At least no one had shot Old Hadley. Yet.

I inched along the adobe and when I got to the living room window I crouched below it and did a duck walk as I crossed underneath. Straightening up on the other side I held my revolver close to my chest with both hands.

Old Hadley, probably afraid that I was going to catch him and put him back in the corral, took one look at me, shook his head in disgust and walked off.

Standing beside the door, with the wall for cover, I listened again. Was someone crying? Thank God. One of them had to still be alive. But which one?

Pressed against the adobe, I reached out with my right hand and nudged the front door open with the barrel of the .38. Nothing. I waited a few seconds and then took a deep breath, mostly to spur my courage, and finally snuck a look around the threshold.

Only the stove light was on, and in spite of Cori Elena's packed boxes of dishes, I could still make out a man sprawled across the floor. He was just in front of the bedroom door, and a dark stain was pooling on the cold brown cement. It had to be blood. He was heavyset and although I couldn't see his face, I knew from looking at his backside that it was not Martín or Juan.

The bedroom was dark and someone in there was crying.

"Cori Elena?" I yelled.

"*Sí, venga*, Trade! *Pronto!*"

I wasn't that eager to madly run into the dark house until I knew what was going on. "What's happening?"

"He's been shot! We need *ayuda*."

Martín had been shot? My heart plummeted to my feet as I fought the urge to rush to him. Christ! But I couldn't risk it or entering the bunkhouse to use the phone to call for help until I assessed the risk. There was no sense in all of us getting shot. If I was dead, I'd be no help at all.

"Cori Elena, listen to me, how many of them are there?" It sounded like I was screaming.

She was crying hysterically now, unable to answer, if she'd heard me at all.

"Think!" I tried to keep the panic out of my voice.

She sounded like she was gasping for air, trying to catch her breath in between sobs. "*Uno*, I think," she finally said in a small voice.

She thinks? Shit. Why didn't she know? *Uno* was okay since I was pretty sure I knew where *uno* was. He was the rug on the floor. But *dos* or *tres* could be major trouble.

The bunkhouse was small. Not counting the bathroom, it was really just two rooms with only the one door coming in from the outside. The living/kitchen area and the bedroom where Cori Elena and Martín were holed up. Surely she'd know if someone else was in there with them. Wouldn't she?

Except for the corner to the right of the front door, I had a clear view of this part of the house, and other than my new friend sleeping on the floor there wasn't anyone else in it. I couldn't quit staring at the silhouette on the cement. He hadn't moved. If she was right about there only being one man, I was pretty sure he wasn't going anyplace.

Holding my .38 in firing position, I ducked and stepped inside, spinning as I aimed at the far, unseen corner. A shadow as large as my own stood there,

nstinctively I fired, realizing too late that I had just shot
carton of dishes, one of the stack of moving boxes that
ad been there when I'd had lunch. Cori Elena probably
adn't gotten around to unpacking them.

The room was empty. Quickly I pulled the front
oor closed and locked it behind me, knowing if there
vas another man in the bunkhouse that I'd probably
ealed our fates.

I could hear Cori Elena whispering in Spanish. Love
vords, telling Martín to hold on, to stay with her, that
he loved him.

About a foot in front of the man on the floor was a
leek chrome-plated automatic, its barrel pointed at the
pen bedroom door. I stepped gingerly around the man,
aking care not to place my bare feet in his blood as I
nelt down and retrieved his weapon. Now, with a gun
a each hand aimed at the middle of his back, I nudged
he intruder hard with the ball of my bare foot. There
vas no response, although his blood continued pooling.

I reached into the bedroom and groped for the light
witch along the inside wall, finally found it, flipped it
nd flooded the bedroom with light.

And got a real surprise.

Cori Elena, stark naked, was attempting to stanch his
leeding by holding a pillow over his stomach. Her
ands were covered with blood and tears ran down her
heeks.

"Trade, for the love of *Diós*, do something!"

I could tell by looking that it was bad. I dashed back
o the kitchen counter, grabbed the phone and dialed
11. As I quickly gave them the situation and directions
o the ranch, I was dimly aware of someone pounding on
he front door of the bunkhouse.

Hanging up the phone, I yelled to the portal. "We're
ll okay. Just a minute!"

Stepping back inside the bedroom, I took another
ook at the man on the floor with the pillow.

Jake Hatcher's color didn't look all that good. His

face was pale, almost the color of his gray-haired che[s]
that until now, I had never seen before. Wearing onl[y]
plaid boxer shorts, his eyes fluttered and he tried to rais[e]
a finger in greeting. I suppose it was a good sign that h[e]
recognized me.

"I'll hold that," I squatted next to Cori Elena and pu[t]
pressure against the thin pillow that was now turnin[g]
pink. The blood had seeped clear through it. "You bette[r]
put some clothes on. Your daughter's at the door."

41

The last sheriff's car left the Vaca Grande at dawn, just as Martín roared in in Prego's Land Rover. The ignition was barely off when he flew out of the vehicle.

"What the hell's . . ."

"It's okay, Martín. Everyone's okay." As I hugged him, I could feel him trembling and his body slumped with relief.

Quinta came up. "We're fine, Dad. Really."

Martín let go of me and embraced his daughter in a huge bear hug. "Freddy Brown was at the Circle K when he heard there were a lot of cops down here." He looked round. "Where's Dad?"

"Asleep," I answered. "Your dad slept through the whole thing and I couldn't see any reason to wake him up."

"Cori Elena?" Martín released Quinta and headed for the bunkhouse, which was surrounded by yellow police tape.

I grabbed his arm. "She's not here and you can't go in here until they're through with their investigation."

"She's at the hospital," Quinta answered the question on her father's face. "With Jake Hatcher."

Martín looked from one to the other of us for an explanation.

"It's a little complicated," I said. "Maybe we better talk over a cup of coffee."

Quinta left us alone and although it was painful for Martín and not particularly pleasant for me, I went through the whole bunkhouse scenario beginning with the shots I had heard and ending with the last sheriff detective leaving the ranch.

"I knew *chiquita*. But I thought it was something she'd get over," he finally confessed. "With Quinta here, I didn't want to think about it."

"Upsetting the apple cart?"

"Something like that. I thought if we could get away, maybe things would be better between the two of us." He got up from the scarred wooden table and retrieved the Mr. Coffee, refilling both our cups. "I guess I was just a coward."

"You're not a coward, Martín."

"Only when it comes to women," he said with a lopsided grin. "I guess he's her hero now."

"Well," I chose my words carefully, "I don't think there's any denying that if he hadn't been here, with you at Prego's, that it would have been a different scenario out there tonight."

He nodded. "And I'm grateful to him for that. For stopping whoever that was from hurting any of you."

"Probably he was just after Cori Elena for Rafael Félix's money."

"We'll never know that, will we?" In spite of the grim discoveries, Martín was actually sounding cheerful.

"Cori Elena told me Félix was dead and the detectives verified that so I'm wondering where the guy came from."

"*Los muertos no hablan.*"

"I know. Dead men tell no tales," I said as I drained my coffee.

◆   ◆   ◆

Although I'd been up for most of the night, I knew I wasn't going to have much luck sleeping during the day so I headed into town. I stopped at the stage stop and grabbed the picture of Abby and Peter that I had taken from her bedside table.

Although the business with Jake Hatcher and Cori Elena had derailed a lot of my thinking about the Abigail Van Thiessen case, still something had been nagging me, tickling the back of my mind. I was sure that the death of Samuel Mullon was somehow connected to her drowning. It was too much to buy into the coincidence of Abby's doctor's being randomly murdered the same day that she drowned. The deaths had to be related. But how? And who was next?

I headed into town, back to the university area. As I drove south on Campbell toward Third, a taxicab, unusual for Tucson, pulled sharply in front of me causing me to slam on my brakes. It then turned into the El Mercado Hotel just past the corner of Campbell and Speedway. As I gripped my steering wheel hard with both hands, the tickle in my head blossomed into a full-fledged theory.

I turned on Third and a half a block later parked in front of Dr. Mullon's house. Nothing had changed except the drought-stressed lawn and trees were now even more desperate for water. The zinnias were beyond salvation.

I grabbed my Circle K jug, which was half full of water and a few surviving ice cubes, locked the cab and headed out.

Since the living room draperies were still closed and there was no hint of human habitation, I dispensed with the doorbell formalities.

I didn't linger long where Mullon had been shot, preferring to take the small brick walkway next to the patio wall. Neglect was apparent here too as weeds struggled to peek through the used bricks.

This time I picked the area closest to the carport an
flattened my back against the wall, feeling the scorchin
heat of the masonry through my thin T-shirt. I closed m
eyes and tried to imagine how Mullon's killer could hav
stood in the exact same spot, in the dark, waiting for th
doctor to get home. It wasn't much of a stretch as th
scenario played out in my mind.

It was too hot to stay against the wall for long, s
once the image was set, I walked slowly north along th
path until it spilled out into a back alley that ran th
length of the block. The battle-scarred garbage cans tha
I'd seen earlier were gone—either taken in by someon
or stolen.

The alley was open, not sheltered by oleanders c
walls or homes, and the noise from the traffic o
Campbell was louder here. When I'd been here before I'
envisioned an easy getaway by the killer. He could hav
easily parked in the alley, hovered along the patio wa
until Mullon returned home, shot him and then jumpe
into his car and taken the alley either down to Campbe
Avenue or up to Tucson Boulevard.

That scenario had been incubating for a while an
now, perhaps prodded by my near miss with the taxica
at the corner, I found myself exploring a different theory

Instead of walking either east or west in the alley,
crossed it and walked between two houses that fronte
on Second Street. I crossed Second and repeated th
process until I was on the last alley before Speedway, th
one just north of First Street.

Now I had no choice. The neighborhood had ende
and only a chain link fence separated me from the con
ference center of the El Mercado Hotel and its parkin
lot.

Sweat was pouring off me as I took a long drink c
water and took the alley down to Campbell Avenue
Once there, I hit the sidewalk and walked the short dis
tance to the hotel.

Stepping into the refrigerated lobby was like enterin

walk-in freezer. I headed to the ladies' room where I lashed cold water on my heat-flushed face and refilled y water jug.

Looking at my reflection in the mirror I knew that I dn't look like an official anything—not a cop, a reporter even a private eye. In deference to the heat I'd piled y long hair on top of my head, but sweat-soaked ten- ils had escaped and long, wet ringlets framed my face. : least my mascara hadn't melted into raccoon eyes.

I was wearing a Zimectrin horse wormer T-shirt, a ir of old denim shorts and last year's Birkenstocks. ell, I didn't even look like a dirty-shirt cowgirl. I just oked hot.

Back in the lobby I skipped the registration desk en- ely. I knew that even if they had the information I was oking for, they'd be unlikely to share it with a private vestigator. Maybe Charley Bell would have luck with s sources. If not, eventually the Pima County sheriff's fice would come snooping around and the guest regis- r would then miraculously open. Even if that informa- on became available I knew that the name I was oking for would probably not be found on the guest g.

I picked up a brochure touting the amenities of the El ercado and found what I expected. Jumping on an ele- tor I rode up to the fourth floor.

Once there, I headed to the end of the hall and let yself through the glass door welcoming me to the EL ERCADO FITNESS CLUB. It was nearly empty this morning ith an overweight man doing very little damage to a ationary bicycle and an anorexic Japanese girl doing me stair step thing.

I approached the counter, which was bare except for plastic box with brochures advertising the fitness club d a sign-in ledger that was opened flat.

A bored young man with a shaved head and a dia- ond stud in his left ear sat behind the desk. As the door osed behind me he looked up from his *Ironman* maga-

zine. A television set behind him showed a group ⌐
string-bikini-clad young women doing something wi⌐
beach balls to jazzy, upbeat music. He reached over ar⌐
put the set in mute mode so the straining women we⌐
all prancing to inaudible music.

"Can I help you?"

"I hope so." I gave him my most engaging grin,
heat-rumpled card and thirty seconds to assimilate th⌐
information on it. Then I pulled a copy of the picture ⌐
Abby and Peter out of my hip pocket and slid it acros⌐
the desk. "I'm wondering if this man"—I talked very qu⌐
etly so the two guests couldn't hear me, and pointed ⌐
Peter Van Thiessen—"has used your facilities in the la⌐
thirty days or so."

"I'm sorry, I can't help you." He didn't even both⌐
looking at the picture. "We aren't allowed to give out ou⌐
guests' names."

"Oh I don't need his name," I assured him. "I ju⌐
need to know if you've seen him."

"I'm not sure I should do that," he said dubiousl⌐
"It's pretty close to giving out a name."

I retrieved the photograph. "Gosh, I was really ho⌐
ing you could help me with this. See, he's my uncle and
think he was in town recently to surprise me and I w⌐
gone, and now I want to surprise him." I was talking fa⌐
and fumbling in my pocket for two wrinkled twentie⌐
He watched with interest as I folded the bills int⌐
the picture. "But I don't want to do it if he didn't do it, y⌐
know?" What I was saying didn't make any sense at a⌐
but was the best I could come up with on short notice⌐
was counting on the twenties to distract him from m⌐
gibberish. "Are you sure you can't take another look?"
held the photograph out again.

He hesitated, but finally took my offering. Placir⌐
the picture under his desk light he studied it for a m⌐
ment before handing it back, along with the twentie⌐
"I'm sorry, but he sure doesn't look familiar." Regret wa⌐
genuine in his voice.

It was a dead end, but hunches frequently are.

I thanked him for his time and started to leave. My
nd was on the door when he said, "Wait!"

I turned back as he motioned me over to the desk,
ot eager to draw attention to his indiscretion. "Is there
ny chance he would have used the club after hours?"

I thought about this for a minute and then nodded
y head. "Sure, I suppose so."

"Do you have any dates?"

"Somewhere around June 5th or 6th."

He opened the cabinet doors on the video console
hind him and thumbed through a string of videotapes,
ally withdrawing one. After checking the date on the
ine, he turned back to the television set, withdrew
e beach ball bunnies and slipped the console tape into
e VCR.

"We have the video on when the club isn't staffed,
om eight to eleven at night," he said in a low voice. "For
curity and liability reasons."

In spite of the refrigeration, my heart began beating a
tle faster.

Glancing at the television monitor I was now looking
an empty fitness club. Other than a scroll across the
ottom of the tape with the date and time on it, there
as no one in the health facility, no moving machine,
d not a hint of life.

"It's empty," I whispered.

"The recorder's triggered by the front door. It keeps
ack of entries and exits, and it's supposed to go off
hen the last guest leaves the facility, but there's a little
t of a delay so you may get some empty space." He
ld up a remote control. "This one's the fast forward,"
e pointed to a black button toward the bottom of the
ntroller. "Stop. Pause. If someone comes in, be sure
ou hit stop immediately."

"Got it," I said, taking custody of the clicker.

He went back to his magazine and I started in on the
deo. I was surprised at how many people were using

the El Mercado's fitness facilities after hours. It was
slow process for me since I had to check every nev
comer. Then I'd try to fast-forward so I wouldn't have
witness their workouts, but another person would con
into the picture and I'd have to hit the rewind button a
then move slowly forward again.

I watched a strange assortment of people—all colo
ages and sizes—sweat and struggle with the machin
adjust their jock straps, pick their noses and scrat
themselves. My viewing reminded me to always keep
mind that someone might be watching what I was doi
and I made a silent vow to never readjust my underwe
in an empty elevator again.

My video sleuthing was interrupted several times
I managed to hit the stop button right before Your
Blood grabbed the remote control. Two women had no
captured the fat man's bicycle and one other and a tri
black man was on the Nautilus. Miss Japan was still d
ing her stair thing.

Finally after thirty minutes or so of video juggling
hit the jackpot.

"Yes!" I whispered.

"Ssh." My earringed friend looked up from his mag
zine to admonish me and then looked at the televisi
set. "Is that your uncle?"

He pointed to a tall, thin man with a deep tan and
shiny silver crew cut. The lighting picked up his uncor
monly high, chiseled cheekbones and the sunken ho
lows beneath them.

I nodded and watched as Peter Van Thiessen, dresse
in white gym shorts and a Hard Rock Cafe T-shi
signed the logbook. Across the bottom of the scre
snowy white letters read "June 6, 10:21 P.M." Now h
back was to the camera as he scanned the room for
suitable piece of exercise equipment.

Peter was a runner so I was pretty sure what h
would choose. I smiled as he selected the treadmill, b
my elation quickly evaporated when I realized that th

equipment was not in good camera range. It was in the far corner of the room and the only thing I could now identify was the fact that there was someone walking on the damned thing. Someone. Not a man or a woman. Just someone. While I was disappointed, I knew that with the proper equipment the video could easily be magnified and enhanced.

I sat through Peter's entire workout and then watched as he stepped off the treadmill and wiped his face and neck with a white terry cloth towel. He threw it in a bin in the center of the room, walked straight for the camera and disappeared.

I didn't have to rewind the tape to know what I'd seen. For although his time on camera hadn't amounted to much in the scheme of things, it was enough. There was no doubt in my mind that Peter Van Thiessen had been in the El Mercado Hotel Fitness Center on the night that Dr. Samuel Mullon had been killed. The same night that his sister, Abigail, had drowned in a remote stock tank in the Baboquivaris.

The other thing I was sure of was that Peter had neglected to share his early Tucson visit with anyone. Not with me. Not with the cops.

I hit the stop button.

"You have a log that they sign in? That thing he signed?"

The young man let out a deep, resigned sigh.

"In for a penny, in for a pound," I said, giving him a wink.

He reached for the ledger on top of the counter and shoved it over to me, hitting my elbow with the edge of it. He didn't apologize. "You know, I could lose my job over this."

"Hey you're doing your civic duty," I said, not eager to give him more than forty dollars. Besides, the police would be here soon enough and they'd get the information for free.

I thumbed through the ledger until I found June 6.

Everyone who had used the fitness center that day had presumably signed the book. I ran down the list of sign-in times until I got to 10:21 P.M. Written to the left of it was a scribbled scrawl that would put most doctors' prescription orders to shame. I studied the writing for a minute, but could not make out a capital P, V or T. The place for the room number was left conveniently blank. Somehow, Van Thiessen had neglected to sign himself out.

Clever. Not only was the name he'd signed illegible and the room number missing, but other than whatever name he'd registered in under downstairs, there would have been no way to trace him on paper to the El Mercado Hotel. Except for the videotape.

He'd had no clue that his exercise session had been recorded. Still, the scrawled name could have meant he was covering his bases. Otherwise, why would he have bothered to sign in at all? Could he have been afraid that an employee would have come in and notice his oversight and remember him for it? Or was it a CYA move in case he had been traced to the El Mercado? Of course I was there, he'd say, after all I signed in at the Fitness Club. Why would I do that if I was a murderer?

I closed the book and handed it back to the attendant. "You'll need to put that video"—I pointed to the television set—"and this in a safe place."

He opened up the ledger and put it back on the counter. "This is our sign-in book," he said smugly. "We don't put them away until they're filled and this one was only started in April."

"Suit yourself," I said. "But that may become state's evidence."

Leaving him with a stunned look on his face and forty bucks in his pocket, I was out the door.

42

By the time I made the trek back to Mullon's house on Third I found an empty Tucson police department black-and-white parked behind Priscilla. The officer was nowhere in sight.

I gingerly slipped the key in the driver's door and opened my truck, using the bottom of my T-shirt as a hot pad. We do that in summer here, for the metal on our cars gets hot enough to burn. I turned the ignition key and hit the power windows to let the hot air out.

Taking a healthy slug on my water, for I was drenched again with the heat and getting dehydrated, I pulled my registration out of the glove compartment and my driver's license out of my wallet. Then I sat on the parched grass under the shade of a palm tree and waited, for I was under no illusions that the police car had serendipitously appeared at the doctor's house.

A few minutes later a young red-faced male cop appeared, an opened notebook in hand. He looked kind of cute, but it was hard to tell with the blue cap shading his face and his mirrored shades shielding his eyes. Still, he was probably young enough to be my son, if I'd had one. It really is true that cops are getting younger all the time.

I liked it better when they made good fantasies. Hell, now even the police chief's too young.

He hovered over me for a minute. "Why don't you stand up?"

The thought had occurred to me, but for some reason I didn't like his suggesting it. "No, I'm fine."

The muscle in his jaw twitched.

"That your truck?" He pointed to Priscilla.

"Yep."

He jotted something in his pad.

"And you're . . ."

I handed him the registration and my license. I was still sitting on the grass and he was hovering over me. I was reasonably comfortable with the trunk of the palm tree supporting my back so I stayed put.

"Is this a moving violation?" I asked, immediately regretting my smart mouth.

He said nothing as he recorded my information on his pad. It seemed a painfully slow process. I suspected he'd gotten As on the Silent Sam routine but hadn't aced his Documents Class.

Finally done, he handed me back my paperwork. It was all bullshit since I was sure he'd already called in my plate. This was verified by his not returning to his car and radioing in my information.

"Ma'am, are you aware that this is the site of a homicide?"

Although death is not usually comic, he was entirely too serious. I read his badge number and name. George X. Houston.

"What's the X stand for?"

"What?"

"That X in your name. What's it stand for?"

Unless you're asking directions, cops usually don't like to be quizzed.

"Are you aware that a homicide was committed here?" He ignored my question and repeated his own.

"I didn't see any yellow tape like on TV."

"That's all over. A man was killed here. Right over there." He pointed to the carport.

I plucked dried grass off my shorts. "Samuel Mullon, July 6th, or maybe 5th."

"How do you know that?" I imagined his eyes narrowing behind the mirrored shades.

"Public record. I read the papers."

"Yes, ma'am, a lot of people do just that, and then they break into the deceased's house." The disgust was evident in his voice.

"Do I look like a burglar?"

"You'd be surprised what burglars look like. That truck of yours could hold a few things." His head jerked toward the street.

"Priscilla? Pilfered TVs and stereos?" I laughed.

"What's so funny about that and who's Priscilla?"

I stood up slowly and as I did so I realized he was about my height, five foot seven. I think he became aware of this at the same time and he took a couple of steps backward.

"Priscilla's my truck."

"I see," he said, although I was sure he didn't.

It was really too hot to continue the interrogation, so I came clean. "I'm here on business. I wanted to see where Dr. Mullon was murdered." I saw no reason to share with him that this was actually my second Third Street visit.

"Business?" Maybe he did have a sense of humor after all because the way it came out sounded a little bit like I imagined a guffaw to be. "What do you mean?"

"I'm a private investigator. I've been hired to look into Abigail Van Thiessen's death."

He didn't have to ask who she was.

"Hired by who?" He was definitely taken in by either the horse worming T-shirt or my hippie sandals.

"Hired by whom."

"What?"

"Whom. It's hired by whom."

His response was to cross his thick arms across his chest. "Just answer the question, ma'am."

"I'm sorry, I'm not at liberty to say." It was a deliberate taunt, but I didn't feel like sharing anything I didn't have to with him. I don't have anything against cops; I just didn't like this particular one.

"I didn't see you around the house or the yard."

I said nothing.

"So where were you?"

This was getting ridiculous. Sometimes cops think they have to know everything we're doing. Unfortunately a lot of people give them this information gratuitously so they've become accustomed to getting it.

"I went for a walk."

"In hundred and ten degree heat?"

"I like to walk." I shrugged and gave him a smile. When I got around to sharing what I had learned at the Mercado Hotel it wasn't going to be with some overzealous, bullying young beat cop.

I took some satisfaction in watching trickles of sweat slither down his cropped sideburns onto his face. He had to be a lot hotter in his uniform, wearing a forty-pound belt with flashlight, gun, billy club and what-not attached to it and heavy black shoes, than I was in my shorts. Why not prolong it?

"Do you like being a policeman?"

He slammed his notebook closed and glared at me. "You're free to go."

"Thank you, officer," I said sweetly as I headed back to my truck.

43

As I drove back down Campbell I thought about Peter Van Thiessen's staying at the El Mercado Hotel. None of it made sense. First of all, with his money wouldn't he have opted for one of the tonier resorts around town—Ventana, La Paloma or the Arizona Inn? The El Mercado catered to people on lower-end budgets who were visiting the University of Arizona or the Cancer Center. It was also far from Abby's home so if visiting his sister was the goal of his visit, why stay in a hotel miles from his destination? There were similar accommodations a lot closer to Oracle. Unless he wanted to be anonymous. Then the El Mercado made sense.

But why come in the weekend that Abby and J.B. were going to be gone? If he'd called his sister to suggest a visit, wouldn't she have told him their plans? Of course Peter could have told her he was staying at the El Mercado, but now with Abby dead, I'd never know. Still, if that was the case, why hadn't J.B. mentioned it? I'd get in touch with María López Zepeda and have her find out for me.

Hadn't Peter also told me that he'd been competing in a marathon in Silver City that weekend? That would be easy enough to verify.

But what if Peter hadn't told Abby about his visit to Tucson?

While I wrestled with that possibility, I could only come up with two scenarios. Maybe he'd come in secretly to see Laurette Le Blanc.

Or maybe he'd come to Tucson to murder his sister.

Forty minutes later I was walking down a corridor in Northwest Hospital looking for the ICU. I rounded a corner and ran smack into my Uncle C.

"Damn!" he said, wiping at the warm coffee that spilled onto his wrist.

"Sorry."

"Oh hi, sweetie. God, I'm glad you're okay."

I felt guilty. I hadn't checked my messages since leaving home. I imagined that there had been a few from Aunt Josie and my cousin Bea once they'd heard the news.

As Uncle C gave me a quick squeeze, my eyes caught the uniformed sheriff's deputy standing outside the intensive care unit. Cori Elena, dressed in the same clothes she'd left the ranch in earlier that morning, was doing her aren't-I-adorable? routine on the cop. He looked as though he was eating it up.

My attention was not lost on my uncle.

"He's coming around, but his only visitors are family for five minutes every two hours."

"I didn't know Jake had much family."

"His ex-wife's been in to see him, but she had to go to work. He has a son in the Coast Guard who's flying in later this afternoon and . . ." He jerked a thumb in Cori Elena's direction.

"The damsel in distress gets in?"

He nodded.

"So I guess you haven't been able to talk to him?"

"I didn't say that," he said with a twinkle in his eye. "Come on, I'll buy you a cup of coffee."

I could use one since I was starting to run down from my lack of sleep.

While waiting rooms at Northwest Hospital, unlike those at the Tucson and University medical centers, are not usually crowded, my uncle blocked the side view of my body with his own as we quickly passed an opened lounge door. "Goddamed reporters," he growled, probably temporarily forgetting that his daughter, Bea, was one.

We finally found an empty corner in a secluded waiting room. I helped myself to a Styrofoam cup of sludgy-looking coffee as Uncle C refilled his own.

"You're sure you're okay?" he asked, settling his bulk into one of the metal-framed chairs.

"Yeah, I'm fine. The bunkhouse's a mess, but I imagine Quinta will take care of it."

"And Martín?"

"Shaken, but not surprised." I sounded like I was giving the recipe for a James Bond martini.

"He knew what was going on?"

"Sure. He hoped she'd get over it."

There was an uncomfortable silence between us. It was finally broken by my uncle.

"Cori says you knew about the Rafael Félix business." He was trying to keep the accusation out of his voice, but I still heard it.

I sipped the hot coffee and carefully considered my answer. "I only knew that there was a *possibility* of trouble from Mexico."

"But she told you that the Mexican authorities wanted to question her about her husband's murder and that Félix suspected her of taking his dough?"

"We have no extradition with Mexico."

"We do on murder."

"But not on drug stuff. And we wouldn't have been interested in extraditing an American citizen just for questioning about a murder, right?"

My uncle nodded wearily. "Still, you should have told me."

"Why? So you and Aunt Josie could stay up night worrying about something that was probably never going to happen?"

"Yeah, well, we've passed that bridge now, haven't we?" He swirled the coffee around in his cup.

"What's the story on Jake?" I asked.

"Punctured lung, shattered left arm, and he's got a bullet lodged near his spine."

"Oh God, will he—"

"Yeah, yeah, he'll walk. No problem there. They're keeping him in ICU for a few days until he stabilizes. He was in shock and he lost a lot of blood."

"But you talked to him?"

"A little. Cori Elena told him about Félix."

"You're not gonna tell me he was at the ranch last night guarding her?"

He gave me a big grin. "Nope. Just happened to be in the wrong place at the wrong time. Amazing the amount of trouble a man's pecker can get him into. He figured he could grab a few more minutes with Cori Elena since Martín was in La Cienega trying to get that old truck running. With them leaving, poor old Jake wanted to stretch out the time he had left with his sweetheart. But then all hell broke loose."

I could use another cup of coffee, but I stayed put, not wanting to interrupt my uncle's story.

"He heard the guy work the lock. By the way, you need better ones. Think about upgrading to Schlages or something."

"We've never had a problem before. I'm surprised the bunkhouse was even locked."

"Cori Elena took care of that. She didn't want Martín walking in on them. The brand inspector figured that if it was Martín, he'd have a key."

Not likely since we rarely lock the doors on the ranch. With so many of us around, someone's usually al

vays home to intercept potential burglars. Still, Jake
Hatcher wouldn't have known that.

"But he didn't want to call out, because if it was
Martín, then he'd know that Jake was there, what they
were doing. So he kept his mouth shut."

"And waited?"

Uncle C gave me a disbelieving look. "We're talking
seconds here. Sure Jake waited. For all he knew it was
Martín coming home in the dark, and he didn't want to
murder the guy whose wife he was screwing. I'll give
him that."

I shuddered, thinking of Cori Elena and Jake waiting
in the dark bedroom for Martín to turn on the light. I
found myself wondering if Jake had shot Martín if that
would have been self-defense under the Rafael Félix circumstances.

"Once the guy was in, it didn't take him long to hit
the bedroom. There's no lock on that door. He opened it
slowly, stood to one side and fired. It was dark. When he
saw Jake go down, he probably assumed he'd hit Cori
Elena. That hesitation cost him."

"Lucky that Jake had a gun."

"His .357 was on the nightstand. Even down, he was
able to grab it and fire." There was something close to
admiration in my uncle's voice. "He said he would have
normally left the gun in his truck, but he was a little
spooked because of the Félix business."

"I never saw his truck."

"He left it out near the shipping chutes and walked
in. After all, he wasn't supposed to be there."

With all the commotion of the morning, the thought
had never occurred to me to seek out Jake's pickup.

"Is the guy dead?" I found myself hoping that he
wasn't so his part in the story would come out.

"Which one?"

I choked on my coffee.

"Yeah," he grinned. "The Bunkhouse Bozo was
DOA."

"Was there really another one?"

"Parked in an old Impala down near the mailboxes. When the call came in, one of the guys from the SO was out patrolling near the cottonwoods so we caught him in a pincer movement. It was unplanned. We just got lucky."

"He's in jail?" It sounded too good to be true.

"Oh yeah." He shifted in his chair.

"I'm waiting with bated breath."

"Pretty textbook, although stupider than most. The guys came up from Mexico three days ago to find Cordelena for Rafael Félix. Fortunately, only one speaks English, the shooter, and he didn't read the papers so he missed the story on his boss.

"The lucky thing for us was the radio on the Impala was shot and they couldn't even tune in a Mexican station."

"So they didn't know that Félix was dead?"

"Yep. Wish they were all this easy."

I hadn't been aware that I'd been holding my breath but a heavy sigh escaped me.

Uncle C reached over and patted my knee. "I'm just glad they got the son-of-a-bitch."

"Me too," I said in a quiet voice that didn't sound quite like my own.

After my uncle left to go back to work, I used the phone in the waiting room to call María López Zepeda. She was in court, so I left a message with her secretary asking her to check with J.B. about Peter's earlier visit to Tucson.

I called my answering machine and checked messages. I'd been right about the one from Aunt Josie so quickly returned her call. Uncle C had already been in touch with her so I didn't stay on the phone long. There were calls from reporters from the *Arizona Daily Star* and the *Tucson Citizen*, one from Emily Rose and one from Bea's television station, Channel 4, asking for an inter-

ew before the five o'clock news. I returned none of
nem.

After hanging up, I grabbed another cup of rotten
offee and headed out of the hospital.

It seemed a real anomaly to be taking a steaming cup
f coffee out into a blast furnace, but I was hoping that
ne caffeine would keep me on my feet for at least a few
nore hours. Staying up all night never used to be a prob-
m when I was younger. Now, over forty, every minute
was awake after midnight took a heavy toll. I was a
usy Cinderella. My eyes burned and in spite of my
nower that morning, I felt used and dirty all over. My
lass slippers seemed like concrete work boots as I
udged across the hot parking lot. In spite of my exhaus-
on, it was no trick to see the layers of heat rise from the
nn-softened asphalt.

While I'd thought about sharing what I'd learned at
ne El Mercado Hotel with Uncle C, I knew the informa-
on wasn't going anywhere and I wanted a little more
me to explore my theory.

A couple of things were bothering me about the sce-
ario of Peter Van Thiessen in the starring role as Abby's
nurderer. First, if he really had killed Dr. Mullon, why
vould he stay in a hotel just blocks from where the mur-
er took place? While it would have been convenient—
e could have easily walked undetected to Mullon's
ouse—it was also very risky. Could Peter Van Thiessen
e that arrogant?

And, if he was the murderer, how did he get out to
ne Baboquivaris? Had he driven in to Tucson and used
is own car? If that was the case, it might be hard to
rove he'd made the trip. But he would have had to
now a picture ID if he'd flown and that would have left
n easy trail to follow. Van Thiessen wasn't a stupid
nan. Maybe he had fake identification. What credit card
nd name had he used to check into the El Mercado?

The second thing that was bugging me was motive.
y mutual agreement, if I was to believe Jim Carstensen,

Abby's lawyer, Peter wasn't going to inherit anythin
from his sister. By all accounts he and Abby had bee
very close. He loved her. So what motive would he hav
for killing his sister?

It just didn't make sense.

I started up Priscilla, threw the air conditioner o
high and rolled down the windows to let the hot air es
cape. I drained the coffee and thought more about m
case before pulling out of the hospital parking lot. Whil
there were still a few holes, I'd learned a lot over the las
few weeks. About J.B. and Jackie Doo Dahs, Lateef Wise
the Covarrubiases and Samuel Mullon. But now I wa
zeroing in on Peter Van Thiessen. I thought about m
conversations with Abby's best friend, Clarice Martínez
and what she had told me about the Van Thiessens' sib
ling relationship.

As I pulled out of Northwest Hospital, a fast ambu
lance, lights twinkling and siren blazing, turned into th
drive.

And then I had my answer.

Peter wasn't really a bad guy after all.

44

ARRIVED AT HER HOUSE JUST AS CLARICE MARTÍNEZ PULLED
. She waved gaily. "Hi there, Girl Detective."

I met her at the front door, which was opened by the
me maid who had been there on my earlier visit.
larice ushered me into the cool house.

"Whew! It's hot out there. Let's get something to
ink."

I followed her back to the kitchen.

"May I help you?" I asked as she pulled a couple of
ll glasses out of the cupboard.

"Heavens no. I've been at exercise class lifting body
arts all morning." She slapped herself on her tiny rear
nd and winked at me. "Those people are slave drivers.
xing tea is nothing."

She poured the glasses half full of tea and then
ached into the refrigerator and pulled out a chilled can
f mango juice. After opening it she topped off the
asses with the juice and then stirred them.

"Jamango tea," she said.

I took a sip. "Delicious."

"I brought that back from Guam with Three.
ourtesy of the Jamaican Grill."

"Three?"

"Colonel Jergensen. Sweet George. That one on
lasted a year."

"But did you like Guam?"

"Loved it. You know they like to say there, 'Guam
where America's day begins,' but it really should b
'Guam, America's best kept secret.' It's better tha
Hawaii. But I guess you didn't come here to hear m
prattle on about Guam, did you?"

I smiled.

She walked over to the glass top table in her brea
fast nook and nodded for me to sit down. I left her th
chair with the best view of the finch aviary.

"So, what brings you back to my neck of th
woods?"

"Abby again. I've been thinking about some of th
things you told me and had a few questions."

"Shoot."

"I wanted to ask you about her relationship with h
brother," I began. "Can you tell me more about that?"

"What's to tell? In spite of his being her half-broth
they were very, very close. I remember one time askir
her about that and she said, 'In this family we don't hav
halves.' She spent a lot of time with him, and for yea
he was like her doll. She'd dress him up and mother hir
In some ways, I think Abby, even though she was on
three years older, was like a mother to him, more so tha
schizo Madeleine ever was. He absolutely adored her."

"Did they see each other very often?"

"Lately, not much. Not since Abby married J.B."

"Did that bother Peter?"

Clarice shrugged. "I doubt it. He has his own lif
he's very physical. Runs all the time, works out and l
spends a lot of time at his place on the Amalfi coast :
he's back and forth to Italy a lot. They kept in touch o
the phone though."

"Does he have a girlfriend?" I wondered what sh
knew about Peter and Laurette Le Blanc.

"Honey, for which night?"

"But not a steady?"

"I doubt it. Peter's into trophies. He's like a big-game hunter, once he's bagged them, he moves on down his list. Sort of like Warren Beatty before he married Annette Bening. Only difference is, Peter's never married."

This confused me for a minute. Could Peter have already dumped Laurette? And if he had, would there have been any percentage in Laurette's killing Abby? After all, she *had* fled back to St. Martin to visit her ailing mother right after Abby's death. But still, Charley had checked that out and Mrs. Le Blanc had had a legitimate heart attack.

"Are you all right?"

Clarice brought me out of my reverie. I pushed Laurette to the back of my brain and returned on track. "When we talked before, you mentioned that Abby was terrified of growing old."

"Petrified, but aren't we all?" Clarice said with a twinkle in her eye. "Criminy, my plastic surgeon brigade depends on me for their boats and summer homes."

"But didn't she also tell you that she was afraid of getting incapacitated in any way?"

"Surely that was one of her terrors." Her eyes looked red, as though she was going to start crying. "And that disease . . ."

"The Lou Gehrig's?"

"Uh huh. That really, really bothered her. She knew she was never ever going to get better. Then when Ruth Whitney died of it, I think the hopelessness of it all really hit home."

"Was she a friend of Abby's?"

"Oh, no." Clarice was laughing now, a light tingling giggle. "Ruth Whitney was an editor at *Glamour*. She was the first person with the guts to put a black model on the cover of a big woman's magazine."

I sipped my tea before asking the next question.

"Do you think Abby could have committed suicide?"

"Suicide? Are you crazy? Abby most certainly did not commit suicide."

"No, no, I'm not saying she *did* commit suicide, I'm only asking if, in your opinion, as the Lou Gehrig's got worse, she would have considered it."

She thought about this for a minute. "Consider it, sure. Under the circumstances, wouldn't you?"

Without hesitation, I nodded.

"But to actually do it, no. She would not have committed suicide."

"You're sure about that?"

"As sure as I can be. Abby was a Catholic."

I raised an eyebrow. Her minister, Lateef Wise, was not a priest, nor his church Catholic.

"A very lapsed one, I'll give you that, with all of her spiritual quests. But those early years of being raised Catholic sunk in. Abby believed suicide to be a mortal sin. She never, ever would have done herself in."

"Even though she was suffering from a debilitating disease?"

"She knew it was a dead-end street. Her doctor went through all of it with her. Her arms and legs were bothering her, getting more tired."

"And she was dropping things."

Clarice nodded. "Abby'd done her homework. She knew that eventually she wouldn't be able to walk, or dress herself or do any of the other things she took for granted."

"When did she find out about it?"

"Couple of months ago. She told me the day she found out."

"So how long did she have?"

"Honey, who knows?" Clarice shrugged. "Some of them go a few years, others ten or more. Eventually you can't swallow or chew and you need a ventilator to breathe, but you still have all your senses about you. It's a horrid way to die."

"Or live."

"Yes, or live. But even facing all of that, she didn't kill herself. And if she had, she sure wouldn't have picked some crap-filled pond to do it in. You have any idea what kind of self-discipline suicide by drowning would take?"

"Not very feasible," I admitted.

"Add to that burning in hell, and I promise you, there's just no way she would have done it."

I left Clarice's with no real answers other than her firm conviction that Abigail Van Thiessen had not committed suicide. It had been a real stretch to even consider it, but that hadn't been the reason I'd gone to see her. I'd wanted to reconfirm that the bond between Peter and his sister had been as strong as I'd been led to believe on my first visit to Abby's oldest and dearest friend.

As I drove home I kept the air conditioner in Priscilla as cold as it could get in an effort to keep alert. My sleepless nights were catching up with me and I found my eyelids as heavy as they'd been in a long time. I shifted and stretched as I drove in a further effort to stay awake.

When I finally drove into the Vaca Grande, Blue and Mrs. Fierce trotted slowly out to see me, their tongues hanging out, panting in an effort to keep cool. Petunia ignored me, content to wallow in the mud at the edge of the pond. I was jealous. The water looked so inviting. I briefly considered jumping right in, but opted for a hot shower instead.

The dogs followed me into the screened porch and then into the house, where they flopped down, feet sprawled out as their bellies flattened against the cool saltillo tile floor. I had just turned the cooler on when I heard a car drive in. Dog-tired, I found the thought of drop-in company very discouraging. Still, maybe the caller would be for Quinta or Juan. With all of last night's excitement it could have been anyone.

I peeked out the kitchen door and saw an unfamiliar faded blue Bronco pull up near the pond. A minute later

Peter Van Thiessen stepped out of the ratty vehicle. I wondered why he was driving that it when he could have had his sister's silver Lexus.

Shit. Just what I needed. My spent brain was still sorting out the information I'd gleaned from my visit to the El Mercado Hotel and I wasn't eager to get into any conversation with Peter. If I let him come in it would prolong his visit so I left the dogs inside trying to get cool and quickly stepped back outside.

"Trade! I'm glad I caught you." I met up with him halfway between the pond and the house. "I stopped in the other day."

"Yeah, I got your card. But things have been so crazy here . . ."

"I heard. Are you okay?" He gave me a quick hug and just as quickly released me.

"Nothing a good night's sleep can't cure."

"And your help?"

That was the difference between the Van Thiessens of the world and me. While it was true enough that Martín and Juan were on the payroll, they were family, not help. "Everyone's fine. Jake Hatcher, the brand inspector, is a little the worse for wear, but he's coming out of the woods."

"Glad to hear it."

The sun was beating down on both of us. Exhausted, feeling filthy and hotter than hell, I longed to step into the shade of the cottonwoods. I didn't, though, since I didn't want to prolong his stay. Better to sweat it out under the grueling sun. After all, the Arizonan should win, right?

"God, that's great news about the eyewitness, isn't it?"

"What eyewitness?" I played dumb in an effort to find out where he'd come by his information.

"J.B. called and told me you'd found someone who was there the night my sister . . ." He hung his head and uddered, but with his dark glasses on I couldn't tell if e was crying or not.

"We're working on it, but I'm not sure it will pan ut."

"Well he's plenty excited about it, I can tell you that. isten, if there's anything I can do, if I can talk to the per- on, or you need money, anything at all, just let me now."

"Did you talk to J.B.'s lawyer?"

"No, should I?"

"Well, you might. She's the one who's trying to work ut the arrangements."

"Arrangements?" He looked startled. "What's the roblem?"

"Look, Peter, I really can't talk right now." My anten- ae were beginning to twitch. It wasn't that I was afraid f him, I just didn't want to share anything. Not just yet. ot until I talked to Uncle C.

"Trade!" In spite of the heat, Quinta came running up ith a roll of Vet Wrap in her hand. It was cold from be- ng in the refrigerator. Summers in southern Arizona are ot kind to the adhesive in Vet Wrap and when we leave e rolls in the barn the tape sticks to itself, making it seless for doctoring. "Excuse me, but can I ask you a vor?"

"Sure," I said, grateful for the interruption.

"Dad just called and he wants me to pick up a part in own so he and Prego can fix the truck. I just looked out e window and Chapo's bandage came loose." She anded me the Vet Wrap. "Would you mind wrapping it I can get to the parts store before it closes?"

"No problem."

"I don't know where my mother is."

"She's still at the hospital. I just came from there."

"Tata's taking a nap. I think all of this was too excit- g for him."

"Trade, I've got to run too," Peter said, extending his

hand. I shook it and watched him walk back to the ol
Bronco and drive out.

"Is Jake going to be okay?" Quinta asked.

"It looks that way."

"Thank God. I'll be back in an hour and a half or so
And with that she followed Peter out.

I was dog-tired and doctoring a horse was one of th
last things I wanted to think about. Still, it needed to b
done and I figured I might as well rewrap Chapo as lon
as I was still filthy.

When I got out to the pasture Martín's horse cam
walking up, the bright pink Vet Wrap fluttering like
party streamer attached to his right rear leg. It had ju
started to unwind and I was relieved to see that a goo
portion of his wound was still wrapped. We weren't :
crisis mode yet.

I grabbed a rope halter off the fence post and broug
him out to the tack room where I tied him to the hitc
ing post. After gathering my supplies—the aloe vera g
cotton, Teflon bandages, gauze and the fresh roll of V
Wrap Quinta had given me—I removed what was left o
Chapo's old bandage and doctored his leg.

Dream and Gray had been up in the far corner, bu
when they realized that I was out there and somethir
was going on, they came up to the fence line, nickering
didn't have to be a horse to know that they weren't gi
ing Chapo encouragement, but were begging for a snac

Finally done with my doctoring detail, I treate
Chapo to a horse cookie and turned him back out in th
pasture.

After I put the vet supplies back in the cabinet
started to go back to the house, but then I remembere
that Martín was still working on the truck at Prego's ar
I had no idea what time he'd be home. I thought, wh
the hell, even though it's a little early I might as well fee
the horses as long as I'm out here.

This decision was a welcome one for the begg

oys at the fence. Nickering and grunting their approval, ꭞey chatted heartily to encourage my progress toward ꭞe hay barn.

There were no alfalfa bales open. Although Martín nd Quinta had cleaned the barn floor not long ago, the ꭞose hay was beginning to pile up again. Briefly I ꭞought about scooping it up for the horses, but frankly, would take too much effort, so I opted to open a new ale instead. As I reached for the knife on my belt, my ꭣeary brain remembered that I had been to town and ꭣas not wearing a belt, or a knife.

I stepped over to the post where the survival knife ꭣas usually hanging and was greeted by an empty nail. ꭝamn. The knife was probably somewhere in the barn, ꭞut where? I tugged briefly on the taut, bright yellow ꭞring that wrapped the heavy three-wire bale, but it ꭞidn't budge.

Nothing's ever easy when you're tired and now I'd ꭞave to go to the workshop and get something to cut the ꭞew bale of hay with.

As I turned to leave the hay barn a shadow blocked ꭞe light.

There, framed by the late afternoon light, stood Peter ꭞan Thiessen.

45

WHAT WAS HE DOING HERE? HADN'T HE LEFT?

"I need to talk to you."

"I'm sorry, Peter, but this really isn't a good time. I'm exhausted from last night and all I can think about is getting my chores done and crashing into bed. How about breakfast tomorrow?"

He quickly covered the distance between us. "No, I really need to talk to you *now*." There was a fevered look about him. I was surprised that I hadn't seen it before, and it scared me.

I edged back to the stacked hay. "All right, all right, we can talk." What I had suspected was quickly coming true. Unfortunately before I'd had time to share my suspicions with anyone. Alone at the ranch, with Blue and Mrs. Fierce confined to the house, I was on my own now.

"Not here."

"Let's go inside then, have a glass of iced tea, or a beer." I gave him a smile I did not feel.

"Not there."

I was beginning to not feel good about this.

"You've got to come with me."

"I . . . I can't. I've got chores to do. But I can meet

ou in a half hour or so, anywhere." I was trying to stall,
though I suspected it was useless.

"No. Now." He grabbed my arm roughly and started
pull me out of the barn, but I grabbed the twine on the
le of hay behind me and tried to anchor myself as I
ug my heels into the loose alfalfa. Still, he was stronger.

I screamed.

He slapped me hard across the face. "Shut the fuck
ɔ!"

The harsh taste of the iron of my own blood flooded
y mouth. Terrified, I ran my tongue across my teeth.
'ere they all still there? I spit onto the barn floor and
atched, dismayed, as red iced the fallen alfalfa. My lips
lt rubbery and fat as I watched my blood drip onto my
shirt.

Releasing the hay twine I swung at him and landed a
ood one on the side of his face and followed it up with
kick to his knee. He buckled only momentarily and
renched my arm, pulling me in close to him.

I was fighting for my life now, and I knew it.

His grip dug into my flesh and I was dimly aware of
s left hand coming back in another hard swing.

But I was wrong. Instead, his hand dropped and
nded on the upper part of my bare left thigh. For a split
cond I heard a crackling sound and then I collapsed in
e most excruciating pain I had ever felt. Gripping my
igh with both my hands I was surprised to find myself
ying.

As I lay crumpled in the loose hay he hovered over
e. I couldn't move or think. I tried to move my arms
d legs and couldn't. What had paralyzed me so
ickly? What had made that sound?

It seemed like an hour passed, but it was probably
ily a minute or two, before my leg started twitching
acontrollably. I felt as though I'd fallen off the barn
of. My senses were a blur as my heart pounded faster
an I thought possible. What in the hell had happened
me?

My stomach was doing flips as I shook my head, tr
ing to get a sense of normalcy. My battered mouth w
nothing compared to the pain I had just felt.

Head down, trying to collect my wits and a sense
physical well-being that had all but drained from me
snuck a peek out of my eye to his hand, hanging by tl
blue horse logo of his white Ralph Lauren shorts. Nestl
in his fist was a small black box, not much bigger than
pack of cigarettes.

The fucker had zapped me with a stun gun!

"You play fair, don't you?" I gasped.

"Look, I'm sorry. I'm really sorry, but I need you
come with me, out of here, in my car."

I was taking deep breaths now and when I final
quit shaking I rolled over and sat up slowly in the ha
still dazed.

Peter reached down and pulled me to my feet. N
balance was totally off as I staggered into him. My l
leg felt like mush, weak, unreliable as I struggled to mal
it work.

"Okay," I said, having no intention of going wi
him.

He seemed relieved and he took me by the elbow
though he were escorting me across a street. Such a ge
tleman. But I was painfully aware that the stun gun w
still secure in his left hand.

We were almost to the opening of the hay ba
when I decided to run for it. Twisting away from him,
the same instant I brought my left heel down hard on tl
instep of his right foot. I heard him yell as his fingers l
their grip on me.

I was free!

Running was my only chance because I knew
couldn't have contact with him or I'd get electrocut
again. While my leg was still shaky I prayed it wou
hold up as I dashed for the opening. I was just short of
when he tackled me from behind. I went down hard, n
chin skittering off the hay-padded concrete. The alfal

as probably the only thing that saved me from a cracked skull.

He was on top of me, straddling me. He snapped my head back by yanking my hair and then I almost blacked out as he pressed the stun gun hard against my back.

Excruciating pain again flooded my body. The high keening I heard could not be my own, could it? Had an animal been wounded? I flopped on the ground like a fish out of water, gasping for breath and praying for the pain in my back to go away. I was convulsing dryly, trying to throw up and trying not to, and beyond embarrassment as I became dimly aware that I had just wet my pants.

If I'd thought my heart was racing before, it now threatened to leap out of my chest. Couldn't stun guns cause heart attacks? Was I having one?

Minutes passed before I got some measure of control again. When I was able to, I curled into a fetal position in a desperate attempt to be safe. Tears were running down my cheeks, the salt from them neutralizing the copper taste in my mouth as my muscles twitched and spasmed.

I was dimly aware of Peter's hands on my back, rubbing where he had last applied his miserable weapon. His hands were deceptive. They felt strong and caring as they massaged my back, but they were also the same hands that had brought me down and taken most of my spirit with them.

"I'm sorry, I'm really sorry about this. Please don't fight. Just come with me." He sounded like he was almost pleading, but then he was the guy with the stun gun so he could sound any way he wanted to.

I nodded slightly, fighting the bile in my throat. I didn't trust myself to speak, or to stand. It was all I could do to get my brain synapses to work. I tried to focus my mind, but all I could think of was getting nailed again. The sweat that was pouring off me was from fear, not the heat.

I was again breathing deeply and after a minute or

two, I whimpered, "Please, just . . . just give me
minute."

"It's okay, everything's going to be okay."

I knew it wasn't, but for now I was content just to l
quietly on the hay. Funny how we take the little thing
for granted. Like not being tortured.

"Take your time, catch your breath," Peter said er
couragingly.

I stayed curled up on the wet alfalfa, which w.
damp and thick with the acrid stench of my own urin
and tried to think. But it was hard. My head was thro'
bing, whether from the slap, the hit my chin had made '
the floor, or the stun gun, I couldn't say.

How long had Quinta said she was going to b
When would Cori Elena be home? Where were the dog
My mind was murky and as it slowly came around I rea
ized that the dogs were in the house and that not muc
time had passed since Quinta had left the ranch. As f
Cori Elena, who could tell?

Time passed and finally Peter stood. "We should t
going pretty soon."

I rolled over on my back and stared at the barn ro
and wondered if there really was a heaven. All I cou
see from this vantage point were a few empty bird nes
up on the rafters. Had God put them there? The bird a.
gels had fled the coop. Like rats leaving a sinking ship:
wondered numbly.

My eyes rolled to the side and I saw the hay hool
nestled on nails on one of the barn timbers. If only
could get to them they'd make a weapon. But that w.
impossible. At least as long as Peter was so close wi'
that damnable stun gun.

I brought my good leg up, bending the knee, ar
then slowly moved the left one, the one that had gotte
zapped. It still felt funny, but not as bad as it had.

I was keenly aware of my back. It twitched ar
burned and I felt an unrelenting stiff ache. I shifted m
weight a little and still couldn't get rid of the stea

rob against it. It felt like a huge welt was rising on my
esh, as though my skin had hardened and was ready to
op open.

I didn't trust myself to stand yet, so I reached behind
y back and tried to feel for the damage. What was I ex-
ecting? Blood? A wound? Ridiculous, since a stun gun
ouldn't leave a hole the way a gun would. This was an
sidious pain that left no obvious sign.

The good news was I knew the damage wouldn't be
ermanent. At least not this time. But Peter Van Thiessen
ad other, more serious damage plans for me, I knew.

As my fingers groped my back searching for the
elt, I was surprised that the hardening I'd felt was not
y flesh. There was something stiff and hard against the
ack side of my hand, between my back and the cement
arn floor. Flipping my hand over, and praying that Peter
dn't know what I was doing, my fingers felt hard rub-
er.

The knife!

It was the rubber haft of the knife we used to open
ales of hay. My fingers walked down the haft to the
lade.

"You'll live," Peter said. "Now let's get going."

"I . . . I need a minute, please."

My plea must have gotten to him because he looked
way.

I was careful sitting up, scooting my rear end as close
the knife as I could, while secretly brushing hay back
ver it.

Finally in the sitting position, I plopped my butt on
p of the knife blade and kept my right hand behind my
ack, rubbing the place where he had zapped me.

Peter reached for me.

"No!" I gasped and threw one hand up to my mouth.
. . . I think I'm going to throw up!"

He stepped back, apparently concerned that I was
ing to barf on his Topsiders.

I made gagging noises, dangerous since I hadn't been

that far away from doing the real thing, and as I did so, scooted around so I was still sitting, but facing him now and more importantly, was off the knife.

As I continued with the godawful noises, my right hand dropped down to the weapon in the hay. The blade was sharp against my fingers, and while I would have preferred handling it by the haft, I didn't have that luxury. I arched my aching back and slipped it up under my shirt, and dropped the knife down my denim shorts.

It wasn't perfect, but it was as good a job as I was going to be able to do. It was a struggle until I finally got to my feet, without his help. As I walked I felt the tip of the knife nudging the soft place between my shoulder blades. Peter's hand pinched the soft skin above my elbow as we walked out of the barn.

And in his other hand was the gun from hell.

46

HERE WAS NO QUESTION IN MY MIND THAT I WOULDN'T GO
ith him. My two encounters with the stun gun had left
e dazed and weak. I had the knife so I might have a
ance, but I also needed my strength, which as long as I
as getting zapped would continue to ebb. Realistically,
I have one shot at him and I had to make it count.

I'd often in the past daydreamed about someone ab-
cting me in a shopping center parking lot. You know
e drill. Bad guy comes up with a gun and either jumps
your car or makes you get back into it and then drives
ou out in the toolies somewhere, far from other people
 help, and then proceeds to rape you and then kills
ou. I'd play the mental game with myself, *what would I
?*

Given that scenario, my solution was always that I
ould stay in the parking lot and fight like hell or run
d take my chances of a bullet in the back. I'd risk all
at for the benefit of being in a populated area where
meone might see fit to give me aid or at least call 911.

Yet here I was, on my home ground with a man who
d caused me more physical pain than any man ever
d, and I was actually thinking it was a good idea to

leave with him in his car. More than likely to go to a re
mote place where he would try to kill me.

Real life.

Getting zapped with a stun gun can do that to yo
And hope can drive you to places where you nev
thought you'd go.

As we neared the ancient, faded Bronco I notice
that even the tires were old, with cracked, split sidewall
Peter opened the driver's door and got in, sliding acro
the console to the passenger's seat as he pulled me in be
hind him. As he dragged me into the tattered driver
seat, the blade of the knife shifted. Although I tried
hunch my back to catch it, I felt the knife slip deeper
my shorts. The tip was now near my bra line and th
rubber haft fell below my waistline.

"Pull the door closed," he ordered.

I did as he said, moving carefully so the knif
wouldn't stab me.

"You're driving."

As though I hadn't figured that out.

The interior of the car was shot. The cloth seats we
ripped and torn and I could see the foam padding unde
neath. A gaping hole was all that was left of what ha
been a radio. The windshield was a road map of crack
and glass starbursts. While I thought ranchers were ha
on trucks, this one was a real beater.

The dashboard looked as though someone had take
a knife to it, a victim, I suspected, of being left unpr
tected in the hot Arizona sun. Glued between two of th
long, wide dashboard slits was a faded plastic Madonn
She'd pulled off miracles before and I said a silent pray
that she could do it again. For a Presbyterian. For me.

"Nice car," I said.

"It's not mine."

No kidding.

I was praying that Juan had awakened from his afte
noon nap and was out in the garden. Not that I'd expe
him to do anything, but I was hoping for the solace th

e could at least tell someone that I'd gone off in the
ronco. But it was not to be. As we drove slowly past the
egetables, there was no one there but the birds pecking
t the bright, ripe tomatoes.

I drove out the dirt lane a lot slower than I ever had,
arely distracted by the pair of bouncing foam dice that
wung from the cracked rearview mirror. Peter said noth-
ng, seemingly content with our pace. When we passed
he turnoff to Sanders's ranch I threw a longing glance in
hat direction, wishing I could mentally make him ap-
ear.

Unfortunately we made it all the way out to the
ighway passing only one person I recognized, Ginny
ske in her Blazer with her passel of kids. She drove past
ot noticing me. But then, why would she? I was piloting
strange car, not Priscilla.

While I'd had trouble staying awake on my drive
ome from town just a short time ago, my priorities had
hifted and, although exhausted, my adrenaline had
icked in. Now that I was worried about sleeping perma-
ently, I was eager to stay awake as long as I could.

I didn't talk and neither did he. While I was full of
uestions, I was still trying to get my mind back on track.
Ay eyes drifted down to the console between us where
eter's tan hand clutched the thing that looked like an in-
ocent TV remote controller. The problem was, I knew
etter. And I was terrified of getting zapped again. I'd
hought I was having a heart attack when he hit my
ack. Was there a cumulative effect to those things? Is
hat what he planned, to zap me to death? Was that posible with a stun gun? I shuddered.

"Are you cool enough?"

"Pardon me?" I stole a quick glance at Peter, who was
djusting the controls of the refrigeration unit. It was one
f the few things in the old car that seemed to be in good
hape.

"It's on high," he said, almost apologetically.

What in the hell was going on? He'd just zapped the

shit out of me twice with a stun gun and now he was so
licitous of my comfort? What was I going to tell him
The temperature's fine but I have this stupid knife poking
me in the back and my legs feel sticky and itchy from
where I wet myself. And I'm worried that you're going
to kill me. Hardly.

Although it was as much of a rush hour as we ever
get when we drove through La Cienega, as near as I
could tell, no one noticed us.

We were just through town, nearing the County Line
Road, when he said, "Turn here."

I did as he asked and headed west across Big Wash
toward the Tortolita Mountains. The road hadn't been
graded in a long time and we bounced and rattled over its
washboard surface. I dropped the speed down to
twenty-five and tried to get a grip on my possibilities.

So far, I'd only seen the stun gun. Could he have an
other weapon? While I was sure that I'd read somewhere
that you couldn't kill a person with a stun gun, hadn't I
also read that the electrical impulses could cause heart at
tacks? Was that what he planned? To heart attack me to
death? While I knew I didn't want to go through getting
zapped again, I felt slightly encouraged. In order for the
thing to work, he needed to have physical contact with
me. If I could just distance myself from him, the stun gun
would be useless. *If*.

The knife prodding me in the back reminded me that
I wasn't entirely defenseless.

We passed no one on the long, lonely dirt stretch
That didn't surprise me, since the mine at the end of the
road had closed long ago and there were no residences
out here. This was all state land, empty but for the graz
ing bald-faced cattle and the normal desert denizens
Occasionally on the weekends, or during hunting season
groups of four-wheelers would come out, but today was
neither.

Remembering the cracked sidewalls I found mysel
hoping—for the first time in my life—for a flat tire.

The road was getting progressively worse as we neared the mountain. In my fatigue, I missed a washout on the right-hand side and the Bronco lurched and bucked hard, sending both of us bouncing in our seats. As I came down, there was a soft pop, like a balloon bursting, as the blade of the knife jabbed me hard in the back.

"Arrrgggh," I yelped. As I shifted my weight to redirect the knife the vehicle swerved across the road.

"Watch it," Peter growled.

Tears flooded my eyes along with the awareness of a searing burn just below my shoulder blades. I gripped the steering wheel and fought the urge to pass out. Flattening my upper torso against the seat, I felt a cool spot spread in the middle of my back. I didn't have to look to know what it was. Blood. Shit! I'd managed to stab myself in the back.

As I pressed my shirt against the seat it didn't feel as though I was gushing blood. I increased the pressure in an effort to stop the bleeding, praying the blade wouldn't poke out my shirt and get entangled in the foam cushion of the torn seat.

My back hurt like hell and there wasn't a thing I could do about it unless I wanted Peter to discover the knife.

We passed several dirt turnoffs but he didn't say a word so I just continued driving west. I had a pretty good idea of where we were headed and I was not happy about it.

My suspicions were confirmed when we reached the old abandoned mine at the end of the road. A heavy steel cable was strung across the entrance, and a small dim two-track split south from there. He motioned for me to turn down it.

We drove another quarter of a mile or so when the road turned back to the north. Making a half circle we ended back at the mine property. All we had done was skirt the barricaded entrance.

"Over there," Peter said, waving the stun gun in the direction he wanted me to go.

We stopped in front of a barbed wire fence bearing painted signs cautioning KEEP OUT and DANGER! OPEN MINE PIT!

It was a popular spot as evidenced by the myriad broken beer bottles, faded Slurpee cups and cheer Budweiser cans. An old abandoned stained mattress leaking its stuffing, was propped against a mesquite tree and what looked like the carcass of a dead dog was not far away. Not to mention a deep mine pit to put a body in that might never be found.

Peter reached over and pulled the keys from the ignition. He opened his door and hunched out of the car so he could keep his eyes on me. "Get out."

Not eager to show him the huge bloodstain I knew must be on the seat, I kept my back pressed against it as long as possible and then swiftly bounded out of the car. My strategy worked, as his head popped immediately up above the car roof. "What do you think you're doing?"

"Getting out of the car." As I stepped away from the Bronco my eyes drifted inside where a bloodstain the size of a five-pound sack of potatoes spread across the back of the driver's seat. Seeing my own blood magnified the pain in my back, which was now throbbing, in addition to burning. The blood was slowly trickling into my underwear, which wasn't having a good day.

Briefly, I thought about running right then, but knew that it wouldn't work with the knife stuck down my pants. It was a damned if I do, damned if I don't decision. I hadn't been thinking clearly before when I thought I could distance myself from Peter and his stun gun. He was a runner. A marathon runner, for God's sake. I'd never outrun him.

My only chance was the knife in my back if I could just manage to not stab myself again.

Although it had to be close to six o'clock, it was still blistering hot. But not too hot for the flies who buzzed around the dead dog and were now acutely aware of our arrival and the fresh meal I was offering on my back.

"Walk toward the fence," Peter demanded.

He was coming around the car now and I knew that if he saw the back of my T-shirt, he'd see the blood and find the knife. My brain kicked into gear and I formulated a quick game plan.

A huge mesquite tree was next to the car and a large flat boulder was nestled under it.

I backed away from him and sat on the boulder. "I . . . I have to sit down," I said. "I'm not feeling well."

My news meant nothing to him.

Keeping my back straight, I held my head in my hands, being careful not to touch my throbbing chin as I willed him to come closer.

I stared at the ground until I saw his Topsiders through my fingers and then looked up. As I did so, instantly there was a cold, raw fear in the pit of my stomach.

Peter Van Thiessen, dressed in his spiffy Ralph Lauren shorts and polo shirt, held the treacherous stun gun in his left hand.

And in his right, a small, sleek, deadly .22.

47

"LET ME GUESS, YOU WERE THE ANONYMOUS CALL ON THE KE-
tamine, weren't you?" I swatted at the flies hovering
around my face.

"I had to do it to protect myself."

I knew it wasn't just that. He'd been covering his
bases from the beginning. Otherwise, why would he
have even used the veterinary drug? He'd planned on setting J.B. up. It may have been a just-in-case scenario, but
it was a setup nonetheless.

"I guess she was terrified, huh?" I asked, wishing I
could see his reaction behind his mirrored shades.

"I'm not a murderer, Trade." He sounded almost
apologetic.

"You must have loved her very much." With my
swollen lip, the "very" sounded like "berry."

"Loved her?" He laughed. "She was everything to
me. When Momma Mad locked us up in the closet Abby
told me stories to keep me from going crazy and gave me
her water. I don't think I would have made it without
her."

"You had a rough childhood."

"You have no idea. No one does, except Abby."

"No, no one could know."

"And then when she found out she was sick, everything just fell . . . apart." He wiped his moist face with the stun gun hand and I couldn't tell if he was smearing tears or sweat.

"She was very afraid, wasn't she?" I asked as gently as I could.

He nodded. "She didn't want to get old and ugly."

"It must have been horrible to see Madeleine's cancer disfiguring her. To see her live with that lingering illness. That's been part of your life for a long time, hasn't it?"

"It didn't bother me as much as it did Abby. Sometimes she had to clip Momma Mad's toenails and help bathe her." He shuddered and I suspected he was more affected by his mother's illness than he was willing to admit. "She didn't want anyone having to do those things for her."

"No, I suppose she didn't."

"She talked to the doctors. We had the money."

"But there wasn't a cure."

"No. And having the money when you're faced with that doesn't mean a damned thing. Not one damned thing."

"Did she help you plan it?" I asked softly.

"God, no." He was horrified. "She didn't want to know. Not how, not when. She just wanted it done unexpectedly."

"Why now?"

"I was in Silver City for a marathon when I got the call about the trip."

"From Gloria?"

He nodded. "It seemed like a perfect opportunity. They were in a remote spot, there'd be no witnesses, easy in and out."

"But there was a witness," I reminded him.

"Which is why we're here now. I need the name." He was slapping the stun gun against his muscle-corded thigh, seemingly oblivious to the flies that were landing on him.

"I don't have it. He was with an Indian woman camping out near the stock pond."

"I don't believe you."

The flies were buzzing around my back, landing on my shirt, attracted by the blood. They were mean, biting my arms and legs.

"It's the truth. The man is from Mexico and was in this country illegally. There's a strong possibility that he won't testify at all."

Peter took a step toward me. "And the woman's name?"

"Stella Manuel." The lie came easily off my lips. Sometimes it's easier if you combine it with truth as I'd just done with the real Stella's first name. "She works at the public health department." I was on a roll.

"But the lawyer knows her name?"

"No." I continued the lie. If I couldn't get out of this, there was no reason to jeopardize María López Zepeda. "She's working on the immunity thing and I didn't want to give her my source until that was settled."

He shook his head and I couldn't tell if he was buying it or not.

"How'd you do the bull prints?" I asked, swatting at the flies. A couple of red ants were trudging across the dirt and I moved my feet out of their way.

"Padded fabric shoes. Custom-made."

"By Gloria."

His mouth twitched in surprise. "How'd you know about that?"

"Three months ago, some very large sums started appearing in her private checking account. They had to come from someone with money. You were one of the candidates. As for Gloria, the prints were the size of Brahma bulls, and Gloria could have gotten the pattern from Double Indemnity. Trouble was, the land where you killed Abby was leased to a rancher with smaller cows."

"I didn't think of that."

"Why would you? You're not a cowboy. Neither is he."

"Gloria deposited that money?"

I nodded.

"I told her not to. She shouldn't have done that."

From what I'd seen of Gloria I doubted that she would have paid much attention to anything Peter said to her.

"Maybe she didn't want to leave it in her house."

"José doesn't know about any of this."

"I didn't think he did."

"If we'd had decent laws in this country . . ."

"But we don't."

"They convicted Kevorkian, did you know that?"

"That was a little close to home, wasn't it? That whole bit with the video on TV?" I hadn't watched the *60 Minutes* show, but I'd read enough about it to be pretty sure of my ground. "That guy he killed had Lou Gehrig's, didn't he?"

Peter took a deep breath, but didn't answer me.

"That must have really gotten your attention, with Abby's diagnosis. And that's what this is all about, isn't it? The lengths you've gone to to save your own ass."

"You don't . . . don't understand, Trade."

"Oh, but I think I do."

"I can't go to prison for this."

He was terribly mistaken; in fact, he could definitely go to prison for this. But I knew that wasn't what he meant.

"Which is why you killed Dr. Mullon."

"God, I had no choice. He was the connection, don't you see? The link between Abby and her disease . . . no one else knew."

Interesting that Abby had told both Clarice and her brother about the Lou Gehrig's disease, but had also told each of them that they were the only ones who knew about it. She'd been abusive in her own way, for each one had thought that they were her only confidant.

"And if Mullon talked, your mercy killing woul[d] have been discovered, is that what you thought?"

He exhaled sharply. "It's been hell." He used the stu[n] gun hand to remove his sunglasses briefly and I saw [a] nervous tic under his right eye. He swiped his arm acros[s] his face before replacing the glasses. "You have no ide[a] what it's been like."

"Killing your sister?"

"Killing both of them. I never thought about her doc[-]tor, but driving home that night, I knew that it had to b[e] done."

"You must have thought about it some, you knew where he lived."

"Only because Abby and I were there for a Christma[s] last year and I remembered the house. I didn't prepla[n] that, Trade."

He was getting agitated, as though it were really im[-]portant that I believe him. He fidgeted and looked at hi[s] watch.

"And you waited for him to come home?"

"No. He was already there."

I was surprised I didn't know this. There'd bee[n] nothing in the newspaper about it, and Uncle C sur[e] hadn't shared this inside information with me.

"I called him from the alley on a cell phone I picke[d] up with fake ID and a fake name." He was pacing; hi[s] left hand held the stun gun to his ear as though it was [a] phone. "Told him that Abby was having a problem an[d] we needed him at the ranch. He was very good that wa[y] about making house calls."

Another little detail Uncle C hadn't shared with m[e] for surely the cell call had shown up on Mullon's phon[e] records.

Peter was mumbling into the imaginary phone, no[t] paying much attention to me. My hand drifted to m[y] back where the knife was, but then he looked up. I pre[-]tended I was scratching my hip.

"I waited for him to come out." He pointed the stu[n]

un at me and jerked his hand twice as though he were
hooting me.

I was glad it was the stun gun hand as I wondered
ow far he was going to take his reenactment.

It seemed like he was starting to cry, while at the
ame time trying not to let me see that he was. "God, it
was just awful."

Tiny gnats had moved in, joining the flies in attack-
ng my eyes, nose and bloody mouth.

"Not as easy as drowning your sister?"

A muscle twitched above his left cheek. "You'll never
inderstand. That wasn't easy. It was the beginning of
ny descent into hell."

"And was it just a coincidence that you took a hotel
oom at the El Mercado, a couple of blocks away from
Mullon's house?"

"You're really not going to believe this." He laughed,
ut it wasn't sincere. "But it was. When I checked in I
adn't thought about killing Sam."

"So you parked the car, walked over from the hotel,
ut a couple of slugs in him, went back to your room and
vent to bed."

"Not exactly. That's not my car." He nodded in the
lirection of the Bronco.

"You said that." A gnat flew into my mouth and I
hoked on it.

"It belongs to a neighbor of Gloria's."

My heart sank. Even with my fingerprints all over
he car, the police would probably never find it. "Nice of
iim to lend it to you."

"He doesn't know. Gloria borrowed it because hers
s on the blink."

"Or because she didn't want you using hers."

He gave me a sly grin, as though I'd just solved a
omplex part of a puzzle.

"She's been manipulating you, Peter. She's the guilty
one."

"Is not! Don't you say that!" His lips curled back and

his teeth looked like they wanted to bite me. "We didn'
want anything traced to her."

"Which is why the ketamine was planted in J.B.'
bull riding gear." I'd already figured out that Gloria ha
planted the drugs in J.B.'s and Abby's whiskey. Why thei
plan worked so well was that different drugs had bee
planned for each of them. J.B.'s to totally knock him ou
Abby's to make her woozy, but still awake enough tha
even after the ketamine injection she could help he
brother carry her off.

He nodded, a little bit calmer now.

"And you conveniently removed the doctored Jac
Daniel's bottle and replaced it with a clean one."

"I was just covering all the bases. I really didn't wan
J.B. to get arrested."

"But if it was between him or you . . ."

"I hoped it would be seen as an accident. Abb
wouldn't have wanted people to know she was mu
dered."

"Because she wouldn't have wanted you to b
caught, Peter," I said as gently as I could. Suddenl
Abby's logic made sense. She didn't tell Clarice that Pete
knew because she wanted to protect him after he kille
her. On the other hand she didn't tell Peter that Claric
knew because she didn't want him to be afraid to do it.

"How'd you know which night they'd drink it?" Thi
was a question that had been bugging me all along.

"It didn't matter. If they'd had some Friday nigh
they would have slept it off and had a couple of goo
hangovers the next day. I figured I could pick the night
could do it."

"Why Saturday?"

He gave me a look that said, how stupid are you? "
was running in the Silver City marathon Saturday morn
ing."

Jesus, he really was a sick puppy, planning his sister'
death around his running schedule. "It was a good alibi.

He smiled.

"How'd you know about the stock pond?"

"Topo maps."

It made sense. He was a runner who trained on country trails. Reading a topo map wouldn't have been any great trick for him. As for acquisition, Gloria could easily have gone into Tucson Map and Flag and picked one up.

"So you used the neighbors's car and then what?" If I was going to die out here in the hot Arizona desert, I at least wanted to die with the full story that had killed me. And for some reason, I sensed that Peter wanted to tell me everything. I straightened my back and was amazed to feel my T-shirt feeling a little stiff. Had I stopped bleeding? I sat very still, not wanting to break things open again or increase the pain I was feeling.

"I left my rental at the hotel, ran to Gloria's where I grabbed the Bronco. Then I went out to the Baboquivaris, came back, dropped the Bronco off and ran back to the El Mercado. Got the .22 out of the rental car that was parked in the garage and then went over to the doctor's." He shuddered, as though the memory of killing Mullon really bothered him.

"And if anyone saw you in your running clothes, hot and sweaty, they wouldn't have thought a thing of it. Nice plan."

"Just another nighttime jogger," he said with a sad smile. "I checked out, drove back to Silver City and was in my room when the call came about Abby."

"Very neat," I said.

"But you know . . ." There was a catch in his voice. "Do you know the worst thing of all?"

I shook my head.

"Giving her that shot." He was crying again, making no effort to hide it from me this time. "When she was a little girl, she hated shots. It was the only thing I really did better than she did." In spite of the heat, he was beginning to shake. "I was always a brave boy when it came to shots." There was a faraway wistful tone in his voice. "Wasn't I?"

"Yes, Peter, I'm sure you were."

"And you know the other bad thing about all this?"

I could think of several bad things, but kept my mouth shut.

"Is that I can't talk to Abby about any of this, not anymore. She can't help me decide what to do." He sounded puzzled now, as though he didn't have a clue what his game plan was. I didn't know whether to be alarmed, or relieved.

"How about Gloria?" I asked softly.

"She was a bad girl," he said. "She made me light those matches, I knew it was a naughty thing to do."

"The fire in the closet," I whispered.

"Uh huh. She was wearing Momma Mad's gloves and poof! They just caught on fire."

"But you saved her, Peter. That was a very brave thing to do."

"That was, wasn't it?"

"Yes it was."

"She never told on me . . ."

Something was crawling on my foot. I looked down to see a red ant creeping across my flesh just above the strap of my Birkenstock. Without thinking, I leaned down to brush it off before it bit me.

Immediately Peter was thrust out of his reverie. He lurched forward. "What's that . . . ?"

He'd spotted the bloodstain. I straightened up quickly and thankfully the knife remained in place. My right hand flew around to my back, and I reached up quickly and pulled down, retrieving the survival knife cleanly from my clothing. As I did so my back ripped open again and I was aware of a fresh gush of blood coming out of my tortured body.

Peter realized too late what I was doing and was

backing up as I instinctively slashed the knife hard against his shins. He shrieked and faltered, but his left hand came down with the stun gun in an effort to zap me.

The son-of-a-bitch wasn't going to get his chance as I dropped and rolled on the ground, coming up underneath him as I slashed upward into his armpit. He shrieked and I was immediately rewarded with a bright gush of blood. Still he held both guns, and in a further effort to disable him, I slammed the knife hard into his left thigh as he collapsed in the dirt, screaming. He dropped the stun gun as both hands, including the right one, which still held the .22, clutched his thigh. The rubber haft of the knife trembled from my effort.

Standing now, I snatched up the stun gun and pressed it into his neck.

"Now we're going to start being kind to one another, aren't we, Peter?"

The blood was gushing out over his hands and I wondered if I'd severed an artery. Could there be one on the top part of the thigh? Why didn't I know that? Maybe there wasn't. Still, it seemed like an awful lot of blood. But then again, I'd also slashed his armpit; maybe some of it was from that.

Keeping the stun gun in place I reached around the front of him and pried his fingers off the .22. "Give me the gun, Peter."

His fingers were slick with blood as he loosened his grip on the pistol. Before I traded weapons I needed to be sure the gun was properly loaded, so I stepped back from him. Since I was fairly handicapped with my wounded back, and not wanting to set the stun gun down, I fired the .22 at a prickly pear several yards away. A clean hole appeared in the slim green tuna pod of the thirsty cactus.

"This will do," I said, pointing the gun back at him.

"You went right through my goddamned muscle." Peter's voice had raised an octave and it came out sounding like he was whining. He was still on the ground, bending over his leg and trying to stanch his bleeding with the shank of his right arm.

"Uh huh." It seemed as though my back was throbbing in tune with my heart and my shorts felt like they were also filling with blood. I ran my tongue over my parched, dried lips. The tip probed the crusted blood of my lower lip, the one that felt like a water balloon. "I think we'd better leave the knife in there. If we pull it out, you'll probably bleed to death." I had no idea if that was the case or not, but his leg seemed to me like a good place for the knife to stay. "Take your shirt off and wrap it around your thigh."

He did as he was told and fashioned a makeshift tourniquet. Ralph Lauren had never looked so earthy.

As for my back, there was no way I could tourniquet my torso. I only prayed that things weren't as bad as they felt and that I could make it back to the highway.

"Get up," I said.

He wanted me to help him up, but frankly I wasn't in the mood. I watched him roll around on the ground and try to get his balance. It wasn't that I was all that mean. I hurt and I was in control and I wasn't about to threaten my advantage by giving him one of my arms.

There was an old dried saguaro on the ground and walked over to it and found a stout, dried rib and threw it over to Peter. "Use that as a walking stick."

He'd taken orders from women all of his life and had no trouble following mine. He braced himself against the boulder and by leveraging the saguaro rib, he finally managed to get upright. Blood was still seeping from his leg wound.

"Now, give me the keys."

It was difficult, but he managed to retrieve them from his front pocket.

He hobbled over to the car with me behind him. opened the driver's door, and nodded. "You're driving."

"You've got to be kidding," he said, his face ashen.

"Shut up, Peter. Don't be a wimp. Hell, it's an automatic. You won't even have to move that leg."

I held up the stun gun and turned it on for good measure. It snapped and crackled as an impressive electrical arc leapt across the two black posts.

He got in the Bronco.

I walked around to the passenger side and climbed in. Keeping the .22 on him, I slipped the keys in the ignition and started the car.

"I don't think I have to tell you not to fiddle with that knife," I said.

He drove slowly out the dusty, rutted road. Every time we hit a bad place we both moaned and groaned.

Halfway to the highway I said, "It's cold in here."

He didn't argue and I noticed that his tanned face was the color of unbleached flour.

As I turned off the air conditioner the thought occurred to me that we were both probably going into shock.

Twenty minutes later we stumbled into the Riata Bar, the first place on the highway that we came to after leaving County Line Road.

The barroom became very quiet as we hobbled in. Even the few friendly faces I recognized didn't come rushing up right away.

If the barmaid was surprised to see two bloody patrons, one with a bruised chin, fat split lip and bloody back holding a gun on the other, who had a knife sticking out of his thigh and blood leaking from his armpit, she didn't show it. She was even kind enough to not point out my wet pants.

"If you'll call 911, I'll have a Canadian Club and water," I said. "My friend here will have a Shirley Temple."

EPILOGUE

THE CASE AGAINST PETER WAS EASILY MADE, IN LARGE PART B
his own confession, which he seemed eager to make
Cops will tell you that murderers frequently want t
confess their sins, and Peter, never a real seasoned kille
to begin with, fell right into that mold. The scary thing i
he might have gotten away with it if J.B. hadn't hire
me.

After a battery of psychological testing it was discov
ered that Peter had temporary disassociation problem
and was easily manipulated by women. Imagine tha
With his troubled childhood it came as no surprise tha
he never knew how to trust anyone, which is why h
had a string of sexual relationships but could never be in
timate with any of his partners. Except for Abby. Killin
her was the ultimate intimacy.

Because of Peter Van Thiessen's confession, Stell
Ahil's friend never had to come forward, and as far as
know, never got into any immigration issues.

Gloria Covarrubias was something else. Althoug
she would not cave in, the police quickly made a cas
against her. A hard nut to crack, she held firm in her con
viction that she had had nothing to do with Abigail Va

hiessen's murder. She had no idea that Peter Van
hiessen had used the neighbor's car that she had bor-
wed, although a deposition was taken from a me-
aanic who had serviced her own vehicle. He said it was
operable because someone had poured sugar in the gas
nk. Frankly, I didn't imagine that Gloria was too wor-
ed about that bill, what with the money she'd received
om both Peter and Abby.

She also maintained that the money in her separate
ecking account came from an old, and untraceable,
oyfriend. And while she admitted packing up the food
r J.B. and Abby for that fateful horseback trip, she
vore that she had no idea how any drugs got into their
hiskey. Gloria Covarrubias refused to take a polygraph
st. Because the evidence against her was largely cir-
amstantial, the charges were dropped. I have no idea
here she is now. Unfortunately, good guys don't al-
ays win, and evil isn't always punished.

The good Reverend Lateef Wise, aka Bobby Bangs,
ot his new day care center and, as far as I know, is still
tending anger management classes every Tuesday
ght.

Jodie Austin has given up bull riding for good. She's
anning on marrying her Sullivan and Cromwell lawyer
is fall.

As for me I learned more than I ever wanted to about
un guns and about being stabbed. As I suspected, both
ter and I were in shock that day—he from the leg and
m wounds—I'd nicked his ulna with the blade—and I
ith my back.

I didn't sever any of his arteries, just a few of his
verdeveloped muscles.

And, of course, I had stabbed myself in the back.
ortunately the two ambulances arrived at the Riata at
oout the same time, so I didn't have to arm-wrestle
ter to see who could go first. I was thinking I'd go to
e emergency room and be released, but the cut be-

tween my shoulder blades was more serious than tha
They did some exploratory surgery and hooked me up t
IVs.

On the fifth afternoon I was released from the hosp
tal and Martín picked me up. I thought he'd be pretty de
pressed because when Jake Hatcher got out of the sam
hospital the day before, Cori Elena moved out of th
Vaca Grande and in with him. But it didn't seem t
bother Martín at all.

We drove home to a great show of pregnant thur
derclouds shrouding the Santa Catalina Mountains, wit
lightning bolts piercing the dry desert earth. Three day
later, the rains came.

I couldn't wear a bra for about ten days and that wa
probably the toughest part of the whole thing.

Oh, and the barmaid did blab so I'm still gettin
teased about wetting my pants.

Which brings me to stun guns. Dreadful things. Hu
like hell. And I discovered that they leave little mark
that look like vampire bites for days afterward. I can als
now attest that a zap to the torso is more painful tha
one to the leg.

J.B. not only got out of jail, but also gave me a $5,00
bonus. Can you believe it? Guess it was just a drop in th
bucket for a wiry little bull rider with sixty million do
lars to spend.

Although Jackie Doo Dahs still asks him out fror
time to time, as far as I know he's not interested. To h
credit, in spite of all the money he inherited, he's st
running his bull riding school.

While I was recovering at home, Quinta helped m
out a lot. Not only with my household chores, but she
also taken on some of my detective work. Frankly,
think she's got a real knack for the job and I'm lookir
forward to maybe using her on some of my cases.

Little did I know then that my next case, runnir
down a kid named Eddy Gallegos, would come fror
her . . .

ABOUT THE AUTHOR

SINCLAIR BROWNING'S FIRST TRADE ELLIS MYSTERY, *THE LAST SONG DOGS* was nominated for a Barry award and for a Shamus award for Best Original Paperback of 1999 by the Private Eye Writers of America. It was quickly followed by *The Sporting Club*.

Browning is a "dirty-shirt cowgirl" whose family ranched for years. Having lived in, and ridden, the Sonoran desert for most of her life, she still breaks her own horses, rounds up cattle and team pens.

sinclairbrowning.com